SAVAGE PRIDE

CASSIE EDWARDS

LOVE SPELL BOOKS NEW YORK CITY

A LOVE SPELL BOOK®

October 2000

Published by

Dorchester Publishing Co., Inc.
276 Fifth Avenue
New York, NY 10001

ISBN 0-505-52406-6

The name "Love Spell" and its logo are trademarks of Dorchester Publishing Co., Inc.

Printed in the United States of America.

CASSIE EDWARDS

THE *SAVAGE* SERIES

PARADISE AND MORE

Red Wing lifted Malvina onto his lap and tremored with rapture when she twined her arms around his neck and looked adoringly up at him.

"Red Wing, I am so weary of fighting my feelings for you."

"We shall spend tonight alone, away from my people and their questions," Red Wing said, his hands framing her face between them. "My sweet mystery woman, I will build a lean-to for us. I shall build a comforting fire. Tonight is ours and all that we wish it to be."

His eyes wavered. "There is one thing we have forgotten," he said thickly. He turned her so that he could see her shoulder. There were bloodstains on her dress.

"The pain?" he said softly. "Does your wound pain you?"

"It comes and goes," Malvina murmured. "Now, while I am with you in this way, I hardly know the wound is there."

"I shall give you cause to forget it is there," Red Wing said huskily. "If you will allow it, Red Wing will transport all your senses to paradise."

With affection, I dedicate Savage Pride, *my Choctaw book, to my dear friend Mark Abbott—who takes much pride in his Choctaw heritage—and to Mark's children: Marcus, Josh and Heather. Also to my dear friend Yvonne Strawser.*

I, my father
in that unseen place,
Cry from the cheeks
of my mother's face.
To know your help,
to run my race,
My wound aches within.

Can flesh endure
a soul's torment,
Or words that calm
when breath's all spent?
No heart can beat
when it's been rent,
The loss of my friend.

Not death but life
now steals my day.
And night so bright,
I lose my way.
I act these lines
of one dark play;
To pay the unknown sin.

In mercy's hope
I call your name.
Let love not be
my greatest shame.
But its true form
my only frame,
And I shall live again.

—Mark Abbott,
Choctaw

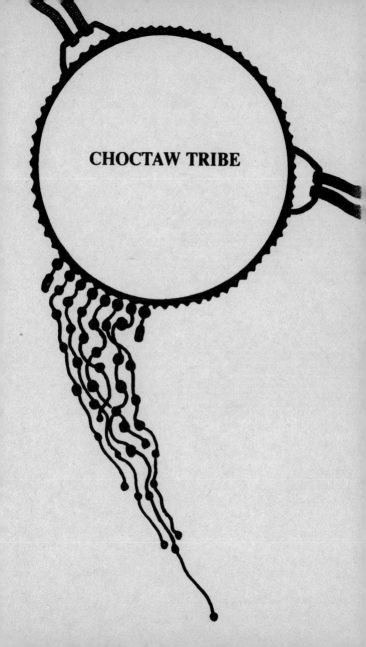

CHOCTAW TRIBE

Chapter One

One chose my time,
And I must live it.
One gave me gifts,
So I must give it.
To sit and ponder,
For what reason,
The answer comes,
In its due season.
So watch my soul,
And let us see,
To know my heart
And let it be.
—MARK ABBOTT, *Choctaw*

Indian Country, The Arkansas Territory—1846

The land was covered with low, rolling hills, blanketed with pine trees. Hardwoods lined the many

11

creeks and rivers that flowed from the land. The forest was a chorus of songbirds, their melodies soft and tranquil. The scent of flowers wafted through the air, some sweet, some spicy.

"Are you sure the moonshiners aren't here? That they are in town?" Daniel O'Neal whispered as he sidled closer to his sister Malvina outside a cabin nestled deep in the woods. "If they catch us, they'll kill us for sure."

Malvina, eighteen and a year older than her brother, gave Daniel a scowl. Her eyes and the sheer loveliness of her face were shadowed by the wide brim of a hat. Tied up in a tight swirl, her lustrously long, reddish-gold hair lay hidden beneath the hat.

"Daniel, you said you watched while I took a nap, so you shouldn't be the one asking *me* if *I'm* sure if the moonshiners are in town or not," she whispered back harshly, her voice softening when she saw the instant hurt that leapt into his eyes at her brusque words.

Her brother had already been through enough without her scolding him. They had both recently lost everything precious and dear to them when men came to their home several miles from Fort Smith, killed their parents, and ransacked their cabin before burning it.

Malvina carried guilt like a dead weight on her heart because she and Daniel had not been there to help protect their parents. Instead, they had been riding free as the wind on horseback, only stopping to fire at tin cans they had placed on stumps of trees to see who was the most accurate shot.

Their papa had taught them both how to shoot,

enabling them to protect themselves from the outlaws in the Arkansas Territory. They took much
delight in using that excuse to challenge each
other in target-practice each day.

Their father's teaching had not saved himself
and his beloved wife.

But now the skills he had passed on would
avenge their deaths.

Malvina and her brother were hell-bent on finding the family's precious heirlooms—a small
chest of jewels her father had brought over
from Ireland when he and his young family
had come to America to spread the word of the
Lord among the new communities springing up
everywhere.

Because he had heard of the hardened criminals that ravaged the Arkansas Territory, he had
chosen that area for his ministry. He had planned
to save the outlaws' criminal hearts.

Instead, he had become a target of their hate.

"If Father hadn't preached so strongly against
moonshining, none of this would've happened to
us," Malvina said to Daniel, her voice breaking as
her thoughts came alive in words.

"But he *did*, and nothing is going to change the
fact that it got him and Mother killed," Daniel
said bitterly. "The moonshiners grew to hate
Father. His words and persuasive personality
were making him too powerful in the community. He had too many people up in arms against
the 'shines."

"But Daniel, if you were in Father's shoes and
were preaching in these parts, don't you think
you'd do the same as he in how you prepared
your sermons each week?" Malvina asked, looking

wide-eyed at her brother. "If you ever do get the chance to enter the ministry, *please* don't return to the Arkansas Territory to do your preaching. Since you are of the same breed as our father, I know you'd follow in his footsteps and also condemn the 'shines and outlaws in the eyes of the community."

"Malvina, chances are I'll never get to preach anywhere," Daniel said solemnly. "As each day passes, I see my opportunity to enter the ministry as something I shall always only dream of, not do."

Malvina understood his disappointment, so much that she could not find the right words to reassure him.

She only nodded. But the angry fire that his solemn words had lit in her eyes said more than any words ever could.

She venomously hated what the 'shines had done to her and Daniel's lives. But what she hated most was that their lives were now guided by revenge. She didn't like what it was doing to her *or* to Daniel.

But most of all, she wanted the family heirlooms back where they belonged. With her and Daniel!

The night the outlaws came and murdered and plundered, the funds saved for Daniel's future had been snatched away from him as fast as a whipcrack.

Until then, Daniel had been planning to enter the ministry in Saint Louis. With the savings gone, the family jewels were now Daniel's only hope, or he was right—he would never get the chance to follow his dreams.

Before he could preach, he needed schooling. And without financial backing of some sort, there could be no means to attend a seminary.

As it was, they were penniless except for their beloved horses and prized pistols. They lived in the out-of-doors, from campfire to campfire, searching for the men responsible for their parents' deaths. When they found the men, they could only pray that the jewels would also be found and returned to their rightful owners.

Thus far they had escaped harm, but they knew that the time would come when they might get caught—even killed.

Malvina sucked in an uneasy breath as she looked guardedly around her again.

She found everything peaceful, even beautiful, a mockery of how she truly perceived life to be for her and Daniel today.

Butterflies flitted about; insects buzzed and frolicked. A lively little lizard scurried with a sudden rush in front of her, seeking shelter beneath a scattering of dry leaves.

Malvina squinted her eyes and gazed through the dizzying rays of the sun toward the entrance of a cave only a few feet away.

This wilderness area was known for its many big caves and crystal-clear, swift streams, a perfect hideaway for the 'shines to brew their white lightning in illegal stills and to participate in the other underhanded activities that went hand-in-hand with moonshining.

Sniffing the air, Malvina recognized the familiar odor of the moonshine. As they had the others, she and Daniel planned to destroy the still that the moonshiners had left behind. It had tak-

Cassie Edwards

en some searching, but in the end, the long days of hunting for it would be worthwhile.

She and Daniel were an extension of what their father had started in this area. He had preached against the moonshine. They were destroying it.

But as always, they first hunted for the jewels among the moonshiners' personal possessions inside the cabins.

Malvina so badly wanted to go to Saint Louis and live a fine life as her brother studied to be a minister. In addition, she and her brother wanted to leave the Arkansas Territory to get away from their Uncle James, their father's younger brother.

James O'Neal had come to America long before Malvina's family had crossed the ocean from Ireland. After his arrival, he had found it hard to secure a job that would make him wealthy as quickly as he had wished. As a result, he had been lured down the wrong road of life—he had become involved in outlaw activities.

When Malvina's father arrived in the Arkansas Territory, her Uncle James had pretended to be a man of God. Having never expected that his preacher brother would come to America, James had told Malvina's father in his many letters that he had planned to enter the ministry as a ploy to hide from his "holier than thou" brother the true way he was making a living.

Then, when Malvina's family arrived, James had been trapped into taking the pulpit at his brother's church often enough to make Malvina's father believe that James *was* a man of the cloth.

Malvina's father had never known the true James. Reverend O'Neal had died before the ugly truth had been revealed to him about his only brother. James's wanted posters now hung in every sheriff's office and on buildings in every town in the Midwest.

Only occasionally did Malvina and Daniel see James, whose nickname was "Preach." He would just appear out of nowhere when they needed shelter and food and provide both for them.

Only out of desperation to survive had they accepted his offerings, for the moment closing their minds and hearts to the knowledge of where he had acquired what he shared with them.

Malvina ached inside when she thought about how her Uncle James chose to live. She turned wide eyes to her brother.

"Let's go," she said, her pulse racing.

She whirled her pistol from the holster belted at her waist, pausing only long enough to look down and grimace at the sight of herself in a man's denim breeches.

For her outing with her brother on the day of her parents' massacre, she had worn comfortable denim breeches and a shirt. She had also chosen ugly, uncomfortable boots over her pretty dainty slippers, all of which made riding a horse more practical. And although she hated these clothes with a passion, they were all she had left. Everything else had gone up in smoke the day her parents died.

Ironically, as it had turned out, wearing such unladylike clothes had made it possible for her to travel these parts less conspicuously.

But, oh, how she hungered to wear a dress.

How she wished to once again feel lace spilling around her ankles!

17

"Sis, I thought you said it was time to go on inside the cabin," Daniel whispered harshly, bringing her mind back to the present. "Come on. Let's get this over with. We may have waited too long as it is. What if the moonshiners are through gambling and drinking at Fort Smith? It's time! Now!"

She nodded, firmed her jaw, then ran around the corner of the cabin and burst through the thin strip of buckskin that served as a door.

Her pistol aimed straight ahead, Malvina stepped inside the cabin, her eyes eagerly searching.

Malvina's nose instantly curled at the vile smells that emanated from all corners of the filthy cabin. She covered her nose with a hand as she discovered half-eaten food in tin plates on an unpainted, hand-hewn table. Flies buzzed around the food.

Her eyes shifted and she shivered when she saw strips of deer meat that seemed to have been recently hung from the rafters, blood dripping onto the filthy planked flooring.

Her gaze shifted again, and she was disgusted to see chickens moving idly around the room, leaving their droppings. Roaches also scampered around, obviously enjoying themselves.

"I think I'm going to puke, Sis," Daniel said, gagging. "Dogs couldn't survive as much filth as this. How could any humans?"

"We're not dealing with humans," Malvina said, slowly inching her way around the room. "We're dealing with two-legged vermin."

She used the barrel of her pistol to uncover rags and push aside wadded-up yellowed papers. An occasional tin can tumbled from a shelf, rattling along the floor until it came to a halt amidst the other litter that had been aimlessly tossed there by the moonshiners.

"Sis, the jewels wouldn't be here," Daniel quickly surmised. "It's plain to see that these hooligans don't have any money to spare, or surely they'd move out of this squalor."

"Daniel, there are those who consider this way of life as normal," Malvina said, bending over a bed. She winced when she had to touch the stinking yellow mattress to toss it aside to see what might be beneath it.

"Malvina, come on," Daniel persisted. "There's nothing here worth spit. Why risk our lives by staying any longer? Let's blow up that still and hightail it outta here. I'm sure it's time for the ferry to come to this side. We can't miss it, Malvina, or we'll be stuck on this side of the river with these moonshiners and the Choctaw."

"I'd feel less threatened with the Choctaw than the 'shines," Malvina said, stopping to take one last look around her. "If the Choctaw knew there was moonshine on their land, they'd do worse than we plan to do. They'd hunt the men down and make them pay with their lives. We plan to destroy only their livelihood."

"We might even find ourselves being condemned by the Choctaw too, if they find us traveling on land that's theirs by treaty," Daniel continued to worry aloud. "Malvina, let's go. Let's get on that ferry before the moonshiners *or* the Choctaw get wind of us."

"Perhaps it's best not to set fire to this still," Malvina said, rushing outside with Daniel. "We could be placing ourselves in jeopardy. The Indians may see the smoke and come to see what's on fire. They might catch us before we make it to the ferry."

"The Choctaw village is far enough away— maybe they won't notice," Daniel said, going to his horse to take two torches from the side of his saddle. "We'll be on the ferry and in Fort Smith before anyone realizes what's happened."

"You *hope*," Malvina said, laughing nervously. She slipped her pistol into its holster.

She held one of the torches as Daniel lit it, then waited for him to light his. Together they ran toward the cave.

They pitched the burning torches inside, ran hard back to their horses, mounted them in a mad scramble, and rode off at a hard gallop.

Able to hear glass breaking as the fire spread inside the cave, they gave each other victorious looks.

They laughed when they heard small explosions, knowing that one by one the jugs of moonshine were being destroyed.

"Ride hard, Sis!" Daniel shouted. "We've got to be aboard that ferry before the major explosion shakes the countryside!"

"It might take a while, Daniel," Malvina shouted back. "If the 'shines store the largest supply in the farthest reaches of the cave, it might take at least an hour before the fire reaches it and sends it up in a ball of fire and smoke."

They rode until the shimmering blue of the Arkansas River came in view through a break in the trees a short distance away.

"We've made it!" Daniel shouted, sinking the heels of his boots into the flanks of his horse. "I see the river. Do you see the ferry?"

Malvina searched the riverbank for the ferry landing.

Her heart sank when she discovered that the ferry wasn't there waiting to transport passengers over to the Fort Smith side of the river.

"It's not there!" she cried. "Lordy, I hope we don't have to wait too long."

She paled when, out of the corners of her eyes, she saw movement, then heard the thunder of hoofbeats.

She turned wild, frightened eyes over her right shoulder, paling when she discovered three horsemen bearing down on her and Daniel from the rear.

"Where did they come from?" she cried as Daniel looked over his shoulder and saw the approaching men.

"It's the 'shines!" Daniel shouted, yanking his pistol from its holster even though he did not want to shoot it. The Choctaw village was too close.

The last thing he wanted was to get their attention!

A thought came to him suddenly, and he felt some relief. Surely the 'shines also knew not to fire their guns. They had more reason to dread the Choctaw than himself and Malvina.

"Daniel, we can't wait for the ferry!" Malvina cried, her eyes desperately searching the riverbank for a boat—for *anything* that might take them across the river.

She sighed with relief when she discovered several moored canoes, probably belonging to the Choctaw. And there were so many. Surely they wouldn't miss just one.

21

She wheeled her horse to a stop only a few yards from the canoes. "Daniel, hurry and get in a canoe," she said breathlessly, dropping her horse's reins.

"We can't leave our horses, Malvina," Daniel said, sliding from his saddle. "Without our horses, we'll be helpless. We won't have a way to travel the countryside to continue our search."

"We'll not be without horses long," Malvina cried, choosing a canoe and giving it a shove into the water. "We've been forced into this sort of life. We'll make the best of it. We'll steal a horse. The Lord will understand. Now get in the canoe."

She plopped down on the seat in the canoe. As Daniel sat down beside her, she handed him a paddle. "Now, sweet brother, paddle with every ounce of strength you have and get us away from the 'shines," she said.

She stopped to give him a motherly pat on his cheek. "I love you, Daniel," she murmured. "This is all going to work out for us. You'll see. The Lord is looking down on us. He'll make everything right."

"He's certainly taking his time," Daniel grumbled.

He then looked ashamedly into the sky. "Sorry about that little slip of the tongue, Lord. I do trust you and your reasons for making us wait for things to get better."

Just as the canoe got far enough away from shore into deeper water, where it was impossible for the 'shines to come after them on horseback, the moonshiners' horses stopped on the riverbank.

"Thank God they know that to shoot at us would

mean to bring the Choctaw down on them like the plague," Malvina said, laughing over her shoulder as she looked at the moonshiners' angry glares.

"Paddle on, dear brother," Malvina said, sighing heavily. "We've done our duty today. Let's find a place to rest for the night. Just before dawn, we'll steal more horses. After we find the chest of jewels and turn them into cash, we'll pay for the horses double what they are worth to help make up for the theft."

A long drawn-out whistle from a paddlewheeler filled the air.

Malvina turned her eyes toward the bend in the river, shrugging. The riverboat was still far downriver. She and Daniel had nothing to fear from it.

Then she saw it rounding the bend sooner than she expected. Her heart skipped a beat when she realized the paddlewheeler was moving much too quickly.

She eyed the other side of the river. Did she and Daniel have time to get there and out of the way of the boat?

She eyed the paddlewheeler again. Its great smokestack was sending off large, billowing columns of black smoke as it came closer and closer, bearing down on the flimsy canoe.

"Faster, Daniel, faster!" Malvina screamed.

Daniel turned his eyes toward the paddlewheeler and broke into a nervous sweat.

Chapter Two

Dogwood blossoms whitened the forest as though snow covered the trees. Dogtooth violets, bloodroot, and dwarf iris carpeted the ground.

His long and flowing black hair hanging past his waist, Red Wing rode tall in his Indian saddle on his white stallion. Headed for the ferry that would take him to Indian Country, he was absorbing the beauty of the land as he traveled leisurely beside the Arkansas River with his friend, Paul Brady.

But Red Wing was not traveling with gentle thoughts. A Choctaw brave and the grandson of Chief Bold Wolf, he was disgruntled over the moonshiners and outlaws who threatened the peace of the Choctaw Nation.

The United States government had granted the Choctaw a vast area in the new frontier territory, a part of which was in the southwestern Arkansas Territory and the Kiamichi Valley area.

Red Wing's village lay just across the river a short distance from Fort Smith, where he had placed the goose quill on treaty papers himself, along with his chieftain grandfather. The purpose of the treaty was to give the Choctaw a measure of peace without interferences from the white nation. But each day he felt this promised peace slowly slipping away.

Red Wing gazed overhead and watched a cardinal flitting from tree to tree in crimson movement. "My people are not like a bird," he suddenly said, giving Paul Brady a solemn stare. "We will not be forced to flit from place to place. We will never again leave land that belongs to us. And we refuse to share it with 'shines or outlaws."

Red Wing paused and lowered his eyes. "My parents died at the hands of outlaws." He looked again at Paul. "My grandfather is chief. I will not allow *anyone* to shorten his life. It is my duty as his grandson to protect him. He and my grandmother took me in as a small boy and cared for me. My grandmother is no longer with us, but my grandfather's lungs still breathe life into his body. And so they shall for many moons to come."

"Any man who dares place a still on Choctaw land proves he wasn't born with brains," Paul said, as solemnly. "Everyone who has any sense knows that liquor was outlawed for the entire Indian nation in 1826. As I see it, placing a still on Indian property is the same as signing a death warrant."

"Yet there are those who will try," Red Wing said. "White men *are* allowed to pass through

Indian Country to get from one place to another.
I imagine that is going to have to change. I will
position braves in strategic places to question all
travelers on our land. That is the only way to
keep away those who have no true reason to be
there."

"I appreciate being free to come and go to your
village when I please," Paul said softly. "As you
know, I've got my eyes on a particular Choctaw
lady."

Glad to have cause to talk of something besides
that which disturbed him to the core, Red Wing
smiled slowly. "It does seem right that you would
prefer a Choctaw woman," he said. The fringe of
his buckskin clothes fluttered in the soft breeze
of early afternoon. "Your feelings for my people
are sincere."

"Sincere enough to want to be taken into your
nation as one with the Choctaw," Paul said sincerely. "Your people are honorable and peace-
loving. The world *I* was born into seems crazed.
The outlaws and criminals outnumber the decent
white folk in this area."

"And I would welcome you into our nation,"
Red Wing offered. "But marrying a Choctaw is
the only way a white man can enter our nation
to live as a Choctaw."

"Yes, I know that," Paul said. His eyes twinkled
as his thoughts wandered to the Choctaw woman
of his desire.

"Pretty Cloud of my village cares not that you
are white," Red Wing said, as though he had read
Paul's thoughts. "It is the hair on your face that
makes her frown when she looks your way. I
always look to beards myself as a mask to hide

behind. Perhaps Pretty Cloud feels the same."

Paul paled and cleared his throat. He reached up and stroked his sandy-colored beard, then his mustache. "You think I should shave it off?" he asked, to take attention away from his uneasiness.

He was a tall, big-boned man with a square-set jaw. His skin was sun-bronzed a mahogany color, out of which a pair of extremely light blue eyes gleamed in startling contrast. He always wore black, from his wide-brimmed hat, to his shiny, sharp-toed boots.

"Does being a white man require one to have facial hair?" Red Wing teased back.

Red Wing thought back to when he had first met Paul. It had been by accident that their special friendship had been born.

One summer ago, Paul Brady had happened upon Red Wing just in time to see Red Wing thrown by his stallion after it had been spooked by a copperhead snake.

Paul had killed the snake with one shot from his derringer and had offered Red Wing a hand at corraling Red Wing's horse, which had gone into a frenzy over the snake.

From that point on they had been fast friends . . . brothers.

"If you think shaving would get Pretty Cloud to take more notice of me, then by damn, I'll shave tomorrow," Paul said, nodding.

"Tomorrow?" Red Wing said, chuckling. "I believe I have heard that before from a man who takes pride in his facial hair as much as I take pride in the long hair that trails far down my back."

27

They rode onward, and the ferry landing where Red Wing and Paul would go their separate ways slowly came into sight.

"Seriously, Red Wing," Paul said as he changed the subject back to moonshining. "Who do you think is behind this new rash of rot-gut whiskey sweeping the area? We've not been able to find even one of the stills in operation."

"As long as the stills are on your side of the river, it is not my concern," Red Wing said. "But any still discovered on Choctaw land will be a different matter indeed."

Red Wing was proud to be the one his grandfather depended on to keep firewater off Choctaw land. By doing so, he earned the clout that was needed to eventually be chief of his clan.

Although chieftainship was not hereditary, his grandfather had already spoken in council of his wish for Red Wing to be chief after him.

Chieftainship was earned by deeds accomplished. Keeping firewater off Choctaw land was essential in order to keep the Choctaw children's lives free of its evil temptation. If Red Wing achieved this, he was almost assured of one day being chief of his clan of Choctaw.

"And it would make no difference to me how many stills brewed whiskey on white man's soil if the whiskey did not get in the hands of our young Choctaw," Red Wing said.

His eyes filled with fire at the recent memory of finding two young Choctaw braves passed out in the forest, an empty jug beside them, the stench of rot-gut whiskey on their clothes and breaths.

"It's almost an impossible task to rid the land of all stills," Paul said, his eyes watching a paddlewheeler make the turn in the river. "As more land is developed and towns are established, whiskey peddlers, gamblers, prostitutes and other unsavory characters flock to them." He paused. "And along with them come Indian-haters."

"I will keep stills and those responsible for them off our land," Red Wing said firmly. "The fox is smart, but he gets caught in the trap just the same. The white man who tampers with the youth of my village is sly and tricky now, but he will get his own medicine in the end."

Having reached the ferry landing, Paul and Red Wing locked hands.

"My friend, one thing for certain—as certain as the very air I breathe—is that I can trust you," Red Wing said. "If only all white men were like you."

Paul's eyes wavered. He shakily eased his hand from Red Wing's, then wheeled his horse around and rode away.

Puzzled over Paul's strange behavior, Red Wing watched him for a while, then jerked his head sharply at the sound of a whistle as the paddlewheeler completed rounding the bend in the river.

He watched it straighten out to follow the center path of the water on its way to Fort Smith, its huge wooden wheel spinning around on the river, biting into the water.

In the middle of the boat, a tall smokestack extended to the sky; black smoke puffed from it.

Something besides the white river vessel soon grabbed Red Wing's attention. He felt a quick panic when he realized that the steamboat was bearing down on a canoe that had appeared out of nowhere. The steamboat captain seemed hell-bent on ramming and capsizing the canoe!

Just as those thoughts entered Red Wing's mind, the steamboat, coughing out more smoke and churning more water, plowed into the canoe, throwing its two occupants into the water.

Red Wing's heart skipped a beat as he watched, as though in slow motion, the canoe being torn in half.

He looked frantically into the water for survivors and saw none.

Sliding quickly from his saddle, Red Wing ran to the wooden pier that jutted out from the land. Breathing hard, he stopped, then dove into the water head-first.

When he came to the surface, he took powerful strokes, over and over again. He swam as fast as he could toward the site of the tragedy, his eyes searching the water as the steamboat trudged downriver as though nothing had happened.

Red Wing paused and treaded water, while bits and pieces of the canoe floated past him. He gazed wildly all around him, but still he saw no survivors.

When he reached the place where the canoe had capsized, he dove down into the water and searched for those he might yet be able to save.

Feeling helpless, and hating the white men who had so thoughtlessly rammed the canoe, he dove over and over again into the depths of the river.

One thing for certain, Red Wing had had time to see that those who had been in the canoe were not Choctaw.

They had been white.

But the canoe was Choctaw.

He burned with anger inside, for the captain of the riverboat surely thought he had capsized a canoe of Indians, thinking them too worthless to care about!

Then another thought came to him. Why had those in the canoe been white? And why had they stolen a Choctaw canoe?

But he doubted he would ever know the answers, for he doubted he would ever find any survivors.

He searched a while longer but still found no one. Too exhausted to search any longer, Red Wing swam back to the ferry landing.

Joe, the hefty, white-haired man who ran the ferry, stood with his hands in his front breeches pockets, idly smoking a cigar.

"Wastin' your time," Joe said, peering up at Red Wing through thick-lensed glasses as Red Wing pulled himself up onto the pier. "Seems they all died 'cept one."

Joe gestured with a nod of his head to one side. "Over yonder," he grumbled. "It seems at least one of the passengers in the canoe was able to swim to shore. See over there, Red Wing? A white couple are seein' to the survivor."

His chest heaving as he tried to get his breath, Red Wing smoothed his wet hair back from his face and gazed at the man and woman who were bent low over the person they had dragged from the water.

From this distance he could see the survivor's face. He was surprised to see that it was a woman. She had a long coil of hair the color of a sunset. And he could see that she was unconscious.

But that fact was soon forgotten in his wonder at how beautiful she was. Never had he seen such perfect features on a woman's face. And she looked so vulnerable and innocent.

Yet he had to wonder about a woman who wore men's clothes. Why would she hide her loveliness in such a way? Her clinging clothes revealed her gentle curves and her generous breasts.

His eyes drank in the delicate beauty of the woman, even as he wondered why she had been in a canoe—and one stolen from Choctaw land.

He looked across the river and saw two stray horses. Why had she and her companion seen the need to steal a canoe instead of waiting for the ferry?

All of this made him want to go to the woman and offer his assistance, so that he could eventually find the answers that would appease his curiosity.

He started toward her, but the man had picked her up in his arms and was carrying her to his buckboard wagon.

His woman companion, who followed close behind, looked genuinely concerned as the unconscious woman was placed gently in the back of the wagon and covered with a blanket.

"Seems she's bein' seen to well enough by her own kind," Joe said. "You'd best be on your way and mind your own business, Red Wing."

Red Wing turned with a start and found Joe behind him. He glared down at him for a moment, then went to his horse and led it onto the ferry.

As the ferry began its slow trip back across the river, Red Wing watched the wagon until it moved into the dark shadows of the forest.

"Do you know the people who took the woman away in their wagon?" he asked as Joe came and stood beside him and lit another cigar.

"Sure do," Joe said, flicking the burned-out match into the river. "I make it my business to know everyone in these parts. Those two are newcomers. Been here for only a short spell. You saw where they went into the forest? Their cabin is only a stone's throw away from there."

"What has brought them to this area?" Red Wing asked, slowly stroking his horse's thick mane.

"Who can say?" Joe said, idly shrugging. "As far as I know, they're good Christian folk who won't cause no one any bother. Take that woman they took in today. Don't that prove they are kind-hearted, lovin' people?"

"Perhaps," Red Wing said, nodding. "Perhaps."

When the ferry reached the other side, Red Wing led his stallion to the land. He tied his horse's reins to a low limb, then rounded up the other two horses, one by one.

Their reins finally tied in with his, Red Wing took the strays to his village and placed them in his corral with his others.

"And whose horses do you bring into our village?" Chief Bold Wolf asked as Red Wing went inside his grandfather's lodge to check on his welfare. "I watched you bring the horses to the corral. Where did you get them?"

"Grandfather, two white people stole one of our Choctaw canoes," Red Wing began, then told his grandfather of the tragedy he had witnessed.

"Those whose canoe was destroyed can take possession of the horses belonging to the thieves," Chief Bold Wolf said matter-of-factly. "Spread the word. Soon it will be known whose canoe, and who should be two horses richer."

Red Wing nodded and left his grandfather's lodge. Word spread quickly through the village about the stolen canoe and about what had happened in the river.

But all that Red Wing could think about was the woman and all the questions he wanted to ask her. He had to find the answers!

And he would.

Mounting his white stallion, he again rode toward the river.

Chapter Three

"Ain't she a beauty, Gerald?" Sally asked, reaching across the dinner table for another piece of cornbread. "I don't think I've ever seen anyone as pretty as her."

Malvina still hadn't regained consciousness. Gerald had carried her into his cabin and placed her on his bed. The shimmering light from the fire in the stone fireplace wafting over Malvina made the pale skin of her face take on a golden glow.

His dirty black hair hanging in greasy wisps over his lean shoulders, Gerald slumped over the table in his chair. He stared at Malvina and sipped a mug of moonshine whiskey, then gobbled down some more spatchcock-style beef.

He nodded toward Malvina. "I've got plans for 'er," he said, his mouth full. "She'll make us some money, Sal. Cain't you jist see those men at the brothel standin' in line to have 'er?"

"I wonder if she's a virgin?" Sally said, stuffing more cornbread into her mouth. Her jowls filled, she talked as she chewed. "Want me to check her and see?"

"Naw," Gerald said, washing the last of his food down with more whiskey. He scooted his mug aside and rose slowly from his chair, wiping his hands on his faded blue corduroy trousers that were worn thin at the knees.

He stood over the bed. "She's young and unused," he said huskily. "A man can tell."

He cast Sally a mischievous gap-toothed grin over his shoulder. "Maybe I oughta try her out myself," he said, snickering. "You could watch, Sal."

"Just you dare mount 'er and see what I'd do about it," Sally warned. She ran her fingers through her thin, graying hair. "Don't you ever think on two-timin' me or I'll cut your throat. Do you hear?"

She pushed herself up from the chair and stretched her arms over her head. Her breasts were heavy and thick and pressed tightly against the inside of her faded cotton dress. "Shove her aside," she said, yawning. "Let's get some shut-eye. Surely by tomorrow she'll be awake. We'll take her into town. I know who'll pay top dollar for 'er."

Gerald rolled Malvina over to the far edge of the bed next to the wall, then lay down beside her, leaving just enough room for Sally.

When Sally stretched out beside him, she pressed her breasts against his chest and reached down and squeezed his manhood through his breeches. "Give me a poke, Gerald?" she whispered huskily.

"The woman . . ."

"She won't know," Sally whined.

Gerald shoved Sally beneath him. He lifted her skirt and tore her bloomers off and thrust himself deeply into her. He closed his eyes and clenched his teeth as he moved within her. Sally clung to him and closed her eyes, her body moving with his, meeting his every thrust.

Malvina's eyes opened slowly, then more widely and desperately when she recalled what had happened in the river.

The groans of pleasure beside her and the movement of the mattress on which she lay made her slowly turn over.

She froze when she discovered the two strangers beside her and was appalled by what they were doing.

She inched her way toward the foot of the bed; then her heart leapt into her throat when a hand grabbed her by her wrist. Malvina turned frightened eyes up just as the man dislodged himself from the woman and gave Malvina a slow, wicked smile.

Gerald rose away from Sally and kept a firm grip on Malvina's wrist. "Sally, get off yer butt and find somethin' for this lady to wear," he ordered. "We've got to shed her of them breeches and shirt. Surely you can find somethin' suitable among them dresses you used to wear at the saloon when you was young and pretty. Make sure it's one that'll make the men at the brothel take a second look at her."

He never took his eyes off Malvina. "Our little waif here is awake and ready to go and take her place among them other *ladies* at the brothel," he said huskily. "When the men hear she's a virgin, they'll be fightin' over who's to take her to bed first."

Sally scooted from the bed, kicked off her torn bloomers, and straightened her dress. She knelt down on her knees before a trunk at the foot of the bed and opened it. "Don't you think we'd best wait until tomorrow to take her to the brothel?" she asked as she slowly sorted through her dresses. "She'd be more rested and presentable. Damn it, Gerald, we only awhile ago fished her out of the river."

She cast Malvina a glance. "The pitiful thing," she said, her voice softening. "She's scared speechless over the accident. Don't you know she probably lost loved ones in the river today?"

"Wife, you'd best save your pity for them that deserves it," Gerald warned. "Like *yourself*, if you don't hurry up with that dress for the wench. The sooner we get her off our hands, the better. Who's to say who'll come lookin' for her?"

Malvina tried to jerk her wrist free, disgusted at the way these people talked about her as though she weren't there. Despair then rushed over her like nausea at the thought of losing her brother in the river.

"Let me go," she cried. "Let me return to the river to see if—"

Gerald interrupted her as he yanked her closer and spoke into her face. "Why, she *does* talk," he said, chuckling. "And she's mighty good at it, I'd say."

"Yes, I can talk," Malvina said, shoving at Gerald's chest with her free hand. "I imagine I have more education than *you*, you filthy, stinking man."

"Did you hear that, Sal?" Gerald tossed over his shoulder. He pulled Malvina to her feet as he rose slowly from the bed. He peered more intensely into her eyes. "Would you look at her green eyes, Sal? Ain't they sparklin' and pretty?"

Again Gerald yanked Malvina close to him. "Who'd you get them pretty eyes and hair from?" he taunted. "Where's your parents? Who are they? What in the hell was you doin' in the river in a damn canoe, dressed like a damn *man?*"

"Nothing about me is any of your business," Malvina spat out, the Irish blood running through her veins fueling her fiery temper.

"Missie, you became my business when I fished you outta the river," Gerald said, giving her a slight shake. "And you owe me, do you hear? You're gonna do as I say, or—"

Malvina interrupted him. "Or *what?*" she said, lifting her chin defiantly. Her eyes glittered mutinously into his. "What are you going to do about it when I refuse to do anything you tell me? If you knew who I truly was—"

She stopped in mid-sentence. She didn't want to reveal to anyone that James was her uncle. That wasn't anything to boast about.

On the other hand, she thought, tilting an eyebrow, perhaps it might be. If this evil man knew that the hardened criminal James O'Neal was her uncle, he'd probably get scared right out of his breeches for having manhandled any of James's relatives.

Deep down she was glad that both creatures standing before her had not caught her slip of the tongue. They were more determined to get in the last word than to listen. And she still did not want to discuss James with anyone. Especially with them!

"What are we going to do about your insolence?" Sally said darkly. "If you're not careful, you'll soon have a hole through your heart, *that's* what." She yanked a pistol from Gerald's gunbelt which hung from a peg on the wall at her right side. Over her arm lay a brilliant red dress, sequins reflecting the shine of the fire in them.

Malvina stared at Sally, her eyes widening, her throat dry.

"And she'd as soon shoot you as look at you," Gerald said, shifting his eyes Sally's way. "You see, she's a little unbalanced. A bit tetched in the head, some say. One minute she's sweet as syrup. The next she's mean as a skunk caught in a trap."

Malvina experienced a momentarily feeling of unreality, as if none of this was truly happening. Only a short while ago, she and her younger brother had been together, trying to make things right in their lives. The next? Daniel was gone!

Malvina squeezed her eyes closed, but even that did not erase from her mind's eye the image of her brother falling into the river.

A sob lodged in her throat when she recalled her brother quickly disappearing from sight. And yet, she had somehow found the strength and courage to swim to shore.

Gerald released his hold on Malvina. He took the pistol from Sally and motioned with it toward Malvina. "Get into that dress, Missie, and let Sally make your hair and face pretty," he said. "Then we're all gonna take a trip into Fort Smith. Jason

Hopper will pay me well for the likes of you."

"I'm not going anywhere with you," Malvina said, throwing the dress back at Gerald. "I wouldn't be caught dead in Jason Hopper's brothel. He *and* his whores disgust me."

"Spoken like a preacher's daughter," Gerald said, laughing throatily. "But you ain't no preacher's daughter. No preacher'd let his daughter go out lookin' like sin, now would he?"

Malvina paled and a melancholy washed over her at the memory of those carefree days when her father had been alive, when everything in life was good. In a blink of an eye that had all changed.

She had given a solemn oath to her brother that one day their lives would be all sunshine and roses again.

Now she doubted she would ever see her brother again, much less make things right in the world for him, as she had promised.

Gerald picked the dress up from the floor and shoved the barrel of his pistol into Malvina's ribs. "I ain't foolin', wench," he said, his teeth clenched angrily. "You see, if you don't cooperate, I ain't losin' what I ain't never had, now am I? So get dressed or don't. Your life is in your own hands."

Malvina's eyes wavered. She looked slowly from Gerald to Sally, then back again at Gerald. Did she dare test this man's ability to speak the truth? Or was he trying to trick her with words that he did not mean?

Malvina concluded that she would not be worth anything to him if she did not do as he said, and she imagined that he *would* kill her. She had too much to live for to chance that.

She must search for her brother to see if he could have survived the terrible river ordeal.

And she must reclaim the family heirlooms!

"I shall do as you say, if . . ." She paused as she looked guardedly from one to the other.

"This ain't no bargaining session," Gerald quickly said. "Either you cooperate, or you don't."

"If I am allowed to go to the river and search for my brother first, then and only then, shall I go on with you into Fort Smith," Malvina quickly said back to him.

In her heart, she knew that what she said was not altogether the way it would be. Yes, she would search for her brother, but later, somehow, before the evil men at the brothel were able to lay one hand on her, she would find a way to escape.

Gerald shrugged. "I see no harm in that," he said. "But, mind you, it will be a quick look."

Her reddish-golden hair coiled lustrously down her back, Malvina slipped into the gaudy red dress. She cringed when Sally fussed over her face, making it just as gaudy as what she was being forced to wear.

"See how she fills out that dress?" Gerald said, gaping openly at the tantalizing cleavage of her full, young breasts. "Reminds me of when you were young and shapely, Sally. Too much pork fat, oats boiled with sugar, and cornbread filled you out in places I never knew you had." He chuckled, then paled when he glanced at Sally, who was eyeing him venomously.

"Husband, it's best you keep your opinions to yourself," she warned as she coiled Malvina's hair up into a bun atop her head. "Or I'll just tell you a few things about how I feel about *your* looks these days, fat, slobbering pig that you are."

When Sally gave Malvina a mirror with which to look at herself, Malvina turned her eyes away. She was ashamed to look like those whores her father had preached against so often from his pulpit.

But she had to play this game just a little longer. The first chance that she got, she would escape.

"Please, let us go to the river now," Malvina said, giving Gerald a pleading look.

"Yes, to the river," Gerald said in a grumble.

Sally grabbed Malvina roughly by the arm and led her out to the buckboard wagon. She forced Malvina onto the seat and sat down beside her, Gerald on her other side.

Gerald shoved his pistol into Sally's hand, then took the reins and rode off.

"Remember, Missie, you have only one look and then we're on our way to the brothel," Gerald said, giving Malvina a heated stare.

"I understand," Malvina said, clasping her hands tightly together on her lap as the team of horses galloped along a crude dirt road.

Her insides tightened when she got her first glimpse of the river. She wanted to continue hoping that she would find her brother alive. He could also have made it to shore. If the Lord was willing, she would find him.

A strange stillness, a tangible presence surrounded Malvina as she watched the river growing closer.

A fat brown rabbit watched from the side of the path.

A pheasant dressed in its rich Oriental-lacquer colors pranced.

A chipmunk scurried across the road in the wake of a horse's hoof beats.

But all that Malvina could see was the water, the rippling silver-blue of the water.

Chapter Four

Just as Red Wing was leaving the village to go and find the woman he had seen rescued, he wheeled his horse to a quick stop. Several of his warriors were riding toward him, three white men on horses in their custody.

Stands Tall, one of the Choctaws' most devoted warriors, sidled his horse up next to Red Wing's.

"While out on the hunt, we heard an explosion and went to find the cause," Stands Tall said, giving an angry yank on one of the white men's horse's reins. "We found these men hiding near the scene of the explosion. They did not have to speak for us to see the guilt in their eyes."

"What are they guilty of?" Red Wing asked, backing his horse up slowly to get a better look at the men. They were all bearded, their eyes cold and shifty. He recognized none of them.

"These men built a lodge on Choctaw soil," Stands Tall said tightly.

"And that is where their guilt lies?" Red Wing asked, inching his horse up next to Stands Tall's again. "That they wrongly claimed Choctaw land to live upon?"

"There is more," Stands Tall said, barely controlling his anger.

"And that is?" Red Wing asked, looking over his shoulder at the captives again.

"The smoke you now see in the heavens?" Stands Tall said, gesturing with a hand toward the sky. "It comes from a cave where the explosion originated. I suspect the cave was being used for making firewater."

Red Wing gazed up at the billowing smoke in the sky, and a quick anger seized his insides.

He wheeled his horse around and studied the white men's eyes as he questioned them. "You bring moonshine to Indian Country?" he asked, his voice slow and measured. "You are responsible for bringing this evil into the lives of our innocent young ones?"

The white men were silent for a few moments longer; then one of them began to speak, but just as quickly stopped when one of the other men warned him not to say anything.

"Being silent condemns you twice in the eyes of Red Wing, three times in the eyes of my chieftain grandfather," Red Wing warned. "Best you confess to me, a mere grandson, instead of to my grandfather, who is chief."

"We meant you no harm," one of the men blurted out. "I didn't even know we were on Indian land. I'm from Missouri. As far as I know, there ain't no land there allotted to Indians. How was I to know things were different here?"

"You are a most ignorant man," Red Wing said, his eyes narrowing. "Or you are a liar. Which is it?"

"Oh, hell," one of the other men grumbled. "We took a small piece of Choctaw land to squat on. It was worth taking a chance. We built it close to a cave. It was a perfect place to make our moonshine. But, hell, the fun's over. What'cha gonna do about it? Scalp us?"

The two other men laughed raucously, then went stone cold when Red Wing grabbed the most boisterous man by his hair and gave it a yank, bringing the man's face closer to Red Wing's.

"You think Indians are savages?" Red Wing said from between clenched teeth. "You think savages always take scalps? Perhaps we should this time. It might teach others like you a lesson."

"There *are* others you'd best concern yourself with," the man gasped, his eyes wide and bulging with fright. "Who do you think destroyed our still? If it weren't Indians, it had to be whites."

"And those whites did the Choctaw a favor," Red Wing said, releasing his hold on the man's hair. He smiled ruefully as the man wove his fingers through his hair to straighten it.

"I think not," the man said smugly. "There were two men. We chased them to the river. They stole a canoe and escaped our clutches."

Red Wing's heart skipped a beat at the mention of those who stole the canoe.

One of them had most definitely been a man.

The other was not.

And she had been most intriguingly beautiful.

"What about those you chased?" Red Wing

47

prodded, scarcely breathing as he awaited the answer. "Why did you?"

"They destroyed our still," the man grumbled out. "And why do you think they would do that? Because they are competition, that's why. They surely have their own still somewhere in these parts. They didn't like having us so close, I reckon. If I ever find out where their still is, by God, there'll be nothing left of it but rubble."

Stunned by the idea that the beautiful white woman was involved in the illegal trafficking of firewater, Red Wing sat in his saddle and stared at the river.

In his mind's eye he recalled seeing the paddle-wheeler crash into the canoe, the occupants of the canoe spilling into the river.

In his mind's eye, and feeling every heartbeat that he had felt when he had first seen the face of the rescued woman, Red Wing saw the accident again, as though it were branded on his brain forever.

It did not seem right that this woman, whose face was all sweetness and innocence, could be dealing in moonshine.

But why else would she and her companion have destroyed another man's still, if not because they were the competition?

Red Wing could still feel the intense pressure inside his lungs that he had felt as he dove over and over again into the murky depths of the Arkansas River, searching endlessly for survivors.

Coming out of the river empty-handed had made him feel as though he had lost a battle with an enemy.

Today the river was the enemy!

"Take them away," Red Wing ordered suddenly, motioning toward the captives. "Take them from my sight. Let the soldiers at Fort Smith deal with their own filth."

"But Red Wing, their still was on Indian soil," Stands Tall argued. "The pony soldiers have no jurisdiction over them."

"Take them to Fort Smith and you will see," Red Wing said. "The soldiers do not take kindly to men like these any more than we do. They will incarcerate them to keep them from participating in illegal activities on their side of the river."

He paused. "I do not want the hands of our people dirtied by the likes of them," he said flatly. "I especially do not wish to hold them as captives. Why take food from our people's mouths to feed such men as these?"

Stands Tall nodded.

Red Wing watched the men being taken away, then somberly followed. When they all reached the river, the ferry was waiting for passengers.

Red Wing reined in his horse and waited until the captives were led aboard by the Choctaw warriors, then boarded the ferry himself.

"You again?" Joe said, squinting his eyes up at Red Wing. "Can't make up your mind where you want to be?" Joe shrugged and shoved a pole into the river that started the ferry moving toward the other side.

Red Wing had scarcely heard Joe. He dismounted and led his stallion to a far corner of the water vessel, where he could be alone.

Again he was plagued with thoughts of the accident and the woman, wondering why and when she had turned to the ugly side of life.

Surely she was no older than eighteen winters. She had so much life ahead of her. Would she again, once she was well enough to fend for herself, choose the life of crime?

Or could the accident have frightened her enough to make her change her life path?

One thing was certain—Red Wing could not deny how intriguing the white woman was to him. He had never met such a woman before, someone who placed herself in danger as though she had the fire and spirit and backbone of a man. She had to know the dangers of what she did, yet did it anyhow.

This was a woman of much bravery, yet she was surely corrupt to the very core. He had to discover what had made her that way, what had led her into the life of crime.

Ah, he thought to himself, she did have the face of someone too innocent to be guilty of such a crime as moonshining.

The ferry bumped against the end of the pier on the other side of the river, and Red Wing was jolted back to the present.

He waited for the Choctaw warriors to lead the prisoners from the ferry, then yanked on his horse's reins and walked his stallion toward the plank that led to dry land.

Red Wing tossed Joe a coin as payment for the ride, mounted his steed, then rode off toward the forest where he had last seen the wagon earlier in the afternoon.

When he came to the only cabin in sight, he rode a short distance more, then dismounted and secured his horse's reins beneath a stone on the ground.

His hand on the knife sheathed at his waist, Red Wing moved stealthily toward the cabin. When he reached it, he leaned his back against the wall and crept to the window and took a quick look inside.

Discovering that no one was there, questions ran through his brain in a rush. He was certain this was the cabin. Yet where was everyone? Why would they have left so soon after finding the unconscious woman?

Determined to find answers, Red Wing went inside the cabin and found the discarded clothes that the woman had worn. He gathered the breeches and shirt up within his powerful hands and studied them. The last time he had seen the white woman, she had been unconscious. She had surely been weakened by her ordeal in the river.

How then could she have the strength to leave the cabin again so soon?

"Unless forced to . . . ?" he whispered to himself.

Then something else came to his mind. "Doc Rose," he said, turning the clothes over and over again in his hands, again recalling how petite and lovely the woman had been, even in these white man's rags.

Perhaps she had been taken to Doc Rose in Fort Smith for medical attention, he thought.

Red Wing started to toss her clothes aside, then decided not to.

Not yet, anyhow.

Slowly, his fingers trembling, he lifted the clothes to his nose and sniffed. He was not sure what he had expected to find by smelling her clothes, perhaps a whiff of the white woman whose fascination was a battle within his very soul, yet still he held the clothes to his nose.

Suddenly feeling foolish and glad that none of his warrior friends had seen his moment of weakness, he tossed the clothes to the floor and stamped from the cabin.

Breathing hard, knowing he should return to his village, to his way of life, and leave the woman to hers, Red Wing rushed to his horse and yanked the reins from beneath the rock.

He swung himself into his saddle and jerked the reins to take himself far from the cabin.

But he did not return to the ferry.

He headed for Fort Smith.

He was too restless to return to his village, his thoughts still troubled by the beautiful white woman whose face seemed branded on his mind.

When he reached Fort Smith, Red Wing led his horse into a slow trot down the center of the street. The fort was at the far end of the town, on the bluffs of the river.

Red Wing rode past a handful of crude, false-fronted buildings that sat on each side of the street. There were mainly saloons and brothels, but there was also a general store and cotton gin. Fort Smith was the leading attraction for trappers, hunters, and farmers in the area.

His eyes and ears ignored everything and everyone who was traveling down the street on horseback or by wagon, except for one building in particular that sat squeezed between the other false-fronted shacks.

Doc Rose's office.

Was the woman there even now, perhaps close to death?

Then he slowed his horse's pace when he realized that there were no horses at the hitching rail outside Doc Rose's building.

No horses.

No buckboard wagon.

The man and woman who had rescued the beautiful lady had traveled with a team of horses and a buckboard wagon. If they weren't there with the woman, then where were they?

The sounds of the town came to him now— loud, raucous, and ugly. The tinkling of pianos. The giggles and laughter of women. The jeers of men.

His eyes were drawn to one establishment in particular. This raw-looking building with its swinging gate entrance was known as a brothel.

He had never been inside such an establishment before, but he had heard about the sorts of women who lived there in their skimpy, strangely colored gowns, their faces painted in a way to make them look grotesque and ugly.

His spine stiff, his jaw tight, Red Wing wheeled his horse around to leave Fort Smith.

The woman wasn't his concern.

He would place her from his mind.

And never allow himself to think of her again.

Chapter Five

Malvina glared at Jason Hopper as he gripped her arm and led her into the midst of the throng of men and women at the brothel. Those who had sold her, as if she were nothing more than a slave, had fled as quickly after the bargain had been sealed between them and the owner of the brothel.

Malvina had played along, knowing that no one could enslave her for long, especially not here among brothel women dressed in their skimpy, gaudy clothing. Never would she be a part of such a life. She would die first.

Malvina cringed when one of the men came up behind her and smacked her playfully on her behind, then stumbled drunkenly away and grabbed another woman and kissed her, his hands fondling her breasts, his body gyrating into hers.

"Just simmer down, will you?" Jason Hopper

hissed at Malvina. "You're not going anywhere, you know."

His steely gray eyes bored into hers as he gave her an icy stare. "You might as well get used to being here with the other wenches," he said flatly. "Pretty thing, you are bought and paid for. And no one'd better try and lay claim on you, either. You're the youngest and the prettiest of all the women under my employ."

"You were foolish to pay those two loathsome creatures anything for me," Malvina said, her chin lifted. "I belong to no one. Not them. Not you. I'll leave here the first chance I get."

She gazed at Jason, finding it hard to believe that such a refined-looking gentleman could be in charge of a house of ill repute. He was dressed in fine Eastern clothes, his boots so polished that they could reflect his image back at him should he bend over to take a look.

A diamond stickpin glistened in the folds of his maroon cravat. His golden hair was smoothed back from his face and hung only part-way to his white shirt collar.

Her gaze lingered on the huge pistol holstered at his waist. If only she could grab it!

"You can't get past my bodyguards," Jason boasted, nodding toward two burly men flanking the entrance of his brothel. "So just smile real sweet for my customers, pretty lady. I'll make sure the first man to take you to bed is nice and clean. How'd you like that? I'll even make sure he's not drunk. Men have more sense with ladies if they aren't filled with spirits."

"No man is going to touch me tonight, or any

other night, unless he is a man of my own choosing," Malvina said, wrenching herself free of his clutches. She swung around and faced him, her fists on her hips. "Now listen well to what I have to say to you. Let me walk free from this hellhole, or you'll regret it."

Jason threw his head back in a fit of laughter, then turned cold eyes down at Malvina. He gripped her shoulders and yanked her close. "You little spitfire—if you don't behave, I'll lock you in a closet until you beg for your freedom," he threatened. "The closet is dark. It's cold. And I do believe a rat or two occasionally visits there."

Malvina paled, then lowered her eyes in defeat. "Please leave me be," she said, her voice breaking. "I need to go and search for my brother Daniel. He . . . needs me."

Jason gave her a gentler shake, sending her eyes back up to stare into his again. "I know of several men who need you, but in ways different than a brother's," he said, laughing cynically.

His gaze raked over her, the very sight of her making his blood pound through his veins. Dressed in the skimpy red-sequined dress, its bodice cut low, revealing the tantalizing cleavage of her well-rounded breasts, she seemed to him nothing less than ravishing.

The flames of the many lanterns brought out the streaks of gold and red in her hair. Her eyes were blazingly green. They were the mirroring of her spirit. Of her courage.

And she looked innocently virginal.

Jason had never made it his practice to take his own whores to bed. But this one was different. It was apparent that she had never been touched by vile, filthy hands.

And perhaps she never would be.

He might take her away and make her his wife. He had waited long enough for the right woman to come along.

"I've changed my mind," he quickly said, smiling down at Malvina. He took her by the hand and began ushering her through the crowded room. "Come on. I'll take you upstairs to my private quarters. You can get out of those dreadful clothes. I'll find you something decent to wear."

Malvina grew breathless at the thought of soon being free of this life that was steeped in sin and damnation. "You are so kind," she said, her eyes shining into his as he glanced down at her. "Thank you, sir. Oh, thank you. I'll find a way to repay you."

Jason's eyes widened; then he realized she might have mistaken his change of plans. "You thank me perhaps too hastily," he said, chuckling. "Pretty lady, I'm not going to set you free. I'm keeping you for myself."

Malvina's lips parted in a light gasp. "No, you can't," she protested. "You must give me my total freedom. I must go and search for my beloved Daniel. It might already be too late!"

"Daniel, *Daniel,*" Jason said, his eyes narrowing. "I'm sick to death of hearing about Daniel. For now, you'd best be concerned about my feelings for you. If I take you from this room, you'll be saved many a night of different hands touching you, of different men taking a taste of you. As my wife, I won't make many demands of you. I don't have a thirst for women as most men do. I would like to have you mainly to look at—and to dispel certain rumors."

"Rumors?" Malvina asked, her voice dry and scarce. "What sort?"

"In time you shall know," Jason said, as he started forcing her up a staircase. "When I send you from my bedroom and you see certain gentlemen enter, then you shall know the difference between myself and the men who pay me well for the services of my ladies."

Having heard her father preach against such things as Jason was referring to, Malvina was aghast at finally knowing such a gentleman.

Then something else alarmed her. Just brushing past her on the staircase was one of her uncle's friends, Burk Sampson. He was a member of her Uncle James's outlaw gang. She couldn't allow him to see her, or know that she was there. He would tell her uncle.

She didn't ever want to see her uncle again. He was someone she no longer knew, nor wished to. She knew too many details of his hideous activities.

She watched over her shoulder until Burk left the brothel.

Then, realizing that once she got upstairs and was locked in Jason's room she would never be free again, Malvina whirled around on the stairs. She yanked Jason's pistol from its holster and gave him a shove that sent him sprawling back down the steps.

She ran down the steps and past him, keeping everyone at bay with the pistol as she aimed first at one, then another.

She knew that she had two major obstacles in

her way—the guards at the swinging doors at the front of the room.

She turned the pistol on them.

"Let me pass!" she screamed. "Or I'll get at least one of you. Which one wants to take the chance of getting shot?"

She motioned with the pistol. "Get away from the door!" she cried at the men. "Get over there with everyone else."

She was surprised that they did as she asked.

When everyone was standing together, perhaps stunned at seeing a woman being this bold, this daring, she slowly backed up to the swinging doors.

She took one last guarded look around the room, then turned and lunged forward through the doors.

Meanwhile, Jason pushed himself up from the floor. He ran over to one of his bodyguards and yanked his pistol from its holster.

Taking off after Malvina, he stepped outside just as she ran into the road. "Stop!" he shouted. "Damn you, bitch, stop!"

When he fired a warning shot in the air, Malvina turned and gave him a haughty look over her shoulder.

Then as she turned to get farther away from him, she ran directly into a horse.

The collision knocked her backward.

She fell clumsily to the dirt road, the pistol she had been brandishing rolling from her hand.

Red Wing steadied his stallion to stop it from being alarmed by the woman's collision.

Then he stared down at the woman. She was the very one he had decided never to think about again. Here she was, sprawled on the street in a sequined dress, staring up at him with her green eyes, a deep pleading in their depths.

He let himself gaze at her strong young breasts, her long slim legs, her velvety skin with the whiteness of new pear blossoms.

Her face radiated a natural, enchanting beauty, and he felt a deep warming coming up from the very pit of his soul, yet he could not help but be confused by her.

First she was dressed like a man.

And now she was dressed like a white whore?

"Come back here, bitch!" Jason shouted, running into the road, his pistol aimed at her. "If you don't, by God I'll shoot you dead."

Red Wing stared from Jason to Malvina. It was apparent now that she had not been in the brothel by choice. She was running from it.

This made Red Wing even more confused.

But the most important thing now was to help her escape. Perhaps she would be grateful enough to open up to him and explain why she was—the way she was!

Malvina scampered to her feet. "Please help me," she cried as she gazed into Red Wing's midnight-black eyes.

It took only an instant for her to realize that this Choctaw was someone special. He was a nymph of the woods, with his coal-black hair that trailed long down his back, and his muscled physique, which showed through the tightness of his fringed buckskin attire.

The kindness in his smile, the cleverness, boldness and confidence that seemed to radiate from him, made Malvina glad that it was he who had seemed to materialize out of nowhere to save her, and not a white man, most of whom she had recently grown to distrust.

She did not have to ask him twice to help her.

He reached down and swept a powerfully muscled arm around her waist and swung her up behind him in his saddle.

Malvina clung to his waist as he rode away on his white stallion at a hard gallop.

More gunfire resounded through the air just as Red Wing swung his horse around a bend in the road. But the horse had not moved quickly enough. Malvina winced when she felt a stinging sensation in her left shoulder. She had been shot!

But she didn't tell the Indian.

She didn't want him to slow down.

She bore the pain, glad that Jason at least had given up and was not chasing her down like a wanted criminal.

The pain in her shoulder was so intense it dizzied her.

Fighting unconsciousness, she slumped against Red Wing's back.

Chapter Six

Red Wing was glad when the ferry came into sight. He snapped his horse's reins and sank his heels into the flanks of his mighty white steed.

When he reached the pier that stretched out to the ferry, he wheeled his horse to a shuddering halt. He started to dismount, then to help the woman from his horse, but stopped.

He only now realized that she no longer had a firm grip around his waist and that she lay limply against his back.

His throat dry, he turned and grabbed Malvina, just as she was drifting off into total unconsciousness.

He gasped and his heart seemed to drop to his feet when he saw the blood on the back of her left shoulder. While he had tried to get her to safety, one of the shots he had heard fired back at Fort Smith must have found its target.

Joe idly scratched his brow as he watched Red Wing gently take Malvina from the horse. "Red Wing, what in tarnation are you up to now?" he asked, flipping a half-burned cigar over the rail of the ferry into the river. "Why'd you bring that whore here? How'd she get shot?"

Red Wing turned blazingly impatient eyes down at Joe. "Get this ferry out in the water—and *fast*," he said, his voice low and measured.

"But, Red Wing—"

"Joe, just this once try not to meddle in my business and get this ferry to the other side."

Joe frowned up at him, then turned and grabbed his long pole that reached to the bottom of the river and gave several heaving shoves.

Not until the ferry was out in deep water did Red Wing feel safe enough to lay the woman down on the floor and to check her wound.

Gently, he turned her on her side and discovered, to his relief, that the bullet had only grazed the flesh of her shoulder. She had not lost that much blood. He felt that her unconsciousness was due more to the shock of the shooting than the actual shooting.

Yes, she would be all right.

If he could keep the white brothel owner from causing her any further trouble, he thought angrily to himself.

As he gently turned Malvina over onto her back, Joe came to him with a blanket.

"I thought you might need this," Joe said, bending a knee beside Malvina. "Is she going to be all right?"

"Her wound is not fatal," Red Wing said, looking over at Joe.

Joe nodded, lit a cigar, and sauntered away.

Before placing the blanket over Malvina, Red Wing could not help but again drink in her loveliness. His gaze took in her long, tapering calves and silken legs, her slim shoulders, and her delicate cheekbones.

There was such a satin smoothness to her skin. Her hair had fallen from its tight bun and now lay in soft, reddish-golden swirls around her shoulders.

His jaw tightened and his eyes narrowed when he saw the way her face had been painted. He would rid her face of the ugly, gaudy paint as soon as he got her safely to his cabin.

Before drawing the blanket up over her, his eyes were drawn to her full breasts. He knew that to touch them would be the same as entering paradise.

But knowing he should not be thinking such things, Red Wing forced his gaze elsewhere and saw the daintiness of her slender fingers.

He wanted to lift her hand and kiss each finger.

He wanted to grab her into his arms and let no more harm come to her.

He wanted all these things, but felt as though they were forbidden to him. It was apparent that she lived some sort of outlaw life.

More than likely she was mixed up in moonshining.

She might be even worse than those women she had been forced to mingle with at the brothel.

Yes, forced. He knew now that those two innocent-appearing strangers who had taken her from the river had done so for profit only. They had taken this little thing to the brothel and sold her as though she were nothing more than a piece of meat.

As he drew the blanket over her, up to her chin, his thoughts lingered on what had become of the land that had at one time solely belonged to men with red skins.

Everything seemed wrong with the Arkansas Territory today. Too many white men came there for the wrong reasons.

This land, with only a few soldiers to keep law and order, had become a magnet that attracted fugitives from justice.

It had become a sort of island, a sanctuary outside the reach of law enforcement for moonshiners, horse thieves, bandits, murderers, and all other sorts of white hoodlums.

It had become almost too great a challenge for Indian tribal law to deal with the criminals who trespassed onto Indian territory. It was also too much for the white pony soldiers and United States deputy marshals to handle on their allotted lands.

It was a place where innocent people turned criminal in the blink of an eye.

He gazed down at Malvina again. How had *she* been introduced into a life of crime? And what of the other person she had been traveling with in the stolen Choctaw canoe? Who was he to her? Perhaps her husband? Or some sort of blood relative?

He could not help but hope for the latter.

"Red Wing, we've reached the other side," Joe said, coming to gently tap him on the shoulder.

65

"Best you leave her here. I will take her back across the river and bring her to Doc Rose. She's pale as a spook."

Knowing that speed was of the essence, Red Wing ignored Joe. He snaked his horse's reins around his right wrist, then quickly lifted Malvina into his arms.

Watching Malvina's face, he carried her across the platform that led from the ferry, his stallion dutifully behind him.

When he reached the embankment, he slid the reins from around his wrist and gave his horse a soft pat on the rump, sending the horse off alone to his village.

Holding Malvina gently in his arms, Red Wing then broke into a run.

Stands Tall soon came riding like thunder toward Red Wing. When Stands Tall reached him, he wheeled his steed around and rode beside Red Wing as he ran.

"Your horse arrived without you in its saddle," Stands Tall said, his eyes cautious as he stared down at Malvina. "I saw blood on the white mane of your stallion. I thought it might be yours."

"It is the white woman's blood," Red Wing said, giving Stands Tall a quick glance. "While trying to escape the clutches of an evil white man, she was shot."

Red Wing stopped long enough to take a deep breath, then once again looked up at Stands Tall. "Go and alert our shaman, Bald Eagle, that I am arriving with someone who needs medical attention," he said, his voice, in its hollowness, showing his concern. "A bullet grazed her flesh. Herbal medications must be readied. Go now,

Stands Tall. See that everything is readied for this woman to take my bed in my lodge."

Red Wing could see much questioning in his friend's dark, studious eyes. And he understood. Who would not question a Choctaw brother who carried a white woman dressed as a whore and whose face was distorted with such ugly paints?

But now was not the time to explain. Now was the time to act, to care. Everything else, the answers to questions, would come later.

Red Wing himself had many to ask.

Stands Tall nodded and rode away, as Red Wing continued to run breathlessly onward.

Red Wing was relieved when he finally arrived at his village. He looked straight ahead when women, children, and elders came from their cabins to stare and to wonder after their chief's grandson, who brought a white woman into their midst. It was not a usual thing, especially not for a man who aspired one day to be chief.

Red Wing ran onward until he came to his one-story log structure built on a slight rise of land that overlooked the meadows, fields, and river beyond.

Stands Tall was already there with Bald Eagle. He held the door open for Red Wing as he entered.

The fire in the fireplace had burned down to dying embers.

Stands Tall lit a candle and placed it on a table beside Red Wing's bed as Red Wing gently placed Malvina on the soft, cattail-down mattress.

They both then stepped back as Bald Eagle, a man in his sixtieth winter, his head as bald as his shaven chest and face, came and knelt beside the bed.

Red Wing patiently waited as Bald Eagle rubbed herbal medications into the fresh wound. He winced when Malvina moaned with pain in her unconscious state. He wanted to comfort her, to tell her that she was going to be all right.

But still he had to wait until Bald Eagle finished performing his healing ritual, which consisted of a low chanting over the woman, his hands in the air, his head bowed.

And then Bald Eagle and Stands Tall were gone. Red Wing was alone with the white woman. For the first time in his life, he felt awkward and at a loss over what to do next. He knew what *must* be done. The dress had to be removed. It must be burned. It represented all that was evil in a woman!

Red Wing was also going to remove the paint from her face and revive the sweet innocence he had seen that first time he had laid eyes upon her.

But to remove her clothing would mean seeing her body totally nude. The way he felt about her, the deep desire he felt for her whenever he looked at her, made it seem wrong for him to undress her.

Yet he did not want to ask any of the women to come and do this for him. He did not want to involve any more of his people in this predicament he had innocently become involved in.

He knew that from this time forth his life would change, all because of his curiosity about this white woman.

He feared it would not be changed for the better.

Being the gentle, caring man that he was, Red Wing put his best interest second to this white woman's and willed himself to keep his feelings at bay as he removed the dress. Once removed, he tossed it into his fireplace where it quickly took flame.

Red Wing stared down at the strange-looking undergarments that the woman wore, which differed greatly from the Choctaw women's attire. He ran his fingers gingerly over the lacy garment that partially covered her breasts, then touched the gathered undergarment that appeared to be a second dress, yet came only to her waist.

This piece of clothing was stiff and bounced as he touched it. Yet it was delicate enough that he could see through it. He stared at the lacy bloomers that came half-way down her thighs, her knees and the skin above them still very much exposed.

His gaze moved lower, where sheer black stockings did not do much to cover her lily-white legs.

And the shoes that she wore were black with a strange sort of heel, nothing like the buckskin moccasins that the Choctaw women wore.

When she moaned, and he thought that she might be coming out of her unconscious state, Red Wing hurriedly removed the rest of her clothes and covered her to the chin with a soft buckskin blanket.

He waited a moment longer, to see if she would wake up.

When she didn't, he proceeded to cleanse the paint from her lips and cheeks with a damp cloth that the Shaman had brought with a wooden basin of water.

Slowly, almost meditatingly, Red Wing renewed Malvina's face to something soft and sweet, the true colors of her lips and cheeks coming through.

The longer Red Wing was with the woman, and the more he gazed at her, the more he realized that he was totally captivated by her.

And lying there helpless, she was so vulnerable.

But in his mind's eye he recalled how she had rushed from the brothel, her eyes and attitude defiant. Not only had she learned the hardships of life, but also what she must do to get by. Although small and delicate, she seemed filled with spirit and courage.

Red Wing brought a chair over to the bed. Again he watched her, so taken by her that he could not will himself to do anything but gaze at her. When he thought that she might be feverish he, took the damp cloth and caressed her brow.

He jerked his hand back with a start when she began talking out of her head, mumbling things that he could understand well enough if he held his head close to her lips and listened.

"Mama, I'll find them for you," she whispered. "Oh, Daniel, Daniel. I let you down. I'm sorry . . . I'm sorry."

When she fell back into a silent sleep, he straightened his back and stared down at her. He had to wonder where her mother was, and who was this Daniel she had been speaking to? And what was she promising to find for her mother?

All that he was certain of was that she was the embodiment of all temptation. As no other woman before her had been able to, she turned him strangely warm with her closeness.

How could he turn his heart away from her? He could not help but love her.

Chapter Seven

Dressed in a long-tailed plum coat with very tight-fitting fawn trousers and a top hat shadowing his narrow face, Jason Hopper swung his horse and buggy to a halt in front of Gerald Smythe's cabin. He left the buggy in a hurry, and with a wide, dignified stride, entered Gerald's cabin without knocking.

Gerald and Sally were at their kitchen table counting the money they had received in payment for Malvina. Gerald knocked his chair over backward when he jumped to his feet in alarm to stare, slack-jawed, at Jason.

"You double-crossing sonofabitch," Jason growled, taking a swing with his fist and slamming it into Gerald's jaw.

Gerald's body lurched with the blow. His hip caught the side of the table, toppling it and spilling the money on the floor.

Sally rose quickly from her chair and backed away from Jason as he glowered at her. "You ain't got no right comin' in here like this," she cried, her eyes wide with fright. "You especially ain't got no right to hit my husband."

"Shut up, you snaggle-toothed witch," Jason stormed back at her.

Gerald rubbed his jaw and stepped out of the way as Jason came toward him again, his fists still doubled at his sides.

"What the hell's the matter, Jason?" Gerald whined, still rubbing his throbbing jaw. "Why'd you hit me? I ain't done nothin' to deserve it."

Jason swung around and hit Gerald again, this time knocking him to the floor. He placed a foot on Gerald's chest, holding him in place. "Which Indian did you pay to abduct that girl I paid top dollar for?" he demanded heatedly. "I'm new in these parts. I don't know any Indian by name. All Indians look the same to me. Who was that Indian, and where did he take the girl?"

"I don't know what you're talkin' 'bout," Gerald said, blood trickling from the corners of his mouth.

Jason fell to his knees and yanked Gerald up with one hand while hitting him again with his other. "I don't take to anyone lying to me," he hissed. "Now, Gerald, I'll ask you again. Where's the Indian you paid to take the girl from my brothel? Do you think I'm dumb enough not to see a suckering when I come face-to-face with a swindler? You sold her to me, then paid the Indian to take her away, with plans to sell her again to someone else. Now 'fess up, Gerald. I want to know everything. I mainly want to know where I can go and collect what still belongs to me."

"She . . . escaped?" Gerald gasped. He winced when Jason dared him with another fist close to his face. "Honest, Jason. I don't know anything 'bout it."

Sally crept slowly over to the wall and slipped one of Gerald's pistols from a holster. Scarcely breathing, she inched her way over toward Jason.

"Get away from my husband or I'll plug you in the back," she said when she got close enough to keep her aim steady on him.

Before she could blink her eyes again, Jason was on his feet and backhanded her, sending the pistol flying across the room.

When it landed, it went off, sending a bullet whizzing just past Jason's head.

He went to Sally and hit her, leaving her sprawled half-conscious across the floor, Gerald cowering against the wall as he watched.

"I want all of your money," Jason said, grabbing the pistol and aiming it at Gerald. "Gather up what fell on the floor. Then get the rest of what you have hidden in the house."

"You cain't leave us penniless," Gerald whined, bending to pick up the coins that had scattered across the floor.

He inched his way toward Jason.

"Place the coins in that coffee can over yonder," Jason flatly ordered. "Then get the rest of your money and also place *it* in the can."

"Why take everything?" Gerald asked, the coins rattling as they fell into the empty can.

"As payment for my inconvenience," Jason said, laughing raucously.

Gerald frowned, then went to his bed and raised the mattress. A cigar box came into view. He took the box and placed it beside the can, then stood back and waited for the money to be taken away.

But Jason wasn't finished with him. The brothel owner came over to Gerald and, with the butt of his pistol, knocked him across the head.

Dizzy, Gerald slumped to the floor. He was scarcely aware of Jason leaving. He could only faintly hear the horse and buggy as it rode away.

Stumbling and holding his head in the palms of his hands, Gerald rose to his feet. Cursing beneath his breath, he went to Sally. He fell to his knees beside her and shook her. "Sal, wake up," he said, his voice drawn. "Sal, damn it, wake *up*."

Gerald was more angry at what had happened than afraid for his wife. And his thoughts centered more on the Indian whom he held responsible for this beating, than on the man who had done the actual beating. Somehow he would find out which Indian had taken the pretty woman from the brothel.

He would find her as well. He would abduct her. There were other men who would pay an even higher price than Jason for such a young, sweet thing.

She would make one lovely slave in a tobacco field!

Sally stirred. She leaned up on an elbow and began to cry as she gazed at Gerald.

He was stunned. Never before had he seen her cry. Normally she was as hard as sin. Nothing could stir her feelings into a need for crying!

"My mama warned me that you were a no-good sonofabitch before I ran off with you and got married," Sally said, inching her way up from the floor. "She was right. I've had enough of your sort of life. I'm going back to Kentucky and live my life out in a more peaceful, respectable fashion."

Gerald rose to his full height over her. "You think I care?" he shouted. He gave her a shove. "Good riddance. I've got other things on my mind besides you, anyhow. You only get in my way. I aim to have me a still. I'll make a killin' off moonshine."

"You just have yourself a still and see if I care," Sally said, stuffing clothes in a rag bag.

Gerald went to her and grabbed her by the back of her hair. "You'd best not come back and beg for what you feels is yours after I get rich," he warned.

"Rich?" she said, cackling.

She spat in his face.

He slapped her and stormed from the cabin.

Chapter Eight

The throbbing in Malvina's shoulder awakened her. Moaning, she slowly opened her eyes.

When she discovered that she was in a stranger's cabin, her eyes jerked open with a start.

Her first thoughts were of those two hideous people who had taken her into their cabin under the pretense of caring for her, when in truth they had only seen her as a way to put the rattle of coins in their pockets.

What if they had somehow managed to get her back in their clutches again? What would their plans be for her now?

They had done what seemed the worst thing possible when they had forced her into the brothel. What more could they possible have in store for her now?

Although it pained her, Malvina leaned up on her right elbow and looked slowly around her.

To her great relief, she realized that she was not in the cabin that she remembered with loathing. This cabin was neat and clean. There was a pleasant odor of cedar wafting through the air, not of something unclean.

Where was she? she wondered to herself.

Suddenly, the memory of what had happened came to her in flashes.

Her escape from the brothel.

Jason Hopper chasing her, firing his pistol in the air, warning her to stop.

Then she gasped when her recall brought Red Wing to the forefront of her memory. The last thing she remembered was the Indian pulling her onto the back of his horse.

Soon after, she had been shot as the Indian carried her on his horse through Fort Smith.

Knowing that the Choctaw lived in cabins instead of tepees, Malvina's insides grew cold with a quiet terror.

Was she in an Indian's cabin?

Had the man who rescued her brought her to his lodge?

She glanced down at the buckskin blanket drawn over her, paling when she realized that she wore nothing beneath it.

Who had undressed her?

Surely not the Indian!

If so, had he brought her to his cabin to wait for her recovery so that he could punish her for having stolen a Choctaw canoe?

Surely she was his captive!

Fighting the pain in her shoulder, Malvina moved slowly to a sitting position.

As she clutched the blanket to her chin, she

looked slowly around. The log walls were mellow with flickering light from the great fireplace. On a table beside the bed a candle sent its faint light out across the room.

On the fireplace mantel, several pine knots burned unwinkingly with their smoky flame. The glow of the lights made it possible for Malvina to see that the Indian was not there.

She took this opportunity to see how he lived, in hopes that when she was physically able, she would already have arranged a plan of escape.

Several straight-backed chairs with rush seats were positioned neatly around a hand-hewn kitchen table. A storehouse of bundled corn hung from the rafters overhead, and a stew pot hung on an iron arm over the glowing embers in the fireplace.

By Indian standards, she realized that the man who lived in this lodge was wealthy.

A writing desk sat against the far wall. Next to it was a small cherry corner cupboard.

She was on a comfortable bed. And over the bed hung storage racks and even more long strings of dried corn and crescents of dried squash.

She shifted her gaze to the open door that led outside, realizing that she had been unconscious for a full night. It was now morning, and everything was wrapped in fog. She could smell the acrid wood smoke from hundreds of cooking fires.

The cool morning air carried the barking of dogs, the clicks and thumps of people cutting firewood, and many voices.

When a shadow filled the space of the door, Malvina gasped and tried to scoot back onto the bed, but found herself in too much pain to move.

Her heart pounding, she stared as the Indian came into the cabin, his arms filled with firewood.

Breathlessly, she awaited his next move, wondering what her fate was at the hand of the Indian. She was most certainly at his mercy. Escape would be impossible. She had surely lost a lot of blood. Just sitting up in bed made her feel dizzy and lightheaded.

Having seen that the white woman was finally awake, and obviously going to be all right, Red Wing's heart warmed. He went on to the fireplace and placed his armload of wood with the rest that he had chopped and split earlier, to the right of the fireplace, on the floor.

He then laid two split walnut chunks against the backlog in the fireplace, and the flames quickly took hold.

Red Wing stared a moment longer into the fire. Then he rose to his full height and went and stood over the bed.

His eyes locked with the woman's. He could see that she was still filled with defiance.

That was best, he thought to himself.

She was not afraid of being there.

"It is good to see that you are finally awake," Red Wing said, admiring her slender neck, the pride with which she held her chin.

"Why have you brought me here?" Malvina demanded, still clutching the blanket to her chin. "Am I . . . your captive?"

"I am Choctaw. My name is Red Wing, and I do not take captives," he said tightly. "Do you not know that the Choctaw are wholly unwarlike?

We devote our time to agriculture and trade. Not warring or taking captives."

"Then if I should ask to leave your village today, you would allow it?" Malvina asked guardedly.

"I would say yes, but I do not believe you wish to ask that of me just yet," Red Wing said, bending to rest on his haunches beside the bed. "Can you not feel your weakness from having been wounded? Or are you wanting to leave my lodge so badly that you are blinded to the truth?"

"You did not bring me here to punish me for the crime I committed against your people?" Malvina asked, her eyes wavering into his.

She wanted to think that he held no grudge against her for having stolen one of his canoes. The very instant that she had seen him, just before he had pulled her onto his horse with him, she had been captivated by his handsomeness, by his eyes that even now melted her insides.

Never had she seen a man who possessed such perfect facial features. Today he wore no shirt, revealing his broad chest and muscled shoulders. He was graceful and tall. Intelligence showed in his deep black eyes.

"The crime you speak of is canoe stealing?" Red Wing said, his jaw tightening.

"You do know about the canoe," Malvina said, her heart sinking. "Do you plan to punish me for having stolen it?"

"I would like to know the reason why you chose it over traveling across the river on the ferry with your horse at your side," he said.

Malvina's eyes widened. "My horse!" she cried. "Daniel's. Where are they?"

"This Daniel," Red Wing said, recalling that

81

she had spoken this man's name more than once while she was unconscious. "Who is this Daniel you speak of with such fondness?"

Malvina lowered her eyes. Tears streamed down her cheeks. "My brother," she sobbed. "My beloved brother."

Red Wing's heart lurched with gladness at discovering that the man he had seen with this woman had not been a husband or lover.

"You know so much—about the canoe, about *me*—perhaps you know of my brother's fate?" she said, her eyes wide and imploring.

In his mind's eye, Red Wing was recalling the accident, seeing both this woman and her brother spill into the water. He recalled searching endlessly for them in the depths of the river and not finding a trace of either one.

He had been relieved when at least one of them had survived.

"I know nothing of your brother," he said, flinching when a renewed stream of tears flowed from her mystifying green eyes.

He did not want to tell her that his search for her brother had been in vain. He knew that she was grasping on to a measure of hope that her brother might still be alive.

Feeling the defeat of having lost so much these past months—first her parents and now possibly her brother—Malvina eased back onto the cattail-down mattress and drew the cover protectively back up to her chin again.

"What is your name?" Red Wing said, not wanting to end this conversation with her so abruptly. "Tell me your name."

Malvina sobbed for a moment longer, then

turned slow eyes up at Red Wing. She knew already that she had nothing to fear from him. He was too gentle in manner and in speech. It was apparent that he had her best interest at heart.

She felt lucky to have been rescued by him rather than another of the vile, drunken louts who frequented the streets of Fort Smith.

"Malvina," she said softly, her eyes again locking with his, warmed through and through by how he gazed at her, so intensely and with something more than any other man had. "My name is Malvina O'Neal."

"The name is pretty," Red Wing said, relieved that she felt no fear of him. "I am Red Wing, grandson of Chief Bold Wolf. In Choctaw my name stands for "He Who Flies With The Wind." What is the meaning of *your* name?"

"Strange how I have never wondered about that," Malvina said. "I just accepted the name my parents gave me as something ordinary, not something to wonder about."

She winced when a sharp pain shot through her wound and tried to position herself so that she would not be lying directly on it. She realized suddenly that it was not bandaged, yet seemed protected enough with something hard and crusty that was dried over it.

"How badly was I wounded?" she asked softly.

"The bullet grazed your flesh," Red Wing said, feeling her pain as though it were his own. "Herbal medication has been applied to your wound. It will heal much more quickly than it would have with white man's medicine. Also, the herbs will soon pull the pain from the wound."

"You did all this for me?" Malvina said, turning to her right side to face him. "Why? Because you wanted me in your custody for having stolen one of your people's canoes? Or was it something more?"

Red Wing went and stood by the fireplace, his back to her, his eyes watching the fire. He leaned an arm against the fireplace mantel. "It is never good to steal from the Choctaw," he said tightly.

He cast her a quick look and turned to face her again. "Unless there is just cause," he said. "The men who chased you. They were moonshiners. What were they to *you?*"

"You even know that my brother and I were being chased by those men?" Malvina gasped. "How can you know so much?"

"It is my place to know these things," he said flatly. "But I do not know everything I wish to know."

Malvina's insides tightened. "What do you need to know?" she murmured, fearing his answer.

"Why you and your brother were being chased by the moonshiners, and why you, a beautiful woman, were dressed as a man."

Unable to trust anyone, even this man whose heart and feelings for her seemed in the right place, Malvina turned her eyes away.

"You choose not to answer now," Red Wing said, his voice solemn. "I will wait and question you again."

Malvina turned anxious eyes up at Red Wing. "Nothing is important except to search for and find my brother," she cried. She tried to get up, but the pain sent her back down on the bed again.

"Daniel. I must go and search the riverbank for Daniel."

"You spoke Daniel's name over and over while you were in the deep sleep," Red Wing told her. "This gave me cause to know his importance to you. I sent many warriors out to look for him. They are at the river now. Soon word will be brought to me as to whether or not he has been found."

"You have also done this for me?" Malvina asked, in awe of his total kindness. "Why would you?"

"Why would I *not?*" Red Wing said, not daring to allow her to know his true reason for bringing her into his life—that he had fallen in love with her the moment he had first laid eyes on her.

He had to keep reminding himself that she was a maiden of mystery, that the hidden, mysterious side of her might reveal what he did not want to know—that she was no one he should lend his heart to.

If she was involved in making and selling firewater, or was even a part of an outlaw gang, he would want no part of her.

She had worn the clothes of a man as a disguise for *some* reason.

Yet how could he deny this need of her that was growing within him?

"Are you hungry?" he blurted out, feeling the need to change the subject to something less personal.

"Very," she said, once again managing to move into a sitting position. Her face grew hot with a blush when she again looked down at the blanket, the only thing covering her nudity.

"Who undressed me?" she quickly asked, her eyes searching his eyes for answers she might not want to know.

"Does it matter?" he said, going to the fireplace, bending down to place two wooden plates on the hearth. "The clothes you wore are now burned."

He cast her a glance over his shoulder. "And the paint from your face is also removed," he said. "Whenever you wish, I will give you a Choctaw woman's dress. It will suit you much better than the clothes of a whore—or those you wore that were meant to be worn by a man."

She paled. "How can you know so much about me, yet still know so little?" she said softly. "You saw me dressed in men's clothes? That had to mean you saw me—"

"I witnessed the paddlewheeler capsizing the canoe in which you traveled," he said, interrupting her. "I tried without success to rescue both you and your brother. When I swam back to shore, I saw you being taken away by those people who pretended to be your friends. After your brother spilled into the river, I never saw him again."

Malvina stifled a sob behind a hand, then drew the blanket around her shoulders. "Thank you," she murmured. "For everything."

Red Wing nodded, then ladled elk stew from the cooking pot into two wooden bowls. He carried a bowl to Malvina and placed it on her lap and gave her a wooden spoon. Then he sat down on a chair beside the bed with his own bowl of stew.

Clutching at the corners of the blanket with

one hand to keep it snugly in place, Malvina ravenously ate the stew with her free hand, realizing that she had never been as hungry as she was then.

Seeing her exuberance at eating, Red Wing laughed beneath his breath. "You soon will be well," he said, his eyes dancing into hers as she gave him a winning smile, her cheeks glowing, her eyes sparkling.

Chapter Nine

Standing before a mirror in his cabin, carefully plucking stray gray hairs from his beard, Paul Brady turned with a start upon hearing a sudden knock at his door.

Slipping his suspenders back into place over his shoulders, he lumbered toward the door.

When he opened it, he found an outlaw friend standing on the small porch, his face well hidden behind a full beard.

"What is it, Burk?" Paul asked, stepping aside so that Burk could come inside his cabin.

Burk made himself at home as he went to the fireplace and lifted a pot of coffee from the hot coals. "I've got news that won't much please you," he said, turning to pour coffee into a tin cup on the kitchen table.

"Oh?" Paul said, sitting down as Burk settled himself on a chair across the table from him.

"What sort of news? A planned heist gone bad, or what?"

Burk's steel-gray eyes peered into Paul's. "It's about Red Wing," he grumbled. "I didn't witness it, but I heard that he was in town and got mixed up in some fracas over a woman and was shot."

Paul scrambled so quickly to his feet that his chair fell over backward. "No," he gasped. "Not Red Wing. How bad? Is he dead?"

"I don't know any details," Burk said, taking a sip of his coffee. "You know how gossip gets all twisted up and crazy as it spreads down the grapevine. All's I know for certain is that Red Wing got mixed up in gunfire in Fort Smith. What actually happened you'll have to find out on your own."

"And I sure as hell plan to," Paul said, slipping a shirt on and placing holstered pistols at his waist.

He started to leave, then stopped and turned to Burk. "Anything else?" he said tightly. "Any plans for raids? Don't leave me out, Burk. I'm not here just to be a sounding board for our outlaw gang. I want a piece of the action. Always remember that. You understand?"

"Yeah," Burk said, nodding.

Burk gave Paul a mock salute; then Paul ran from the cabin and mounted his horse in one leap and rode hard toward the river.

When he finally arrived at the riverbank, Paul led his horse onto the ferry, then impatiently waited as it started its slow trek back across the river. His thoughts were on Red Wing, and how much he would miss him if anything truly happened to him.

Cassie Edwards

Their bond was close.

It was unique, especially since it was between a man of honor and a man whose moral code was less than satisfactory.

Paul's constant dread was that Red Wing would discover the truth about his white friend, a friend he considered a brother.

Chapter Ten

It was growing dark. Robins warbled as they settled into their nests for the night.

Troubled by his thoughts about his friend Red Wing, Paul sent his horse in a hard gallop away from the moored ferry and headed toward the Choctaw village. He felt that if anything had happened to Red Wing, he would feel in part responsible. Red Wing knew nothing of the dark side of Paul's nature, and Paul wished he would never have to find out.

But it was this side of Paul's personality that would be to blame if Red Wing came to harm. Paul was a big part of the ugliness that had seized the Arkansas Territory. He was an outlaw just as vicious and mean as a man might come face-to-face with.

The sporadic gunfire at Fort Smith was usually caused by Paul's unruly friends. Perhaps one of his outlaw buddies had pulled the trigger on the gun that had shot Red Wing!

His only hope was that the gossip had been wrong, that he would find Red Wing well and alert when he arrived at the Choctaw village. On the banks of the Arkansas, in a peaceful little valley, the Choctaws' lives were guided by the tribe's peace-loving and home-loving nature. Everyone looked up to Red Wing. He was beloved by his people. He would one day be chief.

And it was only right that he should be, Paul thought. Red Wing made sure his body was supple and strong, not that he might conquer in war, but that he might be a great leader and the father of many strong sons!

Finally at the outskirts of the village, Paul drew a tight rein and led his horse past a scattering of log cabins, his eyes intent on one cabin in particular at the far end of the village.

He occasionally looked from side to side, to smile at those in the village who saw him as a friend and ally. He clasped a quick hand of friendship with young braves as they reached up for him, smiling, their eyes trusting.

Then he rode onward and dismounted in front of Red Wing's lodge.

As he swirled his reins around a hitching rail, he looked up at the chimney. Smoke was spiraling smoothly, which meant that the lodge fire was burning.

And there seemed to be no unusual activity around Red Wing's cabin or in the village which might indicate grief over a fallen hero.

Paul took wide strides toward the entrance of Red Wing's cabin. The door was agape. He leaned his head inside and peered through the soft candlelight and found things quiet and serene.

Then he was taken aback when he saw Red Wing sitting beside his bed, staring down at someone on the bed who seemed terribly quiet, perhaps injured.

To Paul's relief, Red Wing was all right.

But he had to wonder, then, who had been shot and why this person was brought to Red Wing's private lodge.

"Red Wing?" Paul said, his voice hardly more than a whisper.

Red Wing turned with a start, then smiled when he discovered Paul standing at the door. He rose from the chair and gave Paul a friendly hug.

"My friend, what brings you here?" Red Wing said, motioning for Paul to take a seat before the fireplace. Red Wing followed Paul there and sat opposite him. "You look troubled. Why are you?"

Paul nervously stroked his beard as he glanced over at the sleeping bench, then turned questioning eyes back to Red Wing. "Word was brought to me that you had been shot at Fort Smith," he said. "Of course I came immediately to check on your welfare."

"The bullet was not meant for me," Red Wing said, turning slow eyes toward Malvina. She had fallen into a soft, peaceful sleep. He had enjoyed sitting there watching her, studying her, his thoughts concerned not so much about her wound, but who she was, and why.

"Oh?" Paul said, following Red Wing's gaze. "Who then was shot?"

Paul could not tell who was on Red Wing's sleeping platform. But he could tell that it was a woman. Her long reddish-golden hair cascaded down from the platform, the very ends curling across the floor. He knew a woman with such hair.

But surely this wasn't Malvina. Why on earth would she be in the company of Red Wing?

And who would want to shoot her?

Unless she had gone too far in snooping into other people's affairs. She and Daniel were hell-bent on finding those responsible for killing her parents and setting fire to their house.

Yet it made no sense that her search would involve Red Wing.

No, it couldn't be Malvina.

"She calls herself Malvina," Red Wing said casually, not seeing Paul's reaction since his eyes were still on Malvina, who turned slowly over onto her other side in sleep, her beautiful face now where Red Wing could see it and be warmed through and through by her innocent loveliness.

Paul paled. His eyes wavered as he gazed at Malvina. He was stunned to know that she had been shot.

Even more so that she had been brought to Red Wing's lodge.

There were many dangers in that for Paul. If she awakened and saw him there, she would quickly recognize him as one of her Uncle James's closest allies and one of the most notorious outlaws in these parts.

If she told Red Wing about the darker side of Paul's life, his friendship with the Choctaw warrior would abruptly end. Paul would be forever condemned in the eyes of his best friend.

Furthermore, Paul would never get the chance to court Pretty Cloud and take her as his wife.

"How did this happen?" Paul asked, his voice drawn. "Why did you bring the woman here?"

Red Wing proceeded to tell Paul everything that had happened, yet did not reveal to Paul his suspicions about Malvina—that she was either mixed up in moonshining or part of an outlaw gang.

"And no one has seen her brother since the accident?" Paul asked, hoping Daniel was dead. Daniel had been a thorn in Paul's side ever since he could remember. Daniel, a man who aspired to enter the ministry, was quick to condemn those he thought were the devil in disguise.

Paul had felt lucky that Daniel hadn't turned him in to the authorities. The only thing saving him had been his association with Daniel and Malvina's uncle. For they did not wish to see their very own uncle captured and sent to death at the end of a rope.

That was the only way Paul could continue being free and able to continue leading the life of an outlaw.

If he stayed in James's shadow.

"Many warriors are searching for her brother," Red Wing said solemnly. "But as each hour passes, I feel there is less chance that he survived the accident."

Paul rose from the chair and placed his back to the warmth of the fire. He stared at Malvina, his heart pounding with the knowledge that if she awakened and saw him, she could that quickly change his life.

He didn't want to lose Red Wing's friendship.

95

Nor did he want to lose the chance to marry Pretty Cloud!

His only recourse was to turn Red Wing against Malvina so that he would no longer concern himself over her welfare. He could see in Red Wing's eyes how he felt about her. It went much deeper than just caring for another human being.

He cared for her as a man cares for a woman.

Yes, he had to change that, Paul concluded. And *quickly*. Before she awakened and pointed an accusing finger his way!

"Red Wing, now that I've had the chance to study this woman's face, I recognize her," Paul said, looking guardedly at Red Wing as he rose from his chair to stand beside him.

"You know Malvina?" Red Wing asked. "Then perhaps you can tell me about her, about her family. Am I wrong to think she is involved in underhanded activities? I wish to hear you say that she is innocent of those things I feel inclined to condemn her for."

"I'm sorry, Red Wing, but what I have to say about her is not going to please you," Paul said. "You see, her uncle James is one of the most notorious outlaws in these parts. If I were you, I wouldn't concern myself over her. She's rotten to the core."

Red Wing's eyes widened and his heart seemed to plummet to his feet. "Surely you are mistaken," he said, his voice thin and drawn. "She looks so innocent."

"Looks are often deceiving," Paul said, nodding. "You've heard of her uncle. The outlaw

James O'Neal. His wanted posters are plastered on the walls of all business establishments in Fort Smith and all over the Arkansas Territory."

As Paul explained who Malvina's uncle was, Red Wing grew numb inside. He had heard about the notorious outlaw James O'Neal. He knew that he was known to many as "Preach" because it was said that he had at one time studied for the white man's ministry.

"Preach" was a hardened criminal, known to terrorize settlers and rob banks.

Thus far, as far as Red Wing knew, "Preach" had not brought his treachery to the Choctaw side of the river.

And Malvina was this man's blood kin?

The knowledge tore at the very core of his being, because surely his suspicions about her had been true, that she was someone perhaps as evil as her uncle.

"For all I know, Malvina might even make residence with her hoodlum uncle," Paul persisted, satisfied to see how his words were affecting Red Wing.

He went and slung an arm around Red Wing's shoulder. They turned and faced the fire. "Surely she condones how her uncle chooses to live and how he chooses to make a living," he said smoothly. "Surely she even rides with him sometimes when he is wreaking havoc along the countryside."

Red Wing still could not believe this to be true about Malvina.

She looked so vulnerable.

So innocent.

So *frail.*

Yet had not the captured moonshiners said that she was more than likely the competition for having destroyed their still?

The drone of voices awakened Malvina. She stiffened and stifled a gasp behind her hand when she recognized the voice of the man who seemed intent on destroying her standing with Red Wing.

It was Paul Brady, none other than one of her uncle's sidekicks. He was one of the most hardened criminals of all.

And it was obvious that Red Wing saw Paul as a friend, a friend who knew betrayal as well as he knew the nose on his face.

But she knew not to warn Red Wing about this man. In doing so she would place herself in danger. She knew too much about this particular outlaw's activities. If she spoke against him, he would kill her. For now, she would feign sleep and keep her opinions and knowledge of this man to herself.

Red Wing eased away from Paul and turned suspicious eyes his way. "Paul, how is it that you know so much about Malvina and her uncle?" he asked, suddenly realizing that Paul seemed too knowledgeable about things that to most people were unknown.

Paul's eyes wavered. But then, being the clever, calculative manipulator that he was, he smiled slowly at Red Wing, knowing that he had come up with a quick, convincing answer.

"I used to be a member of Malvina's father's church where James occasionally preached before he became an outlaw," Paul said suavely. "That's where I saw Malvina. That's how I knew of her relationship with James."

Red Wing turned quick eyes to Malvina. "Her father was a preacher?" he asked softly. "A man who preached of the white man's God?"

"One of the best," Paul said, nodding.

Red Wing turned to Paul. "Malvina told me that her parents were killed," he said, his voice drawn.

"Her father was killed because he preached hard against moonshining," Paul said. "He became a threat to the 'shines, so they killed him and his wife. The shock of her parents dying in such a way apparently hardened Malvina. She followed her uncle's footsteps into outlawing."

Malvina had to bite her tongue to keep from speaking out and calling him a liar.

But still, she feared him too much to reveal any truths about him.

Just yet.

In time, yes, in time, she would make him pay!

Paul felt as though he might be close to overstepping the boundaries of what he should reveal to Red Wing about Malvina.

He felt as though he was already on shaky ground with Red Wing—especially if Malvina suddenly awakened and found him there.

"I must go," he said, turning to walk toward the door. "I've already stayed longer than I had planned."

"You may as well spend the night," Red Wing said as he walked Paul outside. Red Wing smiled at his cousin Pretty Cloud as she came walking toward him and Paul, a fresh pot of stew for his lodge swinging at her side.

"I don't know," Paul said, though he found the invitation more than tempting. He felt that perhaps it was best for him to stay close by. That way he could keep an eye on Malvina.

But Paul feared his presence at the Choctaw village might eventually bring doom to them. If James were to come looking for him, he would discover that the Choctaw were wealthy by Indian standards—*and* vulnerable, since they were peaceful in nature.

Although Paul was as hardened an outlaw as James, he *did* have much affection for the entire Choctaw Nation. In Red Wing he had found a genuine friend. In Pretty Cloud he had found someone to love. He could not jeopardize losing Pretty Cloud before he gained her love in return.

Pretty Cloud smiled bashfully from Paul to Red Wing, then took the stew on inside the lodge and hung it over the fire.

When she left again, Red Wing nudged Paul in the side with an elbow. "Go after her, my friend," he urged.

Paul watched Pretty Cloud walk away. She turned to look at him as she sat down beside the fire outside her cabin.

His loins ached to have her.

Her hair was long and free of braids and ornaments.

Her cheeks were well pronounced and colored with a faint hint of vermilion.

Though perhaps only seventeen years of age, her well-formed breasts pressed against the inside of her buckskin dress.

He hoped to one day be able to caress the soft contours of her well-developed mounds.

But now was not the time. He had other things on his mind.

What if Malvina should mention him as she talked with Red Wing?

What if Red Wing should mention *him*, and tell Malvina of his visit and the talk they had shared about her?

Yet Paul knew that it was best that he leave.

He turned to Red Wing, gave him a hug, then walked toward his horse. "My friend, it's best I return to my own lodge tonight," he said. "I shall tell Pretty Cloud of my feelings later. Now does not seem the appropriate time."

"You should not keep putting off that which might turn your life around," Red Wing said, thinking about himself and Malvina, and how he wished that everything that Paul had said about her was untrue. "Life is fleeting, my friend. Take from it what you can when you can."

Paul mounted his horse, gave Pretty Cloud another quick glance, then turned his gaze back to Red Wing. "In time, she *will* be mine," he said, then wheeled his horse around and rode away.

Red Wing watched Paul until he left the village, then sighed heavily as he went back inside.

Full of regret, and torn with feelings about her, he stared down at Malvina.

When she opened her eyes and smiled at him, he could not see how anything about her could be ugly.

Chapter Eleven

The fact that Paul had told Red Wing about her black-sheep relation made Malvina feel apprehensive as Red Wing came into the lodge, his eyes never leaving her.

She was glad when someone else entered behind Red Wing. That gave Malvina a reprieve of sorts, at least for a while, in case Red Wing was planning to question her.

Malvina gazed in wonder at the lovely Choctaw woman. She had been there only moments ago when she had brought a fresh pot of stew to hang over the fire. This time she not only carried a platter of varied foodstuffs, she also had a beautiful buckskin dress slung over one arm and a kind of a chemise over the other.

Malvina only now spied a pair of intricately beaded moccasins that sat on the floor beside the bed, thinking that this young maiden must have brought them while she was asleep.

The lovely maiden turned smiling eyes up at Red Wing. "Cousin, as you requested, I have brought clothes for the white woman," she said, setting the platter of food on the hearth. "I have also brought you something besides stew for your evening meal."

"You are thoughtful," Red Wing said to Pretty Cloud, his eyes still on Malvina.

The woman turned to Malvina and smiled down at her as though they were fast friends. "I have brought you clothes that I made for myself, but are now yours," she said, bending to a knee beside the bed. "I even made the moccasins I have brought for you to use when you are well enough to leave the bed."

She allowed the dress and the chemise to slip from her arms, then spread them neatly at the foot of the bed so that Malvina could see them better. Then she placed the moccasins on the floor so that all Malvina had to do was step into them when she left the bed.

"Thank you," Malvina said, swallowing hard when she realized that Red Wing still watched her, his eyes questioning. "You are very kind.

"Your name," she murmured. "What shall I call you?"

"Pretty Cloud," she replied. "I am called Pretty Cloud."

"What a lovely name," Malvina said, wanting to prolong Pretty Cloud's time there, fearing her next private moments with Red Wing.

"Your name, Malvina, is pretty and intriguing," Pretty Cloud said, her dark eyes wide. "I have never heard the name before."

"Neither have I," Malvina said, laughing softly.

"Shall I help you into the chemise?" Pretty Cloud asked.

"That would be nice of you," Malvina said, glancing guardedly over at Red Wing.

Pretty Cloud looked over her shoulder at Red Wing. "Cousin, if you will turn your back, I shall help your guest get more comfortable."

Red Wing stared at her for a moment, then smiled and turned his back to Pretty Cloud and Malvina.

He leaned his arm against the mantel of the fireplace, his thoughts swirling like the flames sweeping upward over the logs on the grate. How could he openly condemn Malvina, whose very presence made a different man of him? He had never met a woman who made him feel this humble.

She played the role of innocence so very well!

After what Paul had told him about her, how could he feel anything but loathing for her? Yet he did. He wanted her now, as much as before he had heard who she was related to, and even knowing the sort of life that she led.

If she were an outlaw, or one who practiced the art of moonshining, she belonged behind white man's bars, not in the house of a man who aspired one day to be a powerful chief.

He shook his head and inhaled a deep breath; he heard Pretty Cloud giggle as she talked with Malvina.

He listened, his spine stiffening as Malvina's soft, sweet voice sent his heart spinning with a passion he did not want to feel.

"The chemise is so soft, Pretty Cloud," Malvina

said, running her hand over the buckskin fabric as it clung to her bosom. "I have never felt anything so wonderful against my skin. And you say you made this dress yourself?"

"Choctaw women make their own clothing, yes," Pretty Cloud said, pleased to make this better acquaintance with the white woman.

For the most part, Pretty Cloud had been sheltered from white people. She had been taught that it was best to stay with her own kind. They were the true people, whom she could trust. Red Wing had taught her the white man's language, which he had learned from his chieftain grandfather.

And although Pretty Cloud had eyes for Paul, because he was white, there was always something about him that made her uncomfortable. That was why she had not openly given him cause to approach her as a man approaches a woman. Something about him made her feel as though, just possibly, Red Wing trusted him too much.

But she had kept her thoughts to herself.

She never wanted Red Wing to think that she did not trust his judgment about everyone and everything. She loved her cousin too much to feed doubts inside his heart and brain.

"I noticed the dress," Malvina said, so glad to have someone else besides Red Wing with her in the cabin. Had Pretty Cloud not been there, Malvina would have been questioned by Red Wing and not known how to answer. "It is also made of buckskin. Do you Choctaw women always wear buckskin?"

"Our attire is varied, as I am sure the wardrobe of the white woman is varied," Pretty Cloud said, helping Malvina back down onto the bed and drawing a blanket up past her breasts. "Each Choctaw woman has her own spinning wheel. We make many clothes by spinning and weaving."

"You are wearing a long calico dress of bright colors today," Malvina said, admiring not only the dress, but also Pretty Cloud's jewelry. She could tell that Pretty Cloud was fond of shiny objects like rings, bracelets, and broaches, all of which she wore today.

"Yes, my father and I made trade for this dress. Sometimes I also wear skirts made of rectangular pieces of deer skin. They are worn wrapped around the body and held in place by a belt," Pretty Cloud said, standing over Malvina. She gave Red Wing a nervous glance over her shoulder, feeling as though she had already worn out her welcome.

"The dress you brought me to wear is perhaps the most beautiful buckskin dress I have ever seen," Malvina said, shifting her eyes to the garment that lay across the end of the bed. "It is so beautifully white and decorated with beads as well."

"The hide was made white by sprinkling white clay on the deerskin while it was being stretched," Pretty Cloud said, lifting her heavy black hair from her shoulders and allowing it to drop in long waves down her back. "The beads I sewed onto the dress, one by one, myself."

"You are very generous to have brought it for me to wear," Malvina said, touched by her kindness. "Again I thank you."

"I must go now and leave you to your evening

meal," Pretty Cloud said softly. She turned to Red Wing and went to place a gentle hand on his arm. "Cousin, did Paul bring sad tidings to you? You seem so lost in your thoughts."

Malvina's insides tightened as she guardedly watched and listened for Red Wing's reply. At all costs she wanted to avoid talking to Red Wing about Paul.

Oh, why had Pretty Cloud brought the name up, to give Red Wing cause to remember all the ugly things that Paul had said about her?

Yet, surely Red Wing had gathered suspicions today about Paul that might warn him that this was not the sort of white man with whom he should share a friendship. Red Wing had surely seen that Paul knew too much about her outlaw uncle.

Most people did not associate *that* James with the James who had spoken on Malvina's father's pulpit. He had not made an impression with the parishioners. Although he was teased and called "Preach" by his outlaw friends, James had quoted scriptures from the Bible far too few times for the community of God-loving people to remember him.

"Paul was here in part, I believe, to get the courage to approach *you*, my sweet cousin," Red Wing said, turning to face Pretty Cloud. "Since you are here in your cousin's lodge, it is obvious that Paul rode out of the camp again without coming to you with his feelings."

"There is nothing more? Paul is all that you have on your mind?" Pretty Cloud persisted, seeing too much in Red Wing's eyes that spoke of his being troubled. He had not encouraged her association with Paul so much to be this concerned over his relationship with Pretty Cloud.

"No, nothing more," Red Wing said, forcing a smile. "Only Paul."

As he drew Pretty Cloud into his arms, he gazed over her shoulder at Malvina. She looked lovely in the chemise, her reddish-golden hair lying beautifully over her pale, slim shoulders.

Yet there was a guarded look in her eyes. Could she have heard his conversation with Paul? Had she been feigning sleep all along, listening to Paul's accusations, trying even then to find a way around these things that Paul had said about her and her kin?

Yet when Red Wing had gone back inside his cabin after bidding farewell to Paul, he remembered Malvina meeting his entrance with the most beautiful, innocently sweet smile.

Again he was torn in his feelings about her.

Was she innocent of all things Paul had said? Or was she perhaps the worst sort of woman, one who sent men to their graves before their time?

"Concern yourself about Paul no more tonight," Pretty Cloud said, easing from Red Wing's arms. "Cousin, I shall, in time, decide whether or not to accept Paul into my life. It is something to be sure of—a man who not only would be my husband, but would also become as one with the Choctaw. This burden lies heavily on my shoulders. I would not want to be responsible for allowing a white man to become as one with our people if he is not deserving."

Red Wing forked an eyebrow. "Is there something about Paul that you suspect, that you have not shared with me?" he said, remembering only moments ago when he had for the first time ever doubted his friend.

Pretty Cloud's eyes wavered. "I have said too much," she murmured, then fled from the cabin.

Malvina scarcely breathed as she waited for Red Wing's reaction to Pretty Cloud's insinuations and sudden flight. She watched his expression change from confusion to a sudden, quiet anger.

She had to wonder if this anger was directed more toward Pretty Cloud, for being so evasive with him, or toward Paul, whom he might now be doubting.

She was glad when Red Wing's mood changed into something more pleasant and he gathered up two wooden plates and two wooden spoons, and came to her, a smile having replaced his brooding frown of only moments ago.

Malvina watched him fill both plates with piles of food, then go to a shelf and bring down a jug, pouring something from it into two tin cups.

This he also brought to her, offering one of the cups. "Honey water," he said, watching her as she gazed into the yellowish liquid in the cup.

"I haven't drunk honey water before," she said, giving him a curious look.

"It goes well with the foods my cousin Pretty Cloud brought for our evening meal," he said, setting his cup on the floor next to the bed. He scooted a chair close to the bench, then sat down and reached for a platter of food and gave it to Malvina.

He reached for the other platter and motioned with his free hand toward her. "Eat," he said softly. "Drink. We will talk later."

"Talk?" Malvina said, her voice drawn. "What about?"

He didn't respond to her question. He scooped food into his mouth with his spoon and chewed, once again motioning for her to eat also.

Starved, Malvina didn't have to be asked again. She enjoyed the succotash, wild rice, persimmon bread and ash-lye hominy. Even the honey water pleased her, and she drank it down in thirsty gulps.

Wanting to build her strength so that she could leave soon to continue her search for her brother, and then the family heirlooms, she ate another plate filled with food.

She finished off her meal with several plump, juicy strawberries.

She had not been this pleasantly filled for so long that Malvina felt drowsy as Red Wing took her empty plate away, and then her cup.

She watched him through droopy lashes as he took the soiled eating utensils over to the kitchen table and set them there. He was so handsome it made her heart race. He was the very embodiment of a noble Indian. She had known him for such a short time, yet she knew already that he was a man of integrity and dignity.

When he came back to her and sat down beside her in the chair, his direct, deep black eyes seemed to penetrate her soul as he silently gazed at her. It was as though he was seeing her for the first time.

Uncomfortable under such close scrutiny, Malvina wished that she wasn't too weak to get up from the bed. She felt trapped, for slowly but surely, she was falling in love with Red Wing.

For the very first time in her life, she felt something for a man.

But she knew that he would not love someone like her—someone he couldn't trust.

And she doubted if she could ever feel free to tell him what drove her to the actions that made him doubt her, that she was searching for those responsible for her parents' death. She wanted to see them punished.

And she wanted to reclaim the family heirlooms.

This was her business, not Red Wing's.

"Are you ready now to tell me more about what has happened in your life to force you into wearing clothes of a man?" Red Wing asked, gazing at her face, aglow from the soft firelight. "Tell me why you burned the moonshiners' still."

Malvina was shaken by his question, stunned to know that he knew about her and Daniel setting fire to the still.

What might he be thinking about her? He not only knew that she was a thief who stole a Choctaw canoe, and that her uncle was a notorious outlaw. He also knew that she set fire to stills!

Setting her jaw firmly, she refused to answer him. She knew for certain that she must escape at her first opportunity. He demanded more of her than she was willing to give. Answers!

And perhaps even more.

The way he continued looking at her was very unnerving! Could he see how she felt about him?

Oh, she must forget how he affected her heart.

Oh, Lord, surely she *was* falling in love with him.

Her heart cried out to tell him everything, to ask for his help.

But no, this was her private battle.

Her own sought-for revenge.

When he realized that Malvina was not going to answer him, Red Wing leapt from his chair. He towered over her, his face solemn. "You are a most stubborn woman," he said, glaring at her. "Do you not know that answering me is more beneficial than staying silent? Your silence condemns more than condones in this Choctaw's eyes!"

He swung around and left the cabin.

Trembling, Malvina stretched out on the bed. She pulled the blanket snugly around her, yet could not ward off the chill that Red Wing's hasty, accusing words and abrupt departure caused inside her heart.

Never before had she wanted someone's love and understanding more than now.

Yet she feared opening up her life and her heart to him. What if he didn't understand her need for revenge—that although good to the core, she was eaten away inside with vengeance?

Tears came easily.

She cried until she felt drained and fell asleep.

Her tears dried on her cheeks and a soft smile lifted her lips when her dreams brought Red Wing back to her. In her dreams, she snuggled in his arms as he embraced her.

Her insides melted as he kissed her.

She had never felt as needed, or as protected.

She awakened, disappointed that what she had experienced with Red Wing had only been a dream.

"If it could only be real," she whispered, again drifting off to sleep.

Chapter Twelve

His carrot-red hair neatly trimmed to his shoulders, his thick red beard equally well groomed, James O'Neal sat before the fireplace in his cabin, cleaning his rifle.

Coffee brewed in a pot in the coals of the fire, overpowering the stench of the whiskey that Paul's outlaw friends had spilled the previous night while gambling at his kitchen table.

Yawning and casually stretching his suspenders away from his chest, Steve Parker sauntered over to the fireplace and stood beside James's overstuffed chair. "Preach, it may take the rest of the day for the cobwebs to clear outta my head," he said, chuckling. "That moonshine was mighty fine last night, partner. Where'd you say it came from?"

"It doesn't truly matter, now does it?" James said, giving Steve a frowning glance. "It's best to forget where we got this or that, wouldn't you say?"

"Sometimes," Steve said. He sauntered over to a basin of water and splashed his face, then soaped it well, leaving a thick enough lather for shaving. "But only if we got a good store of the moonshine before we destroyed the damn still." He took a swipe of whiskers from his narrow face with his razor, then turned to James. "Preach, we *did* take enough to last us a while, didn't we?"

"You know as well as I do that we toted off enough to last a damn year," James grumbled, now shining the barrel of his rifle with a smooth, clean rag.

Burk Sampson came into the cabin and poured himself a cup of coffee. He settled in a wooden rocker beside James. "Preach, last night when you all had your noses stuck in cards and drinkin' moonshine I went into town and did a bit of noseying around," he said, his eyes narrowing as James gave him a hardened look.

"And?" James said softly. The shadows were muted in the cabin by black cloths covering the windows.

James took every precaution not to allow anyone to find his hideout that was hidden in the depths of the forest. But if someone did find it, he would have a hard time finding out what was inside.

It was not so much what was there, since most of what he accumulated from his raids on the settlers was hidden elsewhere, where no man would find it. It was just that his face was known now by too many people. He thought it best to keep himself hidden in the cabin when he was not riding the midnight hour, wreaking havoc on the countryside.

"I saw your niece at Jason Hopper's brothel in town," Burk said guardedly, knowing that even the mention of Malvina stirred James's very soul into feelings he wished to leave behind in the other world of his past, when he was a peace-loving man in Ireland.

But Burk knew that James would want to know what had happened to Malvina. Although he did not talk about it, nor would he confess to it, James kept track of Malvina and Daniel's activities.

James turned flaming eyes to Burk. "You're mistaken," he said, his heart having leapt at the very mention of Malvina.

"I must confess that I didn't believe my eyes when I saw her," Burk said, pouring more coffee into his cup. "I ain't never seen her in anything but men's clothes."

His eyes sparkled and his white teeth shone against his wind-tanned face as he smiled. "Believe me, Preach," Burk said, chuckling. "She wasn't wearin' man's breeches last night. I scarcely recognized her in that sequined dress that showed a good portion of her breasts. And, damn, what long and beautiful legs."

An instant rage lit up James's face. He threw his rifle down and leaned over to grab Burk by the shirt collar, causing him to spill the scalding hot coffee onto his lap.

But Burk didn't yelp with pain from the coffee seeping through his clothes, scorching his flesh. The anger and rage in his boss's eyes made him too afraid to think of it.

"Don't talk about Malvina like that," James said, his words a low hiss as he spoke through clenched teeth. "Give her the respect due her, do you hear?"

"I didn't mean anything by what I said," Burk said, his voice trembling. "Honest, Preach, I only wanted to tell you that I saw her. I figured you'd want to know."

James released the shirt collar, then rose tall and square-shouldered over Burk. "Tell me everything," he ordered. "I want to know everything. Why she was there and with whom?"

"It was plain to tell that she wasn't there 'cause she wished to be," Burk said, standing to remove his coffee-stained breeches. "Someone forced this on her."

"Jason Hopper?"

"I'd reckon so."

"But how'd he manage it?" James said, pacing back and forth, one hand feverishly stroking his beard. "Malvina wouldn't step one foot inside that place. Surely he threatened her with her life."

Then he paled, stopped pacing, then turned to Burk again. Without thinking, he once again grabbed Burk by the shirt collar. "Daniel," he said, his voice breaking. "What of Daniel?"

Burk stumbled backwards with the force of James's grip. "Preach, get a hold of yourself," he said, fumbling to grab the back of the rocker to steady himself. "I'd never have brought this news to you if I'd thought it'd turn you into a wild man."

"Malvina and Daniel are all the family I have left," James said, dropping his hands to his sides. "I know they don't claim me as their kin any

116

longer. But that doesn't make me love them less and not want to protect them."

"Preach, wouldn't you say you're a bit late for that?" Paul Brady said, as he entered the cabin.

After thinking over his predicament the whole night through, Paul had decided that it was best for James to know from him what had happened to Malvina. Paul felt as though he might be able to talk some sense into James about the matter. If James went off half-cocked and blinded by rage after hearing where Malvina was staying, and with whom, a damn Indian war could erupt in this area.

"Paul?" James said, his eyes narrowing. "Where in the hell have you been these past nights? And what is this about Malvina? About my being a bit too late? What gives you the right to tell me anything about Malvina?"

"Because I've watched you hungering to make things right between the two of you, that's what," Paul said, placing his fists on his hips as he glowered at James. "Now, Preach, I've come today to talk with you. And I don't want to see you go into a fit of rage over what's bein' said. I've come to talk sense with you. And damn it, you're going to listen."

James glowered back at him, then reached down and picked up his rifle and brushed past Paul. "I don't have time for lectures," he said. "I've got to go and get Malvina out of that hell-hole of a brothel."

"Preach, you never let me finish what I was saying about Malvina," Burk said, drawing James around to stare at him.

"What the hell's going on here this morning?" James shouted, flailing a frustrated hand in the air. "Is this some sort of conspiracy? Have the two of you got together and decided to take me off guard by telling me these things about my niece?"

Paul went to James and placed a friendly hand on his shoulder. "There's no conspiracy here, James," he said, his voice drawn. "I'm not even sure what Burk has in mind. But I have a need to tell you what's happened to Malvina *and* Daniel."

James's eyes wavered. "First Burk tells me he saw Malvina in the brothel, and now you are saying you have something to tell me about both my niece *and* my nephew? God-damn it all to hell, spit it out. Tell me."

Paul took James gently by an elbow. "I think you'd best sit down," he said, waiting for James to go into a tirade.

He was glad when James cooperated and sat down across from Paul at the kitchen table.

"All right, damn it, I'm listening like a sane person," James said, his heart pounding in his fear of what may have happened to the only two people on this earth whom he respected and loved. "Tell me, Paul. Tell me about Malvina and Daniel."

Paul nervously shifted his feet on the floor beneath the table. "I'd like some sort of guarantee that you won't do anything rash once you've been told," he said, his voice guarded. "I wasn't going to tell you at first. I thought it best left unsaid. I feared what you might do. I only hope that you have some religion

118

left in you, enough not to do anything foolish after I tell you where Malvina is staying."

"Damn it, she's at the brothel," James argued.
He looked over his shoulder at Burk. "Isn't she,
Burk?"

"No, she ain't," Burk said, scurrying into dry
breeches. "You didn't give me the chance to tell
you everything."

"Where in the hell *is* my niece?" James said,
leaning over the table, his eyes narrowing into
Paul's.

"Give me some sort of guarantee, Preach, that
you'll keep your head once you're told," Paul said,
knowing that he was pushing his luck by forcing
this sort of agreement out of James.

"I never do anything without carefully thinking
it through," James said, his hands doubled into
fists on the table top. "Now, damn it, if you want
to see the light of day again tomorrow, Paul, tell
me where my niece and nephew are."

"I'm not sure about all of the details," Paul
said, nervously drumming his fingers on his knees
beneath the table. "But Malvina and Daniel were
in a canoe in the river. A paddlewheeler capsized
them. Malvina was rescued. Daniel hasn't been
seen since."

James paled. "Good Lord," he said.

"Malvina was taken by those who rescued
her to the brothel and sold to Jason; then by
some stroke of luck, she managed to escape,"
Paul said, his words slow and measured as he
watched James's expression turn to horror. "As
she ran from the brothel, an Indian pulled her
onto his horse to save her as Jason came from

the brothel shooting at Malvina. Malvina was shot."

"Shot?" James said, paling.

"She's all right," Paul said, going around to place a comforting hand on James's shoulder. "The Indian took her to his village. It was only a flesh wound. She's recuperating quite well. She's being fed and looked after."

"I don't have to ask which Indian, since you know so much about this," James said, going to stand before the fire and staring into it. "Red Wing. She's at Red Wing's village."

"That's right," Paul said, feeling as though a weight had been lifted from his shoulders. "Someone brought word to me that Red Wing was shot. I went to check on him. That's when I found Malvina there. She was the one who was shot, not Red Wing."

James turned sulking eyes to Paul. "And you say she is all right?" he asked.

"I'd say so," Paul said, nodding.

He hoped that James would never discover how he had spoken so openly against Malvina, incriminating her in the very same breath he had incriminated James!

Yet Paul knew he would feel compelled to do it again if Red Wing kept Malvina at his village for any length of time. She would draw bad luck to the Choctaw as sure as he was standing there.

And Paul had his own interests to look after at the village. Soon he would take a bride price for Pretty Cloud. What father could turn his back to the sort of bride price Paul planned to offer? And what woman could deny a man who could give her the world?

Yes, soon he would go and claim her as his.

But first he had to make sure that neither Malvina nor James caused any trouble for the Choctaw!

"A village of Injuns isn't where Malvina should be," James said, suddenly stamping over to the wall and grabbing his holstered pistols from a peg. "I'm going for her."

"God-damn it, Preach, that's exactly what I don't think you should do," Paul said, grabbing James by an arm. "I wouldn't have told you had I thought you'd run out of here like a crazed man to the Choctaw village."

"You expected less of me than to protect my very own kin?" James shouted. He yanked himself free of Paul's grip. "I'm going for her and then I'm searching for Daniel."

"Preach, I said she's faring well enough, not *well*," Paul said stiffly. "Preach, didn't you hear a damn thing I said? She was shot. She's recuperating. She's not well enough. Don't go for her. You're only going to stir up trouble between yourself and the Choctaw."

James's eyes wavered. "Yeah, I guess I'd best not go," he said, his voice drawn. He turned flashing eyes to Paul. "Not *yet*, anyhow. I'll give her time to get stronger. Then, by damn, nothing or no one is going to stop me from going for my niece."

"And where do you intend to take her?" Paul scoffed. "She doesn't have a house to go to. She and her brother lived in the out-of-doors."

"I'll bring her here," James said matter-of-factly. "I'll give her this place. I'll find another hideout for the fellas."

"It's best to let sleeping dogs lie," Paul persisted. "She's been on her own for quite a spell now. Leave her to her own destiny, Preach."

"Her destiny isn't with Injuns," James snarled out.

He gave a nod to Burk and Steve. "Come on, damn it," he shouted. "We've got to search for Daniel down by the river."

"It's daylight," Paul argued. "You can't afford to be seen in daylight."

"Then you go and search for me," James said, unfastening his holster. He narrowed his eyes into Paul's. "I *can* depend on you, can't I, Paul? You *will* cover every inch of ground until you find my nephew, won't you?"

"Preach, more than likely he drowned," Paul said, his voice low and measured. "More than likely he's been washed down river."

James spoke into his face. "Go and look for him," he snarled.

"Sure," Paul said, clearing his voice nervously. "I'll do my best, Preach. But that's all I can promise."

"That's all I'm askin' of you."

Paul left, his stride stiff.

James lifted the black curtain and watched Paul ride away. "He ain't much of an outlaw if he can ride free and clear in and out of town and not be recognized," he grumbled as Burk came and stood beside him, also watching. "I'm thinkin' there's more to Paul than meets the eye. I'm thinkin' he allies himself with Red Wing more than he allies himself with *us*."

He gave Burk a frown. "Just how many times recently has he ridden with us?"

"Not enough," Burk said, smiling slowly.

"We're going to have to change that," James said, his mood dark. "Or else he'll have to come up with an accident some night."

Burk chuckled at his side. "Yeah, an accident," he said, his eyes dancing wickedly.

Chapter Thirteen

After spending another night in Red Wing's cabin, and feeling strangely comfortable, Malvina stretched and yawned as she slowly awakened.

When she was finally fully aware of things around her, she found Red Wing placing wood on the fire, his back to her. Just seeing the muscles at his shoulders ripple with each lift of the firewood, her pulse raced and a sensual weakness invaded her.

She knew that her heart was lost to him, yet she doubted that he felt anything for her but a silent loathing. He suspected too many things about her that were not true, and yet she was not willing to share the truth with him.

Not yet, anyhow. Red Wing was a gentle, peace-loving man who might not understand her strong need to avenge the death of her parents.

Sometimes she herself did not understand it.

She had listened to many sermons during her lifetime which should have placed her above the need to harm those who had harmed her and her beloved kin.

But everything had changed the day her parents were slain.

She would never forgive those who had wronged her.

Never.

Not if it even meant sacrificing her chance to be with the man she loved.

"Red Wing?"

A voice speaking so suddenly outside the cabin, breaking through the silence, made Malvina suck in an alarmed breath. She turned on her side, drew her blanket more snugly beneath her chin, and looked toward the door.

When Red Wing's name was spoken again, Malvina's gaze shifted to him as he rose to his full height and went to the door, not even casting Malvina a quick glance to see if she was awake yet.

His quiet aloofness toward her stung her very soul, yet she understood why he was treating her as though she wasn't there. Her silence when he questioned her again last evening seemed more than he could tolerate. She had never seen such anger in eyes that were usually gentle and caring.

And she had also seen a hint of hurt, as though she had wounded, even betrayed him.

Red Wing opened the door and was not surprised to find five elders of his village standing there, their eyes filled with concern.

He was not even all that surprised when, one by one, they brushed past him and entered his cabin without being invited.

He was not taken even aback when they went and stood over his bed, staring down at Malvina.

He only hoped they knew better than to think that he shared the bed with her. He had told them repeatedly that she was there only because she was too injured to go elsewhere.

Even now he saw no future with her. Her silence when questioned about things that he needed to know, to understand her and why she behaved as she did, had placed a wall between them that seemed would be there forever.

Malvina crept slowly to a sitting position and backed up on the bed, her heart pounding, her eyes wide with fear as the elders stared at her.

"What do you want of me?" she asked, her voice quavering. "Please leave."

Red Wing saw her fear. He could even feel it inside his heart, as though it were his own.

This proved to him that he could not cast her from his thoughts and heart that easily. He cared about her so much, and he did not feel comfortable with her being placed in such a position at the hands of the elders.

Red Wing stepped up to the bed and eased himself between the elders and Malvina, forcing them to take a step away from her. "She is still not well," he said politely but firmly. "Must you come with your questions now?"

"Step aside, Red Wing," one of the elders said, his gray hair streaming across his thin shoulders. "It is better to get answers from the woman now than to regret it later."

"She will bring no harm to our people," Red Wing found himself saying, stunned at how the words in her defense slipped so easily from between his lips. "Is that not enough to know?"

"Red Wing, our questions are few," another elder said, his brown eyes almost gray in his half-blind state.

"You come to my lodge, you enter without being invited, and you demand to get answers from my guest?" Red Wing said, his jaw tightening. "I respect you all, but I deserve respect in return. I will one day be the leader of our people. Would you then, when I am chief, make me look foolish in the eyes of our people by making demands in my lodge, where a guest lies injured?"

"This woman is not just *any* guest," another elder said, his voice weak. "She is white. And we do not come here to show you less respect than that which is due you. It is just that we have waited for answers about this woman, and you have not yet willingly given them to us. We are forced to get the answers from her."

"Had I the answers, you would have known them by now," Red Wing said, folding his arms across his chest. "In time, I shall bring them to you. But as for now, I implore you to return to your lodges and enjoy your morning meal with your wives. We shall have council later, where council should be held. In the council house. Not in my personal lodge."

"Red Wing, in time you or we will get answers from her," one of the elders said solemnly. "Even though payment has been made in horses for the stolen canoe, *her* horses, that does not lift this woman's guilt of the crime. And what is her connection to those men who make firewater? These things we must know, Red Wing, or she will be taken from our village."

Malvina now knew where her and Daniel's horses were. In this very village of Choctaw! They had taken them as payment for the stolen canoe.

Knowing this made her thoughts of escape much simpler.

She would steal back her very own horse and take flight on it.

"And who is chief of our people?" a voice boomed from the doorway. "Chief Bold Wolf? Or do you elders who have wrongly entered my grandson's lodge today think *you* are chief?"

Malvina felt more and more trapped by the minute. Her presence in the Choctaw village was causing an upheaval that placed a cold fear into her heart.

But she felt better now that the chief had come to speak his mind against these elders. His word was final, and he was not pressing her for answers!

But knowing that she was responsible for Red Wing's integrity to be questioned filled her with regret. She knew that she must leave as soon as she was able.

Even today, if possible. The pain in her shoulder was no longer as severe. And she *did* feel somewhat stronger.

Yes, at her first opportunity, she had to leave.

Red Wing gazed proudly at his grandfather, who had never once let him down. Red Wing stepped away from the bed and the elders and went to embrace Chief Bold Wolf.

Then he stepped aside and let his grandfather approach the elders, who had turned to face him yet had not offered a response to his demands.

"My elders, who have shared so much with me, this white woman is my grandson's concern, not yours, nor mine," said Bold Wolf, moving from elder to elder, taking the time to rest a comforting hand on each of their shoulders. "Trust his judgment. He will do what is right for our people. Have I not taught him to follow in my footsteps? Have I ever given you cause to regret that I am your chief?"

Red Wing saw a look of embarrassment and shame in the eyes of the elders.

Realizing that his grandfather's prodding had ended, Red Wing breathed more easily, yet he knew he could not allow Malvina's silence to continue much longer. If she refused to answer him, he would have to send her away, and along with her would go his heart.

Each elder humbly lowered his eyes. One by one they brushed past their chief, and then Red Wing, and left the lodge.

Bold Wolf embraced Red Wing, then left.

Malvina stared up at Red Wing, not knowing what to expect from him next.

She scarcely breathed when his midnight-dark eyes locked with hers. She swallowed hard and blinked her eyes up at him, then gasped softly as he turned on a heel and left the cabin.

"Red Wing hates me," Malvina whispered despairingly to herself. And why shouldn't he? Her presence jeopardized his standing with his people. She must find the strength to leave!

Slowly, but determinedly, she left the bed. Lightheaded, her knees wobbling, she reached for the buckskin dress that Pretty Cloud had so kindly given her.

After removing her chemise, she slipped the buckskin dress over her head, then eased her feet into the soft, intricately beaded moccasins.

Not having a comb, she ran her slender fingers through her hair until it lay smoothly across her shoulders. She eyed the breakfast foods that lay on a platter on the kitchen table. Pretty Cloud had brought them while Malvina was still asleep.

Knowing that she might not get the opportunity to eat for hours, and needing the added strength, Malvina went to the table.

She took a piece of persimmon bread and dipped it into a vat of thick, sweet honey. Then she ate several long strips of crisply fried bacon and unpeeled a boiled egg and gobbled it down.

Feeling comfortably full, and knowing that she must leave before Red Wing returned, she crept to the door and slowly edged it open.

Peering outside, she saw that the village women were busy with their chores. The elders, who had only a short while ago stood condemningly over her bed, were sitting beside an outdoor fire, leisurely smoking their pipes. Children ran and laughed and played through the village.

But the person her eyes searched for was nowhere in sight.

She had to think that Red Wing had gone to his grandfather's lodge, perhaps to share his grandmother's morning meal, or to have a private council about *her*.

She was relieved that he was not close by, to catch her leaving. The others seemed too intent on what they were doing to see her.

Malvina waited a moment longer. Then, after taking another quick look outside, decided that now was the time for her escape, or she might never get the chance again.

Having succeeded at getting around to the back of Red Wing's cabin without being caught, Malvina felt the courage to continue.

She had to get to her horse.

She stopped in mid-step when she discovered that the horses were being guarded.

She located her roan, then moved quickly into the forest, knowing that she had no choice but to go onward on foot.

She had succeeded at leaving the village without being caught, yet she did not feel all that victorious about it.

In truth, she hated leaving Red Wing. In him she had found the man she had always dreamed of. She wished that she was free to go to him, to speak her mind about how she felt about him, and confess her secrets to him.

But she wasn't free to love, nor be loved. Not as long as the men who killed her parents were allowed to roam free.

And Daniel!

She had to find Daniel!

She moved relentlessly through the forest now, her shoulder aching so much that she felt ill at her stomach. Her knees were growing weaker by the minute.

And her heart was not in her escape. She kept thinking about Red Wing and what he might feel when he discovered that she was gone.

Would he come after her?

She came to a stretch of meadow. She worried about crossing it, fearing she might be sighted.

But she had no choice. She wanted to get to the point in the river where she had last been with Daniel.

Of course she knew that if he were alive, he would surely no longer be anywhere near the spot of the accident.

And finding him washed up on shore was her worst dread.

Yet she would finally learn what she needed to know—whether he had survived the collision or not.

It was important for her to know.

She stumbled from the timber groves into a sea of green, the grass rippling and waving in the breeze. Flowers dotted the land. She saw the pink verbena, the wild indigo, the larkspur, and the wild geraniums, all of which were woven into a wondrous colorful carpet.

She walked breathlessly past the shy buds of the sweet, wild, pink rose.

Coming to a slope of land which she dreaded having to climb, since she grew weaker and more lethargic by the moment, she slowed to a snail's pace.

Banks of sunflowers flung their yellow banners miles wide before and below her. The sunflowers lay in a ceaseless succession of easy undulations, stretching away to far horizons.

When another pain grabbed at her wound, she cried out and fell to the ground in tears.

Chapter Fourteen

Determined to get answers from Malvina, or take her into Fort Smith and be done with her, Red Wing entered his cabin.

He stopped, startled, when he found that Malvina was gone.

His pulse racing, his eyes darted around him.

The chemise was discarded. The buckskin dress and moccasins were gone.

He gazed down at the food that Pretty Cloud had left on the table earlier.

Much of it was gone. That had to mean that at least Malvina had been smart enough to eat before she left.

His eyes filled with fire, Red Wing grabbed his rifle and left his lodge. He stared down at the stamped-down grass and dirt that edged close to his lodge.

He followed her footprints behind the cabin,

expecting them to go to the corral. But he discovered that she had fled into the forest on foot.

"She cannot get far," he whispered to himself. "She was foolish to try! She is still weak. Pain is her enemy. Her knees will not hold her up for long."

Red Wing went to the corral and saddled his white stallion. He was determined to follow Malvina. Now that she was gone, he grieved for her.

Now, for certain, he knew that life was empty without her. No matter if he never knew the inner self which made her what she was today, he would turn her life around and make her into someone she surely once had been!

Gentle. Caring. Sweet. Loving.

Riding off into the forest, his acute eyes followed the crushed path that Malvina had left behind her. He only hoped that he would find her before someone else did, someone who might not be as patient or understanding with her strange behavior.

Pity anyone who took advantage of her, he vowed to himself.

Chapter Fifteen

Malvina slowly turned on her side, her eyes closed. She was not aware of a horse's approach, nor of when it reined in close to where she lay.

She was only vaguely aware of strong arms lifting her from the ground, too lethargic to care whose they were. She drifted into a black void of sleep, welcoming the peace that it offered.

Red Wing carried Malvina beneath a thick-foliaged maple tree and laid her on a soft cushion of moss beneath it. He sat beside her and watched her, concerned for her welfare. He knew that she could not yet be hungry. She had eaten a good breakfast before she left.

Her lethargy, her need to sleep, was the result of her rash flight long before she was ready to travel.

As he watched her sleep, his feelings overwhelmed him. She was the epitome of woman. Her features were flawless.

As before, when he had first taken her to his cabin, he could not help but take advantage of this moment when he could truly look at her without her being aware of it.

His gaze swept slowly over her, the clinging fabric of the buckskin dress allowing him to see the gentle curve of her stomach, her narrow and supple waist, and her perfect breasts.

He reached a hand to her long and drifting hair. He had never felt anything so soft. The color was the same as he had witnessed many times in the evening's sunset.

Unable to control his desire to kiss her, which had been eating away at him from the very first time he laid eyes on her, he bent over her and brushed a soft kiss against her lips.

He jumped back with a start when she stirred and emitted a low moan in her sleep.

But when she did not awaken, he felt compelled to go farther now that he had already stolen from her a kiss that had left him warm and glowing.

He gently traced her facial features with a finger, then moved his hand lower, smoothing them along her slender neck.

When she sighed in her sleep, he once again withdrew his hand.

But still, when she did not awaken, he touched her again and ventured his fingers lower.

Inhaling a quavering, daring breath, he gently molded one of her breasts within the palm of his hand. Just touching her in such a way made his loins begin a slow ache.

A fire seemed to flicker throughout him, one

that he must ignore, for he had not followed her to seduce her. He had come for her to make sure she was all right and to take her back with him to his lodge. His love for her was too strong to deny.

And he could not help but believe that she felt the same for him. Had he not seen it in her smile and in the way she had softened her tone of voice when she spoke to him?

Even if she did not love him now, she would. He would give her cause never to want to run away from him again!

Malvina spoke in her sleep. "Red Wing," she whispered. "Oh, Red Wing, how can I leave you? I love you. . . ."

Red Wing's eyes widened. He was taken aback by what she said. He was even aware that she seemed to be leaning into his hand, encouraging him to keep it on her breast.

Perhaps she believed she was dreaming? Or was she feeling him there, and urging him onward?

Red Wing's heart pounded like a thousand drumbeats as he lay down beside her and drew her close to his hard, lean body. He held her there, daring not to breathe, daring not to move.

But when she cuddled herself closer to him, reaching up to his face with one hand, touching a cheek, then his lips, he could not help but believe that she was only feigning sleep. She, too, wanted what he hungered for. Why else would she be responding in such a way? Why would she have spoken his name? She had even said that she loved him!

"Malvina," he whispered again, brushing her lips with a soft kiss.

Malvina stirred against him, faintly aware of having heard Red Wing calling her name.

A dream. Surely this was a dream.

If so, she hoped she would never awaken.

She loved the feel of his body next to hers. His kiss made her weak with desire. His hand cupping her breast gave her so much pleasure, she wanted to feel the flesh of his fingers on her bare breast, not only through the fabric of her buckskin dress.

"Malvina, I'm here. I love you," Red Wing said, sending butterfly kisses across her face. "I've come for you. You are going back with me to my village.

Malvina was brought out of her lethargic sleep by those words. She suddenly realized that she wasn't dreaming those wonderful touches, those sweet and gentle kisses, nor the words that he spoke to her with such feeling. He loved her. The same as she loved him! How could he know that she wanted nothing more than to be with him?

Her eyes blinked open. As he held her in his muscled arms, as he gazed back at her with a loving that was so intense, it fueled her desire for him even more, she could not deny herself this man any longer.

He had come for her.

She was glad, so glad that she flung herself into his arms.

"Red Wing, I'm so sorry I've caused you so much hardship with your people," she cried. "I never meant to. That's why I left. I feared your people's wrath. But not for myself. For *you*."

"You have nothing to fear for either of us," Red Wing said, touched to the very core by her caring.

138

That proved that she had a kind heart.

At this moment he saw her as innocent of all crimes. He knew that she had to have some hidden, just cause for behaving as she had.

And in time she would tell him all about it.

She was only waiting for the right moment, when she would feel comfortable with the telling. He would give her all the time that she needed.

"I will keep you from all harm," he then said. "And do not fear how my people perceive my having brought you into my lodge. Their respect for me is too high to condemn me for seeing to, and loving, a white woman."

"Now that I am in your arms, feeling so protected, so wanted, I feel that things will be all right," she murmured. "Thank you for caring enough to come for me, even though I may have caused you some embarrassment among your people."

"You are my destiny," Red Wing said, moving to a sitting position. "I cannot help but love you."

He lifted her onto his lap and trembled with rapture when she twined her arms around his neck and looked adoringly up at him.

"Red Wing, I am so weary of fighting my feelings for you," Malvina murmured. "Oh, how I adore you."

When his lips came to hers, everything—her worries, her fears, and her need for revenge—was swept from her mind. She was not even aware that the afternoon was ebbing and that a chill wind sighed in the grass.

The world was red in late sunlight and streaked

with opaque purple shadows, like deep holes in the world. Long shadows rippled over the ground and bushes. Like a firefly, the moon broke through the trees.

"We shall spend tonight alone, away from my people and their questions," Red Wing said, his hands framing her face between them. "My sweet mystery woman, I will build a lean-to for us. I will build a comforting fire. Tonight is ours and all that we wish it to be."

His eyes wavered. "There is one thing we have forgotten," he said gently. He turned her so that he could see her shoulder. No blood stains appeared on her dress. The wound was not seeping.

"The pain?" he said softly. "Does your wound pain you?"

"It comes and goes," Malvina murmured. "Now, while I am with you in this way, I hardly know the wound is there."

"I shall give you cause to totally forget it is there," Red Wing said huskily. "If you will allow it, Red Wing will transport all of your senses to paradise."

"Will I allow you to make love with me?" Malvina said, her heart thudding at the thought. "Is that what you are asking me?"

"Is that something that would please you or frighten you?" he asked, smoothing a fallen lock of her hair back from her eyes.

"Would it please *you*?" Malvina asked, ignoring his reference to "fright." She had never been taught the mystery of lovemaking, or even of falling in love. She did not see why she would be afraid of something that thus far, while with him, made her feel so deliciously sweet inside her heart.

"So very much," Red Wing said, his pulse racing. His gaze softened even more. "But only if you wish to, and only if I will not inflict pain where the bullet grazed your flesh."

"I wish to lie down with you," Malvina said, timidly meeting his steady gaze. "And please do not think of my pain. That is the last thing on my mind at this moment."

"I will ready things," Red Wing said, helping her to her feet.

Malvina nervously wrung her hands as she watched him gather pieces of fallen branches, placing them together so that there was a roof of limbs and leaves held up by two sides of limbs standing together.

When he went to his horse and removed two bear-pelt robes from a buckskin bag and brought them to the lean-to and laid them on the ground, she was almost numb from realizing why he took such care with spreading them on the ground.

It was for her comfort while he introduced her to the ways of becoming a woman.

She hugged herself as Red Wing made a firepit encircled by rocks, then got a pleasant fire burning within the circle.

When he looked up at her and offered her a hand, she went to him and knelt down before him.

"You are rested enough now?" he asked, searching her eyes for answers. "Do you wish to lie with me?"

"Yes," was Malvina's soft, timid answer to both questions.

Her knees were weak, but not from anything but the building passion that was sweeping through her like wildfire.

Never had she felt like this before, as though she were floating. Never had she been so giddy!

But the feelings were delicious.

And if this was what it meant to be in love for the first time in her life, she was glad that she had waited until now, so that she could experience it with this gentle man, this Choctaw warrior.

With darkness translucent and the blaze of stars above them, Red Wing pulled Malvina down into the robes with him. Slowly he removed her clothes, then moved to his knees and quickly discarded his own buckskins.

When they were both totally nude, the campfire warm on their flesh, they sat down opposite each other. Red Wing ran his hands over Malvina's breasts, making her gasp. She scarcely breathed when his hands moved lower, touching the smooth, flat skin of her belly.

Red Wing gazed at Malvina. Her eyes, shadowed by the firelight, had within them a fire all their own, a fire that warmed him in parts long left cold.

Malvina reached a hand to his chest and smiled at him as she moved her fingers slowly across his muscles, down to his flat stomach, then lower. She had never seen a man naked before, but now that she had, she wanted to know all the mysteries of Red Wing's body.

Her gaze shifted downward as he circled her hand and led it to that part of him that grew, as she watched, to extreme proportions. When he encouraged her to touch him there, she felt a hot blush rush to her cheeks. She heard him groan with pleasure as her slender fingers encircled his thick, long shaft.

"Your fingers are so cool to my heat," he whispered huskily. "Move them over me. Feed my desire."

She did as he asked, and at the same time was aware of his fingers at the juncture of her thighs, touching her where no man had ever touched before. As he stroked her, her senses were ignited. Desire spread throughout her like warm splashes of sunshine.

Then he placed one hand at her waist and urged her down on the bear-pelt robes, his other hand beneath her neck, supporting her. He made sure she didn't lie flat on her back so that her shoulder would not feel the brunt of his weight as he lay over her, a knee nudging her thighs apart.

When he kissed her, an incredible sweetness swept through her. A tremor went through her body, and she gasped against his lips as he slowly guided his hardness into her virginal tightness.

The pain was brief. As his hips moved, coming to her, thrusting deeply, her body became alive to the rhythm, to the pleasure, to the splendid sweetness that was overwhelming her.

And as he kissed her hungrily with a kiss that was all-consuming, his hand kneading her breast, she twined her arms around his neck and leaned her body into his.

His lips drugged her.

Happiness bubbled from deep within.

When she winced and she reached over her shoulder toward her wound, Red Wing drew away from her.

"Should we stop?" he asked softly. "Does the pain take away from the rapture?"

"My wound does pain me, but my heart will pain me more if we don't continue what we've started," she murmured. "I . . . never expected it could be this beautiful."

She placed a hand to his cheek. "Red Wing, please continue," she whispered. "Teach me. Teach me. Make love to me."

Red Wing's lips covered hers. He found her mouth hot and sweet, her body warm and responsive. The curl of heat was growing in his body as he gently drove into her with rhythmic strokes. His world as he had always known it was melting away. His mouth forced her lips apart as his kiss grew more and more passionate.

When he could hardly hold back any longer, he paused for a moment and inhaled a deep, quavering breath. He leaned over her with burning eyes, taking in her loveliness, her eyes sheened with the bliss of the moment.

Then his mouth covered hers with a reckless passion as once again he plunged deeply into her warm and clinging sheath.

Malvina could feel something even more wonderful happening inside her. As he surrounded her with his hard, strong arms, pressing her against him, his heat blending with hers as he sent his constant thrusts into her, the sensations were soaring.

Then everything seemed to explode into a million silver lights within her.

Her body quaked against his.

She clung to his shoulders. She moaned.

The sensations were searing.

They were so beautiful that she did not see how it was possible to feel such things that made her momentarily mindless with bliss.

Red Wing thrust one last time into her, then moaned as the pleasure spilled forth from inside him, sending his seed into her womb as the most magnificent of feelings spread through him.

His entire being seemed to throb from the intensity of their lovemaking.

And his climax had been more violent, more lengthy, than ever before with any other woman.

Their bodies strained together, and as their joy subsided, they still clung to each other.

Malvina was shocked at the intensity of her feelings, stunned to have found such paradise in the arms of a man.

But she reminded herself this was not just any man. This was Red Wing. He was special. In every way imaginable, he was special.

"Surely I am beaming as brightly as a moonbeam," Malvina said, laughing softly as Red Wing rolled away from her.

She turned to him, her eyes taking in his sculpted features, the peace in his eyes. "I never knew being with a man could make one feel totally changed inside. But I do feel changed, Red Wing. I actually *feel* more womanly. Do I look changed, Red Wing? Do you see me now as more feminine?"

"Even when you wore man's clothes, I saw the feminine side of you," Red Wing said, touching one of her breasts, loving the soft feel of it against the flesh of his hand. "But, yes, I see some change in you. My woman, you are more radiant than even the stars in the heavens."

Malvina giggled, then flung herself into his arms. "Tell me over and over again how much you love me," she whispered against his lips. "I shall never tire of hearing it."

"Forever and ever I love you," Red Wing said, forcing thoughts of what they still had to face out of his mind. For now, for this moment in time, they were the only two people on the earth.

There were no doubts.

There were no suspicions.

There was no need to seek answers.

He kissed her, trembling with desire as her fingernails raked lightly down his spine and along his hips, then around to that part of him that was again rising to the occasion when they again would take flight together.

The night was new, as new as their discovery of love.

Chapter Sixteen

Dawn was breaking full upon the woods. The distance was veiled in blue mists as Red Wing awakened and became acutely aware of the soft body pressed against his.

His heart leapt with the memory of what he had shared with Malvina during the night. Even now it sent a rush of desire through him to recall how she gave herself to him so completely, so wonderfully.

Yet with the dawn came renewed doubts that he was truly free to love her as he wished to. He had even gone as far as asking her to become his wife.

Now he was concerned over what his grandfather's reactions might be.

Knowing that he had to have some time with his private thoughts before Malvina awakened, Red Wing reluctantly slipped away from her sweet and shapely body. He reached for his clothes and dressed, then stood over Malvina a moment longer.

He so badly wanted to reach down and touch her fair skin. He ached to awaken her and taste the sweetness of her lips again. He wanted to run his fingers through her sun-kissed hair!

Yet he knew that he must think through not only what he had shared with her sensually, but what he had said to her about being together forever and ever. His decision to take her as his wife might change the path of his future. He had to find a way not to allow that to happen.

His head hung, Red Wing walked through the morning mist until he found the winding river that he had seen when he sought a place for a campsite the previous evening.

The river always filled him with a gentle peace and helped to clear his thoughts.

It showed him the way to decisions that would be for the betterment of his future.

Settling down on his haunches beside the clear, smoothly flowing water, Red Wing took a small pouch from one of his pockets. Loosening its drawstring, he shook some tobacco into the palm of his hand.

Holding his hand over the water, he turned his palm over and watched the tobacco sprinkle slowly into the river. "Old Man River, I have given to you a gift this morning. Please now, in return, allow me to share my thoughts and concerns with you," he said softly, so that his voice would not carry to Malvina.

He slipped the empty pouch back inside his pocket. "I am troubled," he said. "The woman of my heart has been accused of many things. But the more I am with her, the harder I find it to believe that she can be involved in these things."

"And, Old Man River," he said. "Many sleeps ago the elders of my village met in council and agreed that I would follow my grandfather into chieftainship. And I am deserving of such an honor. Not because of being kin with the man who is now chief, but because the title of chief is earned by deeds accomplished. I have won the honor by my valorous deeds for my people."

He paused and sighed heavily. "But now, Old Man River," he whispered. "I am torn with what to do. Does the woman blind me too much to what my world is all about? Should I, Red Wing, choose to have a woman, a white woman, with a questionable past and character, to sit at my side as I rule?"

Red Wing hung his head in his hands. "Give me answers, Old Man River, so that I shall know that my choice in women is wise," he said, his voice drawn.

Chapter Seventeen

Slowly awakening, Malvina stretched. As she opened her eyes, she smiled with the memory of the long, sweet night with Red Wing.

She reached out as she turned over in the warmth of the bearskin robes. "Red Wing?" she murmured, then her eyes widened with fear when she found him gone.

Clutching a robe around her, she bolted to a sitting position, her eyes anxious as she looked for Red Wing. Her gaze went to the campfire. It was now only glowing embers.

"Did he leave me?" she whispered harshly, a sudden anguished pain gripping her heart at the thought. Could Red Wing have reconsidered how he felt about her and left her?

Then a low ninnying sound coming from the brush close by made a smile light up Malvina's face. She turned eager eyes toward the sound, and never had she been so happy to see a horse. Red Wing's beautiful white stallion was still there, contentedly grazing. That had to mean that Red Wing was somewhere close by.

But where?

Her heart leapt with passion when she finally caught sight of him through a break in the trees. Although he was quite far from her, she could see him resting on his haunches beside the river.

Wanting to go to him, to wish him a happy morning, and to be held within his powerful arms again, Malvina reached for the buckskin dress and slipped it over her head. She winced and tightened when the dress brushed against her wound. It still pained her, yet she could tell that it was much better. She was surprised that herbs were the cause. If physicians, who spent many years studying their craft, would listen to the teaching of the Indians, they might discover that a whole new world of medicine lay inside the forests, meadows, and streambeds.

Malvina pulled on her moccasins, then straightened the tangles out of her hair with her fingers.

As she stepped away from the campsite, she yawned and stretched again, her body feeling nothing this morning but a sensual sweetness. Again she was aware of the slight pain in her shoulder, yet all that she could truly feel after her night of being loved by Red Wing was a warmth that seemed to fill her very being.

If this was what love was all about, she thought to herself, she hoped to be in love for the rest of her life!

And why shouldn't she be? She had the most

wonderfully gentle and passionate man in love with *her*.

Feeling like singing, yet not, for fear of looking foolish should Red Wing catch her, Malvina left the campsite. She made her way toward the river, where the sun had now burned away the foggy mist, spraying its gentle light over the land.

The morning was still. Malvina heard nothing but the rustling of the leaves in the trees overhead. The white branches of the sycamores broke the dense, green foliage of the hardwood forest. Wild flowers stood tall, their colors whispering rather than shouting for attention.

The gray-headed coneflower stood highest, offering its yellow rays to the wind. A cluster of monarch butterflies headed for a favorite nectar in the flowers of the blazing star.

As Malvina stepped out from beneath the shelter of trees, something else drew her attention and made her mouth water from hunger. Wild strawberries. Bathed in sunshine, they grew in beds of many acres along a hillside.

Rushing to them, Malvina plucked several large strawberries and slipped them inside the front pocket of her dress.

Smiling, she turned and walked onward in soft steps, her moccasins making no sound. Wanting to surprise Red Wing with her sudden presence, she was glad that he had not yet noticed that she was approaching him from behind.

Stifling a giggle behind a hand, she slowed her pace and crept up behind him. Reaching inside her pocket she took out one of the largest strawberries. She reached around Red Wing and placed the delicious morsel to his lips.

"Good morning, my love," Malvina said, leaning around to face him. "I've brought sweets for my sweet."

Red Wing's eyes danced into hers as he bit into the strawberry, then took another large bite before tossing its stem over his shoulder.

Seeing Malvina this morning, all beautiful and fresh, her hair flowing behind her in the breeze, made Red Wing once again lose heart and soul to her. Casting aside worries of his future, he could not help but reach for her and yank her into his arms.

She settled onto his lap, slinking her body against his as his fingers wove through her hair and drew her lips to his.

Twining her arms around his neck, Malvina melted with the passionate heat of his kiss. She squirmed until she managed to straddle him, her insides feverish for him as she felt his manhood pressed against the fabric of his buckskin breeches so tightly, his hardness well defined against her thigh.

Finding herself becoming mindless again with need of him, Malvina reached down and stroked his hardness through his breeches, then drew abruptly away from him when a fish did a flip-flop in the water behind her, the sound startling her.

Her heart pounding, she turned and stared at the river as the fish swam away, suddenly recalling that day when the canoe had capsized.

Sweat pearled on her brow as she again saw her brother falling over the side of the canoe.

She felt the same anguish, the same fear, as when, after the accident, she had searched frantically for Daniel while swimming toward shore, never even getting that one last glance of him.

Sudden tears swelled in her eyes. She moved away from Red Wing and began pacing back and forth along the riverbank, sobbing.

"Daniel," she cried. "Where is Daniel?"

She turned desperate eyes to Red Wing. "It is so wrong of me to seek such pleasure in your arms, when I should be scouring the riverbank for signs of my brother."

She clutched Red Wing's hands. "I feel so guilty for having made love last night, for feeling so wonderful about having made love, when—when I know nothing of my brother!"

Feeling her despair, and wishing he could make Daniel materialize at this very moment for his beloved, Red Wing drew Malvina into his arms and held her.

"Never feel guilty for what we have shared," he said thickly, having come to some peaceful resolutions within his heart after speaking his feelings to the river. "What we have found between us is real. It is *right*. Nothing shall come between us. Not your concerns over your brother, nor those of my people over my choice of women. We shall overcome all of these things together, my woman."

"I shall never get over losing Daniel," Malvina cried, clutching to Red Wing. She turned desperate eyes up at him. "I'm almost certain now that he is dead. And I am finding it so hard to give him up! Please help me, Red Wing. I loved my brother so much."

Red Wing gazed down at her. He understood that nothing he said would make her feel better, nor would it help her accept what fate had handed her.

All that he could do for her was take her back to the riverbank close to the scene of the accident and once again look for her brother.

Surely once she saw, this last time, that Daniel was not there, she might be able to start accepting that he was gone from her forever.

"I shall take you there," he promised. "Together we shall search one last time for your brother."

"One . . . last . . . time?" Malvina said, her eyes pleading into his. "Red Wing, I shall never stop looking for Daniel. Never!"

Red Wing knew not to argue the point with her. He saw her determination. She was driven by her anguish and by her touching love for her brother.

And he could not deny her anything. If she wanted to search for her brother many times over, he would be there to help her.

"Let us go now, and also all tomorrows, if you wish, to search for your brother," he said.

"Thank you," Malvina said, brushing tears from her face with the back of a hand. "I knew that you would understand."

Feeling the bulge in her pocket, she remembered the strawberries. Hunger gnawed at the depths of her stomach. She reached inside her pocket and scooped out nothing but mushiness, the strawberries crushed when she was held in Red Wing's arms.

"There went our breakfast," she said, giggling as she smiled up at him. "Unless you enjoy crushed berries over those freshly picked and firm."

Surprising her, Red Wing reached for her hand and placed it to his lips. His eyes dancing into hers, he began licking the strawberries from her fingers, slowly, seductively, one at a time.

This caused a sensual thrill to soar through Malvina. She could not help but float into his arms, their lips meeting in a frenzied kiss.

"We shouldn't," she whispered huskily against his lips as he slowly lifted the skirt of her dress, his hands stirring fires as he touched the flesh of her legs.

"We should," he whispered back, now stroking the tender flesh at the juncture of her thighs.

She threw her head back with a guttural sigh as he continued to arouse her. When his hands came to her waist and he pushed her gently to the ground, she clung to him, her eyes filled with want of him.

Red Wing slipped his breeches down to his ankles, then lay over her and entered her with one quick thrust.

Malvina clung to his shoulders, her eyes closed, her lips on fire as he kissed her hard and long.

She melted into his hands as he slipped them up inside her dress and cupped her breasts, his thumbs circling her nipples.

"I love you so," Red Wing whispered against her parted lips. "And I shall make all wrongs right for you, my woman. I shall fill your life with magical miracles."

"Yes, I know that you shall," she whispered back. "You already have." She tremored with ecstasy as she realized again the power of his ways of loving.

They floated above the clouds as they once again found that joyous sharing that made their hearts sing.

And when their tremors had subsided and they

lay in a tender embrace, Malvina could not help but shed a few tears of happiness. Although life had been unkind to her in the past, finally she had found a way to overcome it.

Red Wing was her answer for everything.

Everything!

"I am thoughtless this morning," Red Wing suddenly said.

Malvina's eyes widened into his. "What do you mean?" she asked.

"I did not ask how your wound was," he said. "You lay flat on it this morning as we made love."

Malvina gently touched his cheek, her thumb caressing his lips. "How could you believe I'd feel anything but you while in your arms?" she murmured. "All of my senses were drowned in the wonder of you."

Touched by her words and the sincerity of her feelings for him, Red Wing drew her into his arms again. He cradled her close and kissed her.

The sound of her growling stomach made Malvina giggle against his lips. She eased from his arms.

"I think we are both ready for that breakfast you spoke of earlier," Red Wing said, rolling away from her. He smiled at her as he drew his breeches up his legs, watching her as she straightened her dress. "Let us eat our share of strawberries. Then we shall go and look for your brother."

"I truly don't need any food this morning," Malvina said, smiling at him. "My darling, you were my breakfast."

He kissed her again, then took her hand and helped her to her feet. They went to the wild strawberry patch and plucked several berries. He laughed softly as Malvina ate just as heartily as he.

"And so I was enough for you?" he teased.

"Well, almost," she teased back.

Chapter Eighteen

The ferry was in sight on the far side of the Arkansas River where Malvina and Red Wing held to the riverbank in their search for any signs of Daniel. She sat behind Red Wing on his horse, clinging to his waist, her eyes constantly moving in her search.

"Let's move farther upriver again," she said, her voice breaking.

As each moment passed, she was losing hope that she would ever see Daniel again. And she realized that searching along the riverbank any longer was futile. If Daniel was dead, and his body had made its way to shore, they, or someone else, would have found him by now.

Although she could not tell Red Wing just yet that she wanted to give up the search, she knew now for certain that either her brother's body had washed downstream or he had managed to get to shore and was perhaps in someone's cabin, recuperating.

Oh, Lord, how she hoped for the latter.

But if he *was* alive, how would she ever know where he was? she despaired. How would he know where to find her?

They had had no roots, no true place for either herself or Daniel to return to so that if one of them were missing, the other could be there, waiting. The whole Arkansas Territory had been their home—and their only shelter.

Another thought sprang to her mind. Daniel's objective was to go to Saint Louis, Missouri, to enter the seminary there. Although penniless, he *might* have decided to go there if he were still alive and had lost hope of her having survived the river ordeal.

One day she would travel to Saint Louis and see if that were true. Only then, if she didn't find him there, would she truly ever give him up for dead.

Although he realized that there was no hope of finding Daniel along the riverbank, or perhaps anywhere, Red Wing rode onward to please Malvina. He understood someone who did not want to give up a beloved blood relation. He had gone through his own misery when his parents had passed on to the other side.

The difference for him had been that he had known from that very first moment that they were dead. He had seen them shortly after their last breaths. He had mourned for them for months.

Even now when he thought of them, he was overwhelmed with a deep, cutting sadness.

Yes, he understood Malvina's pain. And now it was also his to suffer through with her. For to see her sadness made him sad. Her emotions were his. He felt bonded to her as though they had never been apart.

It was certain that she made his life complete. Without her, life would be nothing at all for him.

"Let's travel away from the river for a short distance and search there," Malvina said, glad that Red Wing was patient with her.

"You are surely exhausted," Red Wing said over his shoulder to her. "Perhaps we should give up the search today and return to my village."

"Please, let's search for just a little longer," Malvina pleaded. "I hate to give up, Red Wing. I love my brother so."

"I understand your concern over your brother," Red Wing said solemnly. "But *your* well-being comes first in my mind. Your wound could worsen if you do not care for it as you should."

"I'm all right," she said, clinging more tightly when he wheeled his horse around and rode away from the river.

They rode through tall wildflowers, as meadowlarks thronged among them eating insects and singing melodious songs.

The trail steepened, leading into a forest of trees that grew thickly on tangled slopes. They rode beside a thorny cluster of wild crab-apple trees crowded with blushing blooms. Violets and anemones were flowering, brightening the undergrowth.

Still, having found nothing and feeling somewhat defeated, Malvina laid her head on Red

Wing's muscled back. "I am so bone-weary," she sighed, loud enough for him to hear.

This was all he needed to draw tight rein. He led his horse beneath an elm tree and dismounted. His stallion began grazing on the tall bluestem grass, the sound of its chewing revealing contentment for having been given the opportunity to stop, to rest and eat.

Red Wing lifted Malvina from the horse. Holding her hand, he led her to a grove of pines beside a gurgling stream, where he encouraged her to sit.

"We shall rest here for a while, then return to my village," Red Wing said, sitting down beside her. "Pretty Cloud will have food waiting for us. She will have my cabin warm with a fire."

Malvina wove her fingers through her hair. "I feel so empty for not knowing the fate of Daniel," she said, food the last thing on her mind at this moment. "I feel responsible for what has happened. I was the one to encourage the sort of life we led. He always did as I asked. He believed in me. He trusted me."

"Do you wish to tell me about it?" Red Wing asked, his voice drawn.

When she only gave him a shy glance, and he realized that she still did not wish to share this part of her life with him, he tried not to be hurt by her silence. He never wanted to force anything from her. She knew her heart. When she decided to open it up to him, she would; that had to be enough for Red Wing, for he loved her too much to demand more.

They sat in silence soaking up the wonders of the late afternoon.

Their eyes seemed to find at the same moment a bird of mystery to Malvina.

"What kind of bird *is* that?" she asked, staring at the bird that sat in the bare branches of a dead sapling that jutted up out of the brush. It seemed to be the bird's favorite perch, offering a complete view of all that it claimed.

The bird was the size of a mockingbird and powder-white in color. Its wings were black with white patches, and it had another white patch on its back just above its tail. Its bill was hooked, and it had a wide, black face mask.

"To some that bird is known as the winged warrior of the forest," Red Wing said, glad to have something to talk about that broke the strained silence between himself and Malvina. "It is a loggerhead shrike. It is respected by all birds, and feared by many. It is a hunter and lives on insects, small birds, and mice."

Suddenly the shrike began to sing. It imitated the sounds of the bluejay. Often it would add a phrase of its own harsh design to the sound it had borrowed, forming its signature.

Suddenly, the shrike flew into the air.

In its absence, the seed-eating birds appeared. Directly under what seemed to be the shrike's favorite perch, a tiny wren worked its way through the brush.

Red-winged blackbirds flitted about, the red on their wings breathtakingly brilliant.

"And so you can see by the activity of the birds in the absence of the shrike just how dreaded it is," Red Wing said, not surprised when Malvina stretched out on the ground and rested her face on his lap. He knew that she was exhausted.

He regretted not having encouraged her more strongly to give up the long search for her brother today.

"I love it here," Malvina said, sighing as she snuggled more comfortably up against Red Wing. "It's so peaceful. It makes you wonder how there could be any ugliness in the world. Why can't people see the blessings of the trees, of the flowers, of the birds? If they could, there would be no more killings, no more heartache."

"Greed causes too many to look away from the beauty of life," Red Wing said. "White men are the worst. Among the Choctaw, the honor and love of tribe is prized above life, above greed. We live each day for the good in things, not the bad."

He reached behind him and plucked a goldenrod stem, the golden flowers thickly clustered along it. He offered this to Malvina. "Do you see this flower?" he said softly. "Lore holds that whoever carries a goldenrod will find treasure and good fortune. It is good to hope for these things. But it is a different matter when one goes out and steals and kills to have them."

Malvina sat up quickly and began sneezing. Over and over again she sneezed. "Please take it away," she said, laughing softly. "Goldenrod doesn't bring *me* good fortune. It brings me misery. I'm highly . . . sensitive to it."

Red Wing threw the plant into the river, then drew her into his arms as her sneezes subsided. "This Choctaw is glad that you are not sensitive to *him*," he said, gazing down into her watery eyes.

"Never," she whispered, trembling with ecstasy as his lips covered hers with a gentle kiss.

Chapter Nineteen

Gerald Smythe reined in his horse on a butte. He gazed downward and smiled smugly when he saw Red Wing and Malvina embracing.

Now he knew which Indian had rescued Malvina outside the brothel.

Now he knew how to scheme to get her back!

Knowing the customs of the Choctaw, which some white people saw as strange and foreboding, he wheeled his horse around. He knew exactly to whom he must go to get Malvina back. He knew of other ways besides the brothel to get money in his hands for the likes of her. Anyone as beautiful as she was would bring much payment in the white slave trade.

Not only would she decorate the cotton fields for a plantation owner, she would serve him well in his bed at night when his wife was too tired to be bothered by his amorous ways.

"And when I sell her this time, no one is going to take the money back from me," he grumbled to himself. "I'll hightail it outta here as soon as the coins are jangling in my pockets."

He rode hard until a lustrous sunset colored the sky pink and orange. It was then that he caught his first sight of the church steeple in the distance.

"And I ain't goin' there to pray, neither," he said, cackling into the wind.

Finally reining in his horse before the spanking white church, he stopped long enough to spit over his shoulder, then made a wide circle and went to the back of the church and dismounted.

After securing his horse's reins on a hitching rail, he lifted a door from the ground and propped it open. He went down the steps that led to the church cellar.

Not stopping to knock, he went inside, where soft candlelight from several wall sconces reflected off the jugs that lined the walls of the basement. The smell of whiskey was strong in the air.

"Father Christopher!" Gerald shouted as he leaned his head up the inside staircase that led up into the rectory. "It's Gerald Smythe. Can you come down here for a moment? I've somethin' to ask of you."

The door to the basement opened, and a man dressed in a long black gown with a white collar made his way down the narrow steps. He wore gold-framed glasses on a hawk nose. His lips were thick, his cheeks sunken. Hair as white as snow hung neatly to his shoulders.

"And what can I do for you tonight, my son?" Father Christopher asked as he stepped down onto the cold, earthen cellar floor. He peered at Gerald, a gentleness in his gaze. "If you have come to confess your sins, why did you not come into the main part of the church? I rarely take confessions anywhere but there."

"Cut the act, Father," Gerald said, sarcasm thick in his words. "You don't have to put on a performance for my sake. I know the worst about you. Don't you remember when we were youngsters in Kentucky? You stole more candy from the candy jars in the general store than I ever did."

"Yes, you know of my childhood sins," Father Christopher said sullenly. "And I would rather you not shout it from the rooftops."

"Roger, I didn't come here to talk over your sins, nor to confess mine," Gerald said, using Father Christopher's given name, as most would not, out of respect for his being a man of the cloth. "I've come to ask your help."

"Gerald, what is that you need from me?"

Gerald looked slowly around the room at the moonshine, and farther still, at the store of weapons that were partially hidden in a corner beneath a blanket.

He smiled slowly. "If your parishioners knew what you were truly about, they'd hang you," he said. "So, Roger, you'd best find a way to help me, or I just might tell a thing or two about you on Sunday morning."

"You don't need to use threats on me," Roger said, slipping the black robe off to reveal fringed buckskin attire beneath it. "Just tell me what I can do for you. It's the same as done." He swung an arm around Gerald's shoulder. "Isn't that what friends are for?"

Feeling there was just a bit too much cynicism in Roger's words and his sudden forced show of fondness for an old friend, Gerald shifted his eyes. "You've been supplyin' me with moonshine since I've moved to the Arkansas Territory," he said. "And I appreciate it. I'm grateful that you've told me about the outlaw gang and have given your okay for me to be a member. So, as soon as I accumulate enough money to pay you well for what I am about to ask of you, you know you can depend on me payin' it."

"I don't doubt that you will," Roger said, moving away from Gerald. He reached for a small box overhead on a shelf. He took a cigar from the box, a match, then lit up and inhaled deeply.

"You know about the Choctaw and some of their crazy ways," Gerald said, his voice anxious. "I'd like for you to find a way to use some of those practices to condemn them in the face of the law, to rile everyone so much against them that they will have no choice but to leave the area."

"And what do you, personally, have against the Choctaw?"

"Nothing, until today."

"What has turned you against them this much?"

"A lady," Gerald growled out. "Red Wing has this particular lady with him who by right should be mine."

"And what makes her your property?"

"I rescued her from the river."

"I see," Roger said, blowing a slow spiraling of smoke from between his lips.

"So? Can you think of some way to help me?"

"What does setting the white community against the Choctaw have to do with the woman?"

"Only that I need vengeance against that son-ofabitch Red Wing," Gerald hissed. "He should've minded his own business where the woman was concerned. If not for him, she'd still be in the brothel. I'd still have my pockets filled with money. And my wife wouldn't have left me!"

"There is much hate in your heart, my brother," Roger said, assuming his clerical manner.

"Don't 'brother' me, Roger," Gerald shouted. "And don't get holy on me, either. Just find a way to make Red Wing pay for his interference! I'll make it worth your while. Just you wait and see!"

"I'll think of something," Roger said, kneading his chin thoughtfully.

"I thought you would," Gerald said, beaming. "And, being the dark, thieving heart that you are, you'll enjoy it as much as I will."

They both laughed, then took a cork from a bottle of whiskey and took turns lifting it to their lips.

"Ain't this the life?" Gerald said, weaving drunkenly as he went to sit down on a step.

"The best," Roger said, then stiffened when he heard footsteps overhead.

"Lord," he gasped. "Someone's come into the church. Surely it's one of my congregation. I can't let them see me like this. Or smell my breath."

"Then just be quiet and they won't know you are even here," Gerald said, gazing up at the ceiling as the floorboards continued to creak.

He paled when the door at the head of the stairs flew suddenly open. He stumbled to his feet, then smiled awkwardly with relief when he saw someone he knew.

"Paul," he said, heaving a sigh. "It's only you."

Paul Brady sauntered down the stairs. He clasped a hand of friendship with Gerald, then Father Christopher.

Behind him came James O'Neal.

"I need a good stiff drink," James grumbled.

"So do I," Paul said, equally disgruntled.

Father Christopher reached for two mugs and poured whiskey into each. "I can tell something is bothering the both of you," he said warily. "Want to share it with friends?"

James's thoughts were filled with Malvina and Daniel.

But he didn't want to talk about it.

This was his private war.

He just needed the companionship. That was all.

He was going for Malvina soon. He doubted now that he'd ever see his nephew Daniel again.

James shook his head no, showing that he would not speak of his worries aloud, then emptied the mug in one long gulp.

Paul's thoughts were torn between two women. Malvina and Pretty Cloud. He felt nothing but loathing for Malvina. But he felt a deep love for Pretty Cloud. He hadn't known one man could experience such extremes of emotion.

But he didn't want to talk about either woman.

This was his problem to sort through.

Father Christopher and Gerald exchanged puzzled glances, then laughed about it. They poured themselves drinks in mugs also.

"To friendship!" James said, raising his mug in the air. "Shall it be everlasting!"

"To friendship!" the others said in unison.

They downed their drinks, then stood quietly eyeing one another closely, the word friendship lost in the depths of their suspicions about one another.

Chapter Twenty

"After we are married, would you mind if I add a woman's touch to your cabin?" Malvina asked as she looked around Red Wing's cabin.

She loved seeing all of Red Wing's personal possessions. They made her feel closer to him. Yet she had longed for so long for a home like the one her mother had made for her husband and children. Frills and beautiful curtains at the windows always made her feel so pleasantly warm inside.

Red Wing was fashioning a new bow as he sat beside the fire, glad that Malvina was in his lodge again, and certain that she was there to stay. Several days had passed, and she seemed content to be learning the ways of the Choctaw.

Soon he would make her as one with his people by marrying her.

"The house is yours to do with as you please,"

he said, smiling over at her. She was sitting in a chair beside him, spooling beads onto a long string.

Pretty Cloud had brought her a buckskin dress and had instructed Malvina how to place the bead designs on it.

Today was her first try at doing this.

"Please don't think that I don't approve of your cabin as it is," Malvina assured him. "It's you, Red Wing. Everything in this cabin is you. I shan't change much. Only add a woman's touch at the windows. I will also find time to braid a rug to place in front of the hearth."

"When we go to the trading post in autumn, perhaps you can choose some dishes made of something besides tin and wood for your kitchen needs," Red Wing said, enjoying seeing how the suggestion lit up Malvina's face. "They also have kitchen linens in red and blue checkered designs. Would you wish to have those over the plain cloths I have seen you use?"

All of the beads now on the string, Malvina laid them aside on the chair and rushed to her feet. Beaming, feeling perfectly content, she knelt before Red Wing's chair.

"Yes—oh, yes. The suggestion is wonderful. And Red Wing, can't you see? Everything is going to be so perfect between us," she said, looking adoringly up at him. "I shall make you a perfect wife. I shall be a devoted mother to our children."

Red Wing started to reach a hand to her cheek, but sent startled, alarmed eyes to his open cabin door when he heard the arrival of many horses outside.

"No one sent word that they wish to have council with my grandfather," Red Wing said warily, setting his bow aside on the floor beside the chair. "When my grandfather has council, I am a part of it."

Malvina moved to her feet and stepped aside so that Red Wing could get up from his chair. His eyes narrowed suspiciously as he went quickly to the door.

Everything within him went cold when he saw that his whole village was surrounded by outlaws. James O'Neal was edging his way closer to Red Wing's lodge, a small Choctaw brave held hostage on his lap, a knife at his throat.

James stopped before Red Wing's cabin. His eyes met Red Wing's. "Send my niece outside," he said, his blue eyes glittering with anger. "Now, Red Wing, or this child's life is over."

Malvina almost fainted when she heard her uncle's voice and the threat that it presented.

Her knees weak, Malvina crept toward the door.

Breathing shallowly, she stood behind the protective shield of Red Wing's body and poked her head around him to look at James.

A sinking feeling at the pit of her stomach grabbed her when she saw that he held a child hostage on his lap. The fear in the child's eyes sent anguish into Malvina's heart.

"Let Dreaming Shield go," Red Wing said, his voice smooth and even. "You know that if you harm an innocent Choctaw child, your own life will soon be over."

"The child will not be harmed if you send my niece out to me," James said unflinchingly, Red Wing's threats carrying no weight as far as he was concerned.

James knew that he had the upper hand. Out of the corner of his eye he saw his gang members with their rifles leveled on many Choctaw. Red Wing had to know that not only would the child die, but also perhaps most of his people!

Having never thought that her uncle could be this heartless, or this *stupid*, Malvina saw that she had no choice but to do as he asked.

For the sake of the child, for the sake of Red Wing's people, she stepped around Red Wing, her chin boldly lifted, her eyes filled with an angry fire.

"How could you do this, James?" she asked, her voice drawn as an outlaw brought her a horse. "What has happened to you to change you into someone I no longer know?"

"Just get on that horse and shut up," James said, motioning toward the palomino pony. "This isn't the place for you, Malvina. I can't even believe you'd be in that Indian's lodge, behaving as his squaw. In my eyes, that isn't decent."

"I'm *not* his squaw, but when I *do* marry him, it won't be wrong," Malvina said, her voice breaking. "James, when you read the Bible daily and understood its meaning, you were never filled with prejudices."

Malvina angrily yanked the horse's reins from the outlaw and swung herself up into the saddle. "James, what you are doing today is a waste of time," she warned. "I *do* plan to marry Red Wing. You can't keep watch on me every minute of the day and night. I'll come back and live with Red Wing, and there won't be anything you can do about it once I am his wife."

She leaned over and spoke into James's face.

"Or would you also defy God's law and forcefully separate a husband and wife?" she hissed.

"Malvina, just be quiet and ride off with me and don't try anything," James warned. "*And* I'm taking the child to be sure the Choctaw don't follow."

"You can't!" Malvina cried, paling. "Let the child go, James. Please."

Held at bay with too many firearms aimed at him, Red Wing stood his ground, his jaw tight. He knew that James had played his hand well. As long as Dreaming Shield was with him, the outlaw knew that no one would follow. James must surely know that the Choctaw valued their children. They were the future of the Choctaw Nation.

"The child stays with us," James said icily. He turned steel-cold eyes toward Red Wing. "And should any of your warriors follow, the child's life will end as quickly as your warriors are spied on their horses."

"You can't keep the child forever," Malvina argued. "Or do you plan to kill him once you have placed enough space between you and the Choctaw village to feel that he is no longer needed to guarantee your protection?"

"The child will be brought back to his family perhaps tomorrow, or perhaps the next day," James said, answering Malvina, but directing his words to Red Wing. "It is my promise that nothing will happen to this young warrior if you abide by the rules I have set forth today."

Stoic, cold sober, and angry, Red Wing did not offer a response. He would not waste words on this madman.

He shifted his gaze to Malvina. His heart cried out to grab her from the horse.

But he had to be patient and work this out in ways best for everyone. He absolutely knew that she would be safe with James, whose love for her had sent him daringly into a Choctaw village today, proving how he would guard her life with his own.

So then the only one whose life was in true danger was Dreaming Shield.

His gaze went to Dreaming Shield's parents. His father was livid with rage. His hand was on his knife sheathed at his waist.

Red Wing had to make sure that neither he nor anyone else did anything foolish to jeopardize the young brave's life.

If required, Red Wing would stand in the way of their horses if anyone tried to leave the village to go after the child.

He had to believe that Dreaming Shield would be released. If not, the white outlaw must know that the wrath of the Choctaw would come down on him like a swarm of hornets. He would never get away from them alive!

Red Wing also had to believe that Malvina would find a way to escape the clutches of her mad uncle. When she did, she would bring Dreaming Shield home with her.

Then the Choctaw would keep guards posted everywhere to make sure what had happened today would never be repeated. In the future, any outlaw who even got near the village would be shot on sight!

Not wanting any blood spilled, ever, in the Choctaw village, Malvina cast Red Wing a sorrowful

177

look, then swung the palomino pony around and rode off with James. She was amazed at how many men belonged to his gang. She now understood that he was one of the worst outlaws in the history of the Arkansas Territory.

It saddened her to know that he could change so much.

She recalled what Red Wing had said about greed. Greed was the cause of her uncle's change—the need to hear the tinkle of coins in his pocket, to feel the crispness of a bill between his thumb and forefinger, the greed that sent many men to their graves before their time.

The hem of her buckskin dress hiked up past her knees, the sun warm on her flesh, Malvina rode for what seemed to be hours before she saw a cabin nestled deeply within a forest of trees. This was surely her uncle's hideout.

She smiled to herself. She had watched all along the journey to the hideout so she would know her way back once she escaped. If ever she got the courage, she would bring the law down hard on her uncle and his gang.

She had to search hard within her soul for ways to love him as she had when she was a small child, adoring her special uncle. It was hard. He had almost erased from her mind all that was ever good about him.

Finally at the cabin, Malvina reined in beside a hitching rail and slid out of the saddle. She watched guardedly as the child was lifted off James's lap.

Then she ran to Dreaming Shield and fell to her knees beside him, clutching him desperately to her. "Dreaming Shield, don't be afraid," she whispered as he clung around her neck. "I won't let anything happen to you."

Dreaming Shield was only six and knew only ways to love, not to hate. Malvina feared that this might change his whole future and he would never trust anyone again.

She gazed heatedly up at her uncle as he came to place a gentle hand on her elbow.

"Come inside, Malvina," he said, his mood changed to a gentler and kinder one. "Honey, I understand why you are angry with me. But I had to take you from the village so that you can now go on with your life. Find a reputable man for a husband. There are many soldiers at Fort Smith who'd kill to have you."

"And how does bringing me to an outlaw hideout make that possible even if I agreed with you?" Malvina spat out as she stumbled to her feet. She held on to Dreaming Shield's hand as he sidled next to her, his eyes wide with fear.

"I'm going to build you a cabin close to Fort Smith," James said matter-of-factly. "The soldiers won't even know we're related."

"James, you're blind to the truth," Malvina said, going inside the gloomy dwelling with him. "How do you intend to keep me from going to Red Wing once I'm settled into my own cabin? You can't keep me guarded without the soldiers seeing that I am. And if I am kept under lock and key, don't you see that it would be impossible for anyone to come and call on me?"

She laughed loosely. "But I don't know why I'm trying to rationalize any of this with you," she said. "I'll be back in Red Wing's village the first opportunity I have to leave this hellhole."

179

She shuddered as she looked slowly around her. Only candles dimly lit the cabin. Yet the light was enough to reveal that it was unkempt and very harshly lived in.

"If you managed to leave, I'd come and get you again," James said, shrugging.

"You wouldn't get the chance," Malvina hissed out between clenched teeth. "Do you think Red Wing would ever allow this to happen again? You'll be meeting your Maker soon, James, and better that you do. You are living the very life my father preached against on the pulpit. The doors of Heaven will be closed to you, James. And what a pity that is. You once were such a sweet and caring man, a man of God with only pure thoughts."

"Just shut up, Malvina," James said, glowering at her.

"James, don't you even care about Daniel?" Malvina asked, her eyes wavering into his. "You haven't even asked about him. You once loved him as much as you would a brother."

"Malvina, things change," James said, grabbing a pot of coffee from the coals of the fire and pouring himself a cup. "Take yourself, for example. I know that you've been desperately searching for those who killed your parents. I know how intent you've been on finding the family heirlooms."

He turned to face her. "Malvina, it's time for you to get on with your life," he said. "Accept your parents' death. Forget those damn jewels. And damn it, Malvina, accept *Daniel's* death. You know that if you haven't found him by now, he surely drowned."

Malvina paled. She placed her hands on Dreaming Shield's shoulders and backed him up to lean his back against her. She held him in place, to give him a feeling of being protected. "James, how do you know so much about what happened?" she murmured.

Then her jaw tightened and her eyes took on a knowing look. "Paul," she said, her voice breaking. "Paul Brady told you. The scoundrel."

"He's my *friend*," James said, taking a sip of his coffee. "He knew I had to know about you, because no matter what's happened between us, Malvina, I still love you. You're my only niece. I shall always love you."

"You have a strange way of proving it," Malvina said, her voice quavering.

A voice from outside broke the strain between them.

"Preach, can you come out here?" the voice said.

James and Malvina glared at one another a moment longer; then James stamped from the cabin, leaving Malvina and Dreaming Shield alone.

"I want to go home," Dreaming Shield said, turning around to gaze up at Malvina. "Please take me home."

Malvina knelt down before him. She ran her fingers through his dark, shoulder-length hair. "Darling, I know," she murmured. "And I promise you that I will take you home as soon as I can leave this horrid place and these vile, heartless men."

"My uncles are not like your uncle," Dreaming Shield said, his lower lip curving into a pout. "Mine are good. Not bad."

"My uncle used to be good," Malvina said,

drawing him into her embrace. He wrapped his tiny arms around her neck and clung to her. She became aware of his hunger when his stomach growled.

"Dreaming Shield, let me see if I can find us something to eat," she said, drawing away from him. "We need all the strength we can muster so that when the time comes for us to escape, we'll be strong enough to do so."

She stood up and turned toward the fire in the fireplace. A large black kettle hung over the coals. From it wafted an unpleasant odor of what might be wild onions, cabbage, and Lord knew what else.

But it was food. That was all that mattered.

Malvina looked at the table covered with filthy plates, where flies buzzed over half-eaten food.

She shuddered and looked overhead, glad to find some clean tin plates stacked on a shelf. She ladled the stew out of the pot onto the two plates, then handed one of the plates to Dreaming Shield.

"Let's sit on the floor by the fire while we eat," she murmured.

Dreaming Shield nodded and sat down beside her.

So hungry that she did not care what she was eating, Malvina dove into the food and soon emptied her plate. She laughed to herself when she saw that Dreaming Shield had emptied his plate just as quickly.

She was about to place more food in the plates when James came back into the cabin, his eyes filled with anger.

"I've things to attend to," he said darkly. "I'll be

leaving for a while. But don't think about trying to escape. There'll be someone just outside the door waiting for you, should you try."

Malvina looked over his shoulder at a holstered pistol that was partially hidden beneath a buckskin jacket on a peg on the wall. She knew that he had forgotten it was there. It would be her means of escape.

She smiled wickedly up at James. "Whatever you say, Uncle James," she said smoothly, causing him to fork an eyebrow at her cooperation.

"Behave," he said, giving her a lingering stare, then wheeled around and left.

Malvina smiled smugly over at Dreaming Shield. "Honey, we'll be gone from here before the sun sets along the horizon," she reassured him. "Now eat up. Get your fill. I'm not sure when we'll get the chance to eat again."

Dreaming Shield smiled broadly at her and nodded. "Red Wing was right to choose you for his woman," he said softly. "You make life exciting."

Malvina's eyes widened at his remark.

Then she giggled.

"Thank you for the compliment, I *think*," she said, reaching over to tousle his thick head of hair.

He laughed, then held his plate out for a refill.

Chapter Twenty-One

Feeling that enough time had passed for the guard to get drowsy, Malvina tiptoed across the floor and yanked the pistol from the holster that she had spied earlier.

Dreaming Shield watched with anxious eyes as she checked to see if the pistol had bullets in it, then sighed heavily with relief when she nodded and smiled at him.

"Wait while I take a look outside the door to see what the guard is doing," Malvina whispered, now tiptoeing to the door. She flinched when the door squeaked as she slowly opened it.

She gasped with fear when she found Burk, the outlaw who seemed to be everywhere, standing there waiting for her.

But Burk had made a mistake.

He had not counted on her having a weapon.

Burk's was holstered.

Tossing aside the surprise of Burk standing there, as though he had known the very moment she would try to escape, Malvina quickly aimed the pistol at him.

"Hands up, Burk," she said stiffly. "Then step inside."

She was not sure what she would do with him when he followed her commands. She didn't want to shoot him. And she knew that he wouldn't allow her to get close enough to knock him over the head with the butt end of the firearm.

"Don't do anything stupid," Burk growled, raising his hands over his head. "Women don't know enough about firearms to be handling them. You're no exception. One slip of the finger and I'm dead."

"Just remember that, Burk, and we'll get along just fine," Malvina said unflinchingly.

She motioned with her gun toward the door as she quickly stepped outside so that he could enter the cabin. "Go on inside the cabin," she flatly ordered. "But don't forget that I have a pistol leveled at your back. I see you as worthless, so it wouldn't take much for me to shoot you. Especially if doing it ensures our successful escape."

"Step aside, Dreaming Shield," Malvina shouted at the small child, to make sure that the outlaw couldn't suddenly grab him and use him as a shield. "Get to the far side of the cabin. The outlaw is coming in."

Burk frowned at Malvina, then sauntered past her.

The very smell of him made her feel ill. It was a mixture of dried perspiration, horse flesh, tobacco, and moonshine. She coughed and gagged, then followed him inside the cabin.

Out of the corner of her eyes, she caught sight of a coiled rope hanging from a nail on the wall.

"Dreaming Shield, make a wide turn around this man and go to that wall and get that rope," she said, her heart pounding in her anxiousness to leave this place.

Dreaming Shield watched the outlaw as he edged along the wall, his back sliding against it, as he moved toward the rope. When he got it, he looked questioningly at Malvina.

Malvina glowered at Burk. "Dreaming Shield is going to take your firearm from your holster; then he's going to tie your wrists and ankles," she said tightly. "If you so much as *look* like you are going to grab him while he's doing this, you'll get a bullet in the skull."

Burk laughed sarcastically. "Yeah, as though you have the skill to shoot accurately enough," he said.

"My father may have been a preacher, but let me tell you, he prepared both me and my brother for the sort of life we found here in the Arkansas Territory," Malvina warned. "If you don't believe me, give it a try. I swear to you, you'll be sorry."

"Yeah, I should've known that a woman who wore pants like a man might think and act like a man," Burk grumbled, his smile waning. "Just don't get antsy with that thing, Malvina, as men are prone to do. I'd like to see sunup tomorrow."

"Behave, and you will," Malvina said, smiling smugly.

"Now put your arms straight out before you and your hands together so that Dreaming Shield can tie your wrists."

A sudden thought seizing her, Malvina glanced over at Dreaming Shield. The young brave was only six. "Dreaming Shield, you *can* tie a strong knot, can't you?" she quickly blurted.

"In teaching me ways of a warrior, my father taught me how to tie knots in ropes," Dreaming Shield said, inching slowly over to the outlaw.

Eyeing the outlaw warily, Dreaming Shield hurriedly grabbed his pistol from its holster and tossed it over onto a table, then tied the man's wrists together.

He stepped aside when this was done and looked to Malvina.

She motioned with her pistol toward Burk. "Now go and sit down on a chair," she told Burk, nodding toward a chair.

When Burk reluctantly did as she said, she gave Dreaming Shield a quick glance. "Now, Dreaming Shield, take the rope and tie the man's legs to the legs of the chair, and then take several turns in the rope to tie him totally to the chair."

Dreaming Shield smiled at her, then did as she said.

"Now come with me," Malvina said, reaching out to gently take one of Dreaming Shield's hands. "We're leaving this dreadful place."

"You won't get far," Burk warned. "When James returns and finds you gone, you'll have hell to pay."

"If my uncle knows what's best for him, he'll leave me be to my own affairs," Malvina said, stopping to turn and give Burk a stubborn stare.

"You tell my uncle that I won't let him dictate my life. I can do just fine without the likes of Uncle James."

"And so you're going to go and play house with an Injun?" Burk taunted. "You're going to lay with him midst his blankets and make babies? You're a whore, a damn whore, for choosing an Injun for your husband."

"Most white men that I've become acquainted with in these parts are disgusting pigs," Malvina hissed. "Just look at you. You're filthy. You stink. You're disgusting. What woman would want *you?*"

She left the cabin with Dreaming Shield and ran to the corral. She gave Dreaming Shield the gun to hold, then took the reins of the horse that she had ridden on earlier. She quickly saddled it, then helped Dreaming Shield onto the horse.

Hoping she would have no further need of the pistol, Malvina told Dreaming Shield to toss it into the brush. She started to mount the horse, but instead turned and looked at the other horses that were grazing in the corral.

Without much thought to whether or not she should, she opened the corral gate. When she clapped her hands, the horses galloped through the gate and scattered.

Feeling content that she had left no way for Burk to come after her should he manage to escape, she smiled and swung herself up into the saddle.

"Dreaming Shield, let's go home," she said into his ear as the child clutched the saddle in front of her.

The horse blew out a snort as Malvina gave the reins a slap. She clucked to the steed and nudged her knees into its sides, then rode off in a hard gallop through the forest.

She smiled when she thought of her uncle's surprise when he returned to his cabin and found that not only had she and the young brave escaped, but she had also set his horses free.

She knew that he would be beside himself with anger, but hoped that he would now realize how adamantly determined she was to be with Red Wing.

Then her thoughts shifted to Daniel.

Sweet Daniel.

She did not forget him for very long periods of time.

Even now, as she rode free and wild through the forest, it seemed only right that he should be there at her side on his own powerful steed, laughing and joking with her.

"I must take one last look beside the river," she whispered to Dreaming Shield, "Before I take the ferry across the Arkansas to return to Red Wing's village, I must search this one last time for Daniel."

Having memorized the way from the Choctaw village to her uncle's cabin, Malvina made a wide swing with the horse and headed east.

"Hang on tight, Dreaming Shield, we've a ways to go yet before getting home," she told the young brave. "But I've something else to do first. Please be patient with me. As I promised, I'll get you home to your parents before sunset."

"You are a courageous woman," Dreaming Shield shouted back. "As my years lengthen, I will be telling my grandchildren about you."

Cassie Edwards

His words touched Malvina's heart and made her more determined than ever to not let anything stop her from returning this sweet and innocent child to his parents' doorstep.

Chapter Twenty-Two

Red Wing sat staring into the fire in his cabin, burdened with worries and building doubts about Malvina's sincerity. Fearing for the safety of Dreaming Shield and Malvina, Red Wing had not gone after the outlaws to rescue them.

Now he wished that he had. He should have chanced everything to rescue them. No matter what might have happened, it would have been better than having time to think over too many things, finding answers that did not please him.

The more he had time to think about how easily Malvina had left with her uncle, the more he doubted her. He could not help but believe that perhaps what Paul had said about her was true. Why had she left with her uncle, if Paul's accusations were not true?

At first, he saw her willingness to leave as a sacrifice on her part to keep trouble from erupting between the outlaws and the Choctaw. Yet there was the possibility that she knew too well how to fool this man who was blinded by his love for her!

Unable to stay in the cabin alone with his thoughts and feeling a need to go to the river where he had first seen her, Red Wing dressed quickly in a calico shirt, deerskin leggings, and moccasins. He put a Bowie knife in his belt and picked up a rifle.

He spoke to no one as he rode his white stallion hard through the village. Ignoring the questioning stares of his people, he left the village and went to the ferry landing. He found Joe there with the ferry, just getting ready to shove off to travel to the other side.

After taking his horse onto the ferry, Red Wing stayed on the far side, away from Joe. As the ferry made its way slowly across the river, Red Wing stared over to the other side. In his mind's eye he was recalling the two white people taking Malvina into their wagon. He recalled so vividly how beautiful Malvina had been when he first saw her, even while she wore men's clothes.

Shaking these thoughts from his mind, he was glad when he was able to leave the ferry.

Again on solid ground, he mounted his horse and rode slowly beside the embankment of the river. He rode farther and farther, his eyes searching the river bank, his thoughts on how determinedly Malvina had searched for her brother.

Today it was as though Red Wing were searching for something more. Being here, where he had been with Malvina more than once, it seemed only right that he might seek answers about who she was, and whether she had been honest with him.

Sighing, suddenly thinking that what he was doing was foolish and a waste of time, for all it did was confuse and hurt him more, he started to wheel his horse around and return to the ferry.

But he stopped. His heart skipped a beat when up ahead, a short distance away, he saw Malvina. Dreaming Shield was with her. She had not seen Red Wing yet. It was obvious that she had only one thing on her mind as her eyes raked the land an inch at a time.

Again she was searching for her brother.

He wondered if her uncle had allowed her to come here, or—

"She escaped!" he concluded, his voice a harsh, hopeful whisper as the word 'escape' brushed across his lips.

Yet until he questioned her, he would not come to any set conclusions. He did not want to take her back with him to his village until he knew, with absolute certainty this time, that she was worthy of becoming as one with the Choctaw!

His hearing astute, Dreaming Shield looked around and saw Red Wing a short distance away beside the river.

His eyes lit up, and he yanked at Malvina's arm.

"Red Wing!" he cried. "Do you see, Malvina? Do you see Red Wing?"

Malvina was stunned when she looked up and saw Red Wing slowly approach her. "Lord, it *is*," she whispered.

She nudged her horse with her knees and urged it into a soft lope. When she came face-to-face with

Red Wing, she was puzzled by how he looked at
her. He most certainly did not seem all that glad
to see her.

What might he be thinking?

Why would he even be angry with her? she wondered desperately. She had managed to escape her
uncle's wrath and save Dreaming Shield's life at
the same time.

Malvina swallowed hard when Red Wing still
said nothing to her, just stared at her with his
penetrating, midnight-dark eyes.

"Come to me, Dreaming Shield," he finally said,
reaching a hand out for the young brave. "You can
ride with me on my stallion back to the village."

"Red Wing, what's the matter?" Malvina asked
as she helped Dreaming Shield down from her
horse.

She watched the child run over to Red Wing,
obviously delighted to be with him.

"I have had time to think," Red Wing finally
said to Malvina. "To me it seems you left too
eagerly with your uncle. Is it because you wished
to resume the sort of life you led before becoming
acquainted with Red Wing? Tell me I am wrong,
Malvina. I am here to listen."

"You are wrong!" she cried. "I told you why I
left. To keep peace in your village! And can't you
see, Red Wing? I escaped. I've brought Dreaming
Shield with me. Ask him about our time with my
uncle. He will tell you that none of it was pleasant, that I defied my uncle from the moment I
was with him."

"Red Wing, what she says is true," Dreaming
Shield said. "She is a most courageous woman."
He thrust out his chest. "Even I have proved my

194

bravery today. While Malvina held a gun on an outlaw, I took the man's gun from him, and I tied him up so that Malvina and I could escape."

Red Wing's heart leapt with gladness to know that he had been wrong to doubt Malvina. He leaned a hand to her cheek. "My woman, can you forgive this foolish Choctaw warrior for doubting you?" he said thickly.

"Yes, I forgive you," she murmured, her eyes misting with tears. "Darling, please allow me to return to your lodge. I don't want to be away from you ever again."

Certain now that she was a pure-hearted woman, and forgetting all of the questions she had not yet answered, Red Wing twined his fingers through her hair and drew her lips to his and kissed her.

Then he straightened himself in his saddle and looked solemnly at her. "If your uncle comes again to my village, I will fight for you," he said.

"My uncle would be foolish to ever think I would leave with him again," she said, then looked adoringly up at him. "Red Wing, let's go home," she murmured.

He nodded, then swung his horse around and headed back toward the ferry. Malvina rode at his side, her chin proudly lifted, her heart singing.

When they reached the village, the sun was just going down in a blaze of glory. Malvina smiled to herself when Red Wing rode up in front of Dreaming Shield's house. The child's parents came to the door, their eyes wide to discover that their son had been delivered to them unharmed.

Red Wing helped Dreaming Shield from his horse. The boy's father came and swept him up into his arms. Dreaming Shield's mother's eyes filled with tears as she met their approach outside the cabin.

Dreaming Shield turned smiling eyes to Malvina. "The sun is setting," he said, giggling.

"Yes, I know," she murmured, flicking glad tears from her eyes.

"Let's go home, my woman," Red Wing said, taking her horse's reins, leading it beside his toward his lodge. "For having doubted you again, I owe you a loving."

Malvina felt a sensual thrill swim through her at his suggestion.

Chapter Twenty-Three

His eyes smoke-black with passion, Red Wing dried Malvina's creamy skin with a buckskin cloth. Their bath in the river had been quick, since both hungered for more than the caresses the water afforded them. Their mouths, their hands, knew better the art of caressing.

They had rushed back to Red Wing's cabin, their need for one another tonight surpassing the need of the heavens to display their show of flickering stars!

Tonight *they* were the universe. Their love knew no bounds, and Red Wing's suspicions of the woman he loved were cast into the wind.

After the water droplets were smoothed away from Malvina's skin, Red Wing tossed the cloth aside and wove his fingers through her damp hair.

Gently tightening his fingers through her locks,

he drew Malvina closer. "My woman," he said huskily, his gaze taking in her liquid curves, his free hand kneading one of her breasts. "Never will anyone take you from me again. Let those who wish to have you just try."

He paused, then said, "They will that quickly die!"

"I shall fight beside you for my right to stay with you," Malvina whispered, running her hands up and down his muscled back. "Even my uncle shall see the extent of my wrath should he come again to your village with his threats."

"If he should come, he will not only carry threats with him this time," Red Wing said, embracing her, leading her down onto the bed. "He will carry smoking weapons."

As he laid her gently on the bed, his lips curled into a slow smile. "But his smoking weapons will not be enough," he said. "My warriors outnumber his outlaws two to one. You shall see, then, who shall be the victor in the battle fought over you."

"I don't want to be the cause of any battle," Malvina said, shivering at the thought. "If you truly believe my uncle may come for me again, perhaps I should leave on my own this time, Red Wing, to ensure your people's peaceful existence."

"Never," he said, glaring down at her. "Never talk of leaving for *any* reason. My people understand my feelings for you. And from the beginning of time they have fought for what was right. *You* are what is right for me. *You* will make me a stronger leader for my people."

"What if they secretly resent me?" she murmured, then sucked in a wild breath of pleasure when he flicked his tongue around one of her nipples.

It was obvious to her that he was tired of talking.

And so was she.

Her very soul cried out to make love, and not to talk of an uncle whose very name now brought a loathing inside her heart.

As Red Wing blanketed her with his long, lithe body, Malvina reached a hand between them and touched his velvety tightness, in awe, as she was that first time she had touched him, of his length and thickness. When her fingers opened and wrapped around him and he sighed pleasurably, she began to stroke his tender flesh.

At the enticing feel of her fingers where he throbbed with need, Red Wing's senses began to reel. Cradling her in one arm to protect her shoulder, he bent low and rolled her nipple with his tongue, his free hand finding her hot, moist place.

Slowly he stroked her, causing a soft gurgle of rapture to surface from between her lips.

He lowered his mouth to hers and touched her lips wonderingly. He kissed her with a lazy warmth that left her weak, the kiss firing their emotions, their needs.

"I must have you *now*," Red Wing groaned in a whisper against her lips, his heart pounding so hard with want of her that he could scarcely breathe.

"Take me—oh, take me," Malvina whispered back.

When she felt him probing her throbbing center,

she opened herself fully to him as she wrapped her legs around his hips.

She gasped with desire as he plunged into her, withdrew and plunged again.

She rode with him.

She clung to his shoulders, his lips again firing their passions as he kissed her.

As his steel arms enfolded her, and his thrusts became maddeningly fast inside her, the euphoria that filled Malvina was almost more than she could bear. She cried out against his lips when one of his hands swept between them and gathered a breast within its palm, his fingers tweaking her pink-crested nipple to hardness.

Malvina felt Red Wing's building hunger in his fevered kiss.

Then the kiss became a lingering one, soft and sweet, as his tongue explored the inner edges of her lips.

Then once again his mouth closed hard upon hers. She shuddered when suddenly everything within her—the rapture, the euphoria—exploded, dissolving into a wonderful, tingling heat that swept her heavenward.

A wild, exuberant passion overwhelmed Red Wing when he realized that Malvina had reached her moment of glory. Knowing that she was being satisfied, he gave himself over to the rapture.

His release came like the deep rumblings of a volcano within him. He laid his cheek against hers, breathing wildly. He plunged deeply within her, then cried out his pleasure as he released his seed.

His body jolted, quivered, and quaked. His breathing became ragged. And when their bodies subsided together, Red Wing gathered her powerfully within his arms and kissed her again, his mouth urgent and eager.

Malvina responded and moved her body sinuously against his.

Then they rolled apart.

Red Wing smiled at her when he saw how her body gleamed silver in the faint light of the fire. He cupped her breasts and leaned over to flick his tongue across one nipple and then the next.

Malvina's breath caught and held when she felt herself awakening once again to feelings that she had just experienced, a spiraling need for him to fill her with his magnificence.

But laughter outside and the smell of smoke from the large outdoor fire brought them apart.

"My people are gathering for an evening of storytelling," Red Wing said. He leaned up on an elbow as he looked toward his closed door.

Then he gazed down at Malvina and traced her facial features with a finger. "Shall we join them?" he said, his voice still husky from the lovemaking. "It is a time of serenity for my people. They are happy to listen to the heartwarming tales of our village storyteller."

"Yes, let's," Malvina said excitedly.

She was weary of a battle she felt she had lost: That of finding her brother, of finding those responsible for her parents' death, and recovering the family heirlooms.

Before she had met Red Wing, all of those things had been her sole reason for living. But now she looked forward to something else in her life besides sadness and heartache.

And, ah, it was going to be so easy to get used to the peaceful, wonderful ways of the Choctaw, especially being with Red Wing day and night!

He was her lifeline now.

Nothing and no one else.

Malvina rose from the bed. As she slipped the buckskin dress over her head, she recalled something she had seen upon her return to the village. She and Red Wing had become so involved in their wondrous private pleasures that she had not thought to ask him about it, until now.

"Darling, earlier I saw something new in your village," she murmured, now pulling on a moccasin. "A pavilion and colonnade were built in my short absence. The pavilion walls and colonnade poles are painted in red and white. Groups of men were sweeping the stamped-down earth before them."

"My village is readying itself for the Green Corn Ceremony," Red Wing said, now fully dressed. He combed his fingers through his long and flowing black hair. "The colors of red and white are the colors of war and peace. It is a time of joy, a time of camaraderie. It is looked forward to throughout the year. It is the best of times for the Choctaw."

"And I am here to share in it," Malvina said, beaming.

Then a thought came to her which momentarily shattered her lighthearted feeling.

Her uncle.

If he came now, he would spoil everything the Choctaw had worked so hard for all year round.

She cast these thoughts aside. Her uncle had better things to do than to worry further about a niece who loathed him. The time spent with her was time taken away from his raids on the settlers. His greed surely outweighed his concern and love for a mere niece!

Malvina left the cabin with Red Wing. The huge outdoor fire sent its reflection into the dark heavens. The Choctaw people were crowded halfway around the fire, and an elderly man was sitting in the center of the semi-circle on a platform. Malvina surmised that this was the storyteller.

Baskets made of swamp cane were being passed around from person to person. Each person dipped a hand into the basket and took a handful of hickory popcorn.

"Tonight, when the stars hang low and the fire flickers, my people have come to listen to favorite stories about owl and turkey, panther and rattlesnake, opossum and skunk," Red Wing softly explained as he leaned closer to Malvina. "And above all, the storyteller will tell about Rabbit, the trickster."

"Rabbit the trickster?" Malvina said, forking an eyebrow. "I am sure the story will be amusing to hear."

"There will be much laughter tonight," Red Wing explained. "It is easy to sleep after such stories are told."

Malvina smiled contentedly at him. She shivered with joy. She inhaled the night air, sweet and welcome inside her lungs.

She looked farther than the gathering of Choctaw. Horses were grazing in the corral, nipping at the grass. Water cascaded over stairs of stones in a nearby creek. The rich bass of bullfrogs and the staccato of crickets also filled the night air with welcome sounds.

Red Wing took Malvina by an elbow and led her down onto a buffalo robe that Dreaming Shield quickly spread for them.

Malvina smiled a silent thank-you to Dreaming Shield, hoping that one day the child born of her and Red Wing's love would be like this young man in all manner and looks.

Dreaming Shield was a sweet, intelligent, and thoughtful young brave, all that Malvina always wanted in a child.

Dreaming Shield came and gave her a big hug, then ran to be among the other children who sat before the storyteller, anxiously awaiting the first tale.

Malvina settled in beside Red Wing, feeling somewhat ashamed to be so contented.

But it had been so long since she had felt this way.

She would not allow anything to spoil it for her.

As the smoke curled from the chimneys of the Choctaw dwellings and lifted into the sky, the storyteller began his first tale of the evening.

Malvina leaned around Red Wing and gazed at his grandfather as he came and sat down on the other side of Red Wing.

When he glanced her way and gave her a warm smile, everything within her mellowed to something soft and sweet. His smile was that of acceptance. And if he accepted her, how could the rest of the Choctaw not do the same?

She sighed, but still watched him as he lit a pipe with a hot coal that a young brave brought to him in a wooden container.

Puffing on the pipe, the smoke curling upward, his eyes gleamed with delight as he listened to the storyteller.

"The storyteller's name is Lifting Wind," Red Wing whispered to Malvina, drawing her attention away from his grandfather. "The name comes from his voice lifting into the wind as he tells his tales."

Malvina smiled, nodded, and gazed again at the storyteller. He was a lean elderly man dressed in a buffalo robe. His gray hair was tied back from his face with a leather thong. His dark eyes danced as he looked from child to child as he spoke.

Malvina noticed that the elderly man enlivened his tale with a turkey-feather fan, gesturing with it one way, and then another, opening it to fan himself for a moment, then flipping it closed.

Malvina gazed with much interest at the fan. It was made of what looked like many scissortail feathers. The beadwork sewn onto it was blue, black, white, and orange. The feathers were tightly bunched and closely matched, their sheen like a rainbow, yet the fan could also be spread wide in a disc, like a shield.

The beads glittered in every direction beneath the bright rays of the outside fire. Long doeskin fringes hung from the handle.

Something else that drew her keen attention was his pipe, which he rested on his knee as he talked, propped between his fingers. Its stem was four feet long, sheathed in a beautifully speckled snake skin and adorned with feathers and strings of wampum.

Then she became engrossed in what he was

saying, taken by the quaintness of each story, and by its mystery.

"At the beginning of time, there was a great platform mound called *Nanih, waiya,* or "slanting hill", which we, the Choctaw, regard as the Great Mother of the tribe," he said, his old eyes crinkling as he looked from child to child. "At its center, the Great Spirit created the first Choctaw, and they crawled forth into the light of day."

A sudden cracking sound made everyone gasp. Malvina covered her mouth with a hand when she realized what had happened. In Lifting Wind's intensity at telling the story, he had accidentally squeezed the stem of his pipe too tightly between his fingers and had broken it.

Lifting Wind sighed and gazed down at his broken pipe, then looked around at everyone. "It was a good pipe," he said, smiling. "But it lasted more seasons than expected. It is time for a new one." A young brave came and took the pipe away.

"No sleep yet weighs down my eyelids, so I will tell another story," Lifting Wind said, drawing a blanket around his frail shoulders. "I will tell the story of Rabbit the trickster."

The children applauded and drew closer and sat in a tight circle around Lifting Wind.

Malvina looked quickly over at Red Wing. They exchanged smiles at the mention of Rabbit the trickster since they had only moments ago talked about it.

"Once Rabbit swam into a pool with a cord attached to him," Lifting Wind said. "Submerging, he tied the cord to the legs of the ducks resting there. When he surfaced the ducks flew off—taking him with them."

He cleared his throat, then continued. "They flew over Rabbit's grandmother, who was rubbing a pot smooth," he said. "He called to her. She threw the pot over him, and it cut the string so that he fell down. Rabbit had escaped again!"

Everyone laughed, then listened as Lifting Wind went into another tale, and then another, while the moon slowly made its descent.

Chapter Twenty-Four

Daylight was breaking along the horizon when James rode up to his corral and reined in his horse, stunned speechless when he discovered that all of his other horses were gone.

His men wheeled their horses to a halt, also aghast at what they found.

Those escaped horses were valuable to them. They were used while those that had been on a raid rested.

"Who could be responsible for this!" James shouted, then sent slow, glaring eyes toward the cabin.

No smoke spiraled from the chimney.

Burk was not guarding the door.

Everything was too damn quiet.

He slid out of his saddle, handed his reins to one of his men, then ran to the cabin. When he entered, he became enraged to find that Malvina and the young savage were gone.

He stared disbelievingly at Burk tied to the chair, asleep.

James stamped over to Burk and slapped him awake. "How could this have happened?" he shrieked. "How did my niece get the upper hand? How did you allow it?"

His face stinging from the blows, Burk lowered his eyes and gulped hard. "She held a gun on me," was all that he could say.

"Whose gun?" James demanded.

"*Yours*, Preach," Burk said, now looking up at James and nodding toward the empty holster that hung from the peg on the wall. "You were the careless one this time, Preach, not me."

James paled, then shook his head. "Damn it all to hell," he mumbled.

"I'd appreciate it if you'd untie me," Burk said, his voice drawn.

James took his Bowie knife from its sheath and cut through the ropes.

"Preach, what'cha goin' to do about your niece and the kid?" Burk said, rubbing his raw wrists as he rose from the chair.

"Leave them be," James growled out. "If this is what Malvina wants, then let her live like a savage with the damn Indians. I won't waste one more precious moment of my time on her."

"I'd think you'd go after her," Burk said, wanting to get a piece of her himself for having made him look like a fool.

James looked slowly over at Burk. "Think so?" he said, wondering if perhaps Burk was right.

"Yeah," Burk said, his eyes anxious.

"I'll have to think on it," James said. "I've got

some plans I've got to see to first, though, if I *do* decide to go and wreak havoc on the Choctaw."

James laid several logs on the grate of the fireplace. He watched the fire take hold. His thoughts held on Malvina, torn with what, if anything, he should do about her.

A part of him wanted never to let her go because she was family.

A part of him said "good riddance" now that she was gone!

Her decision to leave him gave him an excuse not to worry about her anymore.

Yet he had to think on it and do what was absolutely right for her!

Chapter Twenty-Five

The next day, Malvina got caught up in the activity of the upcoming Green Corn Ceremony. She had gone with Red Wing into the forest in his search for a fairly straight hickory tree, one without knots.

From this he was now making *kapucha*, or sticks, for the game of stickball which would be played during the height of the Green Corn Ceremony. He had been appointed the "stick-maker," an honor that any warrior would hope for.

He had told her that, since he would one day be chief, he had been awarded the honor of making the sticks for some years past. He had proven his skill at making them the first time he had been appointed stick-maker. And his skills had heightened with the years.

Malvina sat in the shade of a tree behind Red Wing's cabin as he split the wood that he had cut from the hickory tree, then began cutting it into sticks, which would be about four feet long.

Knowing how preoccupied Red Wing would be while making the sticks, Pretty Cloud had brought something for Malvina to do to busy her own hands—a basket well along to being completed.

Malvina had gladly taken the basketry materials, attentive while Pretty Cloud took the time to explain everything about basketry to her so that Malvina could finish the basket herself.

Pretty Cloud told her that each original basket was unique, and to those knowledgeable about the baskets, the basketmakers' styles were always evident.

Pretty Cloud warned Malvina that at first basketmaking was difficult. But with practice, it would become much easier.

Pretty Cloud had herself gone and found cane stalks for this basket. After cutting them into strips of the desired size, she had let them dry. She had then dyed a certain number of them to make the designs which was one of the most time-consuming parts of the process.

Pretty Cloud told Malvina that she went into the creation of each of her baskets with a certain design in mind and said that the baskets usually came out just the way she had envisioned them.

Malvina was instructed how to finish an egg basket, one of the smallest and easiest to make.

Pretty Cloud then went on to her own daily activities.

Malvina felt clumsy as she sat there, giving Red Wing some company while he worked. Her fingers weren't as nimble as she wished them to be as she wove the strips of cane stalks in and out.

Having only a few more stalks to weave into place, Malvina held the basket out before her. "I think I've done quite well, don't you, Red Wing, since it is my very first attempt at making a basket?" she said, drawing his attention to her.

He paused at what he was doing and gazed at the small egg basket. "You have done yourself proud," he said, a glimmer in his eyes. "It is good to see you so eager to learn the ways of Choctaw women. My people see this. It will make them accept you even more readily than they already have."

"Have they truly accepted me?" Malvina asked, recalling the previous evening when she sat among them, listening to the storyteller. "I have not been able to tell. I so badly want for everyone to like me."

She reached a hand to Red Wing's arm. "Have they truly forgiven me for stealing the canoe?" she asked anxiously.

"Now that they understand why you stole it, yes, I believe they understand," Red Wing assured her. "And there was payment made. Your horse and your brother's were payment enough for the canoe."

"My horse and Daniel's," Malvina sighed, easing her hand from his arm. She swept a fallen lock of hair back from her eyes. "It seems a lifetime ago when Daniel and I rode free and happy on our steeds before our parents died. It seems so long ago, yet not so long, for I carry my memories of those times within my heart."

"And so shall you always," Red Wing said, his voice taking on a melancholy sound. "As I carry

213

my own memories within my heart of my parents."

"I wish I could have known them," Malvina said. "They must have been fine people to have given birth to such a fine and gentle son as you."

"That was long ago," Red Wing said, changing the subject since it hurt him to linger too long on the past, on those he had been forced to give up to the spirit world too soon.

"A pair of well-crafted stickball sticks are necessary for the success of the game," he said, changing the subject. "Playing the exciting game of Choctaw stickball also requires determination and skill. I carry on the centuries-old tradition of carving hickory wood into the tools of the game so that the players' skills will be enhanced."

"It looks as though you are going to be making several sticks," Malvina said, allowing him to shift the conversation to something less painful. She watched as he began to shave one of the pieces of hickory wood with his sharpened knife. Malvina noticed he had tied his hair back with a headband so that it would not get in the way of his labor.

"That is so, and one always sees the need to have extra sticks because some break during the game," Red Wing said. "Making several ensures that everyone will have a pair to play with."

"When will the game be played?" Malvina asked. She enjoyed being a part of Red Wing's excitement, and she could see in his eyes how he enjoyed what he was doing.

She could also tell that he was enjoying her company in the way he would stop long enough to gently touch her face, or lean over to brush her lips with a kiss.

She would have never thought that stick-making could be so romantic. But just being with Red Wing brought out the romance in her.

And she loved it because she felt more feminine than ever before in her life.

She hoped that nothing else would interfere in the happiness she had found with Red Wing. When her parents died, she had never thought it would be possible to smile again, let alone laugh and feel at peace with herself.

She glanced toward the river. Every time she looked at it, she remembered her beloved Daniel and could not help but momentarily feel sad and alone for him.

"You asked when will the game of stickball be played?" Red Wing said, drawing her thoughts back to him. "Tomorrow. It will be an integral part of the festivities. It is something everyone looks forward to, year to year."

"What sort of ball is used?" Malvina asked, her questions helping to keep her thoughts from drifting to Daniel again. "How is the game played?"

"My woman is full of questions today," Red Wing said, laughing softly. "But that is good. To ask is to know. No one ever has too much knowledge."

He paused and ran his fingers over the freshly carved piece of wood, testing its smoothness, then looked over at her again. "A ball made of deerskin is used," he said. "The game itself is somewhat complicated. As we play, you will see."

He had shaved the piece of wood to the desired thickness for the handle on one end, then shaved the other end until it was about a quarter-inch thick and flexible enough to bend, forming a loop on the end.

After shaping the loop and making holes with his knife in the proper places on the racket end, he threaded in strips of leather to make the webbing that would secure the ball in place during play.

Malvina no longer chattered with him because she thought she might be slowing him down. She resumed her basketry.

After her basket was finished, her heart throbbed with pride to see that it seemed almost perfect.

She looked up at Red Wing to tell him that she was finished. Puzzled by what he was doing, she momentarily forgot about her basket.

"Why are you applying bear fat to the stick?" she asked curiously.

"The bear fat gives the sticks their color. It makes them smoother," Red Wing said, continuing his craft without looking at her. "I take much pride in what I do. Each stick must be not only good to use, but also good to look at. My efforts are respected by the Choctaw, and the sticks themselves are a reflection of pride in the traditions of my people."

Dreaming Shield came running toward Malvina. "Malvina!" he shouted, brimming with excitement. "Pretty Cloud said that you were weaving an egg basket. Is it finished yet? Is it?"

Malvina laughed softly as he half stumbled over her moccasined feet when he came to a quick stop before her.

Dreaming Shield's gaze went to the basket. He took it from Malvina's lap. "It *is* finished, and it is *pretty,*" he said, then grabbed one of her hands. "Come with me. Let us fill the basket with eggs. I found several. The mother pheasant is gone. Let us now get her eggs. They are so good to eat!"

"My goodness, I have never seen a young man so excited over eggs before," Malvina said, laughing softly. "I have seen my younger brother enthusiastic over having found a big patch of mushrooms in the forest, but never over finding eggs."

"That is because white people keep chickens in small cubicles of houses which supply them with eggs," Red Wing said, laying his sticks on the ground. He grabbed Dreaming Shield up into his arms. "Come. We shall all enjoy giving your new basket a try."

Malvina gazed up at him with an intense love, then took his hand. "Where are these eggs, Dreaming Shield?" she asked, so glad that she had been given the opportunity to know this child intimately. It was the way in which it had come about that she regretted, the way they had been forced together by her uncle.

But perhaps it was all worth it to have found a way inside the youngster's heart.

Grateful for Dreaming Shield's attentiveness to her, and what he had brought into her life, she was growing to love him as though he were her very own son.

"Down by the river close to a berry patch!" Dreaming Shield said, pointing.

Red Wing placed Dreaming Shield on his feet. "Young brave, take us to it," he said, tousling the child's head before Dreaming Shield broke into a run through the knee-high blue grass.

Red Wing turned to Malvina. He stopped her and drew her into his arms. "In him I see my own sons," he said thickly. He placed a finger to Malvina's chin and lifted her eyes to his. "In you, I see a wonderful mother."

Malvina thrilled inside as he softly kissed her.

When Dreaming Shield squealed excitedly, Malvina and Red Wing drew apart and walked hand in hand to the pheasant's nest nestled in the tall grass.

Once there, Malvina held the basket as Dreaming Shield began placing the ten roundish eggs inside it.

Knowing Red Wing's love of eggs, Dreaming Shield gave him one of the pheasant eggs.

Malvina shivered somewhat as she watched Red Wing crack the egg and let the nourishment fall into his mouth. She had seen one of her distant cousins place raw eggs in his whiskey in Ireland and drink it down in fast gulps. But never had she seen anyone eat a raw egg. She couldn't imagine herself ever being able to do that.

Dreaming Shield nudged her with his elbow to encourage her to turn her attention back to gathering the rest of the eggs, which she did without hesitation.

Red Wing tossed the empty eggshell to the ground, wiped his mouth clean with the back of a hand, and gazed up at the sun. Soon the naked moon would sneak into place in the heavens.

His gaze shifted. As he gazed at the butte that overlooked his village, he stiffened when he saw a white man ride off on a horse.

He looked quickly toward the guards that were posted in strategic spots around his village. They had not been aware of the man's presence. He had to make sure to post someone on the butte from now on. Whoever had been spying today would not get the opportunity to get that close to his village, his people, or his woman again.

Malvina was laughing and giggling with Dreaming Shield. As he placed the last egg in the basket, she looked over at Red Wing to see if he had noticed.

Her smile faded when she found that he was preoccupied by something else, his mood dark. She followed his gaze and stared up at the butte that overlooked the village.

She grew cold inside to think that he might have seen someone spying on them. Surely it had been her Uncle James, or possibly that terrible man who had sold her to the brothel.

Had he discovered where she was?

If so, what sort of a threat did he pose?

"See the eggs?" Dreaming Shield said to Red Wing as he took the basket from Malvina and carried it over for Red Wing to see.

Dreaming Shield's happy voice drew Red Wing from his reverie. He forced a smile. "You and your parents will have a feast of eggs tonight," he said, placing a hand on the young child's shoulder as he gazed at them.

"I wish to share them with you," Dreaming Shield said. "Can we go and cook them and have them now?"

Red Wing glanced over at Malvina. Her smile and nod was all that it took to make the decision, since she was the one who would be cooking.

"Yes, we will share them with you," Red Wing said, tousling the child's hair.

"We will have such fun preparing them together," Dreaming Shield said excitedly.

Then he frowned up at Red Wing. "Moments ago you were staring up at the butte," he said warily. "Why, Red Wing? Why? Was someone there you did not like?"

Red Wing and Malvina exchanged quick, troubled glances.

"I did not get a close look at the man, so I cannot say whether he was a friend or foe," Red Wing said. "But I did see that he was white."

Malvina swallowed hard, realizing that fear and danger were never all that far away.

Chapter Twenty-Six

The next day, Malvina was amazed at just how much excitement the *Busk,* the Green Corn Ceremony, created. She had been in awe the long day through of the festivities, of the dancers honoring the knee-high green corn with their wild and picturesque dancing.

She had soon discovered that the purpose of the festival was also for tribal renewal and perpetuation of health. This was accompanied by a feast, during which people consumed vast quantities of meat and vegetables.

Malvina had learned that all Choctaw land was held in common by the tribe, but individuals had a claim to any tract they cultivated as long as they did not encroach upon fields already claimed by others.

If a Choctaw abandoned his or her field, control over it reverted to the tribe.

They cleared their fields in mid-winter by burning the underbrush and killing the trees by cutting off a ring of bark near the base of their trunks.

The women performed magic in their preparation of corn. There was always corn bread, corn stew, and corn meal for their dinner tables.

Chief Bold Wolf, with Red Wing sitting dutifully at his right side, had used the occasion to conduct business. Distinguished warriors had been recognized, and youths of all ages had been instructed in Choctaw lore.

Malvina had watched Dreaming Shield with much pride as he had listened intently to his instructions. She knew that one day he might be a Choctaw chief, for even at the age of six he displayed strong leadership qualities.

But for now all serious business was finished.

It was time for the game of stickball.

Malvina sat beside Pretty Cloud on a buffalo robe spread across the ground, her hands clasped softly on her lap. She gazed up and down the long field that had been readied for the game. Goal posts had been erected at each end perhaps two or three hundred yards apart. These goals consisted of two split logs stuck in the ground about six feet apart.

Malvina sucked in a wild breath when the warriors rushed out on the field. Red Wing had not prepared her for how he would alter his appearance for the game of stickball.

He, as well as the others, was magnificently painted in bright colors and entirely naked except for a belt and breech cloth.

"Does Red Wing not look very handsome?"

Pretty Cloud asked. She leaned over and spoke more softly to Malvina. "His body colors of red and yellow are the brightest of all."

"Yes, he is quite handsome," Malvina said, still staring disbelievingly at Red Wing, for she *did* find the way he was painted and dressed quite stimulating.

Especially when he turned his dark, smoldering eyes her way and smiled.

"But is not Stands Tall also handsome?" Pretty Cloud sighed. She looked dreamy-eyed at the warrior as he stood beside Red Wing, huddled with him to work out their game strategy.

"Stands Tall is not yet married, is he?" Malvina asked.

"No, he is not married," Pretty Cloud said, her eyes moving slowly to Malvina. When their eyes met dancingly, Pretty Cloud covered a giggle behind one of her hands. "Perhaps I should persuade him that he should soon take a wife?"

Malvina recalled some of the conversation between Paul Brady and Red Wing the night Paul had come to tell his lies about Malvina. Red Wing had urged Paul to go to Pretty Cloud. He had encouraged Paul to reveal his true, deepest feelings about Pretty Cloud to her.

Malvina was relieved now to know that Pretty Cloud had no true feelings for Paul. Not only was Paul twice Pretty Cloud's age, he was not fit even to speak her name.

If Pretty Cloud was considering marrying him, Malvina would have been forced to reveal Paul's true nature to everyone. She would have made sure that Paul wasn't allowed to become as one with the Choctaw by exchanging marriage vows with one of their loveliest maidens.

Her silence about his treacherous personality would go only so far, and then she would have to reveal to the whole village the true murdering, thieving, lecherous rogue that he was!

She smiled at what might happen then to this man whose smugness sent spirals of rage through her veins!

"If I were you, Pretty Cloud, I would encourage Stands Tall to marry you *soon*," Malvina said softly over at her. "Do not be shy about it. Where men are concerned, sometimes women have to take the initiative."

"Perhaps I shall," Pretty Cloud said, her eyes beaming.

The stickball game began with a tip-off.

Malvina winced as the men ran together in wild charges, tripping and dodging with agility and grace.

She quickly noticed that the game called for restraint as well as skill, for they wore no protective equipment.

She could tell that the players were as careful as possible not to harm each other with their sticks.

When tackling and wrestling takedowns became a part of the game, Red Wing's prominence became more pronounced. In the roughest moments, Malvina gasped and turned her eyes away. Although the players were being as careful as possible, bruises were rising on Red Wing's arms and legs.

"Red Wing and Stands Tall's team is ahead with points!" Pretty Cloud shrieked excitedly. She grabbed Malvina by the arm. "Watch, Malvina. It is something truly wonderful to see!"

Turning her eyes slowly around, Malvina's heart went out to Red Wing when she saw a stream of blood curling from the corner of his mouth.

But the look in his eyes, a look that came with winning, of pride and assurance, made Malvina look past his wounds and to the game as he made another point for his team.

Malvina sighed with relief, though, when it was all over, and Red Wing and his team stood victorious. She was touched deeply by how those who lost embraced the winners. There was such camaraderie among them all that, in truth, one could scarcely tell them apart as winners or losers.

The village was now framed in a vision of a sunset. As those who had participated in the stickball game ran to the river and dove in to remove their paint, blood, and sweat, dancers appeared in a circle around the great outdoor fire.

Malvina wanted to go to Red Wing, to say soothing things to him as he bathed his wounds, but she knew her place was to wait for him.

Patiently awaiting his return to her side, she became entranced by the dances that were being performed. First there were the male stomp dancers. The fire reflected off dozens of copper headdress plates and weapons wielded by costumed bird and animal impersonators. Their movements followed the rhythmic beat of many drums made of hollowed logs and large pottery vessels covered tightly with deerskins, the low tones of cane flutes, the shrill wail of bird-bone whistles, and the staccato rasp of rattles made of polished gourd and tortoise shells.

Wearing smoked-hide leggings and capes, the dancers' buckskin fringes swayed and their hawk and eagle-feather bustles fluttered in the cooling breeze. The dancers spun and twisted, a haze of smoke and dust hanging over them.

The men ceased their dancing and moved away into the dusk of night as female dancers took their place around the fire and began their own version of dancing.

"They do what is called 'the fancy dance'," Pretty Cloud whispered over at Malvina. "Are they not lovely? Are they not light and fanciful on their feet?"

Nodding, Malvina became absorbed in the movements of the women. One day *she* would also be among the women who danced and pranced around a fire.

Some women wore fancy embroidered shawls with long fringes to accentuate their movements. All used intricately fast and acrobatic motions.

Several of the women who were not dancing broke into song. As their songs filled the air, the dancers strained and whirled, twisting and turning in a dazzling explosion of color. They showed an exuberant style of fancy footwork and high-stepping spins.

"Why aren't you dancing?" Malvina asked, leaning closer to Pretty Cloud.

"My courage is not as bold as those who perform before others like peacocks and strut their lovely feathers for the sake of an audience," Pretty Cloud said, looking quickly up when Red Wing came and reached a hand down for Malvina.

Everything, everyone, was lost to Malvina as she rose to her feet before Red Wing.

Her eyes wavered when again she was aware of the many bruises and cuts that came with Red Wing's victory in the game.

"My darling," Malvina whispered, touching a swelling on his arm. "How your wounds must hurt. Surely more than mine ever did."

"The pain is an honor because it comes with the thrill of victory," Red Wing said, his chin lifting with savage pride. He gazed down at her, his eyes smoke-black with passion. "But above all else at this moment—the pain, the pride of victory—comes my need for you, my woman. Let us slip away from the festival and celebrate as only you and I know how to."

A sensual warmth spread through Malvina as he gathered her next to him and swept her away to his cabin.

Standing beside his bed, the embers of the fire glowing in the curling shadows, he grabbed her into his arms.

Fueling her passion, his mouth seized hers.

She felt his hunger in the hard, seeking pressure of his lips.

She returned the kiss hungrily, passionately.

Her hands trembled as she ran them over his hairless muscled chest, then lower, where only his breechcloth covered that part of him that mystified her.

His hand twined through her hair, his tongue flicking between her lips, Red Wing maneuvered his way out of his breechcloth. When it fell around his ankles, and his need for her sprang into view, he led her hand to him.

Her heart pounding, her knees weak from the building rapture at the mere touch of Red Wing's throbbing hardness, Malvina opened her fingers and slowly enwrapped his manhood within them.

Feeling as though he were flying, the pleasure intense, Red Wing moaned against her lips. He gathered a fistful of the hem of her skirt into his hands and began shoving it upward until he had it over her head, then tossed it aside.

Then, feeling the searing sensations building within him and not wanting to receive his pleasure without giving the same to Malvina, Red Wing pressed his body against hers and led her down onto the bed.

Blanketing her with his body, he ran his fingers across the silken flesh of her slim, white thighs, caressing her, making her shiver.

Wanting him as never before, her body crying out for him, Malvina reached for his tight shaft and guided him inside her.

He kissed her long and deep.

Her pelvis lifted to him as he pressed endlessly, powerfully deeper within her in a wild, dizzying rhythm.

She whimpered tiny cries when his burning-hot lips slid down from her mouth and moved over a nipple.

Leisurely his tongue swirled around the nipple, causing a storm of passion to shake Malvina's innermost senses.

Red Wing's fingers bit into the rounded flesh of her bottom and molded her into the shapely contours of his body. He felt the pleasure building as he moved within her at a maddening speed.

So close to the peak of passion, Red Wing

pressed his cheek against the soft flesh of her breasts, his body momentarily stilled.

Then he clutched his fingers into her hips and pressed her more tightly against him as he made a deep thrust that gave him the fulfillment that he needed. She in turn quavered against him in her own release of joyous bliss.

The pleasure subsided into a sweet aftermath. Red Wing rolled away from Malvina, then took her hand and led her from the bed to sit, nude, on a blanket before the dying embers of the fire.

Red Wing lifted several logs onto the grate, and soon flames were lapping around them in hypnotic orange streamers.

"Today was wonderful," Malvina said, cuddling as Red Wing swept an arm around her waist to draw her close at his side. She looked adoringly up at him. "Thank you, my love, for giving so much of yourself to me."

He started to respond, but a voice outside his closed door drew them quickly to their feet. He pulled on a pair of fringed breeches. Malvina dressed as quickly in a buckskin dress.

They went to the door together. She stood aside as he opened it, then moved beside him when they found Stands Tall and Pretty Cloud there.

"Can we share your fire with you?" Stands Tall asked, looking from Malvina to Red Wing. "The festival is over. Everyone has gone to their lodges. Pretty Cloud does not yet want to return to her parents' lodge." He cast Pretty Cloud a smile, then looked over at Red Wing again. "She is too shy to come to mine."

"Yes, do come in," Red Wing said, puzzled that Pretty Cloud appeared to be smitten with Stands

Tall, when before she had spoken of Paul Brady as a woman does a man she wishes to seek a future with.

Had Red Wing misinterpreted her feelings, her stares, when Paul was in the Choctaw village? Red Wing wondered. Or was she a fickle young lady who toyed with the feelings of men who showed interest in her?

He frowned at the thought of her behaving wantonly. Yet she was only his cousin, not someone he felt free to scold. That was her parents' duty, not his!

He and Malvina stepped aside as Stands Tall and Pretty Cloud went past them into the cabin.

"It is good to have your company," Red Wing said, gesturing toward the chairs, and then the blanket. "Sit where you wish."

Exchanging smiles, Stands Tall and Pretty Cloud chose the blanket so that they could sit much more closely to each other than had they chosen the chairs.

"Pretty Cloud and I have chosen tonight to reveal our feelings for each other," Stands Tall said, as Red Wing and Malvina sat down on chairs opposite their guests. "Red Wing, Pretty Cloud and I plan to marry soon. Our visit tonight mainly is to ask when you and Malvina are going to share words of marriage with one another."

"You are going to be married?" Malvina blurted out, recalling how Pretty Cloud had told her only tonight how she felt about Stands Tall, how she wished that he would also feel something for her.

It amazed Malvina how quickly Pretty Cloud had made things work out for herself. Surely she had only given Stands Tall a flirting smile to bring him her way!

"Yes, Malvina," Pretty Cloud said, her voice soft and lilting. "Is that not wonderful?"

"I'm so glad for you both," Malvina said, still stunned over the suddenness of their decision.

"When things are right for my woman, I will marry her," Red Wing said, his eyes locking with Malvina's. "She will choose the time, not I. She has just experienced a tragedy. Now is not the time to speak vows."

"We also are waiting, but not for the same reason," Stands Tall said, reaching to take one of Pretty Cloud's hands. "I want Pretty Cloud to be certain. There are many warriors who are worthy of her love. She must have time to be certain of her choice."

Pretty Cloud smiled bashfully up at him.

Red Wing's eyebrows arched, thinking that perhaps Pretty Cloud had suggested they wait, to make certain she truly wanted marriage to Stands Tall rather than to Paul.

His thoughts strayed to Paul's last visit to the Choctaw village, and his strange insistence about sending Malvina away. That day, while Paul had spoken so heatedly against Malvina, had given Red Wing cause to doubt Paul's trustworthiness. Now that Red Wing knew for certain that Malvina was good to the very core of herself, he knew that Paul had to have been lying.

He glanced down at Pretty Cloud. Had *she* seen something questionable in Paul's behavior and personality before he had?

If so, why had she kept her silence about it?

"Red Wing, Stands Tall said something to you," Malvina said, breaking through Red Wing's troubled thoughts.

"Oh?" Red Wing said, shifting uneasily in his chair. "I did not hear."

"I only said that you played a fine game of stickball today, my friend," Stands Tall said, his eyes twinkling.

"Yes, it was a game won with much enthusiasm and pride," Red Wing said, still not able to shake thoughts of Paul from his mind.

He did not want to think that Paul had the ability to trick Red Wing, a warrior who would one day be chief and should be able to look into the very soul of a man and see whether he was good or bad.

"Red Wing?" Malvina said, when again he did not hear something that Stands Tall said back to him.

Red Wing again stirred uneasily in his chair. He smiled awkwardly at Stands Tall. "My thoughts wandered again," he said.

"Is something troubling you?" Stands Tall asked, his jaw tightening. "If so, tell me what it is. I am always here to help you, my friend."

Red Wing stared from Pretty Cloud to Stands Tall, then gazed into the fire, knowing that neither of them would truly want to know what he was thinking about at this moment.

He was thinking that Paul could be a threat to their dreams.

Chapter Twenty-Seven

Pretty Cloud had come early in the morning to teach Malvina how to prepare various Choctaw foods while Red Wing and several warriors scouted the land to make sure no white men had trespassed on their property these past days. They were going to make sure no more moonshiners placed illegal stills on land that was, by treaty, the Choctaws'.

A popular dish for the Choctaw called *bunaha*, cornmeal combined with boiled beans, cooked in a pot over the flames in the fireplace. Sturgeon, caught in the Arkansas River, sizzled in bear fat in a skillet on the outer edge of the hot coals.

"You are learning quickly," Pretty Cloud said, watching Malvina now wrapping the cooked *bunaha* in corn husks. She laughed softly. "Perhaps I am teaching you too well the art of Choctaw cooking. You will make both Red Wing and your children so fat they will not be able to move around except in a waddle."

The day was exceptionally warm and muggy. Malvina brushed a damp strand of hair back from her eyes, smearing flour across her brow. "I only hope that once I have my own family, they will appreciate my cooking," she said, laughing softly. "It isn't all that easy to stand here preparing food. I am used to being outdoors. When my mother was alive and tried to urge me to stay in the kitchen and learn to cook, I always sneaked out and rode away and enjoyed horseback riding with my brother Daniel."

Bringing Daniel's name into the conversation stung Malvina's heart. She doubted that she could ever accept that he was dead. Even if she knew for certain that he was, she didn't see how she could ever learn to live with it.

Not wanting Pretty Cloud to see the tears that were filling her eyes, Malvina went to a window and threw back the sash. "Let's get some more air in here," she said, her voice breaking.

Pretty Cloud went to her and placed a gentle arm around her waist. "Do you wish to tell me about your Daniel?" she murmured. "Will that help calm some of your pain at having lost him?"

Malvina turned and flung herself into Pretty Cloud's arms. She placed her cheek on her shoulder. "I miss him so," she sobbed, relieved after all to have the opportunity to confide in someone besides Red Wing. "He was such a sweet and lovable young man. He would have made a wonderful preacher. His heart was filled with compassion."

She drew away from Pretty Cloud and wiped her eyes with the backs of her hands. "Why does someone like him have to die, when there are so many heartless, evil men roaming the land?" she said, imploring Pretty Cloud with her eyes. "It isn't fair, Pretty Cloud. Daniel could have spread the word of God to so many who hunger for it. God is needed in this land of killings and robberies."

"The Great Spirit, as well as your God, looks over us all," Pretty Cloud said, placing a gentle hand to Malvina's cheek. "Together they will make wrongs right. It just takes time."

Malvina placed a gentle hand on Pretty Cloud's cheek. "How old are you, Pretty Cloud, in exact numbers?" she asked.

"I have been on this earth seventeen winters," Pretty Cloud said. "Why do you ask?"

"My Daniel was seventeen only a few months ago," Malvina said, her voice breaking.

In her mind's eye she recalled how she and Daniel had celebrated his birthday. They had worked for an inn in Fort Smith. They had washed dishes and cleaned the rooms for one week prior to Daniel's birthday so that they could save enough money to buy a small cake at the town bakery.

When the owners of the bakery learned the cake was for Daniel's birthday, they had generously given them candles for it.

On the big day, Malvina and Daniel had found a quiet stream and had sat beside it, eating the whole cake.

They had both been plagued with stomachaches the next two days.

235

Smoke swirling into the draft of the window made Malvina's thoughts return to the present. She turned with a start.

Her eyes widened and she gasped when she discovered that the contents of the frying pan had caught fire.

She looked from the flaming pan to the flour that she had shaken from a bag into a bowl on the table and suddenly recalled something her mother had done while cooking one day. Food had caught fire in her mother's kitchen, and Malvina had come into the room just in time to see her mother dump flour into the flames, quickly extinguishing them.

Malvina grabbed the bowl of flour and poured it into the skillet, smothering the flames.

"How did you know to do that?" Pretty Cloud said, as she rushed to Malvina's side.

"My mother unknowingly taught me how to put out a cookfire," Malvina said, smiling at Pretty Cloud as smoke puffed in thick clouds between them. "I just happened to see her do it one day. If she hadn't, our whole house would've burned to the ground."

Pretty Cloud coughed as the smoke curled into her nose and down her throat.

"Let's go outside until the smoke clears," Malvina said, gagging.

Laughing softly between their choking, coughing, and gagging, they rushed outside.

Teary-eyed, their eyes burning from the smoke, they were drawn to the arrival of Red Wing and the Choctaw warriors at the far end of the village.

As Malvina's eyes cleared and she could focus on Red Wing, she was taken aback by what he had on his lap—a small white boy who appeared to be about five years old.

Her gaze shifted. On Stands Tall's lap was another white child, a girl. She was perhaps a year or so older than the boy.

Malvina's insides tightened when the horses grew closer and she could see that the children were soaked to the skin, their torn and tattered clothes clinging to their small bodies.

They both looked completely exhausted and drained of emotion. Their eyes were empty, their expressions sad and distant.

"No," Malvina said, her hands folding in tight fists at her sides. "Please, God, no."

"I fear asking where the children were found," Pretty Cloud said wearily. "Their parents are surely dead."

"Yes, and we already know why, don't we, Pretty Cloud?" Malvina said solemnly. "Outlaws. These children and their families were the victims of outlaws."

She could not help but think about her uncle at such a time as this.

If he was responsible . . . !

Red Wing and the others drew tight rein a few feet from Red Wing's cabin.

Malvina ran to him. Pretty Cloud ran to Stands Tall.

"Where did you get the children?" Malvina asked, reaching up to help the young boy from the horse. She grabbed him by the waist, then eased him to the ground.

She sucked in a quavering breath when the child suddenly and desperately wrapped his arms around her legs, sobbing.

237

She wasn't sure if he did this because he was afraid to be with Red Wing, an Indian, and found the presence of a white person comforting, or because he was just glad to have been rescued.

"There, there," Malvina murmured, then moved to her knees before him. She took him into her arms and stroked his back as he clung to her, his body racked with hard sobs.

"Sweetie, things are going to be all right now," she said softly. "Nothing will hurt you ever again. Please stop crying. Please?"

The child leaned away from her. His eyes wavered into hers. "My Mama," he said softly. "My Papa. They are both dead."

Suddenly the young girl came and clasped hard to one of his hands. She gazed at Malvina with such a sadness in the depths of her eyes that Malvina had to look away.

What if her uncle had done this to the children?

Red Wing came to Malvina and sat on his haunches beside her. He reached a hand to the small boy's shoulder and rested it there for a moment, then touched the girl's shoulder.

"Red Wing, where did you find the children?" Malvina asked again, her voice breaking.

"Down by the river," Red Wing said. "We found them wandering aimlessly along the riverbank, wet and shivering."

"Why were you down by the river?" Malvina asked, directing her questions at the girl, since she was the oldest. "Who did this to you?"

"We lived a few miles out of Fort Smith. Outlaws came and murdered our parents, stole everything they could carry off, then burned our house and outbuildings," the girl told her.

Malvina was catapulted back in time, to the night her own family had been torn apart in the same way. She knew that sympathy would never be enough for these orphaned children.

"Then . . . then the evil men took me and my brother to the river and threw us in," the girl said, sobbing. "They wanted us to die. They didn't know we could swim. Papa said that with the river so close, we had to know how to swim in case we fell in."

"And you swam clear to the other side of the Arkansas River, to Indian Country?" Malvina asked, amazed that they had not been swept away by the current.

"We swam partway, then clung to some tree branches," the girl said, tears streaming down her cheeks. "I thought we were going to die. But the branches were swept ashore."

"Can you describe the men who did this to you and your family?" Malvina asked softly, reaching to smooth the tears away from the child's face with the palms of her hands.

"I'll never forget the one who shouted out the order to throw us in the river," the girl sobbed out. "He also gave the orders to kill my parents and to do the burning!"

Malvina's spine stiffened, afraid to hear, then froze when her fears were confirmed.

"He had red hair and whiskers and cold green eyes," the girl said, shivering. "He was called Preach. He's a cold-hearted, cruel man."

Feeling a bitter taste rush into her mouth at the description and the mention of the name and feeling as though she might retch to know that her uncle could be this evil, his mind this twisted, Malvina rushed to her feet and turned her back to the children. She hung her head in her hands and slowly shook her head back and forth.

"How could he?" Malvina harshly whispered. "He's a demon, surely the devil incarnate!"

Red Wing saw Malvina's distress.

Understanding her feelings and sympathizing with them, he pushed himself up and gathered her into his arms. "This is nothing you can change by allowing it to eat away at you," he soothed her. "These children are now our responsibility. Let us think of *them*. Not your uncle."

"At all cost, James must be stopped," Malvina said, jerking her head up to gaze determinedly into Red Wing's eyes. "I now know where his hideout is. I shall lead the authorities at Fort Smith to him. He will get his dues, Red Wing. I shall proudly watch him hang from a rope!"

Red Wing framed her face with his hands. "Do not let bitterness ruin your sweetness," he said, his voice drawn. "We shall go together to the white authorities. But for now, let us think of these children and what must be done for them."

"Yes, I know," Malvina said, wiping her nose with the back of a hand.

She and Red Wing turned back to the children. Red Wing swept the boy up into his arms. Stands Tall held the young girl close.

The people of the village had come from their lodges to see about the children and had listened to their plight.

A woman stepped forth. "As a child, I was always encouraged not to associate myself with white people, to avoid them at all cost, because they could not be trusted," Slender Flower murmured. She looked at Malvina and smiled. "I followed my parents' teaching, but think now that I was misled. Malvina is white. I trust her. I am glad to have met her and to know that there are some whites that are good."

Her husband, Fire Fox, then spoke. "What my wife is trying to say is that we are childless," he said thickly, reaching a hand to the young boy's shoulder and gazing at length at the boy. "We shall take both children into our lodge. We shall care for them. If they are comfortable with us, we shall then adopt them as our own."

"Our very own," Slender Flower said, reaching a hand to the young girl's long and golden hair, running her fingers through it.

Malvina was touched speechless by the offer. She could not help but think back to when she and Pretty Cloud had been talking about the good and bad of people. Today she had witnessed both.

Her uncle was the worst of people.

This Choctaw family who offered to take in the children, the best.

"Would you and your brother go with this man and woman into their lodge?" Red Wing asked the girl. "The woman's name is Slender Flower. The man's name is Fire Fox. Would you share your names with us so that we can know what to call you besides white boy and white girl?"

Malvina had noticed that the girl had not recoiled when Slender Flower reached her hand out to touch her hair. Nor had the boy flinched when Fire Fox placed a hand on his shoulder.

241

That was a good sign that the children might not resent or fear Indians. Perhaps their parents had taught them that it was wrong to be prejudiced against those whose skin color was not the same as theirs.

That might have been one of their most important teachings.

"My name is Dorothy June Martin," the girl said, looking trustingly at Slender Flower. "My brother's name is Howard. Howard Martin."

"Will you go with me and my husband to our lodge?" Slender Flower asked, looking from one child to the other.

The children both nodded their heads, then hung their heads sadly.

Another woman stepped forward. "I shall bring clothes from my lodge for the children," she said softly. "I have both a daughter and a son. Their clothes should fit these children well enough."

Another woman stepped forward. "The children look hungry," she said. "I shall bring much food."

Suddenly voices rang out from all sides, making Malvina full with a mellow warmth.

"I shall bring blankets," one said.

"I shall bring toys," another said.

Red Wing and Stands Tall placed the children to their feet. They began walking away with Fire Fox and Slender Flower; then Dorothy June broke free and ran back to Red Wing.

She flung her arms around his legs and gazed gratefully up at him. "Thank you," she murmured. "Thank you, thank you."

Touched deeply by the tender scene, Malvina again turned away. She felt in part responsible for what had happened to these children and their parents today. The day she had left her uncle's cabin, she should have gone straight to the fort and told the authorities where he lived.

He and his gang would have been arrested.

His murdering and plundering, his reign of terror, would have been brought to an abrupt end.

She decided there and then that she would lead the soldiers to her uncle's hideout soon. She would gladly look him square in the eye as he was taken away to the gallows!

But her thoughts were interrupted by a sharp cry of distress, silencing everything in the village.

Red Wing stepped away from the child and turned in the direction of the mournful cry.

He grew cold inside when he saw an elderly cousin step from his grandfather's lodge. As she wailed and pulled her hair, then began scoring her arms with her fingernails, he knew that had to mean only one thing. If she was behaving this way after having been in his grandfather's lodge, Chief Bold Wolf must have died!

But how could this be? he despaired, seemingly frozen to the ground.

He could not move.

He could not cry out!

His thoughts were too muddled.

His grandfather had been all right this morning when Red Wing went to have an early smoke with him.

So how could he have died?

And why . . . ?

Chapter Twenty-Eight

Lightning flashed overhead in a stormy, dark, and brooding sky as James and Gerald arrived on their horses at Father Christopher's mission.

With nods of greeting, they dismounted and led their horses into a barn at the back of the mission, to hide the animals in case a parishioner might come to light candles for a loved one or to seek solace within the walls of God's house.

James readjusted his gunbelt while waiting for Gerald to settle his horse into a stall. Then they walked from the barn in wide strides.

"Gerald, it's good to have you as part of my gang," James said. "You proved your worth last night. You didn't flinch when I gave you the order to set fire to the settlers' house."

"What I got as payment made up for how I might have felt about doing it," Gerald said, hiding a shiver while in his mind's eye recalling how cold-heartedly James had murdered the mother of the two children they had later dumped into the river.

"I get paid well for following your orders," Gerald said. "And thanks for lettin' me buy into a partnership in the still you just took over."

He chuckled. "I told Sally I'd have me a still and get rich," he bragged. "She didn't believe me. She left me anyhow."

"Gerald, you don't need a wife for your nightly pleasures," James said, his lips curling into a slow smile. "There's plenty of women to choose from in the brothels at Fort Smith. You'd best frequent them now, before your picture gets plastered all over the place on wanted posters."

James's insides tightened when he thought of Malvina being taken to that hellhole of a brothel. Money had actually changed hands for her! If he ever found out who took her there. . . .

Gerald nervously wove his fingers through his greasy hair at the thought of Jason Hopper's anger over the foul-up with Malvina. No. There was no way Gerald could ever go to that brothel.

His eyes flashed. Of late he had watched Malvina from a bluff more than once. So far he hadn't caught her alone.

But there would come a time when she *would* be alone and, by damn, he'd steal her away this time for *good*.

Thunder rolled.

Lightning flashed.

Rain began in a slow mist.

"We'd best get inside," James said, eyeing the sky. "We're in for a whopper of a storm."

They ran to the door that opened into the cellar. Gerald flipped it open and stood aside as James entered ahead of him.

Then Gerald lowered the door behind him as he went down the narrow, dark stairs that stank of rot and mildew.

James opened the door at the foot of the stairs, where kerosene lamplight illuminated the musty room. Father Christopher and Paul were already there, sitting and smoking cigars on stools.

James nodded a welcome to them both, then sauntered over to the supply of moonshine and lifted a jug and tin cup from a shelf and poured himself a cupful.

Gerald followed his lead, then sat down on a stool beside James. He gazed at Father Christopher, who had opted to wear ordinary clothes this evening, instead of his usual black robe.

Then he gazed over at Paul, who did not seem to fit into this scenario. He seemed too proper to be an outlaw.

Gerald recalled that Paul had not been with the gang the previous night when the settlers were slain. The findings had been good in their cabin.

Gerald kneaded his chin, thinking that perhaps Paul *was* different. It was gossiped among the gang members that he was friends with Red Wing and that he had his eye on a Choctaw squaw.

"Roger, we'll be bringing a fresh supply of moonshine tomorrow," James said. He wiped his mouth clean of the moonshine with the back of a hand. "It's brewing now in the cave."

He set his tin cup aside, his eyes twinkling. "I think we can throw out the stuff we stole from that still a few nights ago," he said. "This stuff we're brewing is the best. This batch of our own white lightning is so strong, it will light up a man's insides like a lightning strike."

Thunder shook the mission.

"I'd say lightning is doin' its thing quite well today," Gerald said, laughing raucously, then sobering when no one seemed to appreciate his joke.

"Preach, how was the raid last night?" Father Christopher asked, his eyes intent on James. "Did you confiscate many firearms?"

"We got more than that," James said, smiling smugly. He poured his cup full of moonshine again and took a slow sip.

"Yeah, we got enough jars of fruit and vegetables to last into the winter, didn't we, Preach?" Gerald said, interrupting.

James frowned at Gerald for being so forward, then forgot about him when Father Christopher rose from his stool and stood with his hands clasped together behind him.

"Was anyone killed during the raid?" Father Christopher asked, his voice drawn.

"None of the gang were," James said, pausing to take another sip of moonshine. He looked guardedly up at Father Christopher. "But yes, Roger, killing was necessary last night. A man and a woman were shot."

Father Christopher dropped his eyes to his feet, then looked slowly up at James. "You know that I don't approve of killings," he said throatily.

"You know that most times it's necessary, so don't go bellyaching about it to me *now*," James grumbled. "You knew what you were getting into

247

when you sided in with me and my gang."

Father Christopher inhaled a quavering breath. "It was easy to look past that when I first agreed to allow you to use my church for your meetings and for storing your moonshine," he said. He walked slowly up and down the short aisles and stared at the jugs of whiskey. "My life as a child was one of deprivation. It was by the grace of God that someone came to my rescue and paid my way into the ministry."

He turned and glowered at James. "I've sinned now far too much in trying to make money and also to have close friends that I will never be forgiven. Being poor, the boys my age poked fun at me. It is good to have people with whom I can share conversation, even if it is about things I should be turning my eyes and heart from."

"Preach, tell him about the kids," Gerald said, his eyes dancing. "*That* oughta get him goin'."

"Children?" Paul said, finally breaking into the conversation. He had not been paying that much attention. He had other things on his mind—he had been thinking about Pretty Cloud! "What's this about children, Preach?"

James gave Gerald a scowl, then looked over at Paul, then Father Christopher. "There were two children, a boy and a girl," he said.

"Lord, don't tell me you killed *them*," Paul said, seeing more and more what a murdering scoundrel James was. He wished that he had never formed an alliance with him.

But Paul knew that he was in too thick now to get away from the outlaw gang easily—and live to tell it.

"They were spared," James said, shrugging.

"Where are they now?" Father Christopher asked, pale from realizing the depth of James's evil.

"I imagine drowned," James responded, again shrugging.

"What do you mean?" Paul asked, storming to his feet. "Did you or did you not drown them?"

"What's it to you what happened to them?" James growled. "You chose not to ride with us again last night, so you don't have the right to say much on how I conduct myself, now do you?"

"Preach," Father Christopher said, going to place a trembling hand on James's shoulder. "What did you do with the children?"

James turned slowly around. His eyes met Roger's unfalteringly. "I threw them both in the river," he said icily. "If they knew how to swim, just *maybe* they're alive. But I'd rather think they were washed away in the current. I'd hope they couldn't identify me."

"You should've killed 'em," Gerald complained. "Dead people don't point accusing fingers."

Father Christopher hung his head. He wove his fingers through his gray hair. "I don't know where this is all going to end," he said sadly. "Because of wanting earthly possessions and friendship, I have become someone I don't even know."

He looked slowly up at James. "And *you* studied the ministry. Your brother was a preacher. Where did it all go wrong for you, Preach? Where?"

"I never actually studied to be a preacher. I never wanted to be a man of God," James confessed. "It was all a lie I made up to tell my brother. But now my brother's dead. I no longer have to pretend I am something I'm not."

"Preach, you've been nothing but a hypocrite from the day I first met you," Paul grumbled. "I need some fresh air."

Paul turned and stamped up the stairs. As he threw the door open, he held his face up to the wind and rain. He didn't flinch as a bolt of lightning hit a tree close by, splitting it in half.

He stepped up into the rain and walked slowly toward the barn, then turned and looked over his shoulder at the church steeple. He silently prayed that lightning would strike it and rid the earth of those who were inside, whose very souls were lost to the devil.

But knowing that he was no better, that he had participated in killings and maimings himself, and that he would again in the future, Paul went to his horse, mounted, and rode off in the rain.

James stalked toward the stairs and gave Father Christopher one last stare over his shoulder. "Don't get so weak on me that you'll go to the authorities," he warned. "You'll be sorry, for you don't know the half of how I enjoy making those who cross me pay."

Gerald chuckled and followed James from the church into the storm.

Then Gerald turned cold inside when they reached the barn and James turned to him and grabbed him by the collar. "That goes double for you," he warned. "I don't trust you any farther than I can spit."

James then released Gerald and mounted his horse and rode away.

Savage Pride

His mood dark, Gerald glowered after James. "One day you're going to get yours, and I'll be the first to dance on your grave," he whispered to himself, then doubled over with laughter at the thought.

Chapter Twenty-Nine

Clouds hung low and gray along the horizon. There was a hint of rain in the air.

Sullen, filled with grief over his grandfather's passing, Red Wing had done his duty. He had meticulously painted his grandfather's face with vermilion. When he had finished, he thought that his grandfather's face looked as if it were no longer made of flesh and bone, but of rock—some hard, brown, polished stone.

Gently, Red Wing had placed a necklace of many bear claws around his grandfather's neck and had then dressed his body in a robe of feathers and fur.

The final wrapping of his grandfather's body had been with the hide of the medicine animal, the great bear. He had then been placed on an elevated platform erected near his house, food and drink and a change of clothing and other items placed near the corpse.

This was the second day of mourning for Chief Bold Wolf. While the entire village watched, Red Wing set up a number of poles around the scaffolding on which his grandfather lay. Meticulously and with much love, Red Wing hung hoops, wreaths, and flowers on these poles.

Each day at sunrise, until his grandfather's bones were placed in the bone house, Red Wing would prostrate himself before the poles and scaffolding and utter convulsive cries, to show his grief for the deceased.

Malvina watched Red Wing as he stepped back from the poles now, his face ashen from his deep sadness. His arms reaching toward the sun, his hands palm-side up, he began saying what seemed to be a prayer.

Malvina listened as Red Wing prayed, her heart breaking for him. She felt useless in that she had no way to lift the burden from his heart. He was now chief, but could not celebrate even that in his sadness over his grandfather's death.

As soon as the death of Red Wing's grandfather was confirmed, that he had died due to sudden heart failure, Red Wing had been quickly appointed chief so that this band of Choctaw would not be long without a leader.

Touched to the very core of herself by Red Wing's words, Malvina continued to listen to Red Wing as he now spoke to the Heavens, where his grandfather's spirit walked the spirit path of the hereafter.

"Spirit of Greatness, we mere mortals are constructed like the tree," Red Wing cried. "We are made out of many ideas, like the leaves on a tree, and in time, produce their fruit. In that way we give back to the Earth that which was given to us. Spirit of Greatness, my grandfather walks the spirit path. Soon his bones will become a part of the earth. Then he will have done all that was required of him, his duty as a man. Care for him, Spirit of Greatness. He was a man of peace. Make his journey an easy one."

His head hung, Red Wing turned away from everyone and went inside his grandfather's lodge. His mourning was so deep that he could not see past it.

And Malvina understood. She rose to her feet and walked lightly toward Bold Wolf's lodge. Paul soon appeared beside her.

Her lips pursed tightly, Malvina gave Paul a blistering stare. She did not want to disturb the silence of the mourners by telling Paul that he had no place there, that he was a liar, the worst of pretenders since he had wormed his way into the lives of the Choctaw as though he was kin to them.

If they knew the depths of his evil ways, they would all know just how this man had fooled them into believing that he was someone special, a white man who could be trusted.

Walking ahead of Paul, not wanting to be near him if she could help it, Malvina went inside Red Wing's grandfather's lodge.

She went to Red Wing, only scarcely able to see him since the fire in the fireplace had been allowed to burn down to cold ashes.

But the open door gave her enough light to see what Red Wing was holding. It looked like some sort of shield. She went to his side, drawing his eyes down to her.

"This is my grandfather's shield," Red Wing told her. "It was to be my father's, should he have become chief. But now it is mine."

"It's beautiful," Malvina said, ignoring Paul as he moved to Red Wing's other side.

"It will one day be our son's," Red Wing said, running a hand over the shield. "See the drawings? The unstrung bow, encompassing three arrows and a smoking pipe-hatchet, symbolizes the history and tradition of the Choctaw."

He paused and cleared his throat, then continued, "The three arrows symbolize the three great Choctaw chiefs who signed the Treaty of Doaks Stand in 1820, by which the United States assigned the tribe a vast western domain for a part of the Choctaw land in Mississippi."

Red Wing lowered the shield to his side. He sighed heavily, then smiled at Paul. "It is good that you came to share my mourning," he said, reaching a hand to Paul's shoulder. "Thank you, my friend. Thank you."

Malvina saw how quickly Paul glanced at her, uneasiness in his eyes, for he knew that she could destroy this friendship faster than a whipcrack.

And if she knew for certain that Paul had any part in the massacre those few days ago, when two innocent settlers were murdered and their children thrown into the river to drown, she would not hesitate to reveal his true self to these trusting people.

But now she had her own game to play. She could not let Paul know that she was going to lead the authorities to her uncle. As soon as Red Wing's mourning was over, she planned to go after her uncle and see that he paid for his evil deeds. If Paul was with him, she would happily kill two birds with one stone!

So, she would bide her time. Her focus now was on Red Wing and how to help him through his sad time. He needed her comforting arms.

And she would not bring any more heartache to him now by telling him that he had been duped by a man he considered a close friend.

"I wouldn't be anywhere else," Paul said sincerely. "When I heard of your grandfather's death, I came as quickly as I could."

Paul lowered his eyes uneasily, then looked up at Red Wing again. "I noticed Pretty Cloud sitting with Stands Tall," he said, shuffling his feet nervously as he spoke. "I had planned to bring a bride price soon. Have I waited too long?"

A commotion outside caused Red Wing's thoughts to stray from Paul's question. He laid the shield aside and walked to the door.

Malvina and Paul followed him outside. Malvina looked quickly over at Paul when she heard him gasp at who was there, wondering why he would have such a reaction to Father Christopher's arrival. It was obvious to her that the priest had come to the village to pay his respects to the dead chief. Malvina could not understand why this would have any effect on Paul, or why he should care one way or another about the priest's being there.

She looked at Red Wing, seeing a softness in his eyes at the sight of the black-robed man on horseback. She could tell that Red Wing was moved by the man caring about the passing of his grandfather.

Father Christopher drew tight rein in front of Red Wing's grandfather's cabin, his eyes on the scaffolding upon which lay the deceased.

His gaze shifted to Red Wing, moving slowly on over to Malvina, his gaze lingering on Paul, whose wavering eyes locked with his.

"You have come to pay respects to my grandfather," Red Wing said, taking a step toward Father Christopher's horse. "That is kind of you." He gestured toward the priest. "Would you like to dismount and stand beside my grandfather's resting place? If you wish to say a few words, my grandfather's spirit would welcome it."

"I shall stay on my horse, for I have not come to linger long in your village," Father Christopher said, his gaze shifting quickly to Paul again, then moving once again to Red Wing.

"I do not understand why you have come, yet will not take the time that you might with my grandfather," Red Wing said. He slowly lowered his arms to his sides. "But of course, our beliefs vary. What you white men regard as simply death, the Choctaw sees as the passing into the spirit world of one level of consciousness, and the rebirth of another."

Father Christopher's jaw tightened and his eyes narrowed, both of which Red Wing saw and did not understand.

"You do not feel that the spirit world and the natural world are so close that certain beings can move back and forth between the two almost effortlessly?" Red Wing said warily, feeling that things were not as they had first seemed with this white holy man.

The black-robed man seemed cold and distant.

257

He seemed unfriendly, not sympathetic to Red Wing's mourning, nor to the passing of a beloved one that had sent the whole village into the depths of despair.

When Red Wing's voice faded and Father Christopher still did not reply, Red Wing stepped closer to his horse and gazed questioningly up at the priest.

"You have come to my village at a time when my people are burdened with sadness," Red Wing said, his voice guarded. "If not to pay your respects, then why?"

Paul cleared his throat nervously when Father Christopher looked his way again.

Malvina saw how their eyes locked and lingered too long on each other's. Red Wing saw this too and was puzzled by it.

Then Father Christopher said to Red Wing, "You have misinterpreted my reason for being here."

"Then why *are* you?" Red Wing said. He folded his arms across his massive chest in a sudden gesture of distrust of this man, who seemed less than holy at this moment.

"Word came to me of your grandfather's passing," Father Christopher said, looking again up at the body stretched beneath robes on the scaffolding.

His eyes then searched for a person whose fingernails would be much longer than anyone else's. That would be the Choctaw village bonepicker. When he found the man who stood, short and stocky, dressed in a long robe, with hair as black as midnight and so long it dragged to the ground, Father Christopher visibly shivered. He had been asked by Gerald Smythe to find a way to bring negative attention to the Choctaw.

It was not hard for Father Christopher to use the condemnation of bone-picking as the way to rid this land of the Choctaw. It was known that the general at Fort Smith abhorred the practice. And he himself saw bone-picking as the act of heathens!

"Yes, I am certain that word has spread wide and far of my grandfather's passing," Red Wing said. He was glad when Malvina eased to his side, finding comfort in her presence. "He was a beloved man of peace."

Father Christopher's gaze shifted to Malvina. Could this be the woman Gerald had spoken of earlier? There was something vaguely familiar about her.

Had he seen her before?

Her eyes and the color of her hair reminded him of someone, yet he could not at this moment place who.

He mainly knew his parishioners—and his out-law friends.

Knowing that it was best to get this confrontation over with and get out of the village as soon as possible, Father Christopher turned a livid gaze to Red Wing.

"I have not come to praise your grandfather, but to condemn a practice that comes with the death of a Choctaw," he pronounced, finding the words easy when earlier he had thought that the presence of so many Choctaw would be too threatening.

"And what practice is that you speak of?" Red Wing said, his voice suddenly icy.

"Bone-picking," Father Christopher said angrily. "You do not wish to be looked at as savages? Then do away with such practices as bone-picking that make you look like heathens."

"And what do you know of bone-picking that makes you condemn it so openly in the presence of Red Wing and his people?" Red Wing said, trying to keep his composure.

"I know that after worms have consumed the flesh of the deceased, the entire family of the deceased assembles and watches the bone-picker dismember the skeleton," Father Christopher said, his voice steady. "First the bone-picker tears off the muscles, nerves, and tendons which the worms leave on the body. Only then does the deceased have a proper burial—when the bones are placed in a chest and buried."

Red Wing had explained all about the practice of bone-picking to Malvina, and she too had seen it as so unusual, so *medieval*, that she had felt sick when she tried to envision it.

But she had also known that she would have this, as well as many other customs she might not understand, to adjust to and to accept.

And it seemed strange that only now would the priest come and condemn the practice so openly. As with the white community, there was always someone to bury in the Choctaw village as the old gave way to the birth of new.

So it made no sense for this priest suddenly to condemn bone-picking now, unless for an under-handed, scheming purpose.

Yes, she could not help feeling that something was very wrong here, and that perhaps he had been paid to do this.

She looked slowly from Paul to the priest. Too often, their gazes locked and lingered. It seemed as though they knew one another too well.

If Red Wing didn't get any answers today that satisfied him, then she would have to begin her own investigation.

Perhaps this priest was involved in more things than were godly.

Although the idea might be a bit far-fetched, just perhaps this priest might lead her to who had murdered her parents.

He might even lead her to those who had stolen the family heirlooms!

Yes, she would do some investigating, for she suspected that Father Christopher's visit here was for some other reason than to condemn the practice of bone-picking. And she was determined to find out just why he had come to interfere in the Choctaws' lives.

Suddenly, several other horsemen arrived at the far end of the village. The Choctaw gathered and watched the other white men arrive, the sheriff from Fort Smith at the lead.

Red Wing's insides stiffened when he recognized the sheriff. Thinking that the priest's and sheriff's timely visits were planned, he glared up at the priest.

He then looked slowly at the sheriff as he drew a tight rein beside Father Christopher, his men hanging back on their horses several feet from him.

"Red Wing, word has come to me that your grandfather has died," Sheriff Grinnell said straight out. He rested one hand on a pistol holstered at his right side, his other hand smoothing a wide-brimmed hat back from his wind-bronzed brow. His blue eyes cut into Malvina as he looked slowly at her, smiling smugly as he raked his eyes over her Indian attire.

Then he looked down at Red Wing again, realizing that Red Wing was not going to offer any return remark.

"I've come to pay my respects, Red Wing," Sheriff Grinnell said. "But that's not the only reason. I've come to order you not to use bone-picking in your burial ceremonies anymore. It's not a healthy practice. And it's not good for our children to realize that Indians can get away with such heathen practices. It sets a poor example. So, Red Wing, hear me well when I tell you I'd better not get wind of your people ever practicing bone-picking again."

"You have come on my land during my mourning and you have given orders to this Choctaw chief and you believe they are the last word in the Choctaw community?" Red Wing said in a rush of heated words. "Hear *me* well, white lawman. . . ." He shifted his dark eyes to Father Christopher. "Hear me well, white man in black robe!"

He glared up at the sheriff. "No one comes on land owned by the Choctaw and hands out orders," Red Wing continued. "No one has the right to tell the Choctaw how to live their lives, especially how to bury their dead. The Great White Father in Washington looks over the Choctaw with a kind heart and made laws that gave the Choctaw freedom on their own land to do as they please. There is nothing in the treaty that says the Choctaw cannot practice bone-picking."

Several warriors came suddenly from their cabins, their rifles leveled on the white men.

Red Wing smiled. "I would suggest you who came to disturb the mourning time for my grandfather leave now, or my warriors will escort you in their own way from the village," he said. He frowned at Father Christopher. "You are not welcome ever again into my village."

Again Red Wing noticed how Father Christopher and Paul exchanged quick glances. This gave Red Wing even more cause to believe that Paul was not the friend he pretended, or why would he seem to be the priest's friend, as well?

His thoughts shifted when the sheriff wheeled his horse around and rode away, his men following.

Father Christopher glared down at Red Wing, then at Malvina, then also rode away.

Red Wing turned stone-cold eyes to Paul. "I will not ask you what is between you and Father Christopher, because I do not know if you would be truthful, or if what you say would make me feel foolish for having ever aligned myself with you. Paul, I think it is best that you leave now, also. I shall talk with you later, when my heart is not burdened with so many things."

Malvina smiled smugly at Paul. He caught the smile, then inhaled a quavering breath and turned and walked away.

Red Wing watched Paul until he rode from the village, then reached an arm around Malvina's waist and walked slowly toward his cabin. "Too often I am disappointed in those I have grown to trust," he said thickly. He gazed down at her.

"You have gained my total trust. Never disappoint me."

Malvina swallowed hard, knowing even now that she must find a way to leave the village without Red Wing knowing. Should he find out, would he believe her reason?

Or would he condemn her as quickly as he had just condemned Paul?

It made her heartbeat quicken to think that he might.

Yet she still had her own answers to find out.

Chapter Thirty

Not certain whether or not Red Wing was in a sound enough sleep for her to leave, Malvina watched him guardedly as she lay beside him.

Deeply into his mourning for his grandfather, Red Wing had not eaten, nor had he said much to her when they were alone. He had given her a light kiss after they had gone to bed, but then had rolled over away from her, placing his back to her.

She understood that she would have to accept his more sullen mood for a while, just as she hoped that he would understand why she was driven to do what she must do tonight if he awakened and found her gone.

She just could not let go of the past all that easily. The priest coming to the village, and his and Paul's attitude toward one another, had fueled the fires within her heart to find answers that she had thought she could forget about once she concluded that her brother was dead.

But her brother's death should never have stifled her need to avenge their parents' deaths. They would be alive today if not for those outlaws who so cold-heartedly came that night, leaving death and destruction behind.

Not wanting to think about it any longer tonight, and feeling a desperate need to take action, Malvina slowly moved to her knees.

Scarcely breathing, she leaned over Red Wing and gazed at him. The fire in the fireplace gave her enough light to see that he was sleeping peacefully. Surely she could move around without his hearing her. If he caught her dressing to leave, she feared it would again arouse his suspicions of her.

Would he even listen to reason?

Would he order her to leave his village?

Could he truly turn his back on the love he vowed he felt for her?

Knowing that she must take this chance, and truly hating to leave the warm cocoon of blankets and buffalo robes, Malvina inched her way to the foot of the bed.

The boards of the planked wooden floor were cold to the soles of her feet, causing her to flinch.

She inhaled a quavering breath, then slowly left the bed.

Trembling, her knees weak from fear of being caught, Malvina reached for the buckskin dress that she had left purposely close to the bed. Her heart thudded as she slipped the dress over her head.

After it was smoothed down her body, she stopped to take another lingering look at Red

Wing. When he groaned and mumbled something in his sleep and tossed quickly to his other side, Malvina jumped, her breath quickening.

When he settled in again and was quietly sleeping, Malvina exhaled a breath of relief.

Still watching him, she bent over and fit one foot into a moccasin, then the other.

Straightening up again, she watched Red Wing for a moment longer. She was unable to shake the sudden feeling that she was betraying him by sneaking away in the night without confiding in him why she must.

But she knew this was the only way. He was not only mourning for his grandfather; he was now a powerful chief with the duties that came with being chief! He did not need *her* troubles added to what he already had.

Wanting to do her investigating and get back to the village before Red Wing awakened, she determinedly went to his store of weapons and chose a holstered pistol.

When she placed it around her waist, she frowned down at it. She had forgotten that the gunbelt would probably not fit her. She took the pistol from the holster and, holding it down to her side, tiptoed toward the cabin door. Her pulse raced as she reached for the latch on the door with her free hand.

If the latch or the door squeaked . . .

Slowly she opened the door, breathing much more easily. The moon spilled inside the door as she stepped outside into the midnight hour.

Before going to the corral, Malvina looked guardedly around her for signs of life. She saw no sentries anywhere. Surely their duty to guard the village had been forgotten during their mourning.

She only hoped that the young braves who usually watched the horses through the night were also elsewhere. Perhaps they would be with their parents, to seek solace in the presence of the families over having lost their beloved leader.

Creeping in front of the cabins to get to the corral, Malvina suddenly found herself shadowed by something.

Fear quickened her heartbeat and her flesh crawled when she gazed slowly upward and discovered that she was standing in the shadow of the scaffolding upon which Red Wing's grandfather lay.

Slowly she looked upward, shivering at the sight of the wrapped corpse.

Then her eyes moved over the objects that Red Wing had hung from the poles, and guilt splashed through her for what she was doing behind his back. She could not shake the feeling of betrayal that came with looking at Red Wing's gifts to his grandfather.

In the distance, an owl hooted, causing Malvina to start. She looked over her shoulder when she heard the low, mournful howl of a coyote.

Her gaze followed the sound and found the coyote on the bluff that overlooked the village. His eyes were lifted to the moon, his howls echoing across the vastness of the land.

Inhaling a nervous breath, now a creature of the night herself, Malvina turned away from the scaffolding and broke into a quiet run that soon took her to the corral.

As she had hoped, no one was there. It was as though the Choctaw expected everyone to respect their fallen warrior, so much that they did not guard against any intruders.

Had they forgotten so easily the priest's ugly words and the sheriff's threats? she wondered as she looked through the horses.

She sighed with relief when she found her very own horse that had been taken as payment for the canoe she had stolen.

Had the Choctaw not seen the disrespect and the hate that lay within the threats and demands of those who came today to disturb their mourning? Malvina still wondered about this as she reached for a saddle from the many that were stacked neatly beneath a tree.

After saddling her black roan, Malvina took time to reacquaint herself with him as she allowed him to nuzzle the palm of her left hand, her right hand being burdened with the heavy pistol.

"There, there, boy," she whispered. "It's only me. Malvina. Can you take me away quietly enough so that no one will catch me? We've done this countless times before when I needed a ride after Mama and Papa were asleep. I trust that you remember those long midnight rides. I shall never forget them."

Choked up with memories of those times when life had been simple and sweet, Malvina flicked tears from the corners of her eyes.

Then stubbornly firming her lips, she slipped the pistol into the empty gunboot at the side of the saddle, then mounted the horse and lifted the reins.

Cassie Edwards

"Let's ride, Midnight," she whispered in his ear, patting him.

Following the command of her voice, and the feel of her heels on his flanks, the roan took off and soon jumped the corral fence.

Riding with the skill and daring of a man, Malvina smiled to herself as her roan broke into a gallop across the open meadow.

Then a thought came to her that made her frown. She knew the ferry would not be running this late at night. That gave her only one choice if she was to get across the river. Of late, rains had been scarce, and there had been only one huge downpour in two months. The river was low, so low that the river boats could not make their usual journeys down the Arkansas River to Fort Smith.

But she knew of a small island that appeared in the river when the river was this low. It was called Crow Wing Island because it was shaped like a crow's wing.

Long ago, Malvina had taught her horse how to swim in the river. He would have no trouble getting her to the island, then from there to the other side.

"Again, Midnight, I'm depending on you," she whispered, her hair flying in the breeze, the moon shadowing her and her steed on the ground beside them.

When Malvina reached the river, she was stunned to see that the ferry was tied up at the pier. She drew a tight rein and wheeled her horse to a sudden stop.

She then urged her roan in a slow canter toward the ferry. When she reached it, she dismounted and walked her steed onto the pier, then onto the ferry.

Suddenly Joe was there, a rifle aimed at her.

When the shine of the moonlight revealed to Joe that it was Malvina, he lowered his rifle to his side. "What the hell you doin' on my ferry this time of night?" he said, scowling at her. "Don't you know the dangers of bein' alone?" He chuckled to himself.

"Or did Red Wing send you away?"

"No, Red Wing didn't send me away," Malvina said, throwing her reins over the rail of the ferry. "And you'd better not tell him you saw me, either."

"What sort of game are you playin'?" Joe said, looking her up and down. He leaned his rifle against the rail. "Why are you here?"

"Why are *you* here on this side of the river this time of night?" Malvina asked, tiring of his questions.

" 'Cause I paid him to bring me here, that's why," Gerald said, inching his way onto the ferry, his pistol leveled at Malvina. "Joe, I left my horse on the riverbank. Do me a favor. Go get it for me."

"I ain't paid to do errands," Joe grumbled. "And had I known what you were up to, I'd have refused to bring you to the Indian side of the Arkansas. I should've known you were up to no good."

"Yeah, but the shine of the coin I paid you for your services blinded you to what might be civil or not. Right?" Gerald tormented.

Malvina stood stone cold as she listened to them talking. It was obvious by what was being said that Gerald had been the one spying from the bluff. She had to wonder how many times he had watched her from afar, making plans to abduct her.

And now she realized why he had been there. He had been waiting and watching for the opportunity to accost her!

"You low-down, no-good scoundrel," Malvina said angrily. "I should have known I hadn't seen the last of you."

"You will soon," Gerald said, shrugging. Out of the corner of his eye, he watched Joe go for his horse. "After I sell you to a plantation owner. You'll make a mighty pretty slave, don't you think?"

"Slave?" Malvina gasped, paling. She gazed past him, at Joe. "Joe! Help me! Go for Red Wing!"

Malvina's heart sank when she realized that Joe wasn't going to help her. Then a thought came to her that filled her with hope again. When Red Wing discovered that she was gone, he would search for her. He would question Joe. Surely Joe would be honest enough to tell him what had happened.

That hope was quickly shattered when she heard Gerald warning Joe not to tell anyone about what had happened tonight.

"I'll fill you full of holes, then sink your ferry to the bottom of the river if you tell Red Wing I abducted his woman," Gerald hissed as he leaned into Joe's face. "She ain't worth that, is she, Joe?"

Joe looked clumsily over at Malvina, then silently went to the pole that he used to shove the ferry into deeper water.

"He ain't no fool," Gerald said, keeping his pistol leveled at Malvina.

"Does your wife know you're this mean?" Malvina asked, hoping to find his vulnerable side.

"Thanks to you, I ain't got no wife no more," Gerald growled.

"She—left you?" Malvina stammered.

"Yeah, she left me," Gerald said, his eyes narrowing angrily.

Malvina said nothing more. She watched the other side of the river coming closer, hoping that someone might be there to catch the ferry for a trip back to Indian territory.

But she knew the chances of others being out at this time of night were slim, unless they were outlaws who did their dirty deeds under the cover of night.

She had to wonder where her uncle might be at this moment, and whose lives might be altered tonight forever because of him.

Not wanting to double her feeling of futility, Malvina shook thoughts of her uncle from her mind and concentrated more on how she might escape this horrid man before he did as he threatened.

A plantation owner?

She would be sent into slavery? She had heard of white slavery. The women were used not only to work in the fields, but also in the plantation owner's bed at night.

The thought sent shivers of revulsion through her to think that some other man besides Red Wing would touch her body. Would possibly even rape her!

"Joe, remember what I told you," Gerald said, as he saw the other side quickly approaching. "Not a word to anyone about what you seen tonight."

Joe nodded, then guided the ferry up to the pier.

"Get on my horse," Gerald flatly ordered Malvina. "Get in the saddle. I'm going to sit behind you. Mind you, Malvina, don't try anything. I'll shoot you if you do."

Knowing that this man was capable of anything, Malvina swung herself into his saddle. She stiffened when he mounted behind her and she felt the cold steel of his firearm against her arm as he grabbed for the reins with his free hand.

Her shoulders squared, not wanting to show this man that she was afraid, Malvina rode with him to the riverbank.

She jumped when a horseman rode out from the shadows and she recognized him. Although he had never seen her, she had seen him riding with James. He was a member of her uncle's outlaw gang.

That had to mean that Gerald had to be mixed up with her uncle's illegal activities also!

"You got 'er," Dave said, looking over at Gerald with a surprised, awkward smile.

"Yeah, Dave. I said I would, didn't I?" Gerald said, laughing boisterously.

"What's the boss going to say about you takin' a woman to his hideout as a hostage?" Dave asked, a wariness entering his squinty eyes.

"Preach won't be back for a while, probably not until sunup," Gerald said, swinging his horse toward the road. "I hope to get this woman outta my life for good before then."

"I hope the boss didn't wonder about us tonight, where we wuz and all," Dave shouted at Gerald as they bypassed Fort Smith by taking a narrow path into the forest. "We could be tossed out on our ear, Gerald. I can't afford that happening to me. I need the money that we're both bein' paid, not only to help with the raids, but also with the distributing of moonshine. I've got a couple of kids and a wife who depend on me."

Malvina looked quickly over at the man. He had a family and he was a part of an outlaw gang?

She then looked away in disgust.

She clung to the pommel of the saddle as Gerald sent his steed into a hard gallop. It seemed to Malvina that they rode for hours and hours, then finally stopped before the entrance of a cave.

She didn't have to be told what was made inside the cave. The smell of moonshine was overpowering.

"This is where I leave you for a spell," Gerald said to Dave. He shoved Malvina from his horse. "Take her inside. Tie her up. I'll be back later."

"You'd best get your dealings done quick or we're both dead, Gerald," Dave said as he drew his horse up beside a large oak tree and threw his reins over a branch. He then slipped out of his saddle, his pistol aimed at Malvina.

"The plantation owner is stayin' in a hotel in town," Gerald said, wheeling his horse around. "It won't take long for me to make my bargain with him. I'll be back for Malvina shortly."

Dave motioned with his gun toward Malvina. "Inside," he grumbled. "Missie, do you hear? Follow me inside the cave. I truly don't want to hurt you."

Malvina half stumbled into the cave, then stopped when a campfire farther in revealed the still and the huge store of moonshine lined up against both sides of the cave.

"Sit down beside the fire," Dave said, his voice not so authoritative as it was apologetic.

Malvina nodded and sat down on a blanket, then hugged herself. She shivered when Dave stared down at her, his eyes slowly raking over her.

She kept reminding herself that this man had a family.

He had a wife.

He had no need for *her*.

Chapter Thirty-One

Someone shaking him awakened Red Wing with a start. He looked quickly up as a small face peered down at him, the glowing embers in the fireplace giving off enough firelight for him to recognize Dreaming Shield.

"Young brave, what is it?" Red Wing asked, leaning up on an elbow.

But before Dreaming Shield had a chance to answer, Red Wing suddenly noticed that Malvina was no longer in bed with him.

He bolted from the bed and looked in anxious jerks around him. Then he gazed down at Dreaming Shield again.

"You have come to tell me something about Malvina?" he said, his pulse racing.

Dreaming Shield looked past him at the empty bed, now realizing that his calculations about Malvina were correct. He looked quickly up at

Red Wing. "I came to tell you that the horse that once belonged to Malvina has been taken from the corral," he said, swallowing hard. "My father allowed me to stand guard with him tonight. When he left long enough to look in on my ailing mother, it was my duty to stay and watch the horses for him. I . . . I left long enough to go and look up at the scaffolding upon which your grandfather lies. I . . . I so miss Chief Bold Wolf."

Touched by the child's innocence and his love for Red Wing's grandfather, Red Wing drew him into his arms. "No one will fault you for the horse being taken," he said.

He gave the child a quick, comforting hug. He knew that he needed it since guilt lay heavy on his heart for not having tended well enough to his duties for his father.

Then Red Wing swung away from the child. He knelt down before him and clasped his hands onto Dreaming Shield's shoulders.

"Surely you heard the horse being taken away," he said, his eyes anxiously searching Dreaming Shield's. "How long has it been gone? Did you see in which direction it went?"

Realizing the depth of the error he had made tonight, in that he had not only left his post, but had waited much too long to come to Red Wing to confess, Dreaming Shield hung his head and gulped hard.

"Dreaming Shield, Malvina is gone," Red Wing insisted. "This is no time for silence. Malvina is not in my lodge. I am certain it was *she* who took the horse. I must follow. She could be in danger."

Dreaming Shield lifted wavering eyes into Red Wing's. "I heard the horse ride away," he said softly. "But I did not see who was riding it. And, Red Wing, I did not come right away to tell you. I was afraid to tell you that I had not stayed with the horses as I was told to do. But I knew the other guards had been lifted tonight to mourn with their families for Chief Bold Wolf. I thought . . . that perhaps you saw it was not that important that I stay at my post."

"Dreaming Shield," Red Wing said, his voice drawn. "I am not going to scold or punish you for what you did tonight. Just tell me how long Malvina has been gone. And you heard the hoofbeats of the horse. In which direction did the sound go?"

Red Wing's heart beat more rapidly by the moment in his impatience to get to the answers he needed before going after Malvina. He was confused as to why she chose *now* to leave.

He had thought that they had come to some sort of understanding!

He had thought that she was content to forget the past and instead look toward the future!

He had to wonder what had changed her mind, or if she had ever been truthful with him about her feelings, about her intention to become his wife.

Had she decided to go to live with her outlaw uncle?

He *was* her only living relative.

"She has been gone for some time," Dreaming Shield finally confessed, again lowering his eyes. "And . . . and I was so frightened over having been lax in my duties that I did not think to listen to the direction of the horse's flight."

Tears flowed from Dreaming Shield's eyes as he gazed up at Red Wing. "I am sorry, so very sorry," he said pleadingly, in a way that tore parts of Red Wing's heart away, for he so loved this child.

Red Wing drew him into his arms and stroked his bare back. "Young brave, do not despair so," he said softly. "I hold no one to blame for Malvina's flight from our village except myself. It is apparent now that I did not impress upon her enough my love and need for her. So do not hold yourself to blame for what I myself seemed to lack in the art of persuasion."

Red Wing then rushed quickly to his feet. He slipped into fringed breeches, yanked on a fringed shirt, and slapped a gunbelt around his waist, one pistol hanging heavy in its holster.

"Shall I go and awaken Stands Tall and the other warriors?" Dreaming Shield asked, wiping tears from his eyes as Red Wing slipped into his moccasins.

"No," Red Wing said solemnly. "This I will do alone. It is my woman who has fled. No one but the man she has fled from should go after her."

"But you might be riding into danger," Dreaming Shield said. He realized that he had said the wrong thing when Red Wing frowned at him for voicing his doubts of his chief.

"You have your duties tonight," Red Wing said, weaving his strong hands through his thick hair to straighten it back across his shoulders. "Go quickly and ready my stallion."

Eyes wide, Dreaming Shield nodded anxiously, then turned and left the cabin.

Red Wing turned solemn eyes to the bed. Had it been so long ago that he felt the comfort of his woman's body pressed against his from behind as he lay there quietly and inwardly mourning the loss of his grandfather?

Had she even then been plotting to leave him?

"Why?" he cried in his despair and confusion, lifting his eyes heavenward. "Grandfather, are you there? Can you hear me? Will I ever know Malvina? Truly know her? Should I even want to? Has she deceived me in pretending she loved me? Why would she? Why?"

Knowing that too much time had already elapsed since Malvina's departure from his village, and needing to find her for many reasons, Red Wing swung around and left his cabin at a determined run.

When he reached the corral, Dreaming Shield's father was there. He humbly apologized when he realized what had happened, then handed Red Wing his horse's reins.

Dreaming Shield and his father stood back as Red Wing nudged his horse's flanks with his moccasined heels, yanked on the reins, and rode away through the opened gate of the corral.

Red Wing knew that he had to go to the white man's side of the Arkansas River. The ferry would not be there at this late hour, and he knew of only one place to cross the Arkansas. In her astuteness about the land and the river, Malvina must have gone there herself to get across.

His muscles tight, his eyes alert with angry, savage pride, Red Wing kicked his horse into a hard gallop until he reached the river.

Then he loped along a crusty trail that led alongside the river, where a creamy fog clung like a fallen cloud over the water.

At the place where the river narrowed and close to where Crow Wing Island thrust from the water like a ghost during times when rain was scarce, Red Wing once again sent his stallion into a hard gallop. His horse's wide nostrils flared, its eyes flamed, and its wind-flung mane and tail resembled wings as it thundered through the fog.

When Red Wing came to the place he intended to cross, he yanked on the reins and guided his horse down into the water. The water lapped at Red Wing's knees as the horse swam toward the island.

Then the island was left behind and the horse swam expertly toward Fort Smith's side of the river. Red Wing peered ahead, yet was unable to see the other side due to the fog.

Red Wing was glad when he finally reached dry land. His stallion shook himself dry, spraying water into the air, then followed Red Wing's command and rode off at a brisk clip.

Red Wing had one destination.

Paul's house.

The more he had thought about Paul's attitude while the priest was at Red Wing's village, and about how Paul seemed too knowledgeable about the wrong things, *and* recalling Paul's determination to turn Red Wing against Malvina, the more Red Wing saw him as corrupt and untrustworthy.

Tonight Red Wing would discover just how corrupt Paul was and to what lengths he would go to prove there was still a measure of loyalty left inside his heart to Red Wing.

Red Wing would force answers from Paul by not actually demanding verbal answers from him.

It was what Red Wing was going to ask *of* Paul that would make the difference in their future relationships!

Leaving the fog behind him where it hovered over the river, Red Wing sent his stallion into a neck-breaking gallop across the land.

First he rode down a narrow dirt road past Fort Smith.

Then he wound his way around trees in the depths of a forest.

He then rode across a great, wide meadow where moonbeams played like fairies along the ground.

Then he entered a thicket and saw Paul's cabin a short distance away in a break in the trees.

Eyes narrowed angrily, he rode onward. When he reached the cabin, he wheeled his horse to a shuddering halt, slid from his saddle, and entered the cabin without knocking.

With only the spill of the moonlight to guide him, Red Wing made his way through the darkness.

When he reached Paul's bed, he stood over it for a moment, studying this man who he had for so long assumed was a trusted friend, then bent over and grabbed Paul by the shoulders and yanked him to a sitting position.

Frightened by being awakened in such a way, Paul cried out with surprised fear.

Wild-eyed, he gazed up at Red Wing, his mouth agape. "Red Wing, what the hell are you doing?" he said, his voice high with fear.

"My woman is gone," Red Wing said. "I suspect you can lead me to her uncle. Take me to his hideout. *Now*."

"How should I know where James's hideout is?" Paul asked.

Paul's heart pounded and he cursed himself for lying to Red Wing about Malvina, saying that she was in cahoots with her Uncle James. If he had kept his mouth shut, Red Wing would not have involved him in anything even closely associated with the little bitch!

"I believe you know more than you say about many things. I feel a fool for having trusted you and brought you into my village as I would a red brother," Red Wing said between clenched teeth.

"What makes you doubt me?" Paul asked, glad when Red Wing released his shoulders. His grip had been fierce. Even now Paul's skin burned from it.

"Things I have witnessed and things you have said have made me think twice about this man who has wormed his way into the lives of the Choctaw," Red Wing said, grabbing Paul by an arm and forcefully yanking him from his bed. "Get dressed. You are going to lead me to Malvina's uncle's hideout. And play no more games with me. What you do tonight, you do as one last act of friendship. Then we go our separate ways, forever."

Paul's eyes wavered and he swallowed hard as Red Wing gave him a shove toward the chair where Paul had left his clothes before going to bed. He felt trapped. If he didn't do as Red Wing said, he knew that Red Wing would not believe that it was because he did not know where to take him.

And if he led him there, Red Wing would then know absolutely that Paul had led two lives and had spoken with two tongues.

Either way, Paul realized that he had lost Red Wing's friendship.

He saw it as best to try and help Red Wing find Malvina. Perhaps he would be somewhat grateful and not totally hate him. Paul truly loved Red Wing as he would have loved a blood brother.

"I'll take you to the hideout," Paul said, flinching when he heard Red Wing suck in a quick breath.

Feeling empty over having been discovered as the traitor that he was, Paul stumbled awkwardly into his clothes. When he was fully dressed and he started to reach for his gunbelt, he choked out a cry of pain as Red Wing grabbed him by a wrist and twisted it as he forced him around to face him.

"Do you think I am foolish enough to allow you to carry a firearm now that we are enemies?" Red Wing hissed, his eyes narrowing into Paul's.

"Enemies?" Paul gasped out, wincing when Red Wing's grip tightened on his wrist. "Are we that quickly enemies, Red Wing? We have shared so much. Can you forget it so easily?"

"This sharing that you speak of," Red Wing said, his voice drawn. "It was done when hearts seemed connected. When this Choctaw trusted you, a white man. Tonight we share one last time. And best you lead me to Malvina so that I can save her, or you will see how quickly this Choctaw chief can hate!"

Paul swallowed hard.

Red Wing released his grip, then gave Paul a shove toward the door.

"Go to your horse," Red Wing ordered. "Lead the way. I shall follow."

"Red Wing, I feel naked without my firearm," Paul choked out. "When James finds out that I led you to his hideout, he'll come shootin'. Surely you'll allow me a way to defend myself."

Red Wing thought for a moment, then stamped back to the holstered pistol that hung from a peg on the wall. He saw the logic in what Paul said. And to get Malvina out of the outlaw's hideout, *if* she had actually gone there, there might be a lot of gunfire. He only hoped that she would not be harmed.

He grabbed the holster and took it to Paul. "If there was ever a thread of decency in the friendship you offered me, you will use this firearm for only one purpose tonight, and that is to help me find my woman," he said. "Should you turn the firearm on me, and should I die, I will haunt you from the hereafter until you wish that you had not betrayed me that last time."

Paul's eyes locked with Red Wing's as he slowly reached a hand out for the holstered pistol.

Chapter Thirty-Two

"Red Wing, I'd never do anything to hurt you," Paul said sincerely as he clasped the gunbelt around his waist. "Although you may doubt everything I say from now on, please believe me when I tell you that you are the best friend I have ever had or ever will have. I'm sorry if I've disappointed you."

"I will not ask you why you chose one road of life over the other," Red Wing replied. "And you are not the most urgent of my concerns tonight. I must find Malvina. I first want to make sure she is all right. Secondly, I must find out why she chose to leave."

Knowing that he might condemn himself further in Red Wing's eyes if he said anything about Malvina, Paul said nothing more. He left his cabin and went to his horse and swung himself into his saddle.

"Again, I am sorry for having disappointed you," Paul said, sidling his horse next to Red Wing's.

Red Wing said nothing. He rode off with Paul at his side.

They rode relentlessly until Paul wheeled his horse to a stop. He edged his steed over closer to Red Wing's as he drew tight rein beside him. "The hideout is through those trees up ahead," he said, nodding toward them. "Red Wing, if you go to the cabin and the gang is there, it'll be like entering a hornet's nest."

"If they are there, *we* will have the advantage," Red Wing said, his voice filled with confidence. "It is late. They will more than likely be asleep. If Malvina is there, I *will* get her!"

"Is she worth the risk you are taking?" Paul asked, frowning. "You are now chief of your people. What if you lose your life tonight? What then, for your people?"

"Stands Tall is next in line for chief," Red Wing said matter-of-factly. "The council has spoken this choice. So if I should die for the sake of a woman, best then that he be chief. He would be more worthy than I."

Red Wing headed onward, Paul at his side, then wheeled his horse to a sudden stop only a few feet from the cabin. He looked guardedly from side to side, then glared at Paul. "There are no horses, so my woman is not here," Red Wing growled. "Does Malvina's uncle have more than one hideout?"

Paul's thoughts went to the cave. Although recently acquired, it was now considered James's second hideout. Not only was their still hidden in this cave, it was now being used as a quick escape if the authorities discovered the cabin.

Paul knew, though, not to tell Red Wing about it. Paul would be signing his own death warrant if he did.

He looked guardedly at Red Wing. "No, there is no other hideout," he said. He jumped when Red Wing reached over and clasped a hand around his throat, half lifting him from the saddle.

"I do not believe this could be an outlaw gang's only hideout," he said, his teeth clenched. "A cabin this size is not large enough for a store of weapons *or* for hiding what they steal from innocent settlers."

Red Wing leaned his face into Paul's. His free hand yanked his pistol from its holster. He thrust the barrel of the gun into Paul's stomach. "If you do not take me there, you will die as you sit in your saddle."

"All right, all right. . . ." Paul said, his voice scarcely a whisper from the strain on his throat as Red Wing held him in a tight grasp. "I'll . . . take . . . you there."

"You have been a member of this gang all the while you befriended the Choctaw?" Red Wing demanded, still holding firmly on to Paul's neck. "You had to be, to know so much about them."

"It just happened," Paul said, choking.

"I will deal with that later," Red Wing said, easing his hand away, and also the pistol. "Take me to the other hideout."

"I doubt you will find Malvina there," Paul said, rubbing the raw flesh of his neck. "No one goes there but the gang members."

"You once accused Malvina of being a part of

her uncle's gang," Red Wing said, slipping his pistol into its holster. "Now you are saying she is not? Which lie, or which truth, should I listen to?"

Feeling that he was getting himself more deeply into trouble with Red Wing, Paul tensed up. "I'll take you to the hideout," he said. "You can decide then what you wish. No matter what I now say to you, you will not believe me."

"Yes, that is so," Red Wing whispered to himself, glaring at Paul's back as he rode away. He wheeled his stallion around and followed Paul's lead, disappointed over having discovered that Paul was someone he did not even know.

As Red Wing rode onward, his thoughts shifted back to Malvina instead of lingering on Paul. He had searched and searched within his very soul to find the answer to why she had left his bed tonight.

Was it as simple as her still searching for her brother? Or was it because she could not stay away from the sort of life she had led before becoming acquainted with Red Wing?

Was she a part of this criminal gang after all?

Could she have lied so convincingly?

His troubled thoughts made the miles go by much more quickly. He reined in beside Paul as Paul stopped.

"The hideout is in the cave over there," Paul whispered to Red Wing as he nodded toward the mouth of a cave shadowed by the moon's light. He looked around for horses, finding only one reined to a low limb of a tree just outside the cave. "It seems we're in luck. There's only one outlaw in the cave."

Red Wing was not sure how he felt when he did not see Malvina's horse. A part of him was glad, thinking that he was wrong about her having come to her uncle for reasons that were ugly.

A part of him was disappointed—for he might never find her!

Or worse yet, was she riding with the outlaws tonight, attacking innocent white settlers?

Determined to find whatever answers he could, Red Wing dismounted. He peered intensely into Paul's eyes, making Paul's insides grow cold.

"You will stay outside and keep watch for the return of the outlaws while I go inside and take a look around," Red Wing said flatly. "If you were ever my true friend, you will do this for me."

Touched by Red Wing's show of trust, if only in small measure, Paul eagerly nodded. "Yes, I will do this for you," he said. "Red Wing, I hate losing your friendship. I will do anything you ask to get it back."

"Do this tonight for me, and we can talk later about this thing you call trust," Red Wing said, his voice showing emotion.

"Yes, Red Wing, go on inside and I shall keep watch," Paul said, inhaling a trembling breath. "But watch out as you enter. The horse belongs to Dave Patterson. Although he's constantly whining about being forced to be an outlaw because of his family's needs, he's mean to the core."

His knife drawn from its sheath at his side, Red Wing dismounted and ran to the cave entrance, then stealthily entered.

Paul's eyes narrowed as Red Wing stepped from his sight. Then he looked guardedly from side to side, looked toward the cave again, and wheeled his horse around and rode away. He was afraid that this might be his only opportunity to get away from Red Wing. And be damned with the promise. Nothing would bring Red Wing's trust back again.

Red Wing moved quietly through the darkness of the cave, a campfire ahead throwing its reflection on the walls.

Suddenly, a blow to his head made him cry out. He stumbled awkwardly, then fell unconscious to the cave floor.

Malvina cried out with despair when Dave dragged Red Wing farther into the cave and dropped him beside her. She struggled with the ropes at her wrists as she tried to loosen them.

But her attempts were in vain. The ropes were too snugly tied. She was helpless to help the man she loved, and it tore at her heart to see him lying there, unconscious.

"Red Wing, why did you have to wake up and find me gone?" she cried, staring at the trickle of blood flowing across his brow from his head wound.

"Shut up," Dave shouted as he tied Red Wing's hands behind him.

Malvina sobbed, then stiffened when Gerald came back inside the cave.

Gerald took a startled step backward when he spied Red Wing lying on the floor of the cave. "How'd he get here?" he then said as he eyed Dave warily.

"Hell if *I* know," Dave said, shrugging. "They say Injuns are skilled trackers. I guess he tracked you and the woman here."

"An Injun cain't track across water," Gerald

grumbled out. "He had to cross the river to get here, didn't he? The only way he could know about this cave is if someone led him here."

"You're right about that," Paul said, suddenly stepping into view behind Gerald, his pistol drawn. He stared down at Red Wing, wondering now how he could ever have gone against him. There was a true, honest friend—the only true, trusting man Paul had ever known.

He had only gotten a short distance away when his conscience forced him to turn around, to return to the cave.

But he had been too late. If he had kept guard as he had promised, Red Wing wouldn't have been rendered unconscious.

He glared over at Gerald. "You did this, didn't you?" he snarled, his eyes two points of fire. "I saw you riding toward the cave. You caught Red Wing off guard."

"I found him unconscious," Gerald said, inching back away from Paul. "Dave did it. Now put the damn gun down, Paul. You'll regret it if you don't."

"I'm filled with regrets all right," Paul said somberly. "But not over scum like you."

"Who's callin' who scum?" Gerald said, laughing sarcastically. "You're double-crossing sonofabitch scum."

When Red Wing moaned, Paul turned to look down at him.

Gerald and Dave took advantage of Paul's moment of carelessness. They bolted past him and got lost in the shadows of the cave as they ran toward the entrance.

The sound of scurrying feet caused Paul to look

up to find them gone. "Cowards!" he shouted after them. "You are both God-damn cowards!"

But more concerned over Red Wing's welfare than finding the two outlaws gone, Paul slipped his pistol into his holster and knelt beside Red Wing.

He checked Red Wing's wound, then glared at Malvina. "You've been a thorn in my side since I can remember," he grumbled.

He looked down at Red Wing again when he woke up, groaning.

"Red Wing, we've got to get out of here, and *fast*," Paul said, quickly untying Red Wing.

As Red Wing became more alert, he gasped when he looked over and found Malvina there, Paul now untying her.

Just then, following Gerald's orders to go back into the cabin to get Malvina before Red Wing awakened, and while he only had Paul to deal with, Dave rushed back inside the cave.

When he found Red Wing still conscious, he stopped. Just as he aimed his pistol at him, Red Wing rolled over and kicked him in his groin.

Yelping, Dave dropped his pistol. Losing his balance, he fell backward into the campfire. His clothes quickly caught fire and he ran frantically around the inside the cave, blazing, knocking the bottles of moonshine over. Everything became drenched with alcohol. It ignited.

Red Wing scurried to his feet. He grabbed Malvina into his arms and ran toward the mouth of the cave. Paul followed.

They reached the outside just in time. Everything inside the cave exploded, the impact knocking them all to the ground.

Half stunned, Malvina lay beside Red Wing.

He reached over and drew her closer. "You are all right?" he asked softly.

"*Now* I am, now that you are here," she said, suddenly breaking down into hard, body-racking sobs.

Paul rose shakily to his feet. His eyes wavered as he stared down at Malvina and Red Wing. Although he had done his part to save Red Wing, he did not believe anything could ever be the same between them.

Without stopping to explain why, he mounted his horse and rode away.

Red Wing sat up and drew Malvina onto his lap. He cradled her close. "You left the safety of my lodge tonight," he said thickly.

She clung to him. "I now know that I shall never rest until I find those who are responsible for my parents' deaths," she murmured between sobs. "Please understand that I have tried. Oh, how I have tried to forget. But I just can't."

"Why did you not confide in me?" he asked, stroking her back through her buckskin dress. "Had I known you were still torn inside by not knowing, I would have gone to the ends of the earth to make wrongs right for you."

"You have your own problems," Malvina said, gazing wide-eyed up at him. "You are in mourning for your own family loss. I felt that perhaps I could find the answers myself. I strongly suspect that the priest who came to your village might have something to do with all that is wrong in this area. I was going to his church to look around, to try and find answers."

"You were abducted before you were able to?"

"Yes—by that despicable, filthy man that sold me into that terrible life at the brothel. Gerald. He did this to me."

"Well, now you are safe, and because of Paul, we are still both alive," Red Wing said, suddenly realizing that Paul was no longer there.

He stiffened. Paul's flight meant only one thing—that he did not want to work anything out with Red Wing. He was accepting the fact that they were no longer friends.

"How did you find the cave?" Malvina asked, clinging as he rose to his feet and began carrying her toward his horse.

"Paul . . ." Red Wing began.

"Paul?" Malvina said, eyes wide.

Red Wing had no response.

"Then you know all about Paul, and that he is most definitely a part of the outlaw gang," Malvina said, settling down onto his saddle.

Still Red Wing did not answer her. His set jaw and clenched lips were enough answer for her.

He wheeled his horse around and headed back toward the river.

Daylight was just breaking on the horizon.

Chapter Thirty-Three

As the ferry came into view, Malvina saw Joe slumped strangely over the railing, one arm dangling down close to the water.

"Red Wing, something is wrong with Joe," she said, watching Joe's dangling arm waving slowly in the wind.

Red Wing squinted into the bright sprays of the morning sun, his jaw tightening when he also saw Joe's questionable appearance.

He rode onward and reined in close to the ferry. From this distance, Red Wing could tell that Joe was more than likely dead. Blood dripped in a steady stream from a head wound into the water.

Red Wing looked guardedly from side to side, then dismounted. "Malvina, you stay here while I look around," he said warily.

"He's dead, isn't he?" Malvina said, shivering at the thought. "Who could have done this? He was a gruff sort of man, but he never caused anyone any harm."

Red Wing nodded, then moved stealthily onto the pier. Before going on, he stopped and looked slowly around him again, hoping that he and Malvina had not stepped into some sort of trap.

When he concluded that they were safe, he hurried to Joe. Bending to one knee beside him, he checked for a pulsebeat at the side of the ferryman's neck.

Red Wing's eyes widened with surprise when he discovered that there was some life left in Joe. The pulse was faint, yet he *was* alive. He lifted Joe up from the railing and carried him to a long wide bench. As he laid him down, Joe groaned and reached a slow hand toward Red Wing.

Malvina slid from the saddle and ran onto the ferry and knelt down beside Red Wing.

"Joe," she said, watching his eyes slowly flutter open. "Joe, it's Malvina and Red Wing. Who did this to you?"

Joe gazed blankly from one to the other, whispered Malvina's uncle's name, then slowly closed his eyes again.

"My Uncle James did this?" Malvina cried, almost choking on the words.

"Red Wing, your village," Joe whispered, his voice scarcely audible. "James . . . and his . . . outlaw friends. They were there. I took them across on the ferry. They knew I knew what they were up to. They shot me to keep me silent."

Red Wing's heart lurched at what Joe said.

"Lord, take me home," Joe whispered. His body went into spasms, then lay quiet.

"He's now truly dead," Malvina said, closing Joe's eyes with her fingers.

Red Wing grabbed her hand, yanked her to her feet, and half dragged her to his horse. Her breath was almost knocked clean from her body when he grabbed her by her waist and placed her on his saddle.

"I must get to my people," Red Wing said, quickly mounting behind her. "The ferry is useless to us. We must go downriver and cross by way of Crow Wing Island."

Then he led his horse into a hard gallop alongside the river.

It seemed an eternity until they were finally on the other side of the Arkansas River. Although Red Wing's stallion was galloping as fast as it could, for Malvina and Red Wing it just wasn't fast enough. Both envisioned what might have happened at the Choctaw village.

Malvina was still numb to know that her uncle could be this devious.

But the more she recalled the few sermons that he had spoken, sermons spoken only to fool a godly brother, she could remember how he would often speak of hell and damnation. He had spoken of the devil as though it pleased him more to bring the devil's name into the sermons than God's.

She had not thought much about it at the time, thinking that he was just trying to find a way to individualize his way of preaching, differing from his brother's in every way imaginable. Now she realized that he meant to praise the devil, not preach against him. He had been obsessed by the devil.

Blinded by goodness, those who had listened to her uncle had not even realized that he was playing with their minds and lives in the worst way possible.

Smoke curling up through the treetops a short distance away made Malvina's thoughts leave her uncle. A chill of fear crept into her heart at the sight of the smoke. By the way Red Wing moaned, she knew that he had also seen the smoke and realized that it was more than likely coming from his village.

Malvina's hair fluttered wildly in the wind as Red Wing sent his horse into an even faster gallop, then wheeled his steed to a sudden halt when a small child stumbled out of the forest, his body and clothes blackened with smoke. And it was not just any child. It was Dreaming Shield!

Malvina slid from the saddle as Red Wing secured his reins. She gathered Dreaming Shield into her arms.

Sobbing, his fingers bit into the flesh of her neck as he desperately clung to her. "So many died," Dreaming Shield cried, looking past Malvina's shoulder as Red Wing bent to his haunches behind her so that he could look into Dreaming Shield's eyes. "Red Wing, outlaws came. They killed. They burned. They stole from our people!"

Red Wing hung his head. He tried not to picture in his mind's eye what he would find when he returned home. He wished he did not even have to go and see it. It would tear his heart out!

"Your grandfather's body was taken from the

scaffolding," Dreaming Shield said, shuddering. "Laughing, the evil men took him away. They dragged him behind a horse. They said they were going to throw him into the river." He swallowed hard. "They said no bone-pickers would get at your grandfather if he was in the river."

Malvina closed her eyes and bit her lower lip when Dreaming Shield spoke the name of the leader of the marauding outlaw gang.

"The man who shouted the orders was the same man who came to our village before and took Malvina away with him," Dreaming Shield cried. "It was your Uncle James, Malvina. He did this thing to our people."

Now coming out of his stunned state, and so enraged by it all that he felt he might split open with the hate that was pulsing through his veins, Red Wing jumped to his feet and screamed out a cry of remorse.

"*Aieee, aieee!*" he cried, lifting his eyes and reaching his hands toward the heavens.

Malvina moved clumsily to her feet. She covered her mouth with her hands as she sobbed out Red Wing's name. He gave her an icy stare and then mounted his horse in one leap and rode away.

"He holds me responsible," Malvina said, wiping tears from her eyes as she peered down at Dreaming Shield. "Do you, Dreaming Shield? Do you blame me for all that's happened?"

"Had you never come to our village, many Choctaw would have not died, that is true," Dreaming Shield said solemnly. "Your outlaw uncle never bothered our people until you became involved with our lives."

He reached a tiny, smoke-stained hand out and took one of hers. "But no, Malvina, I do not blame you for anything," he said softly. "You are a victim, as are my people. You are not to blame for having been born into the same family as the outlaw fiend. I shall always love you as though you were born Choctaw, not white."

Malvina fell to her knees and drew him into her arms. "Your words, your feelings toward me, touch my heart," she said, tears flooding her eyes again. "Thank you for caring so much, and for trusting me. I do love your people, Dreaming Shield. I would have never ever stayed one day with the Choctaw had I known my uncle could be this vindictive over my choices in life."

"I think Red Wing will soon need you," Dreaming Shield said, easing from her embrace. Like a gentleman and a boy who was much older than his true age, he again reached a hand out for her. "Come. Let us return to my village."

"Your parents, Dreaming Shield?" Malvina asked softly. "Are they all right?"

As though hearing the mention of his parents' name had catapulted him back into the realization of what he had lost, he became a boy of six again. He hung his head and broke into hard sobs, then flung himself into Malvina's arms again.

"They are dead!" he cried. "That is why I ran from the village. I fear returning. I do not think I can look upon their bodies again."

He left Malvina's comforting embrace. "But I know that I must," he said, wiping his eyes dry with the backs of his hands. He thrust out his chest. He squared his tiny shoulders. "My father taught me to be strong. For him, I must have courage."

The pit of Malvina's stomach seemed empty as she watched this child whose whole life had been torn apart by the acts of Malvina's very own kin. How could she ever make it up to Dreaming Shield?

"I don't think I can go with you," she said suddenly. "Your people will not want me among them. My uncle . . . he . . ."

Dreaming Shield suddenly hugged her legs. "Come with me," he choked out, a keen desperation in his voice. "I need you, Malvina. As you once needed me." He looked pleadingly up at her. "Please come with me. Help me?"

So moved by how much he truly cared for her, Malvina fought back the urge to cry again. She had to be strong, not only for this child, but also for herself. If the Choctaw people's love for her had turned to hate . . . if Red Wing no longer wanted her . . .

"Yes, I shall go with you," she said, fighting her tortured thoughts. "I'll do what I can to help you in your time of sorrow."

"Thank you," he said simply.

Holding his hand, Malvina walked with Dreaming Shield to the village.

Once she was there and saw the utter destruction and chaos, her knees weakened.

She had the strong urge to run in another direction. But Dreaming Shield's grip on her hand gave her the courage to stay.

She soon discovered that the two white children who had been under the protective wing of the Choctaw had been slain, as well as their adoptive parents.

Malvina looked slowly around at the smoldering remains of the cabins that had burned, then gasped and grew dizzy when she saw the destroyed scaffolding upon which Red Wing's grandfather's body had lain. What remained of the scaffolding lay along the ground, smoking. Bodies lay strewn everywhere.

Mourners wailed to the heavens.

Women whose husbands had died had cut their hair and scored their flesh with their knives and fingernails.

Finally Malvina found Red Wing among those who were trying to comfort others who had lost loved ones. He was with Stands Tall and Pretty Cloud, kneeling over a fallen warrior and his wife, both of whom had died clutching one another, their fingers intertwined.

His eyes dark with hate, Red Wing rose to his feet. He shouted out the names of those warriors who still lived. They came to him in a wide circle, their eyes intent on their leader.

"I know the outlaw's hideouts!" Red Wing shouted. "We shall go there now and avenge the deaths of those we love. We must not wait until after our mourning. Too many more innocent people would then be dead at the hands of this tyrant! We shall form a war party. Now! We will kill those who came and left death and destruction at our village!"

Malvina ran to Red Wing. She gazed up at him intensely. "I want to go with you," she said in a rush of words. "I have my own debt to pay!"

When he shifted his eyes downward and locked

them with hers, she felt as though someone had poured ice water through her veins. The way he looked at her! It was as though he hated her, as though he saw *her* equally guilty of this crime with her blood kin.

Eyes wide, her knees trembling, Malvina took a shaky step away from him.

"You *will* leave my village," Red Wing said flatly, his voice void of emotion. "But not at Red Wing's side." He lifted a shaky hand and pointed to the far edge of the village. "You will leave and never return."

"What . . . ?" Malvina gasped, hearing others gasp around her at his command.

Dreaming Shield rushed to Malvina's side and grabbed her hand. "Red Wing, why would you order her to leave?" he asked, his voice soft and fearful.

"Because of my selfish need to have this white woman as my wife, much death has been brought to our people," Red Wing said, his eyes still locked with Malvina's, his guilt eating away at his heart for having been so determined to have her, when all along he knew what her uncle was capable of.

"Leave, white woman," Red Wing said flatly. "Do not turn your eyes back in the direction of me or my people."

Stunned speechless by Red Wing's attitude toward her, Malvina stared up at him.

Then she was shaken out of her trance when he turned and walked away from her as though she no longer existed. She yanked her hand out of Dreaming Shield's grip and ran after Red Wing.

"You can't do this," she cried. "Red Wing, I

understand how you feel, but do not blame me for something I had no control over. Please do not push me from your life. Don't you see? That would only please my uncle. He would have finally succeeded at tearing us apart. Don't allow that. *Please* don't allow that!"

When he turned and stopped, the look he gave her sent Malvina into despair. She placed a hand to her mouth, stifling throaty sobs behind it.

Then she found some fight left in her that had not been swept away by all the terrible events that continued to plague her life. She straightened her back, lifted her chin, and wiped tears from her eyes.

"I will leave," she said, fighting back the urge to break down into tears again at the very thought of never seeing Red Wing again. "I will find my own answers. I still have Father Christopher to question. I will pull answers from him. I *will* prove my worth to you and your people. You *will* have me in your life again, Red Wing. You *must.*"

Her whole body trembling and feeling so empty that she might collapse, Malvina turned and ran from Red Wing. She went to the corral only to discover that her uncle's men had destroyed that too. She ran onward until she found a stray horse.

After mounting it, she took one last look at the village. Red Wing and his warriors were using the ashes of the destroyed lodges to paint their faces for war.

She turned her eyes away. Her heart seemed to be ripping into shreds as she sent the horse into a hard gallop toward the river. She tried to understand why he had cast her from his life.

She lifted her eyes to the heavens. "Please, God, show Red Wing a way to allow me into his heart again," she cried.

Chapter Thirty-Four

Knowing that the cave had been destroyed by fire, Red Wing thought that the outlaws would be forced to return to their other hideout—the cabin.

The cabin was in sight through a break in the trees. Red Wing slid from his saddle and yanked his rifle from the gunboot while his warriors also dismounted and grabbed their weapons.

Red Wing gave the silent command for his warriors to follow him. Stealthily, he moved through the cluster of trees, his eyes on the cabin. But his thoughts were tumbling around inside his head.

He had always aspired to be chief one day. But never had he thought that one of his first duties as the chief of his people would be to paint his face with black ash for warring.

He wished still to be a peaceful leader. He had never aspired to be a war chief who sent his warriors into battles where their lives could be snuffed out in an instant.

But never had he been faced with such a tyrant as James O'Neal before. Too many lives of his people had been lost because of him.

And *that* had been during Red Wing's time of peaceful leadership.

He pursed his lips tightly together as he thought of what this outlaw had done to his beloved grandfather's body! It had been callously thrown into the river! There was no way his body could be recovered. It had either been carried down to the bottom of the river by the heaviness of the robes in which he had been wrapped, or it had been washed downriver!

How could his grandfather's spirit ever rest now?

Red Wing only hoped that the spirits of the river would have mercy on the soul of his grandfather and help lift his spirit from the watery grave into the heavens, so that he could walk the road of the hereafter with those he loved who had passed to the other life before him.

And Malvina!

Because he had been to blame for bringing death and destruction to his people because he had loved a white woman, Red Wing's guilt had forced him to send her away!

Now that he had, he knew that he had done so in haste and regretted his decision.

She had not been at fault. She had not chosen who her uncle would be when she had been born into this world of tragedy and heartache.

Fate had given her a father whose brother was evil to the very core.

Once Red Wing put this tragedy behind him, and the true villain had paid for the crimes against his people, Red Wing would go after Malvina and bring her back into his life and lodge.

He would marry her.

And pity anyone who ever interfered in their lives again!

Now at the outer fringe of the trees nestled around James's cabin, Red Wing stopped and gazed intensely, then realized that there were no horses anywhere.

His gaze shifted upward. There was no smoke spiraling from the fireplace chimney!

He gazed at the door of the cabin. It was partially agape.

Everything was too quiet.

Stands Tall inched over beside Red Wing, his eyes also watching the cabin for any signs of movement. "They have not returned from their nightly raids yet?" he whispered. "When they do, we will be waiting for them. Before they have the chance to wash blood from their hands, we will kill them!"

"Something does not seem quite right here," Red Wing said. "Does it not appear to you that the cabin seems vacated? See the door? It is ajar."

"They left in haste to kill our people," Stands Tall grumbled out. "*That* is why the door is ajar."

"Let us go on to their lodge," Red Wing said. He turned to his warriors, who waited behind him for orders. "All but Stands Tall stay behind and keep watch for the outlaws' return."

Everyone nodded.

Red Wing and Stands Tall moved from the cover of the trees and ran hurriedly to the cabin.

Pausing to take a deep breath, Red Wing hugged the wall of the cabin with his back as Stands Tall stood beside him, his eyes watching all around him.

Red Wing gave Stands Tall a nod.

Together they rushed inside the cabin, stopping abruptly when they discovered that nothing was there.

No furniture.

Nothing that belonged to the outlaws was there.

"The cowards have fled into hiding," Red Wing hissed, kicking at a lone tin can that lay on the board flooring.

"Since they have chosen to flee and go further into hiding, we may never get the opportunity to avenge our dead!" Stands Tall grumbled.

Red Wing went to the door and peered outside into the brightness of the afternoon. "It seems that the outlaws' flight came at an inopportune time for the Choctaw," he said darkly.

He turned slow, burning eyes to Stands Tall as his friend stepped outside with him. "Does it seem that perhaps they may have been warned that we were coming to make them pay for what they did?"

"What are you saying, Red Wing?" Stands Tall asked, his voice drawn.

"Did not Malvina know our destination today, Stands Tall?" Red Wing said, not liking what he was concluding from finding the outlaws gone.

"Yes, and as I recall, she asked to travel with us to settle her own score with her uncle," Stands Tall said, almost warily.

"Yes, that is true. But think about it, Stands Tall," Red Wing said, almost as warily. "How it might have been instead."

"Red Wing, what are you saying?" Stands Tall said. "What are you suggesting?"

"Do not Choctaw blood kin look after one another? Especially if they know that certain death may come to them at the hands of their enemies?" Red Wing said solemnly, in his mind's eye seeing Malvina and her loyalty to her brother.

Why would it not be the same for her uncle if she truly thought he was going to die?

Although she had her own reasons for hating her Uncle James, perhaps after thinking it over she had decided that she did not actually want him to die?

"Yes, our blood kin always defend one another," Stands Tall said, nodding. "Always."

"I am thinking that perhaps Malvina may have warned her uncle that we were on our way here," Red Wing said, the very thought tearing away at his insides.

His heart ached to think that she might betray him in such a way.

Yet he could not shake the possibility from his mind!

"You do not truly believe she is capable of betraying you in such a way as that," Stands Tall said.

He eyed Red Wing speculatively, wondering if his friend could actually think this of the woman he had vowed to love. It had been obvious when Red Wing had ordered her away that he had done so only because of guilt!

Stands Tall knew that Red Wing was torn now by many emotions.

That had to be the cause of his doubts about Malvina.

"Maybe I never knew her at all," Red Wing said, looking heavy-eyed at Stands Tall. "Does a man ever truly know a woman? Especially one whose skin is white and whose blood kin is so evil?"

Stands Tall did not respond. He felt it best not to voice his opinion. This was something for Red Wing to work out inside his soul, for if Red Wing chose to believe the worst about Malvina, he was destroying a future he had so looked forward to.

And even though Red Wing had sent her away only a short while ago, Stands Tall had known even then that he would reconsider and go after her.

Now Stands Tall was not sure about anything. So much had gone wrong these past weeks. His heart was heavy with remorse.

"I do not believe that Malvina has ever been truthful with me," Red Wing said, his voice breaking. "When she spoke of not being involved with her uncle and his outlaw activities, she spoke a lie to me."

He took a step away from the cabin and gestured toward it. "Does this not prove it?" he shouted. "She knew this was our destination. She knew what we had planned for her uncle. She came ahead of us and warned him. That is why he and his gang members have fled. Because of *her* and her devotion to *him*. He is her father's brother!"

Stands Tall doubted that Malvina was guilty of such a crime as this, yet Red Wing was chief now, and out of respect for him, no one should openly doubt his decisions or reasoning.

Red Wing turned troubled eyes to Stands Tall. "She came here and warned her uncle, and then she went elsewhere. Do you recall her saying something about going to Father Christopher's church?"

"Yes, I recall her saying that she was going there to seek answers," Stands Tall said softly. "As we were placing war ash on our faces, she declared this to you and then left."

"Then that is where we shall look for her and demand answers about where her uncle has fled to," Red Wing said. His heart ached even to think that Malvina could be so sweet while in his arms, and so devious while away from him.

Red Wing ran back to his horse and mounted it. He waited for his men to mount their steeds, then gazed slowly from warrior to warrior.

"The cowards they are, the outlaws fled our wrath," he shouted, his eyes glittering. "But we shall find them. We shall not give up until they are all dead."

Not wanting to mention Malvina's name to his warriors and at the same time condemn her for the sort of person she had proved to be, Red Wing turned his eyes away from them for a moment and became lost in thought.

Inside his heart and in his mind's eye he was seeing Malvina reaching out for him. He could feel the warm, sweet press of her lips against his own. He could feel even now the softness of her flesh, his loins aching at the remembrance of how her breasts filled his hands.

He could not believe that was all lost to him

forever! Their feelings for one another had seemed so genuine, so special.

Never had he felt such savage pride as he had felt while sitting at her side during the festival times of his people!

Her eyes had shown her happiness. Her smile had reached inside his very soul and left an imprint there, as a leaf sometimes becomes fossilized and leaves its imprint in stone.

He knew he would have to be strong these next few days. He not only had his people's lives to put straight again, but he also had to forget that Malvina had ever existed.

Yet how could he? If she was truly guilty of betraying him and his people, she also had to pay, along with her outlaw uncle.

If he had to condemn her to death, she would always be there in his mind. He would never have a moment's peace.

Even if he allowed her to keep her freedom and her life, she would be on his mind. He would always wonder where she might be, or with whom. For she *would* seek the arms of another man. She had much to offer in ways of the heart. While they had made love, it had been her endearing, wondrous way of loving that had stolen his very soul.

Yes, even while hating and resenting her, he would always love her.

"Red Wing?" Stands Tall said, breaking through Red Wing's reverie.

Red Wing looked over at him, then realized that his warriors were staring at him.

He did not like feeling awkward in their presence.

He was a mighty Choctaw chief!

Yet at this moment, he felt less than noble.

Firming his chin, Red Wing gave the order that filled him with foreboding. "Ride with me to Father Christopher's mission!" he cried.

"Is that where we will find the outlaw renegades?" one of his warriors asked, his eyes filled with hunger for revenge.

Red Wing was silent for a moment. "We will not find them there, but it is my belief that we will find someone there who will know where their flight has taken them," he finally said.

Red Wing could not help but wonder if he was truly going to the church to find out where the outlaws had fled, or just to see Malvina again, hopefully to find a way to make things right with her.

He was so torn with all that had happened that he could not keep things straight in his mind as to how it should be, or how it might have been. He was unsure of his every word now, and of his every thought!

Never had he thought that his life would become this confused, or this filled with pain.

Again he could not help but cast some blame on Malvina!

Had she not come into his life none of this would have happened.

Yet knowing the devastation that the outlaws left along their trail, he had to believe they would have made it to the Choctaw side of the Arkansas eventually, without having any reason besides wanting to take and kill.

Yes, he had to believe that was how it would have been eventually, or he would go insane thinking it had all happened because of a woman he would love forever and ever.

He raised a fist in the air and whooped out the war cry.

Chapter Thirty-Five

After tossing her horse's reins around a hitching rail, Malvina stopped long enough to take a lingering look at the church. Tears sprang to her eyes when she thought of her father and how beautifully he had preached the word of God to those who hungered for it.

Even though he had not had the money to have a church that was as fancy as this one, with a beautiful steeple reaching into the heavens, the one that he had built with his own bare hands many miles from this church had been enough for those who loved to hear him preach.

Idolizing her father and his ability to reach into people's hearts, she had sat in the pews, proud to know that he was her father.

Overwhelmed with feelings that pained her, not having entered a church since the deaths of her parents, Malvina went to the door of the church and eased it slowly open.

Her knees shook as she stepped into the dark shadows; then her eyes were drawn to a narrow band of light that streamed through a stained-glass window. She followed the path of the light with her eyes and gasped when she saw a statue of Christ hanging from a cross above the pulpit.

Again she was catapulted back in time, to her father standing in the shadow of Jesus on the cross as he had spoken of love and forgiveness.

Forgiveness! she thought angrily to herself. She could never, ever, forgive her Uncle James. He was perhaps even worse than those outlaws who had slain her parents.

Swallowing hard, Malvina looked away from the pulpit, then moved slowly down the aisle where pews stretched out on either side of her. Everything was quiet and serene. Many candles burned beneath the statue of Christ, their flames wavering in the breeze of the opened door.

Then a scent came to Malvina that made her eyebrows fork. She stopped and gazed down at the cracks in the floor boards beneath her feet. She couldn't see between them, but that seemed to be where the strong, unpleasant stench was originating.

She sniffed again; then her eyes widened in recognition. "No," she whispered harshly to herself. "How can it be?"

Then she relaxed. What she had first thought was the smell of moonshine was surely not illegally brewed whiskey after all, but more than likely the church's store of wine that was used for communion on Sunday and Wednesday of each week. She had swallowed many a tiny glass of wine during her father's ministry.

The memories of her father rushing in on her, paining her, Malvina wanted to leave, yet she had to find the priest first.

"Oh, where *is* he?" she murmured to herself.

She saw a small room at the far back of the church, to the right of the pulpit.

"His office," she whispered to herself.

Her pulse racing, Malvina went to the door and slowly opened it. It led into a dank, dark room. She tiptoed into the room and felt around until she found a candle and match.

After the candle was lit and positioned safely in a holder, Malvina held it out before her and looked slowly around the windowless room.

A cluttered desk was the most prominent piece of furniture, with shelves of books on the wall behind it.

Malvina went to the desk and brushed papers around and studied them. She found nothing suspicious. They were notes used for preparations of sermons.

Then her eyes widened when she found traces of gunpowder loosely scattered across the top of the desk, beneath the papers.

Her gazed moved slowly to the side.

She held her candle out and gasped when she found a holster hanging heavy with two large pearl-handled pistols on a peg on the wall. They seemed out of place. Her father had never taken any of his firearms into his rectory. Although he had seen the need to teach his children the art of shooting for their protection, he had always said that firearms represented the worst in man.

Renewed thoughts of her father caused Malvina to feel alone, empty, and sad. She blew out the candle, set the candle holder on the desk, and fled from the church.

She slowly wandered around the church building, finding a strange solace in its shadow. For a moment she enjoyed the wildflowers that hugged the log walls of the church. From the forest came the call of the robins, the squawk of the blue jay.

When she reached the back of the church, she stopped and stared at the trap door that led down to the cellar.

Curious to see what might be stored in the cellar besides the wine that was used for communion, and having no one there to stop her, she opened the door and laid it aside on the ground.

Her moccasins making no sound, she walked softly down the rickety stairs.

When she reached the door that led inside the cellar, she hesitated for a moment. It did not seem right to trespass, yet she did not see how it could matter.

Scarcely breathing, Malvina opened the door and stepped into total darkness.

And what she thought she smelled while upstairs in the church now proved to be something even stronger. Now that she was close to it—for it was apparently all around her—she knew that it most definitely was not wine.

It was moonshine!

Her heart pounding, thinking that she might be close to uncovering something that had no association at all with the church, Malvina stumbled through the darkness in an attempt to find a lantern.

She breathed with relief when she found one, matches lying beside it. Her fingers trembled as she struck the match and placed it to the wick of the lantern. She watched the flames take hold, then lifted it and looked slowly around her.

She was struck numb by the number of jugs of moonshine that lined all four walls.

"Lord," she gasped, now knowing for certain that her suspicions of Father Christopher had been correct, that he was certainly not a man of God. Just like her uncle, Father Christopher had somehow gotten caught up in greed.

But in even a worse way. He allowed the moonshine on the premises of his church.

She gasped when she also found a huge store of weapons partially covered at the far back wall of the cellar.

"Well, I believe it's time for the truth to come out about *this* preacher," Malvina said, walking slowly around the room.

Then something caught her eye that almost made her drop the lantern from the shock. She reached for a shelf with which to support herself as her knees almost buckled from the sight of the small chest resting among the jugs of moonshine and stacked journals on a shelf.

"Our family heirlooms!" she whispered. "Oh, Lord, Father Christopher is mixed up in more than moonshining. He's an outlaw. He also kills. He also steals from the dead! He is part of the gang who killed my parents!"

She set the lantern down, then picked up the small chest. As she opened it and gazed down at the pieces of jewelry that she remembered so well from the times her mother had shown them to her, tears flooded her eyes.

"I can't believe I have found them," she whispered, reaching in to run her fingers over and through the various glittering jewels.

There were many necklaces, bracelets, and rings.

One broach, in particular, caught her eye. It had been her precious grandmother's.

She gazed at them all again. Everything was beautiful and breathtaking!

The creaking of the steps that led down to the cellar from the interior of the church made Malvina turn with a start. When a large shadow filled the door, she squinted to make out who it was.

She gasped and felt lightheaded when James stepped into full view.

"You just couldn't leave it alone, could you?" James said, his pistol leveled at Malvina. "You had to come snooping around, didn't you? Why couldn't you have been content to just stay with me and let me look after you? First you decide to stay with the Indian, and then you decide that isn't enough." He reached his free hand out for her. "Give them to me, Malvina. Give me the family jewels."

"James, if you are here, and you know about the jewels, then . . . that has to mean that you had a part in stealing them," Malvina gasped, paling at the thought of the true meaning of what she said. "That means that you had a part in killing your very own kin! James, how could you? You had a part in choosing the very moment your own brother would die. Did you set flame to our cabin after stealing the chest of jewels? Did you?"

"And so now you know the worst of my secrets," James said, smiling crookedly. "Didn't you know that I've always been the black sheep of our family?"

"Father didn't know," Malvina said, aghast at her discovery and sickened by it.

"No, he wouldn't have," James said. "He always wanted to think the best of everybody. But he made the worst in me come out when he began interfering too much in outlaw activities."

"It wasn't moonshiners at all who killed my parents?" Malvina asked, her voice almost failing her.

"I truly didn't want him to die," James said, his voice breaking. "It just happened. I only . . . wanted to frighten him that night. When he saw my face, I had to silence him."

"You're disgusting," Malvina gasped, shivering. "You are repulsive."

"Give me the jewels, Malvina," James said flatly, gesturing with his free hand toward her. "That's all I want from you now. Just the family heirlooms. They're my ticket out of the Arkansas Territory."

"Just like you killed your very own brother, you'll have to kill me to get them," Malvina said, hugging the chest to her. "And you will, won't you?"

"Don't tempt me," James said, placing his finger on the trigger of his pistol.

"How could you be so evil when your very own brother was so good?" Malvina cried.

"There is one more secret I guess I may as well share with you today, Malvina," James said, his voice void of feeling.

"I don't want to hear it," Malvina said, trembling inside.

"You're going to, anyhow," James said. "Malvina, your parents never told you that I was adopted. I am truly no relation to you at all. When I was two, my parents left me on your grandparents' doorstep. I was raised in the shadow of your father. I never felt as though I belonged. I began to resent everything and everyone. It is easy to hate, Malvina, when one discovers one's very own parents don't give a hoot."

"You are . . . adopted?" she gasped.

"So you see, Malvina?" James said. "I have bad blood running through my veins from some relative in my past I never even knew."

"How horrible," Malvina said, covering her mouth with a hand.

"Enough talk of such nonsense as this," James said darkly, then stiffened when he heard footsteps coming up behind him.

"It's only me and Father Christopher," Gerald said as he and the priest came down the steps and entered the room. They stood together at James's right side, their eyes locked on Malvina.

"I saw a horse outside when I arrived," James said. "I found Malvina down here snoopin'. Seems she's found our little treasure, gents."

"What treasure?" Gerald asked, forking an eyebrow. He leaned closer to Malvina. "What's in that thing? Looks like a jewelry chest of some sort."

"It *is* jewels," Malvina spat out. "It belonged to my parents." Her eyes narrowed as she stared at Gerald. "I had no idea you knew my uncle. Were you a part of the gang that killed my parents? Or are you involved in something that you had no idea was this vicious?"

Gerald paled and took a step away from James. "She's your niece?" he asked, his voice guarded. He knew that if this were true, and if James had ever had any true feelings for Malvina, he would not appreciate the fact that Gerald had sold her to the brothel owner as though she were worthless trash.

"And why does this come as a surprise to you?" James asked suspiciously. "Unless . . ."

Gerald now realized that James might be putting two and two together too quickly. He had no choice but to get out of there and disappear from these parts so that James, the heartless killer that he was, would not be able to kill *him*.

Gerald swung his pistol from his holster and quickly grabbed Malvina. He placed her in front of him to use as a shield while he fled.

Malvina screamed and dropped the chest to the floor. The lid popped open. Jewels of all sizes and shapes scattered everywhere, twinkling and sparkling in the lamplight.

"Drop your gun, James," Gerald said, trying not to let the sight of the jewels distract him.

When James didn't do as he asked, Gerald thrust the barrel of his pistol in Malvina's back. "I don't truly think you want her killed, do you, James?" he asked dryly. "Now do as I say or I'll kill her; then I can get a shot off at you way before you could at me."

"James, please?" Malvina pleaded. "For all that we were before, please don't let him shoot me. Remember in Ireland, when I was small and you sat me on your knee beside the hearth as Papa read to me and Daniel? You were more like a brother to us then. Let those times make you want me alive, James, not dead. For God's sake, please have some portion of goodness left inside your heart. Please?"

James lowered his pistol to his side and slowly stepped aside. "I'll get you for this, Gerald," he hissed. "You'd better have a place to hide, for I'll hunt you down until I find you. Then I'll kill you slowly, one bullet and body part at a time, so that you can know suffering before you die."

"I've already known my share of suffering," Gerald said. "I've hardly known nothing *but*. Life hasn't been sweet to me. Never will be. But that don't mean that I'm ready to die, neither."

Gerald backed up the stairs, clumsily half-dragging Malvina.

Malvina's heart pumped blood wildly through her veins as she watched James inching his way toward the stairs, watching, his eyes squinted up at her in the shadowed darkness of the staircase.

Finally she was out in the brightness of the day. She fell to the ground as Gerald gave her a shove.

By the time she was on her feet, Gerald was gone from her sight on his horse and Paul was suddenly there on his steed, gazing questioningly down at her.

"What's going on?" Paul asked, quickly dismounting.

"As if you don't know, you fiend," Malvina said, running her trembling fingers down the front of her buckskin dress, smoothing out wrinkles and brushing grass from it. "You're surely a part of this outlaw gang or why else would you be here? You are most certainly not the sort who frequents a church. Especially not for the right reasons."

Father Christopher quickly following behind him, James rushed from the steps and looked frantically around him. "Where'd the sonofabitch go?" he cried, his pistol raised to fire.

"If you are speaking of Gerald, he's smart enough to put many miles between the two of you," Malvina said, placing her hands on her hips as she glared up at Paul.

Approaching hoofbeats made Malvina turn with a start. Her eyes widened when she recognized Red Wing and Stands Tall riding on their steeds ahead of many Choctaw warriors toward the church, their rifles raised and ready for shooting.

James stared, wild-eyed, at the approaching horsemen. Knowing that he didn't have a chance in hell defending himself against so many Choctaw, he turned and began running.

Father Christopher ran beside him, the hem of his black robe slowing him down as it wrapped around his ankles.

Malvina paled when Red Wing wheeled his horse to a stop a few feet from her. Dazed by all that was happening, she watched, unable to move or to speak, when Red Wing raised his rifle and aimed at James.

"Stop or I will shoot!" Red Wing shouted at James.

When James stopped, turned on a heel, his pistol aimed at Red Wing, Red Wing immediately pulled the trigger.

James dropped his weapon, and his body lurched with the impact of the bullet in his chest.

Then he slumped over forward and fell on the ground in a pool of his blood, dead.

Father Christopher stopped and grabbed a pistol from inside his black robe. He raised to fire but was downed when Stands Tall shot him.

Everything was suddenly quiet.

The smoke from the guns scorched Malvina's nose.

Her eyes stung with tears as she stared down at James.

She wasn't crying because he was dead, but because he had turned into someone so horrible.

And yet she remembered he had protected her. He had not wanted her to die.

He could have ignored Gerald's warning.

He could have not cared if Gerald killed her.

In a sense, he had saved her life.

Paul looked desperately at the bodies, then turned wild eyes to Red Wing as Red Wing dismounted and came to stand next to him, his eyes filled with a dark hate.

"Red Wing, don't do anything hasty," he said, his voice anxious. "I—came to help Malvina. She's no outlaw. I swear she has nothing to do with the gang. When I discovered that she was here today, I came to help her get away from—from that uncle of hers."

"You're a liar," Malvina hissed. "You had no idea I was here. I had just gotten here. I only came to question Father Christopher about things I thought he might know."

She turned anxious eyes up at Red Wing. "And I was right," she cried. "Father Christopher was involved with my uncle in everything ugly. There's a huge store of moonshine in the cellar. And—and Red Wing, I found my family heirlooms in the cellar."

Her eyes lowered and she swallowed hard, *still* finding it hard to believe her uncle's association with those who had killed her parents.

Then she looked up at Red Wing again. "Darling, my uncle was the leader of the gang who killed my parents. He stole the family heirlooms."

She glared at Paul. "And *he* was in on it all, also," she said icily. "Or else why would he have been here today except to have a meeting with the others?"

"Red Wing, no. . . ." Paul said, edging slowly away from Red Wing. "She's wrong."

But knowing that he was caught, and knowing that he had no other choice, that he had lost everything, and that Red Wing would never believe he was turning over a new leaf, Paul had no choice but to try and escape his wrath.

He grabbed Malvina, and again she was used as a shield as he drew his pistol and aimed it at her back. "I'll shoot her, Red Wing, if you don't let us ride away," Paul said thickly.

"You kill her, and you will die many deaths before actually dying," Red Wing hissed, certain that he had been wrong again about the woman he loved.

She was everything good on this earth, not bad!

Paul inhaled a shaky breath. "I'll do what I must to survive," he said. "Shoot me to get to her, and by God, Red Wing, I'll manage to shoot her before I take my last breath."

Red Wing held his pistol to his side. His eyes met and held with Malvina's as she was forced on Paul's horse.

"Red Wing!" she cried as Paul rode away with her.

Chapter Thirty-Six

Malvina struggled to get free of Paul's grip, but his arm was like steel around her waist as he held her against him in the saddle. She yanked at his arm. She sank her fingernails into the flesh of his hand.

Yet he still would not flinch or budge.

As she turned and gazed into his eyes, she shivered at what she saw—a total emptiness, like a man who had lost everything.

And in a sense, he had.

Losing Red Wing's friendship would have to be the same as losing the world, for Red Wing was a genuinely kind, compassionate person whose friendship was all-encompassing.

When Red Wing befriended someone, it was with his whole heart and soul.

As it was also when he loved.

Tiring of trying to remove Paul's arm from

331

around her waist, Malvina sighed heavily and tried to relax until she found the opportunity to get away from this dreaded man.

Her thoughts returned to Red Wing. Had he truly heard and believed Paul when he told him that Malvina was innocent of the crimes of which he had accused her?

Had Red Wing seen her innocence in what she had said today? Even in her behavior?

Then her thoughts shifted to her Uncle James. It did not seem possible that she could be relieved that he was dead, when not long ago she had cherished him.

Yet she *was* glad. She knew that the world was a better place without him. She did not even want to think about how many families' lives he had destroyed—worst of all, her very own!

She hung her head when she thought of Daniel. She could hardly bear the thought of never seeing him again. Today had brought it all back, why he was no longer with her, and who was truly to blame. James was to blame for all the recent tragedies in her life.

Oh, but if only sweet Daniel's life could have been spared!

Paul led his horse onto a path that led into the forest, where trees stood like sentinels on each side. The coolness of the shade from the trees touched Malvina's face, somewhat invigorating her. The musty scent of the dried leaves that had fallen in the autumn months of last year was overwhelmed by the sweet fragrance of the wild roses that crept up the tree trunks in bright pinks and reds.

For now Malvina tried to concentrate on the

flowers, on the sweet side of life, to make her captivity more bearable. She *would* find a way to escape. There was no way that Paul could keep his eyes on her twenty-four hours of the day.

And she knew that Paul might not even get the chance to imprison her somewhere, or murder her. Red Wing was surely even now gaining on them from behind. There was no way Red Wing would allow Paul to get away with this. Red Wing now knew the absolute truth about Malvina.

Yet another thought stung her heart. He had cast her from his village not so much because he did not trust her, but because he blamed her presence there for the recent tragedies that had befallen his beloved Choctaw people.

She was not sure if he could ever accept her into his life again if he kept harboring the guilt that he felt over bringing her into his life and that of his people.

The sun flickered its brilliant rays through the treetops overhead. Robins warbled. Chipmunks scampered across the path of the horse.

Then something else stirred at the right side of the path. Malvina's eyes widened and she screamed when someone stumbled out in front of Paul's horse, then jumped away just in time before he was run over.

The suddenness of the appearance of the man frightened the horse. It whinnied, shook its head, then reared.

Malvina clung to the pommel of the saddle as Paul was thrown from the horse. Feeling herself slipping and ready to fall, she frantically reached for the horse's reins.

While she was trying to steady the horse, her

heart was pounding with wondrous delight, for she had recognized the man who had frightened the horse.

Daniel!

Her beloved brother Daniel!

He wasn't dead after all.

He had survived!

As the horse came to a nervous halt, snorting, Malvina gazed down at Daniel as he came and peered up at her.

"Malvina?" Daniel said, his voice weak. "Lord, Malvina, it *is* you."

Malvina slid quickly from the saddle and grabbed Daniel into her arms. "Daniel, my Daniel," she said, sobbing, clinging to him. "I thought I was never going to see you again."

Daniel held her tight. "I thought I would never see *you* again," he said thickly. "I looked often along the riverbank. I . . . couldn't . . . find you."

"I searched for *you*," Malvina said, easing from his arms.

With eager eyes she looked him up and down. To her relief, he seemed to be in good enough health, but he wore clothes that were black with smoke, ripped and torn.

"Where have you been, Daniel?" Malvina asked. "The clothes you are wearing are not yours. And how did they get torn? It also looks as though you have been involved in some sort of fire."

"A family took me in shortly after our tragedy in the river," Daniel explained. "For so long I fought for my life. When I was dragged from the river, I was half dead. I almost drowned. A kind family took me in. They gave me lodging, clothing, and food. When I was well enough, I looked for you, but I finally gave up when I couldn't find you."

"Did you ever happen upon Uncle James in your search?" Malvina asked softly. "Did you tell him about the tragedy?"

"You know how I feel about Uncle James," Daniel said. "He's not worth talking about."

They got no further with their conversation. Red Wing rode up and dismounted, Stands Tall with him.

Red Wing went to Malvina and drew her into his arms. "You are all right," he said, looking past her shoulder at Daniel.

Then his gaze shifted to Paul, who lay on the ground, blood curling from a head wound. A rock lay close by, blood covering it.

"Yes, I'm fine," Malvina said, then turned back to Daniel. She placed an arm around his waist. "Red Wing, this is my brother, Daniel. He's alive, Red Wing. Can you believe it? He's truly alive!"

"And so you are Daniel?" Red Wing said, looking Daniel up and down. He reached a hand of friendship out toward him. "It is good that you are alive. Your sister has looked for you often. She is only half a woman without you."

Stands Tall knelt down over Paul. He checked for a pulsebeat at the base of his throat.

Finding none, he gazed up at Red Wing. "He is dead," he said, his eyes locked with Red Wing's, glad to see that he had no remorse for the man who had betrayed him.

"Daniel stepped out in the path of Paul's horse," Malvina said, turning to stare down at Paul. "The horse threw Paul. I guess he hit his head on a rock when he fell."

335

"Dying in such a way is too merciful, too quick, for a man whose heart was black," Red Wing said, not allowing melancholy to seep into his consciousness over his prior camaraderie with Paul. He now knew that it was all falsely done on Paul's part. It was better that he was dead in this way, than to die at the hand of Red Wing!

"I recognize the man," Daniel said, frowning down at Paul. "He . . . he was with those who came and killed the people who took me in. He set fire to their cabin and their barn. I was gone to look for you one last time. When I returned, I saw it all. I could not stop the outlaws. There were too many. I hid until they rode off. Then I ran into the burning cabin and dragged the bodies free. That is how it looks as though I have been a part of the fire myself."

"Paul did that?" Malvina said. She felt ill at her stomach when she turned and stared at Paul. She knew now that she was lucky to be alive.

"James was also one of the outlaws I saw riding away from the massacre," Daniel said solemnly. He hung his head. "I've been wandering since. I guess I was in a state of shock until now, until I saw *you*, Malvina."

Malvina drew him into her arms and held him tightly. "Daniel, it's all over now," she murmured.

Then, with brightened eyes, she shoved him gently away from her. "Daniel, I found the chest of jewels!" she said, her voice brimming with a sudden excitement. "You can enter the seminary for theological training after all!"

Then she whitened and wheeled around to gaze up at Red Wing. "Red Wing, the jewels!" she cried. "They are in the church cellar! What if someone discovers them and takes them?"

She ran for Paul's horse. "Come on, Daniel," she said determinedly. "Get on the horse with me. Let's go and make sure no one else steals our jewels! They are your future."

Before she swung herself into the saddle, she turned back to Daniel. "I can't believe you are actually here and that you are going to be able to have your dream after all," she cried, giving him one last squeeze of a hug.

She quickly mounted. Daniel mounted behind her and took control of the horse's reins.

Before they rode off, Malvina gazed down at Red Wing. "Please come with us," she murmured. "I've so much I want to say to you."

Red Wing became choked up with emotion. He nodded. "I shall follow," he said, then reached a hand to her cheek. "My woman, I want you to return to my village with me. I want you to be my wife."

Melting inside when she realized that Red Wing no longer held her responsible for the sins of others, Malvina bent low and kissed him. "Thank you," she whispered against his lips.

Daniel watched, stunned speechless; then Malvina turned to him.

"I shall explain everything to you soon," she said softly. "First we must see that the jewels are finally ours to keep. They should have never been anywhere but with us. James took them from us, Daniel. Our own Uncle James."

Daniel paled.

"Yes, Daniel, Uncle James," Malvina said when she saw his reaction.

Then another thought came to her. "And Daniel, we have worried so much about James being our blood kin, and wondering how he could be so different from the rest of our family," she blurted out. "Daniel, he was adopted. He was truly no blood kin of ours whatsoever."

Daniel stared at her for a moment as the reality sank in; then he laughed.

"Let's go, Daniel," Malvina said. "It's time we set our sights again on our future, a future without the likes of James to darken it for us."

Daniel slipped a protective arm around Malvina's waist. He snapped the reins, sank his heels into the flanks of the horse, and turned it back in the direction of the church.

Red Wing watched Malvina and Daniel until they became lost to sight.

Then he went solemnly to Paul and stood over him. "I never thought I would see the day I would part willingly with you in this way," he said, his voice drawn.

He looked over at Stands Tall as he came to stand at his right side. "Did you ever suspect that he was anything but a good man, a friend?" he asked, his voice breaking.

"I did not spend as much time with this man as you, so I did not have much cause to wonder about him one way or the other," Stands Tall said, staring down at Paul. "I had hoped for more for him, for it is good to have an alliance from time to time with some white men. White people outnumber the Choctaw two to one in the Arkansas Territory. Soon that number will more than double. Settlers come every day. Not even the presence of outlaws will stop the white people

338

who are determined to live on land that once was solely the Indians'."

Red Wing bent to one knee beside Paul. He reached inside one of his front breeches pockets and withdrew a small buckskin bag.

He laid the tiny bag in the palm of an outstretched hand and gazed at it. "Many moons ago I gave this to Paul in friendship," he said thickly. "In this medicine bundle made by my own hands are small tokens of the Choctaws' way of life. As though he were our brother, I gave him the medicine of our people."

Angrily he threw it to the ground and stood up and crushed it beneath one of his heels.

He ground it into the dirt until it was unrecognizable.

"It is nothing more now than dust of the earth."

Not looking again at Paul, Red Wing rose to his full height and walked somberly toward his horse.

Knowing not to ask Red Wing if he was going to see to this man's burial, knowing what the answer would be and glad of it, Stands Tall went to his horse and swung himself into his saddle.

Filled with savage pride, and sitting square-shouldered on his white steed, Red Wing rode off toward the mission.

"You are no longer angry with Malvina?" Stands Tall asked, giving Red Wing a questioning stare as they rode out into a sun-drenched open meadow, the Choctaw warriors behind them.

"I was never so much angry with her as I was with myself," Red Wing said back to him. "That is, after I knew she was innocent and deserved more from me than I was giving her after ordering her from our village."

"You will marry her?" Stands Tall persisted.

"Will you marry Pretty Cloud?" Red Wing asked, his eyes smiling into his friend's.

Stands Tall frowned as he turned his gaze from Red Wing's. "I do not believe so," he said throatily. "Her feelings for me do not seem as genuinely sincere as I would wish from a woman whom I wish to marry."

"When did the special feelings change between you?" Red Wing asked, surprised at Stands Tall's answer.

"It was not so much mine that changed, but hers," Stands Tall said. "She is a fickle tease. First she wishes my attention, then she shuns me."

"Then she does not deserve such a man as you," Red Wing said. "There are many others even more beautiful and mature who have openly shown they wish to share your blankets."

Although Red Wing felt sad over Stands Tall's lost love, he was glad to have something besides the recent tragedies to linger over in conversation. Whenever he thought about his grandfather in a watery grave, he grew ill inside.

Whenever he thought about all the useless deaths that awaited mourning at his village, he felt a wave of uselessness flow through his veins.

But now that those responsible for his people's recent tragedies were dead, they could begin life anew, as they had been forced to many times in the past.

Again the Choctaw would prove they were invincible, that there would always be Choctaw people as long as the earth itself survived wars and useless killings.

Chapter Thirty-Seven

Malvina's heart pounded fiercely as she watched Daniel flip the horse's reins around a hitching rail in the front of the church.

Together they ran around to the back, then stopped and stared down at their uncle's body and Father Christopher's.

"Daniel, someone dragged them here, away from where they both died," Malvina noticed.

Daniel didn't respond. He was staring down at James.

"Daniel, Uncle James *had* to die," Malvina said, grabbing one of Daniel's hands. "He was a terrible man who did not think twice before killing men, women, and children. Even those whom he was raised with as family. His mind was twisted. He is better off now, Daniel. So is the world."

"I know, Malvina," Daniel said sadly. "But it's so hard to believe that he could be so wicked."

"He was the worst kind of outlaw, Daniel," Malvina said softly. "The very worst."

Her heart skipped a beat when she saw a horse grazing not far from the church, its reins secured beneath a heavy rock.

Then she eyed the closed door that led down to the cellar. Whoever had arrived before her and Daniel was down in the cellar—with the jewels!

No one could miss seeing them. They had spilled all over the floor when she had dropped the chest!

Hope sprang forth when she thought that it might be only a parishioner, someone who had come to call on Father Christopher and had found him dead.

If it was, they could have gone to the cellar to investigate how this could have happened, or to see if those who had perpetrated the crime were still there.

Yet again, another horrible, mind-grabbing thought came to her.

Gerald Smythe had managed to escape. He was still a threat.

Her eyes glittered mutinously at the thought of coming face-to-face with that evil, vicious man again.

She turned her gaze back to her uncle and rested it on his holster. One pistol was gone. The other was still there.

She shivered at the thought of how many times it had been used against innocent people.

Swallowing hard, her gaze locked on James's face. She couldn't help but feel some remorse over his death, especially knowing what had driven him to madness. He had never been able to live with the feeling of rejection as a child. It had turned him into a tormented man.

But any feeling for James was a wasted emotion. The man had led a wasted life.

Malvina bent to one knee and inched her hand toward his pistol. It was as though she expected him to awaken at any moment and reach up to grab her wrist. Somehow it seemed to her that anyone as evil as he could never truly die! He might have nine lives, like a cat!

But knowing that she was foolish to be afraid, and to think such things that only children thought up at the midnight hour when they could not go to sleep in the darkness of their bedroom, Malvina yanked the pistol from James's holster.

"What are you going to do with that?" Daniel asked, looking quickly over at her.

"Someone is in the church cellar," she said, nodding towards the stranger's grazing horse. "I'm going to go and see who it is. Hopefully, it is someone other than Gerald Smythe."

"Who is Gerald Smythe?" Daniel whispered back.

"It's a long story," Malvina said, sighing. "And because you don't know the man, I must be the one to go into the cellar to see who is there. You wouldn't know if the person there were friend or foe. I will never forget the sickening face of Gerald Smythe."

"You can't go down there alone," Daniel whispered harshly, eyeing the door.

"We can't go together," Malvina said softly. "It would create too much commotion and confusion."

"Malvina, I insist—" Daniel reached for the pistol.

"Daniel, you are a peace-loving man who one day will be in charge of your very own church, or possibly a mission," Malvina explained. "You would not want anyone ever pointing an accusing finger your way, saying that here is a preacher who once shot a man, now would you?"

Daniel dropped his hand to his side. "No, I would rather not have that on my conscience," he admitted. "Yet sometimes circumstances enter into one's life over which one has no control."

"Daniel, I have learned these past weeks to take care of myself despite the worst odds," Malvina said, sighing with frustration. "Now I won't argue with you another minute. I am going to the cellar. You stand guard until Red Wing arrives."

Daniel knew not to argue with Malvina when her mind was made up. He nodded. "Be careful, Sis," he said, grabbing her suddenly into his arms. "Be careful."

Malvina gave Daniel one last hug, then walked away from him.

Sighing with relief that she had convinced Daniel that she must do this, and glad to have the gun for protection—especially against Gerald Smythe should he be in the cellar—Malvina moved stealthily to the door that led to the cellar.

She gave Daniel a nervous smile over her shoulder, then lifted the door and laid it aside. Holding the pistol stiffly at her side, she crept down the steps, wincing when one of the weakened and rotted boards creaked.

Stopping, she inhaled a nervous breath, then

345

took another step downward. She stopped when a thought came to her that put fear into her heart. Surely whoever was in the cellar had heard her and Daniel arrive on her horse. Surely he had even heard her and Daniel talking before they realized that someone else was there!

Yet perhaps not, she argued to herself. The door was shut to the cellar. The cellar was dug deeply into the ground. Surely all outside sounds were muffled by the packed earth that hugged its sides.

Sighing again, hoping that she was right to think that just perhaps they hadn't been heard after all, Malvina crept down the steps.

When she reached the foot of the staircase, candlelight emanating from the cellar gave her enough light to step into the small cubicle of the room.

"Stop right there," Gerald ordered from the shadows to her right.

Malvina was startled by the suddenness of Gerald's voice, yet not so much that she dropped the pistol. Hoping that he hadn't seen the firearm, she inched it behind her back.

"I've been waiting for you," Gerald said, as he came into view. He held a small revolver in his right hand; the small chest of jewels was tucked in the crook of his left arm. "Now I don't have only the jewels, I have *you*." He snickered smugly. "I'm one mighty rich man, don't you think?"

"I wouldn't be too sure of myself if I were you," Malvina said. "You stupid man. Don't you know that you can't leave this place without being shot? Red Wing and his warriors are outside. They have the place surrounded."

Gerald made the mistake of believing her.

He took his eyes off her for the moment it took him to look frantically up the stairs.

Malvina pulled her uncle's pistol out from behind her, took quick aim, and shot at Gerald.

She watched, wide-eyed, as he winced with pain as the bullet entered his right arm just below his elbow, causing him to drop his pistol.

"Now who's got *who?*" Malvina said, laughing softly. "Leave the chest of jewels on the shelf behind you, Gerald; then get out of here. You're the least of my concerns at this moment."

Perspiration poured from Gerald's brow as he was forced to bear not only the humiliation of being taken advantage of by a mere female, but also the pain that the bullet was causing in his arm.

"You're one spitfire of a woman," Gerald wheezed out between his pain. "You're a damn wildcat."

"I'm what I've been forced to become because of men like you and my uncle," Malvina said. "Now do as I say or the next bullet will find your heart."

Gerald's eyes wavered from Malvina to the stairs that led to the outside. "But if I leave, I'll be shot the minute Red Wing sees me," he said, beginning to panic.

"You fool," Malvina said, laughing. "As far as I know, Red Wing hasn't arrived yet. You only have my brother Daniel to cope with, and I shall warn him that a coward is coming outside."

She smiled wickedly at him. "But I'd run like hell past him if I were you," she said, laughing softly. "He's got some of our uncle in him."

Malvina leaned closer to Gerald, enjoying telling a lie that put the fear of God into his eyes and heart. "Why, my brother Daniel is the worst of outlaws," she said, her eyes dancing. "He's killed so many men and scalped so many Indians it'd make your eyes bug out to know the true number."

Gerald paled. He glanced up the stairs, then quickly placed the chest of jewels on the shelf to his left.

Holding his bleeding arm, he crept slowly past Malvina as she made room for him.

"Remember, Gerald," she taunted. "My brother Daniel would as soon eat you as look at you."

"Good Lord," Gerald said, visibly shuddering. "I've never seen such a crazy family as yours. I'm outta here."

He took off up the stairs in a mad dash. Malvina shouted up the stairs at Daniel. "Have mercy on the man, Daniel," she said. "Don't eat both of his legs. He needs one for running away, the coward he is."

Hearing Gerald whooping and hollering with fright as he reached the top step, Malvina could just envision how he eyed Daniel—sweet, gentle, loving Daniel—with wild, frightened eyes as he stepped outside.

Daniel came down the steps, an eyebrow arched. "Who was that?" he asked, brushing his hair back from his eyes again. "What'd you say to him to make him run past me like I was the devil?"

"That was Gerald Smythe," Malvina said, smiling mischievously at her brother. "I told him that you were an outlaw, even worse than our uncle." She laughed. "I told him that you would as soon eat people as look at them."

"What?" Daniel said, his eyes widening. Then he laughed with her.

"I let him go," Malvina said, now sober with thought. "But only because I am tired of seeing people die today, Daniel. You see, sweet brother, I know that his time will soon come. Men like him, who live viciously, eventually die a violent death. I just did not want to be the one who would always have to remember having done it. I'm tired of all of this wickedness, Daniel. I'm ready for good, clean living again, like we knew when we were children."

"It may never be as we both remember," Daniel said, swinging an arm around her shoulder. "Sis, things change. As we grow older, we discover that the memories we thought were so sweet were also flawed in some way."

"Let's no longer dwell on the past," Malvina said, easing from his arms. "Let's concentrate on the future. It is bright again for us both, Daniel."

She went to the shelf where Gerald had left the chest of jewels. She laid the pistol aside, then smiled at Daniel as she lifted the chest in both hands.

"This is a guarantee of *your* future, Daniel," she said, holding the chest out toward him. "Red Wing is mine."

Daniel stared down at the chest. He had never thought that he would see it again. He choked back the urge to cry as he took it and slowly opened it.

The assortment of jewels picked up the light of the candle and glistened up at him. "They are ours again," he said thickly.

He looked slowly up at Malvina. "I remember the first time Mother showed these to us," he said, his voice filled with emotion. "I had never seen anything so beautiful."

He frowned. "The jewels have been in our family for generations," he recalled. "Is it fair of us to use them for my education? Shouldn't we keep them in the family as they have been for so long?"

"Daniel, people like you, who are gentle and loving, are rare," Malvina said, reaching a hand to his cheek. "You must spread your love around to those who are hungry for it. That is more important than family heirlooms. You are the hope of many people's futures. Take the jewels. Do not hesitate to trade them for the money it will take for you to study for the ministry."

Malvina paused, then added, "Don't blink an eye, Daniel, when you exchange these for money that will shape not only your future, but all those people who will depend on you to teach their children not to grow up to be like James, Paul Brady, and Gerald Smythe."

She swallowed hard. "Especially not like the corrupt Father Christopher," she murmured.

"Especially not him," Daniel said, nodding.

"Daniel," Malvina said, as she looked slowly around her at the store of moonshine. "This mission has been used for all the wrong reasons for far too long." She circled her fingers around the candle holder and lifted the candle from the shelf. "Go on outside, Daniel. I have something to do here."

"So you see this as no better than the last still we destroyed?" Daniel said, smiling mischievously at her.

"Exactly," Malvina said, her chin proudly lifted.

"Go to it, Sis," Daniel said, firmly gripping the chest as he ran up the stairs.

Malvina set the lantern down long enough to tear many pages from the journals that were stacked on a shelf. After wadding several together, she took them and the candle up the stairs.

Standing on the top rung, she began lighting each of the wads of paper and tossing them down into the cellar.

When enough smoke was wafting up the stairs, and she began to hear the crackling and popping of jugs breaking, she broke into a mad run and went to stand with Daniel.

Malvina's eyes wavered as she gazed down at James. Should she give him a Christian burial?

She quickly decided that, no, let his and Father Christopher's bodies be erased from the face of the earth as the church went up in smoke.

When the fire did not spread quickly enough to the upstairs part of the church, frustrated, Malvina broke into a run.

Unsure of what Malvina had in mind, Daniel quickly followed her. "Where are you going?" he cried. "What are you going to do?"

"I must make sure this damnable place burns!" Malvina cried as she headed for the front door.

Daniel continued running after her. "No, Malvina!" he cried. "Stop. Don't take the risk. It's not worth it!"

Malvina gave him a frustrated look over her shoulder, then ran on inside.

Daniel laid the chest of jewels on the ground, then ran inside the church. He stopped and stared when Malvina took the many lighted candles from the altar and began throwing them on the pews. The wood was so old and rotted that the fire spread quickly in flickering orange waves along the pews.

"Malvina, come on!" Daniel shouted, feeling the heat on his face as the fire rapidly spread to the walls.

He started to go after Malvina, but the heat was too intense.

"Malvina!" he screamed when he saw a beam fall from overhead, blocking Malvina's way.

Red Wing rode up to the church. His heart leapt when he heard Daniel inside the burning inferno, calling Malvina's name.

Stands Tall rode up beside Red Wing just as Red Wing dismounted and started running toward the mission.

"Red Wing, no!" Stands Tall shouted. "Do not go in there!"

Red Wing ignored Stands Tall. All he could think about was Malvina. She was his life! His very reason for taking each and every breath!

Entering the smoke-filled, fiery church, Red Wing shielded his eyes with the back of a hand. He found Daniel groping through the smoke, his eyes wild.

"Leave!" he shouted at Daniel. "Save yourself. I will save Malvina!"

Choking and coughing, Daniel stumbled past Red Wing. He collapsed when he reached the fresh air.

Stands Tall lifted him into his arms and carried him a safe distance from the burning mission. Stands Tall then ran into the mission, but was soon overwhelmed by the heat and the smoke.

He felt his way through the haze. "Red Wing!" he cried. "Where are you?"

Red Wing moved onward, then tripped over something and fell to the floor, half dazed. When he looked down and saw Malvina lying there, her eyes closed, he found the strength to rise again from the floor.

He swept her into his arms and made his way back toward the door.

Stands Tall was there. He took Red Wing by the arm and led him outside to safety.

Red Wing coughed and sputtered as he carried Malvina away from the danger and heat of the building. He half collapsed beneath a tree with her, where Daniel sat, heaving, his eyes blood-shot.

"My sister?" Daniel said, crawling over to Malvina.

Tears of gratitude flooded his eyes when she awakened and reached out for him, and then Red Wing.

Malvina felt a fierce burning in her lungs. When she tried to speak, her words came out in painful, raspy whispers.

Yet she smiled victoriously when she looked at the church. It was totally engulfed in flames.

"No one will use it wrongly again," she said, then gazed at Red Wing. Tears streamed from her eyes. "Thank you, darling, for coming for me. I'm not quite ready to die just yet. I've a baby to think about."

Red Wing's eyes widened.

Daniel gasped.

"A baby?" Red Wing said, gathering her into his arms.

"Yes, I am almost certain I am with child," she murmured, getting more comfortable on his lap. "And I am so very, very happy about it."

Daniel sat quietly beside her. He did not voice his opinion of a sister who was with child before vows had been spoken. He thought of all of the circumstances that surrounded her pregnancy. Life had been anything but normal for her.

Perhaps a child now was even a blessing, he concluded to himself. Children to him meant purity, hope for the future!

Malvina smiled softly at Daniel when she saw acceptance of the fact that she was with child in his eyes. Perhaps he even saw it as she did, that through the dark days of their sadness had come some sunshine!

"Let us go now to our home," Red Wing said, gently helping Malvina to her feet. "I have much to do in my village to make things right for my people."

Malvina's eyes wavered. "Are you certain that I will be welcomed back among your people?" she said, her voice breaking. "Will my brother? I would like for him to stay with me until he is stronger and can make the long journey to Saint Louis."

"As long as I, my people's chief, have breath in my lungs, you are both welcome in my village," Red Wing said sincerely.

Malvina flung herself into his arms.

Red Wing reveled in her closeness. Too many times he had almost lost her!

Chapter Thirty-Eight

Malvina rode on Gerald's horse. Daniel rode at her right side, Red Wing at her left. Stands Tall rode behind them with the other warriors, who had emerged together from the forest.

Remembering that Joe had been murdered and that the ferry was no longer being offered at this time, they rode past it. When they came to the shallower part of the river that reached out to Crow Wing Island, Red Wing rode his stallion into the water first and went to the island. He then turned to watch and make sure that Malvina crossed safely.

While waiting for her and the others, something out the corner of his eye caught his attention.

He turned his head and gasped when he saw what was tangled in the weeds, broken tree limbs, and other assorted debris at the bank of the island.

"Grandfather!" Red Wing cried, slipping quickly out of his saddle. He ran to the riverbank and waded into the water, his fingers trembling when he tore through the tangled debris to get to the body of his grandfather, the wrappings that had been around him gone. The old man's face was bloated from being in the water for so long, and his clothes clung loosely to his frail, stiff body.

Malvina led her horse onto the island, then, along with Stands Tall, ran over to Red Wing. "Lord," she gasped, paling as Red Wing lifted his grandfather's body from the water.

"My grandfather no longer rests in a watery grave," Red Wing said, carrying Bold Wolf to the sandy bank of the island. "He will soon be back where he belongs. Go ahead to our village, Stands Tall. See that a scaffolding is built for my grandfather."

Stands Tall nodded and motioned for the other warriors to follow him. They rode off into the water and were soon on the other side.

Malvina watched them ride away, then turned to Red Wing, who had already secured his grandfather's body to the back of his stallion.

Daniel edged closer to Malvina. "Tell me what happened that Red Wing's grandfather was in the water?" he whispered.

Malvina proceeded to tell him everything.

"It is a miracle that Red Wing found his grandfather's body," Malvina said at the end of her explanation. Her heart went out to Red Wing as he tied the rope that secured his grandfather to his horse one last time.

"The Lord works in many ways," Daniel said

in a shallow whisper to Malvina.

"Sometimes it seems there is no God at all," Malvina said, her voice trailing off.

"Never doubt that He is always there," Daniel said, taking Malvina by the hand and leading her toward her horse. "Sometimes He tests us far beyond what we think is bearable. But in the end, for those whose beliefs are strong, things are righted."

Red Wing came to Malvina and helped her onto her horse. "My woman, soon our lives will turn around again so that each day when you awaken you will smile," he said. "Time passes quickly. Time *heals*."

She leaned down and brushed a kiss across his brow. "Just as long as I am with you, that is all that matters," she murmured, then watched him walk, tall and dignified, toward his horse.

He swung himself into his saddle, his grandfather tied across the back of his horse behind him.

They were soon back on dry land again and rode quietly until they reached the village.

Malvina was amazed to see that Stands Tall had worked quickly to get the scaffolding built again for Chief Bold Wolf. She was amazed to see that some of the cabins that had burned had already been dismantled and discarded, and new ones were already being built to replace them.

Although filled with mourning, with many burials to see to now that their chief had returned, the Choctaw had learned long ago to look forward. They had been taught that each breath taken was to be looked upon as a new beginning.

Sorely tired, the fatigue of all of the turmoil she had experienced coming down hard on her like a dead weight pressing against her skull, Malvina dismounted.

Daniel came to her, and she leaned against him as he led her through the destruction.

"I am so very tired," she murmured, pointing out Red Wing's cabin to Daniel. It was one of the few that had been spared destruction.

She looked over her shoulder as Red Wing laid his grandfather on the ground beneath the scaffolding. She knew that he would wrap his grandfather as he had been, before placing him on his resting place again.

She could not wait until he was finished.

She felt that she could scarcely take another step.

"Malvina, are you certain that you wish to stay with the Choctaw?" Daniel asked worriedly, then glanced down at her abdomen, realizing the foolishness of the question. Malvina was committed to Red Wing in more than one respect. They had a bond now, a responsibility.

Malvina was about to answer him when she realized that he was looking at where her child lay in its protective cocoon.

She blushed, yet held her chin high. She was fiercely proud to be carrying Red Wing's child! And she would never feel guilty for having conceived before she was married to Red Wing. Who on earth could cast blame in light of the obstacles that had come in the way of a normal life for them? Had none of these events happened, she would already be the wife of this caring, wonderful chief.

No. Never would she be ashamed of this love child. Never!

Dreaming Shield ran up to Malvina and grabbed her hand. "I am so glad that you are home again," he said, smiling up at her. "You have come for me, have you not, Malvina, since I am now orphaned? You and Red Wing will take me into your lodge as though I am yours?"

The eagerness, the savage pride with which Dreaming Shield asked this of her made Malvina stop and move to her knees before him.

Framing his face between her hands, she softly kissed his brow.

She then gazed at him, tears filling her eyes. "Yes, you can live with us," she said, her voice breaking. "I do not even have to ask Red Wing if he agrees with me. I know his answer as I know my own. In his heart he carries much love for you. You will be a brother to our children. They will look up to you as I have always looked up to my brother, though he is one year younger than I."

Daniel came and also knelt beside Dreaming Shield. "Malvina, who is this young man?" he asked, stroking his fingers through Dreaming Shield's thick black hair.

Malvina proceeded to tell Daniel of her and Dreaming Shield's experiences, and about his parents having been killed in the recent massacre.

After hearing it all, Daniel drew Dreaming Shield into his arms. "You can call me Uncle Daniel, if you wish," he said softly. "I am Malvina's brother."

Dreaming Shield clung to him. "I have no other uncles, so, yes, I am glad to take you into my heart as an uncle," he said, then drew away when Pretty Cloud came and stood over them.

Cassie Edwards

Pretty Cloud gazed down at Daniel, her eyes wide.

Daniel moved slowly to his feet, his gaze taking in Pretty Cloud's loveliness, his heart pounding.

Malvina saw the instant attraction. She was not all that happy about it. They were the right age to be interested in each other. Pretty Cloud was one year younger than Daniel, and so sweet, she would make a perfect wife for a minister.

Yet Malvina had seen the fickle side to Pretty Cloud. She had at one time been attracted to Paul Brady. She had also been attracted to Stands Tall and only yesterday had told Malvina that she no longer cared for him.

Remembering these sudden yet brief infatuations made Malvina uneasy. She didn't want her brother's feelings toyed with. He was a sincere, good man whose heart could break easily over a woman who was not sincere.

She cast those thoughts aside and tried to think the best of the situation when Daniel introduced himself to Pretty Cloud and she to him.

"How long will you stay in the village of the Choctaw?" Pretty Cloud asked, her face flushed with the heat of sudden intrigue.

"Until I am a bit stronger," Daniel said, his pulse racing when he realized by her behavior she was attracted to him. He knew that he should have only one thing on his mind, now that the jewels had been found. His ministry!

Yet he had never felt this way before in the presence of a woman. He had the strength and character to care for two important things in his life at once. He would share his loyalties between his career and his woman.

Now he had to make certain that she truly wanted him, he thought to himself. He would stay long enough in the Choctaw village to see whether or not this would work between himself and the Indian woman.

He gazed at Malvina, able to appreciate her feelings for Red Wing more, now that he had his own feelings for an Indian.

Malvina went on to Red Wing's cabin.

Pretty Cloud took Daniel down by the river and gently bathed the smoke from his face, then his hands.

Malvina found a basin of water beside the fireplace. She hurriedly hand-bathed, then slipped a clean chemise over her head.

Yawning, she collapsed onto the bed and soon fell into a sound sleep.

After a while, Malvina was awakened by the gentle touch of hands on her inner thighs and a soft kiss on her brow. She melted inside when Red Wing snuggled onto the bed beside her, nude and dripping clean from a fresh bath in the river.

Chapter Thirty-Nine

Stirred sensually by his hands stroking her throbbing center and his lips kissing the hollow of her throat, a sudden panic nevertheless filled Malvina. She gently shoved Red Wing away and smoothed her chemise down to cover herself, her eyes wide and wary as she looked around the cabin.

"Daniel?" she said, then questioned Red Wing with wondering eyes. "Where is he? I can't let him see us doing—well, you know—*that.*"

"Daniel helped my people build their lodges; then he was taken in by Pretty Cloud's kin, as was Dreaming Shield. They are all now being fed and are listening to stories of our people," Red Wing said softly. "It is good that my people can see beyond their mourning and be generous to a stranger who has come into their lives so quickly."

"Your people are rare," Malvina said, relaxing

now that she knew neither Dreaming Shield nor her brother would enter the lodge during her and Red Wing's lovemaking.

"Dreaming Shield told me that you have said we will take him as a son into our lives," Red Wing said, smoothing his hands over her face. "My woman, your heart is big and generous to a child who has recently lost so much."

"I love him, Red Wing," Malvina said, her voice breaking. "It will be easy to mother him."

"I love *you*," Red Wing said, slipping his hands farther up inside her chemise, cupping both her breasts within the warmth of his hands. "I *need* you. Help lift some of the burden of sadness from my heart. Help me forget. Give me moments to remember forever."

Moved by the quiet pleading in his voice, feeling his pain, Malvina reached for the hem of her chemise and drew it over her head. She tossed it aside.

As he leaned away from her, she gently removed his fringed shirt, then smiled softly at him as she placed her fingers to the drawstring of his buckskin breeches and untied it.

He stood up, allowing her to pull his breeches down, revealing his readiness, his manhood bold and sleek within her fingers as she placed them around him.

Red Wing sucked in a wild breath and trembled as Malvina leaned closer to him and moved her fingers on that part of him that would always fascinate her.

Her fingers continued to move on him, her tongue now flicking around one of his nipples, then the other.

Feeling the ecstasy building much too quickly, setting fires within him that reached into his very soul, Red Wing took Malvina's hands in his.

He leaned his hard, lean body against hers and gently pushed her onto the bed on her back. He raked his eyes over her, his insides blazing as he gazed at her erect rosy nipples that were hard and tilted upward in her passion.

Her hair was disarrayed around her smooth and creamy shoulders, its coppery sheen reflecting the blushing glow of the fire in the fireplace.

He gazed lower, his heart thumping wildly to see how her hips curved voluptuously from her slender waist, framing the cloud of copper hair that screened the warm and wet place he was about to enter.

His gaze went to her lips. They were softly parted.

Her eyes were hazed over with want of him.

His mouth covered hers in a fiery kiss as her soft, full thighs opened to him.

Without any more preliminaries, he entered her, her warm inner flesh clasping to him like a clinging embrace.

As he thrust endlessly into her, reaching the very depths of her being, it seemed, he fought to go more slowly, but his need for her tonight was fierce.

It was so overwhelming that it dizzied him.

His hands cupped the soft flesh of her buttocks, molding her shapely contours with his fingers as he whispered soft words of love to her, then showered her with loving kisses along the gentle planes of her face.

He claimed her lips again, their moans mingling

as the passion rose and spread between them, as though they were one being, one soul, one star in the heavens!

Malvina was swirling in a storm of passion, of sweet remembrances of times not so long past. After she had reached her teenage years, in her soft, pink dreams she had been in a man's arms. Yet she had never been able to make out a face.

It had been the strength of the man's arms as he held her, and the sweetness of his kisses, that had made her feel warm and delicious when she awakened.

So often her brother had noticed her strange behavior while taking their horses out for an early morning ride. When he had asked her about the blush to her cheeks, and the dreaminess in her eyes, she had only smiled secretively.

She had known even then that one day she would find the secrets of that blissful, youthful happiness.

But this was now. Pleasure was spreading through Malvina in a delicious tingling heat. She twined her arms around Red Wing and moaned throatily when his lips moved to her breasts and sucked her nipples one at a time.

Malvina's hips moved and gyrated with his body.

She rocked with him, her pelvis pressed against him.

His mouth once again covered hers. He kissed her long and deeply and with exquisite tenderness, his palms still moving seductively over her satiny body.

Then a great surge of passion swam through Malvina. She clung to Red Wing as his body hardened and tightened. She absorbed his last, bold thrust and followed him down the road to total bliss.

Breathing hard, still floating from the final throes of spent passion, Red Wing rolled away from Malvina and lay on his side facing her. Smiling over at her, he pushed wet locks of her hair from her face.

"You have such pretty and delicate lips," Red Wing whispered, now gently tracing the outline of her lips with a finger. "Do you know what those lips do to me?"

"The same as yours do to me," Malvina giggled as he moved his hand down across her long neck, then lower to cup a breast within his palm. She closed her eyes and shuddered. "Red Wing, your hands are so powerful, yet so very *gentle*. Oh, what they do to me."

"Your hands set me afire," Red Wing said huskily as she reached and touched his manhood. He could feel the heat rising again within his throbbing shaft. He closed his eyes and spread out on his back as she knelt over him and kissed her way down his body to that part of him that was hungry to love her again.

When her tongue touched the tip of his manhood, Red Wing groaned and stiffened.

Then he began a slow melting when she worshiped his flesh in such a way.

Feeling too close again to that wondrous release he had sought earlier from her, he placed his hands gently on her shoulders and guided her down beside him.

The feeling came at once for Malvina, startling her, when Red Wing touched her mound of pleasure with the tip of his tongue. She moaned and closed her eyes when he bent lower over her and pleasured her until her body burst into what seemed many rainbows.

Stunned by the suddenness of the pleasure he brought on in such a way, Malvina looked down at Red Wing, blushing.

Red Wing smiled up at her, then covered her body with his and entered her.

Moving rhythmically, they soon found paradise again.

Tremors cascaded down their backs.

They cried out their pleasure.

Ecstasy spilling over her again, drenching her with warmth, Malvina watched Red Wing as he rose from the bed. She sat up and smiled a thank-you as he brought her a cup of honey water.

Still not taking her eyes off him and how hand-somely beautiful he was, his copper body sleek with sweat from the lovemaking, she drank from the cup.

He came to her and knelt down before her. Gently, he splayed the fingers of both hands across her abdomen. "Inside grows our child," he said softly, then laid his cheek against the flat plane of her belly. "Do you hear me, my child? Do you hear your father talking to you? Your mother is beautiful!"

Malvina giggled. She set her cup aside, then wove her fingers over and over again through Red Wing's thick black hair. "I wish we could have met under different circumstances," she murmured. "When life was simple. When life was sweet."

He gazed up at her with his midnight-dark eyes.

"And when was that, my woman?" he said, his voice drawn.

"For me, it was when my parents were still alive, and my father was a proud minister whose thoughts were always of others," she murmured. "Surely there was a time when you were as happy, as carefree."

Red Wing sighed heavily. He took one of her hands and led her from the bed, guiding her down onto a blanket beside the fire.

Gently he placed a robe around her shoulders, then sat down beside her, shoulder to shoulder, and linked the blanket between them so they could share their body heat.

"When my parents were alive and I was a youthful brave who learned the ways of a warrior from my father, yes, it was a more peaceful time for me," Red Wing said, gazing into the fire as though he saw his past in the flames. "But I grew up too fast and saw that the world was filled with those whose hearts were evil."

He turned to her. "But with you at my side, no matter the pain of living, there will be a spark of sunshine in that pain," he said, his voice breaking.

Malvina flung herself into his arms. "My darling, how I wish I had the power to erase all sadness from your heart forever, not only for the moment," she whispered.

"It is you who bathes my spirit," he said. "While I am with you, it is like coming home from warring to truth and beauty."

"How beautiful," she murmured, touched deeply by his words.

"One day the Choctaw will again find a sense

of the infinite mystery and richness of life," Red Wing said.

He held Malvina tight, yet looked past her, knowing that tomorrow was too close—a tomorrow when many mournings would begin and scaffoldings would be built for the fallen people of his village.

Malvina eased out of his arms. She gazed waveringly into his eyes. "Red Wing, I know how you feel about me," she murmured. "But will your people ever truly accept me? I'm afraid they will look at me and remember too many things that the white people have done to them. Will they be able to see past that which I had nothing to do with? Or will they secretly loathe and hate me?"

Red Wing twined his fingers through her lustrously long hair. "They have accepted you," he said, smiling reassuringly at her. "As I, they have seen your goodness."

Again Malvina moved into his arms. For the sake of this child growing within her body, what Red Wing said *must* be true, she thought. The child born of their love must never know the meaning of the word 'prejudice', whether the child's skin was white or copper.

"It will be all right," Red Wing said, caressing the creamy flesh of her back. "I will make it so!"

Tears streamed from Malvina's eyes. She closed them and clung with all her might to his powerful shoulders, so badly wanting to absorb his confidence.

Thus far there had been many interferences in their happiness. But so many of those who had caused them problems were now dead. She did not want to think about her uncle ever again.

Or Paul Brady.

He could never tell Red Wing any more lies about her.

Her eyes widened and she gasped.

Red Wing realized that something had come to her that startled her. "What is it?" he asked softly.

"Gerald," she gasped. "Gerald Smythe. Red Wing, he is still out there somewhere. I let him go. How could I have let him go free? Why didn't I remember that he was a vindictive man? He'll be back to bring torment into our lives again. I feel it in my bones that he'll be back."

Red Wing's eyes darkened at the thought of what this man had already done to his woman.

His jaw tightened as rage filled his very soul at the thought of this man still being alive.

"He dare not approach you again," Red Wing said firmly.

That was not reassurance enough for Malvina.

Chapter Forty

Several weeks had passed. Life was not as everyone wished it could be in the Choctaw village, but it was better.

The cabins were rebuilt. The burial of those loved ones who had died was far behind everyone now. Although many people would never stop mourning within their hearts, the outward signs of their grief were over.

Malvina awakened slowly from sleep filled with dreams of Red Wing, and of this, her special day, her *wedding*.

More content than she had been in months, she stretched and yawned lazily. When she opened her eyes she found Red Wing sitting on the edge of the bed, looking down at her.

She melted inside when he placed a gentle hand to her cheek, then bent low and brushed a kiss across her lips.

"Were you gathering flowers in your sleep?" he asked, as he drew her into his arms.

"What?" she asked, giggling. "Why would you ask that?"

"You were smiling in your sleep," he said, running his hands up and down her bare back in a slow caress.

They had made love into the wee hours of the morning.

They hadn't bothered to dress.

It had been much easier to fall asleep within each other's arms as they were.

They had been given their full privacy, even though Dreaming Shield had now been adopted by them. He had grown close to Daniel these past weeks and had been staying with him in a cabin that Daniel and he had built.

Because of his attraction to Pretty Cloud, Daniel had not yet left for Saint Louis.

"I was smiling in my sleep because my dreams were filled with you, my love," Malvina said, shivering with desire as Red Wing reached between them and filled his hands with her breasts.

She snuggled closer. "I can hardly believe that our wedding day has finally arrived," she murmured. "It seems forever since we first met."

Red Wing's hands slid lower. He stretched his fingers over her belly, which now showed her pregnancy. "In many ways we are already man and wife," he said wonderingly. "In ways that matter we are. We are already a family. Dreaming Shield is our son, and we have another son on the way."

Malvina leaned away from him. "And you are

so certain that I am carrying a son, not a daughter?" she asked, her eyes dancing into his. "I have been told that by the way I am carrying the child already in my early weeks of pregnancy, so low, that I can expect to give birth to a daughter."

She snuggled against him again. "Would you be all that disappointed if we had a daughter?" she asked poutingly.

"Never will I ever be disappointed in you again," Red Wing said, flinching when he realized what he said.

But Malvina understood. Those many times, when she had fled the safety of his lodge and arms, he was pushed into doubting her, even though he regretted it once he knew why she had been driven to such things that endangered not only her, but also their love.

"I shall never do anything to disappoint you again," Malvina said. "I am content with my world now, Red Wing. My brother is safe. We have the family heirlooms in our possession again. And, my love, I have *you*. We have our son, Dreaming Shield." She placed a soft hand on her stomach. "And the best is yet to come."

He laughed softly. "Today is the beginning of all of our *bests*," he said, leaving the bed.

He went to the fireplace where he had earlier arranged small logs in a circle on the grate. The flames were slowly eating away at the ends of the logs. He pushed enough of them farther into the circle so that they would burn strongly throughout the day.

Grabbing a robe and tying it snugly around her waist with a belt, Malvina went to the door and eased it slowly open. The sun was just rising out of the eastern sky.

And it was *her* day. She had never felt so wanted, never felt so strongly that she belonged among the Choctaw.

Her gaze shifted when she caught sight of Daniel walking toward the cabin, a spring in his steps. She stepped outside and met his approach.

Daniel drew her into his arms. "Sis, you look radiant," he said, gazing down at her with a warm gleam in his eyes.

"Red Wing has brought so much into my life," Malvina said. She laughed softly. "I believe he has even tamed me, Daniel. I no longer have the strong desire to rush outside each morning to ride a horse, to find a touch of freedom in the saddle. I am at peace, Daniel. I am no longer restless."

Daniel smiled at her. "I can tell that much about you has changed," he said. "But I still see what I saw on the mornings of our adventures on horseback."

"And what is that?" Malvina asked.

"You have that same radiance, that same blush to your cheeks, and that softness in your eyes that I used to see and questioned you about," he said. "You didn't know Red Wing then. What caused you to behave as though you might have?"

Malvina laughed softly. "Darling brother, I dreamed dreams that warmed my heart," she said. "I dreamed about being held within the arms of a man, of being kissed. Surely even then I knew it would be Red Wing who would make those dreams turn into reality."

Red Wing stepped outside, the fringes of hïs buckskin breeches blowing in the gentle breeze.

His bare chest was a copper sheen beneath the soft rays of the morning sun.

"I believe I heard my name?" he said, reaching a hand to Daniel's shoulder as Daniel stepped away from Malvina. "Good morning, Daniel. Are you ready to hand your sister over to my care today?"

"Had I been given the opportunity to choose the man for my sister, it would have been you," Daniel said, then turned with a start when he saw Pretty Cloud come from her cabin and walk toward the river for her morning bath.

Daniel's heart frolicked within his chest when she cast him a shy smile, then walked onward. He watched the gentle sway of her hips and her lustrously long, jet-black hair as the wind whipped it around her face.

Then Dreaming Shield caught his attention. He was with a gathering of boys, chattering like magpies, occasionally looking Malvina and Red Wing's way. He knew they were excited about the upcoming event, as was Daniel.

But Daniel had someone else on the mind.

He wished one day soon to have his own wedding ceremony.

Yet Pretty Cloud had not openly shown to him that she was interested in that way. She had looked at him with shy glances, smiling, yet she had never allowed him to be with her alone.

Daniel turned quick eyes back to Red Wing. "What must I do to get Pretty Cloud to not be so shy around me?" he blurted out. "I must leave soon for Saint Louis. I should not have stayed so long. I have been eager to enter the ministry since I was a child. I can no longer delay the teachings that are required. What am I doing wrong? Is there some sort of ritual a Choctaw man performs to attract the attention of the woman he wishes to marry?"

Red Wing chuckled and placed an arm around Daniel's shoulder.

Malvina clasped her hands together before her, proud to see the affection between her brother and the man who would soon be her husband. She could not have asked for more than this. It most definitely made the happiness of her world complete.

"Yes, there is something a Choctaw male can do," Red Wing said, nodding. "I should have told you earlier, but it did not enter my mind that you would not know what a Choctaw woman expects of a man who wishes to marry her. Of course now I realize that your ways differ greatly from ours."

"Tell me, Red Wing, so that I can win her heart," Daniel said, turning to look at Pretty Cloud again, just as she stepped out of sight into a thick cover of brush down by the river.

"Daniel, when a Choctaw warrior finds a girl whom he wants to marry, he catches her eye and nods," Red Wing said. "She will start out running. She will run like a deer until nobody sees her, then will slow down until the man can catch her. He will lead her back to the village where they will be pronounced man and wife."

"That is how it is done?" Malvina said, eyes wide. "But for us, we—"

"Everything has been different for us the moment we realized we had feelings of forever for each other," Red Wing said, turning away from Daniel. "We had no chance to do what is normal. And that does not matter. We will soon reach the same end as those who do."

"Do you mean that today, if I do what you just described, Pretty Cloud and I could become man and wife on the same day as your marriage ceremony?" Daniel said in a rush of words, his eyes bright with excitement.

"There is usually no actual ceremony," Red Wing said. "But today it is different for your sister and I. We have been forced to wait to be pronounced man and wife. I am making certain that much excitement accompanies our wedding. Your sister deserves it."

"Then today I wish to see that Pretty Cloud joins in the excitement as my wife," Daniel said, his pulse racing at the thought.

"But Daniel, I have not told you everything," Red Wing quickly interjected.

Daniel's smile faded. "What have you not told me?"

"That if Pretty Cloud does not fancy you, she will not accept your challenge and will not run," Red Wing said. "*And* Daniel, if you are serious about offering her this challenge, I would advise you to do it after everyone is gathered around for the celebration today. Choctaw women wish for such an audience. They enjoy being seen sought after by a man. It makes them look special in the eyes of those who have not yet had a man's attention."

"But if I am wrong about her, if she does not wish to be my bride, then I will look foolish in front of your people," Daniel said.

"That is the chance men must take for women," Red Wing said, chuckling beneath his breath.

"Daniel, I am certain that you won't be made to look foolish," Malvina quickly said. "Pretty Cloud has talked of nothing else but you to me."

Daniel rubbed his chin, then laughed softly. "I shall do it," he said. He looked wide-eyed at Malvina and then at Red Wing. "That is, if you don't mind sharing this day with me and my antics."

"Not at all," Malvina and Red Wing said in almost the same breath.

Then they all laughed.

Malvina gazed up at Red Wing.

Their eyes met and locked.

Malvina could tell that Red Wing was enjoying finally being able to be carefree.

She most certainly was!

Chapter Forty-One

The day had been long, yet joyful. The night fires were now burning as drums made from trunks of black gum trees beat out their steady rhythm, with the music of cane flutes and gourd rattles to accompany it.

Malvina sat beside Red Wing on a raised platform, wild flowers spread at their feet on the ground. They had been pronounced man and wife many hours ago. There had been much feasting and dancing.

Grass Dancers whirled even now beneath the light of the moon.

Malvina watched them, feeling as though she were in a trance. The melodies of the instruments flowed, ascended, and descended as the dancers reacted to the melodies.

Some of the watching Choctaw people sang in high falsetto voices from deep in their throats, pushing sound from their diaphragms. Others sang at a lower pitch, but using the same basic song structure.

The Grass Dancers were then replaced by those who performed the Jingle Dress Dance.

Malvina watched them with interest, finding them uniquely dressed, their performances special. The Jingle dresses were made of bright cloth with large tin cone "jingles" sewn in patterns on them.

The performers danced in an up-and-down motion due to the tightness of the form-fitting dresses. Their feet lifted in a hopping, rocking manner which caused the jingles to produce a rhythmic clacking.

When the dances were over, the children became the center of the attention, staging mock battles or mock deer kills. Malvina laughed and smiled as Dreaming Shield seemed the most aggressive of all the children. It was apparent that he was trying to prove his leadership, as he would occasionally glance at Red Wing and Malvina to see if they were watching him.

Red Wing nodded his approval. Malvina smiled her own toward him.

Then Daniel suddenly stepped into the circle of people. He caught Pretty Cloud's eye and nodded toward her.

Everyone became quiet.

Waiting for Pretty Cloud's reaction, the crowd held its breath. Malvina's heart beat soundly within her chest as she waited for Pretty Cloud to rise to her feet. Should her brother be humiliated, she would blame herself for encouraging him to chance his fortune.

Then she breathed more easily when Pretty Cloud rushed to her feet and started running away toward the river, Daniel running after her.

At first Pretty Cloud ran quickly; then she slowed her pace. Daniel soon caught up with her and grabbed her up into his arms and carried her back to the celebration.

Bald Eagle, the Shaman, stepped forth and pronounced Daniel and Pretty Cloud man and wife. Daniel would explain to Pretty Cloud later that the ceremony must be repeated in Saint Louis so that he would see it as legal in the white man's world.

The celebration began again. Malvina hugged Pretty Cloud and Daniel, then watched Daniel walk away with his bride toward his lodge.

Tears filled Malvina's eyes to know that her brother's life had turned into something sweet and wonderful. His future was bright, and he had someone to fill his nights. What sister could ask for more for her beloved brother? She was glad that Pretty Cloud had proven that at long last she was serious in her feelings about a man.

Red Wing placed an arm around Malvina's waist. "The celebration is over," he whispered. "Everyone is going to their lodges. My wife, shall we go to ours?"

Malvina moved into his arms. "Today really happened, didn't it?" she asked, gazing up at him. "We are man and wife? And my brother captured the heart of Pretty Cloud?"

"It is all real," Red Wing said, lifting her into his arms. "Let me show you *how* real."

Chapter Forty-Two

When Red Wing carried Malvina inside the cabin, she couldn't believe her eyes. Everything was beautiful. She could tell that Red Wing had gone to great lengths to make their first night as man and wife special.

Clinging around his neck, she turned her eyes up at him. "When did you do this?" she asked, touched deeply by his thoughtfulness.

Still holding her, he smiled. "You were not suspicious when I sent you away to another lodge for your hair and face to be made beautiful for the ceremony?" he asked, chuckling low.

"I wondered about it," Malvina said, laughing softly. "And so Pretty Cloud was in on this also. I couldn't see why she wouldn't come to our cabin to help me do those things. I hadn't expected it was for you to have time alone to prepare a surprise for me."

"I plan to make love to you until the sun splashes the morning sky with its brilliance," Red Wing said, walking slowly toward the fireplace. "I wanted everything to be comfortable for you, yes, to be *special*. I want this to be a night you will never forget."

"Red Wing, every night with you is a night I will never forget," Malvina said, brushing a soft kiss across his lips.

"I wish for tonight to live within your storehouse of memories longer than any other," Red Wing said, allowing her to slip from his arms as he stopped within the dancing shadows of the fire.

"And it will," Malvina sighed as she looked at everything that Red Wing had laid before the fireplace.

A thick layer of bear pelts had been spread on the floor in front of the fire. Flowers bloomed in small wooden vases at one end of the pelts, their colors vivid, their scent sweet. Trays of food lay on the hearth, tantalizingly rich aromas wafting from them.

"It seems you had some help," Malvina giggled as she gazed up at Red Wing.

"Yes, Pretty Cloud picked the flowers and the many women of my village came just prior to the end of the ceremony with the food," Red Wing said.

His eyes lowered to the cushion of pelts, and he smiled slowly at her. "But I am responsible for the pelts on which we will make love," he said huskily. "They will hug your body with warmth when the air cools outside."

"All I need is you, my love," Malvina whispered,

her fingers already at his fringed shirt, shoving it up past his muscled chest. "But I do so much adore what you have done. Shall we now make use of it?"

"You are not hungry after the long evening of celebration?" Red Wing asked as she tossed his shirt aside.

He trembled inside when she placed her fingers at the waist of his breeches and began lowering them over his hips.

"Later," she said, hardly recognizing her voice in its sensual huskiness. "I have waited all day to be alone with you. Would you think me brazen if I confess to you that food is the last thing on my mind?"

"Men are not alone in their desires, their needs," Red Wing said as he stepped out of his breeches and now stood nude before her. "It is just that too often women are made to believe they should not voice such feelings aloud. I am glad that you feel comfortable enough with me to say what you feel when you feel it."

"Before I met you, I would have thought it improper for a woman to initiate lovemaking as I have done tonight," she murmured. "Even perhaps married, I would have thought her a wanton hussy."

"Hussy?" Red Wing said, arching an eyebrow. "I am not familiar with such a word as that."

"That is because you never frequented the brothels in Fort Smith and never *met* such women," Malvina said.

Then she gazed innocently up at him. "You never *did* use such women to quench your desires, did you?" she asked curiously.

When Red Wing's eyes twinkled down at her, Malvina's heart skipped a beat.

"You didn't, did you?" she warily asked again.

"No, I would not want such a woman," Red Wing said, taking her by the wrists and yanking her to his hard, ready body. "I want *you* to fill my arms."

Still not letting go of something she had started, Malvina went on, "Before me, who *did* fill your arms? You are a virile man. Surely you have not done without women. Was there ever a . . . special woman before you met me? One you perhaps considered marrying?"

"Yes, there were women," Red Wing said, slowly shoving her dress over her head. "But none that made my heart thunder inside my chest the way it did when I first saw you. I fought my want of you until the fight was over and you were locked inside my heart forever."

"I am so glad you finally realized that I was innocent of the things I was accused of," Malvina said, shivering with desire as his hands swept the dress away from her.

When he bent to one knee before her and removed her moccasins one at a time, he stopped as each was tossed aside to kiss the soles of her feet.

Then he placed his hands at her waist and slowly lowered her to the plushly soft pelts. As she stretched out beneath him, she laced her arms around his neck.

"I wasted much time that could have been good between us when I suspected you of too many things," Red Wing said huskily. "Let us waste no more time talking about it. It is a thing of the past. Let us keep it there."

He parted her legs with his knee and probed at the center of her desire with his throbbing hardness. "Let us now think of the mysteries of our bodies as they come together again. Our love for each other has taken us beyond that which most know. We are the lucky ones, Malvina. So very lucky."

A surge of warmth flooded Malvina's body when his mouth covered hers with a fiery, trembling kiss, and he entered her in one deep thrust.

She pushed her pelvis toward him and moved her body with his as he thrust rhythmically into her, his hands kneading her breasts, his tongue surging through her lips.

Tremors cascaded down Malvina's back. She was only half aware of making whimpering sounds as the passion built within her when his lips moved to one of her breasts, his tongue sweeping around the nipple, his teeth nipping it to hardness.

And then he slowed his pace and made love to her slowly, gently, scarcely moving inside her.

Malvina closed her eyes as once again he kissed her, leisurely, tenderly, his hands twined through her hair.

Aflame with longing, Red Wing found it hard not to go over that brink that would give him the pleasure he was seeking.

Yet he wanted it to last longer this time than ever before. He wanted to relish her every movement, her every pleasured breath.

Unable to hold back much longer, Red Wing kissed Malvina more fiercely, his mouth urgent and eager, his thrusts now deep and insistent within her.

Malvina's breathing was ragged.

Her heart was pounding.

Her insides were warm as she moved her body sinuously against his.

Their bodies stilled against each other.

Red Wing gazed down at Malvina, absorbing how she looked only moments before reaching total bliss.

Her eyes were hazy.

Her cheeks were rosy.

"You are more beautiful at this moment than I have ever seen you," he whispered huskily.

"I am?" Malvina whispered back, transfixed by the smoldering in his eyes. "My love, never have you been as wonderfully handsome."

She had never felt such sweet, painful longing, as now. "Oh, how I do love you. Please kiss me again. Please fill me. Take me to the stars, Red Wing. I don't think I can wait much longer."

He lowered his mouth to hers. When she parted her lips, he touched his tongue to hers. As she clung to him, he thrust his tongue into her mouth and flicked it in and out, then moved it along her lips.

She clung to him.

She sighed.

She felt her breath catch and hold when he thrust himself even more deeply into her, exquisitely filling her in demanding, hard thrusts which sent her mind into bliss.

Feeling the nearing of his climax, Red Wing paused again to take a shuddering breath.

Again he gazed down at Malvina, seeing her

eyes, lips, creamy shoulders and breasts as an incredible, beautiful dream.

She reached her hands to his sculpted face and drew his lips to hers again.

He came to her with maddening thrusts; her gasps of pleasure became long, soft whimpers.

And then their bodies met in an explosive burst of rapture.

She strained her hips up at him and became lost, heart and soul, to the moment of joyous fulfillment.

She clung to him as he thrust one last time into her, before his body subsided exhaustedly against hers.

They lay there for a moment, their bodies touching, their hands gently exploring and caressing.

Then Red Wing rose to his knees and reached for a long-handled gadget, in which blue kernels of Indian corn lay on a kind of screen.

"What are you doing?" Malvina asked, brushing damp strands of her hair back from her brow.

"We will have fresh popped corn," Red Wing said, sitting nude before the fire as he reached the contraption over the flames.

He smiled at her, his gaze traveling over her, stopping at her abdomen. "Do you think our son will enjoy sharing popped corn with us tonight?"

"He shared more than that," Malvina said, laughing softly.

She scooted close to Red Wing, draping an arm around his bare waist. She leaned against him, placing her cheek on his arm. "I am so perfectly content," she said, watching the kernels of corn start to stir, then pop into something white and alluring, the aroma teasing her nose.

"It is good to see such peace in your eyes," Red Wing said, shaking the popcorn popper one last time. "You have experienced much sadness in your eighteen years of life."

"And so have you in your lifetime," Malvina said, her stomach growling as the scent of the popped corn became overwhelmingly tempting. "But hopefully the worst is behind us."

"Yes, behind us," Red Wing said, knowing that deep inside her heart she knew there was still an enemy out there to deal with.

Gerald Smythe!

Red Wing would never feel at ease allowing Malvina far from his sight as long as Gerald Smythe was alive to bring horror into his wife's life again.

But Red Wing wanted peace as badly as Malvina. He would not let a man like Gerald rule their lives by allowing him to be a central focus of their conversations or fears.

In time, Gerald would be dealt with.

But only if he truly became a nuisance and a threat to his wife's happiness.

Malvina plopped another piece of corn in her mouth and gazed at Red Wing. He seemed immersed in deep thought. There was even a trace of a frown at this moment, when they should be concentrating only on their happiness!

"What are you thinking about?" Malvina asked, unable to cast the wonder aside.

Red Wing looked guardedly at her, then smiled away his frown. "Only that surely you wish to eat something besides popcorn," he said, reaching for one of the platters of food.

"Yes, I would like to sample some of the other

goodies," Malvina said, eyeing the food on the platter. She knew that he was not being altogether honest with her. No one would frown and seem lost in such dark thoughts if he were considering only which food to eat next.

But she would not question him. She would rather not delve into things that might be troublesome. She just wanted to be happy tonight, to let nothing interfere in this happiness!

Her gaze locked on the persimmon bread, and she plucked a piece from the platter. She enjoyed eating that, then ate a few nuts and berries before she realized that Red Wing was no longer eating; instead he was sitting there smiling at her.

"What is it?" she asked, forking an eyebrow.

Then she realized the foolishness of the question.

He was waiting for her to finish eating.

She placed the platter of food on the hearth, then slithered against him so that her breasts pressed warmly against his chest.

With quick, eager fingers, his hands were in her hair, drawing her lips to his.

Their bodies strained together hungrily.

Malvina melted sensually inside when his lips came to hers in a fierce, fevered kiss.

He moved over her with his body, molding himself perfectly to the curved hollow of her hips.

He pressed gently into her and again spun his golden web of magic around her.

Chapter Forty-Three

Several weeks had passed. The cool breezes were blowing in off the Arkansas River. There was a hint of snow in the air. The riverboat from Saint Louis was making its last trip to Fort Smith due to winter's fast approach.

Comfortably snug in a fur robe and knee-high, fur-lined moccasins, Malvina ran to Daniel's cabin. She knocked on the door and waited, glancing at Dreaming Shield as he came toward her with something quite long and large wrapped in buckskin.

Dreaming Shield's eyes smiled into hers as he stood beside her. "I have brought Daniel a special farewell gift," he said, his shoulders squared proudly. "It is something he can take with him when he goes on the hunt."

"What is it?" Malvina asked, forking an eyebrow as she gazed at the long, covered gift.

"It is something I made, but with some help from friends," Dreaming Shield said. "Until it was finished I kept it at my friend Swift Wing's lodge. I was afraid that Daniel might see it in our lodge when he and Pretty Cloud came and sat evenings with us before the fire."

He glanced away from her when the door opened. His smile widened when Daniel stepped into view.

"Well, what do we have here?" Daniel said, looking from Malvina to Dreaming Shield. "A going-away party?"

Pretty Cloud came to his side and linked an arm through his.

"I've come to see if there is anything I can do to help you get ready for your trip to Saint Louis," Malvina said, stepping inside when Daniel ushered her in.

"But I believe Dreaming Shield has a different purpose for being here," Malvina said, looking at the child as he came inside, Daniel closing the door behind him.

Dreaming Shield stepped up to Daniel. "I have brought something for you to have with you when you are far away from Dreaming Shield," he said, his voice breaking at the thought of having to say farewell to Daniel. "I hope you will like the gift. I . . . made it."

Touched by the child's thoughtfulness, Daniel knelt before him. "You've made something especially for me?" he asked, overwhelmed.

Dreaming Shield nodded, then held the wrapped gift out for Daniel. Daniel took it, then rose to his feet and slowly laid the buckskin back a corner at a time.

When an intricately carved bow was finally uncovered, Daniel gasped and stared down at it in wonder.

"When you are on the hunt, you can think of Dreaming Shield," the child said, beaming.

"It is a fine and handsome bow," Daniel said, running his fingers over the carved figures in the wood.

He looked down at Dreaming Shield. "Thank you, Dreaming Shield," he said, his voice deep with emotion. "I think it is the grandest gift I have ever received."

"It is a gift from my heart to you," Dreaming Shield said, then rushed to Daniel and hugged him. "I shall always miss you. You are a brother I never had."

"I will return as often as I can to see you and your family," Daniel said, smiling at Malvina. He knew that Dreaming Shield had adjusted well to living with Red Wing and Malvina since the loss of his parents.

He placed a hand on Dreaming Shield's shoulder and held him at arm's length. "And it won't be long, Dreaming Shield, until you will have a brother in your lodge," he said, giving Malvina a quick, warm glance. "I bet then you won't even think of me."

Dreaming Shield wiped tears from his eyes. "I will never forget you," he said. Then he looked up at Malvina, a slow smile flickering across his lips. "But I do look forward to having a baby brother."

He looked back up at Daniel. "I shall also make *him* a bow," he said proudly. "But one much smaller. I shall teach my brother how to shoot

393

the bow. I shall teach my brother good sportsmanship."

"He couldn't have a better teacher," Daniel said. He chuckled as he once again gazed admiringly at his new bow. "And, yes, a young brave must start with something smaller than this when he is learning to hunt."

"Daniel, I wish you didn't have to leave," Malvina said, looking over her shoulder at the bundles readied for traveling.

"Sis, we both fought tooth and nail for this moment," Daniel said, setting the bow aside. He went to Malvina and drew her into his arms. "We risked our lives more than once for the opportunity for me to go to Saint Louis to learn to be a minister. I want it no less now than the first time we went looking for those who were responsible for killing our parents."

He eased her from his arms and looked over at the chest of jewels. "I wish you would have taken more than our grandmother's brooch from the family heirlooms," he said reproachfully. "There is more than enough to pay for my schooling."

"Then use it to get your bride a pretty home filled with pretty things," Malvina said softly, feeling somewhat guilty for having taken even the one brooch from the chest.

But it was a keepsake, nothing more. She had seen her grandmother, and then her mother, wear it often when she had taken care to look pretty on special occasions.

"Life is going to be hard for Pretty Cloud living among the white community," Malvina murmured. "White men taking Indian brides are not common, Daniel. You and Pretty Cloud are going to have much prejudice to face."

"I'll protect her with my life," Daniel mumbled, then went to the chest of jewels and opened the lid. He stared down at the gems sparkling up at him.

"I tried to get Red Wing to take some of the jewels," he said to his sister. "If the winter is bad, he could use them to provide for his people."

"Red Wing is too proud to accept charity," Malvina said. "He wishes to pay his own way. The hunt is how he does this. He trades for what he wishes his people to have."

She eyed the jewels, knowing it would be the last time she would ever see them. She recalled those times their parents had shown them to her and Daniel, explaining how they had come across the vast ocean from Ireland, and how they would never part with them.

She did not want to feel guilty over knowing that soon they would no longer be a part of the O'Neal family.

But surely even her parents would not object to how they were going to be used. She was certain that her parents would have parted with the jewels willingly, had they known they would help Daniel achieve his dreams, dreams blessed by the Lord Almighty.

Daniel closed the lid as though he were closing the final chapter of his past life.

A knock on the door drew Malvina around. "It's Red Wing," she said, rushing toward the door. "He had business to tend to in the council house. He said he would come as soon as it was concluded."

She swung the door open.

Red Wing stepped inside and embraced Malvina, then Pretty Cloud.

He then went to Daniel and clasped his hands onto his shoulders. "The time has come to say farewell for a while," he said. "Your cabin will be kept clean and ready for your return anytime you can manage to come for a visit."

"The winter ahead will keep me and Pretty Cloud from traveling long distances," Daniel said. "But once the paddlewheelers make their way back down again to Fort Smith, Pretty Cloud and I will be their first passengers."

"That is good," Red Wing said, nodding.

He stepped back from Daniel. "And did my son please you with his gift, Daniel?" he said, his shoulders squared with savage pride.

"It shall always be the most beloved of my possessions," Daniel said, then laughed softly. "Besides my Bible and my bride, that is."

Everyone joined in the good-hearted laughter; then Red Wing spoke of something that made their eyes waver and their laughter fade.

"There is something I must again warn you about, Daniel, while on your journey to Saint Louis," Red Wing said, his voice solemn. "When the paddlewheeler makes its stops along the river, I would advise you and Pretty Cloud to stay aboard. Outlaws are still a threat up and down the river."

"And Gerald Smythe has never been seen or heard from since our uncle's death," Malvina said, shivering at the thought of the vile man. "You're my brother, Daniel. Because you are, that man would love to get his hands on you. He cannot help but blame me for much that happened to him."

Another knock on the door drew the conversation away from the subject that had placed a shadow over the departure of Daniel and his wife.

Pretty Cloud went to the door, then took a startled step away from Stands Tall when she found him standing there.

"I have come to say my good-byes," Stand Tall said, peering down at Pretty Cloud.

Pretty Cloud rushed to Daniel's side and clung to his arm, her eyes closely scrutinizing Stands Tall as he came into the cabin and closed the door behind him.

It was obvious to everyone that his mere presence made Pretty Cloud uncomfortable, since she had at one time promised to be his wife.

"Daniel, we have not had much conversation since you arrived in our village," Stands Tall said softly. "I would not want you to leave thinking I was not a friend. You are Malvina's brother. That makes us friends."

"Thank you," Daniel said, reaching out a hand of friendship toward Stands Tall. "I appreciate your thoughtfulness."

Stands Tall clasped his hand around Daniel's. "Travel with care," he said, then stepped back and stood beside Red Wing.

"Well, I think it's about time for us all to be going to Fort Smith," Daniel said, feeling somewhat awkward in Stand Tall's presence even though he had just accepted his gesture of friendship. It was common knowledge that Stands Tall still had feelings for Pretty Cloud.

Malvina fought to hold her tears back. She felt a strange desperation knowing that she had to part with her brother again. While they had been parted after the accident, she had almost given up hope of ever seeing him again.

She had a strange feeling now—that this might be their last good-bye!

She hoped these feelings were not a premonition of what was to come. Perhaps her brother shouldn't leave today on the paddlewheeler. What if ice had begun to form on the boat and the captain hadn't seen it?

Or what if outlaws forced the paddlewheeler to stop and they ravaged it and the passengers?

"Malvina?"

Red Wing's voice drew her out of her reverie. She looked up at him, her eyes showing her concern and fears.

"Malvina, what is it?" Red Wing asked, taking her hands in his. "You are pale. Your eyes show much that troubles me. What has caused this change in your mood?"

Not wanting to speak out loud what she had been thinking, fearing that might make it happen, she forced a smile. "Nothing," she murmured. "I just hate for Daniel to leave. It will be a long time before we see him again."

Daniel came to her side. She turned to him. He drew her into his arms. She hugged him for all she was worth.

"Sis, except for recently, I know that we've never been apart," he said thickly, stroking her hair. "It's time now for us both to depend on others for our happiness."

"Yes, I know," Malvina said, slowly nodding. "And I am so happy, Daniel. I never thought I could be this content with a life other than what we shared as children. You are such a wonderful brother."

"As you are a wonderful sister," Daniel said, then eased her from his arms. "We have our memories to carry with us forever. Now we will be building on those memories, to make new ones with those we love."

Malvina placed a gentle hand to his cheek. "Daniel, I hope the ministry is all that you hope it will be," she murmured. "I hope that you will find it as rewarding as Father did."

"I shall," Daniel said, then swept her into his arms one last time as the loud sound of the paddlewheeler's whistle wafted through the air from the river. Soon it would be moored at Fort Smith. "I must leave now, Malvina."

She gave him an intense hug, then stepped away from him and moved to Red Wing's side. Fighting back the urge to cry, she watched Daniel take the buckskin bags outside to place them on a horse.

When he came back and took Pretty Cloud's hand and led her outside, Malvina knew that it was truly time for him to leave.

She wiped tears from her eyes, smiled weakly up at Red Wing, then left the lodge beside him.

Dreaming Shield was holding the reins for Daniel as Daniel lifted Pretty Cloud into the saddle, then mounted behind her.

Three young braves brought horses to Red Wing. Dreaming Shield mounted one of the horses as Red Wing and Malvina mounted the two others.

They rode from the village, the atmosphere solemn, their faces drawn.

And when they reached the ferry that was waiting at the riverbank, there were many hugs and kisses. Then Malvina stood between Dreaming Shield and Red Wing as the ferry took her brother and his wife to the Fort Smith side of the river.

Malvina still could not shake the foreboding that hovered around her. She reached for Red Wing's hand and squeezed it as her mood deepened.

"Wife, still something more than saying a goodbye to your brother troubles you," Red Wing said, frowning.

"So much has happened to my family these past months, how can I not fear saying goodbye to my brother?" she said, looking wearily up at Red Wing. "If anything should happen to him . . ."

"You should not worry so much while a child grows within your womb," Red Wing gently scolded. "Let life happen and then if you have cause to be concerned, *then* be concerned."

"And of course you are right," Malvina said, laughing nervously.

Dreaming Shield stepped closer and took one of her hands. "I shall always be near to protect you when Red Wing is called away on the hunt, or into council," he promised.

"And I would feel quite safe in your company," Malvina said, laughing softly. She gazed toward the river, in her mind's eye recalling the day of the accident. It sent shivers up and down her spine to recall the moment she had been spilled into the water, then surfaced to look frantically for Daniel.

"I only wish there were two of you, Dreaming Shield," she said, smiling down at him. "One for me, and one for Daniel."

Dreaming Shield giggled, then grew silent when the paddlewheeler came into view, making its way down the river, its destination Saint Louis, Missouri.

"There he goes," Dreaming Shield said in barely more than a whisper. He reached a hand out toward the boat. "Daniel, I shall miss you so very much."

Smoke puffed black and thick from the paddlewheeler's smokestack. The paddles whipped into the water, making a great splash. The whistle broke through the silence, loud and long.

And then Malvina's eyes brightened. "Daniel!" she cried, pointing, then waving. "Do you see him, Red Wing? Dreaming Shield, do you see him? He's on the main deck waving at us. And see Pretty Cloud? She is also waving."

They all waved until the boat reached the bend in the river that took it from their sight.

"Let us go home," Red Wing said, walking Malvina toward her horse.

He looked over his shoulder at Dreaming Shield, who still stood staring at the bend in the river. "Dreaming Shield, it is time to go to our lodge."

Dreaming Shield turned wavering eyes to Red Wing, then smiled. "I believe he liked my gift, don't you?" he said, mounting his horse.

"The bow made Daniel very proud," Red Wing said, swinging into his saddle. "He will have it with him to hold when he misses you, my son."

"I am now making you one, my father," Dreaming Shield said, gazing with pride at Red Wing.

401

"I will use it well, my son," Red Wing said, nodding. "And what do you make for your mother?"

Dreaming Shield's smile faded. "What does a boy make for a mother?" he said, then smiled again. "I know. And I will present it to her soon."

Malvina was enjoying these moments of family closeness, yet in her heart she was already sorely missing Daniel.

But she knew this was the time for her to place more importance on her new family than her old.

She sighed, knowing that would not be hard at all to adjust to, this life without a brother to dote upon!

"I shall wear it well," Malvina said, giving Dreaming Shield a teasing glance.

"How did you know that I was thinking of making you a necklace?" Dreaming Shield said, his eyes wide.

"What more could boys make their mothers?" Malvina said, then laughed softly along with Dreaming Shield and Red Wing.

They rode into the village as the sky began to turn crimson with sunset.

Malvina took one last glance over her shoulder toward the river.

Chapter Forty-Four

October, "Big Chestnut Month," had come and gone, and winter's approach quickened the pace of the Choctaws' daily life.

It was now November, time for the wild turkeys to emerge from the forests to feed on nettles in the clearings, a signal for the hunter to leave for the biggest of the annual food quests.

Malvina clung to the sides of a sled of bark that was being drawn through a heavy layer of snow by Red Wing's stallion. She had practically begged for Red Wing to take her on the hunt with him today. She was five months along in her pregnancy, and when Red Wing was gone for days at a time on the hunt, she could hardly stand the loneliness that overwhelmed her.

For the most part, even Dreaming Shield was gone more than he was at home. He had many friends, each demanding of his time.

And for the sake of their unborn child after Malvina suffered several sick spells of late, Red Wing would not allow her to do the normal chores that women did each day. Other women came and took turns doing her chores, no matter how much Malvina had fussed at Red Wing for treating her as if she were made of glass.

All that she was allowed to do was beadwork, which had become humdrum to her.

Sewing of any sort was downright tedious!

Especially for a woman who had spent the first eighteen years of her life riding horses instead of training to become a wife, an ambition she had never thought much of.

Until Red Wing.

The warmth from the stones resting against her moccasined feet beneath the layers of warm bear pelts was further proof of how Red Wing doted upon her in her pregnancy.

She was surprised that he had allowed her to accompany him on the hunt today, even though it gave her a reprieve from her daily lack of activities. She was glad, at last, to have something to take her mind off her brother, who had not written to her for several weeks now.

She could not stop worrying about him and his wife. They had, thankfully, made it safely to Saint Louis on the riverboat. But after arriving there, their true troubles had started.

Daniel had written to her about having to face disappointment after disappointment when he and Pretty Cloud sought a place to live while he attended the seminary.

Many would not rent to them because they saw Pretty Cloud, and any Indian, as a savage.

And then Daniel had been faced with worrying about leaving Pretty Cloud alone while he attended school each day, since prejudice followed them everywhere they went. She could not leave the house alone without facing ridicule.

"Are you enjoying the outing?" Red Wing asked as he looked over his shoulder at Malvina from his saddle on his white stallion.

Malvina was shaken out of her reverie by his voice. She laughed softly at his nose which was red from the cold temperatures.

"I am, but are *you?*" she said. "I have the warmth of the blankets and the warmed rocks at my feet. You are only shielded from the cold by one fur coat."

"The fur is worn inside to lend me its warmth," Red Wing said, frowning when he saw her hair blowing in the cold breeze. "And you! Your head is exposed. Did I not tell you to wear the fur hat I gave you?"

"I can't see as well with it on," Malvina argued back.

She glanced over at Dreaming Shield, who rode at Red Wing's right side on his very own pony. "Dreaming Shield, are you all right?" she asked. "You've been so quiet. And are you warm enough? I wouldn't want you to get pneumonia while proving your worth as a hunter."

Dreaming Shield cast her a warm smile. "I am quite content in all ways," he said. "I am silent because I am listening for the call of animals. The snow makes it impossible to hear their movements."

"You are watching for tracks, are you not?" Red Wing asked Dreaming Shield.

405

"Yes, and I have seen many, but most are so small," Dreaming Shield said poutingly. He thrust out his chest. "I do not wish to return home with only a squirrel. I wish to be shouldering a white-tailed deer, or at least a wild turkey."

"It is good that you think in grand terms," Red Wing said, chuckling. He drew a tight rein and stopped, then dismounted. "Come down from your horse, Dreaming Shield, and watch what I will do to try and get the attention of a moose."

Malvina stayed snuggled beneath the pelts on the sled and watched as Red Wing produced a birch-bark moose call from his coat pocket.

"Now listen as I make the call of the cow moose in the rutting season, which is now, next the answer of the eager bull, and then the whining 'hurry-up' of the cow again," Red Wing said as he lifted the moose call to his lips.

Malvina was stunned by his ability to use the moose call, for she had heard these very sounds before coming from the forest.

If *she* were a cow moose, she would most certainly follow the sound.

If she were a bull, she would also be lured by the false sound. She could almost see the two of them coming together, mating.

Red Wing placed the moose call back inside his pocket, then withdrew something else from his saddlebag, something Malvina had never seen before.

"What is that thing?" she asked, leaning forward to get a better look.

"This is a birch moosehorn," Red Wing told her.

He took another pouch from his saddlebag—the one that was used for carrying drinking water—and poured water into the moosehorn.

"Why are you doing that?" Dreaming Shield asked, having never watched this practice before.

"This is another part of the ritual to draw a moose to us if there are any near," Red Wing patiently explained. "Now watch what I do next."

Malvina and Dreaming Shield attentively watched as Red Wing poured the water slowly from the moosehorn onto the snow. The snow made a hissing sound as it melted from the warmth of the water.

"I have watched, yet I don't understand," Malvina said, forking an eyebrow as Red Wing repeated this strange performance.

"Of course, I would not expect you to know, or to guess why I am doing this," he said, smiling over at her. "My wife, I am imitating the urination of the cow moose under the excitement of the coming encounter with her future mate. This also will lure a bull from the thickets to the cow."

Malvina giggled, then blushed as she gazed over at Dreaming Shield. He was taking all this in, his face intent in its seriousness. She realized then that this was not something to laugh at. It was a practice important to all Choctaw.

Hearing a movement at her right side, Malvina turned her eyes quickly toward it. Her heart skipped a shallow beat when she saw the soft eyes of a doe gazing at them through the bushes.

Malvina started to turn to tell Red Wing what she had seen, then realized that he and Dreaming Shield were also aware of the deer's presence.

Both had grabbed their bows from their shoulders. Each had an arrow snugly fit into the string and were moving slowly toward the deer.

Malvina jumped when the deer made a sudden swing around and leapt away over the bushes, Red Wing and Dreaming Shield giving chase.

Not wanting to miss out on the special event of Dreaming Shield's first kill, knowing what it would mean for him to return victorious to the village so that the other young braves could stare after him, Malvina threw back the pelts. She had already lost sight of them, and their tracks were all that was left for her to follow.

Slowly she moved through the snow, for the sake of her child making sure not to lose her balance. She walked through ankle-deep snow, the wind bitter on her cheeks and ears, her hair blowing over her shoulders.

Then she suddenly saw them. She stopped and stared as Dreaming Shield raised his bow and arrow, Red Wing beside him, proudly watching.

Her gaze shifted.

She found the deer nibbling trustingly on the tips of grass that it had found thrust through the snow. It amazed Malvina that the doe's hunger was more fierce than her fear of those who followed her.

That thought was lost to her the instant Dreaming Shield's arrow entered the deer's side. The deer's body lurched with the sudden impact of the arrow; then the doe leapt away again, blood trailing along the snow behind her.

Malvina ran softly onward as she followed Red Wing and Dreaming Shield, who ran in pursuit of the wounded deer.

Again Malvina stopped when she caught sight of the doe as it paused to stumble from side to side in its weakness, Dreaming Shield quickly readying another arrow.

The arrow soon zipped through the air.

This time the doe was downed. It fell to its side, dead.

Malvina shouted at Dreaming Shield. "You've done it!" she cried. "You have your first kill! Oh, Dreaming Shield, I am so proud of you! You will be the envy of all boys your age when you return with your deer!"

Dreaming Shield turned proud eyes to Malvina as she came and stood between him and Red Wing.

"Proceed now, Dreaming Shield, with what I have taught you," Red Wing said, not so much ignoring Malvina as he was eager to get her back to the sled once Dreaming Shield finished the procedure at hand.

Dreaming Shield nodded, then went and knelt down beside the deer and placed his hand on it. "Sister," he said, his small voice filled with savage pride as he spoke to the deer. "Thank you for giving life to me and to my family so that we may survive. We will use you well."

Malvina was touched by what he said and his gentleness toward the doe while saying it.

She covered her mouth with her hand when Dreaming Shield continued with the ritual, this aspect of it making Malvina become somewhat light-headed. She watched Dreaming Shield take a sharp-edged blade from a sheath at his waist and open the deer's belly, then spread the entrails across the snow.

"Little brothers of the forest," Dreaming Shield then said, looking around him into the darker depths of the forest. "I share my kill with you."

Dreaming Shield gazed up at Red Wing. "Thank you for having told me the story about the good hunter who was slain by enemies and brought back to life by the forest animals because he always respected them and shared the game he killed with them."

"There are many more stories to tell," Red Wing said, placing a hand on Dreaming Shield's shoulder.

Malvina was touched almost to tears by the camaraderie between Red Wing and Dreaming Shield. It was as though they were truly father and son. No closer bond could have existed if it were true!

"Now you must prepare the deer for the returning home for all to see," Red Wing said, stepping away from Dreaming Shield. "Proceed, my son."

Dreaming Shield nodded. He knelt down beside the deer and reached inside the opened stomach until he found the heart and then the liver, each of which he placed in a small pouch.

Malvina turned her eyes away. The sight of the blood made her queasy. She grabbed for her stomach when she felt a strange ache at the pit of her abdomen and then sharp pains that shot downward through her womb.

Her eyes widened with fright, knowing that it was too soon to feel anything in her birth canal. She had scarcely even received a kick from her baby from inside the womb.

So what was happening now? she despaired. When another pain grabbed hold, she called out,

"Red Wing, I think I'll go back to the sled." She did not want to tell him just yet that she might be in trouble with their child.

"Do go on, wife," Red Wing mumbled without turning to look her way. He was watching and guiding Dreaming Shield each and every step of the way as he prepared the deer to be carried to his horse. "I am certain it is too cold for you."

"Yes, it is *very* cold," Malvina said, faking how she felt by keeping her voice lighthearted and gay.

Malvina inched her way back toward the sled as she followed her tracks through the snow. She almost doubled over with pain, glad now finally to see the horse and sled.

Stumbling, wincing with each step, Malvina reached out for the sled, then jumped with alarm and turned to stare up at a bluff when a lone gunshot rang out, echoing and echoing through the stillness of the snow-covered trees and ground.

She felt faint when she discovered a man standing on the bluff, his rifle poised for firing again. She could tell that it was aimed directly at her.

"Red Wing!" she cried, fear gripping her insides.

Chapter Forty-Five

A cold terror swept through Red Wing when he heard Malvina screaming his name after hearing a blast of gunfire. He turned his eyes in her direction and saw that she was gazing up with an intense fear at a butte overhead.

He didn't take the time to look at the butte.

He dropped his bow and arrow and ran toward Malvina, the ankle-deep snow an impediment.

Another gunshot ripped through the cold, still air.

Red Wing heard the bullet whiz past his head, missing him by inches.

He watched, numbly afraid, as Malvina screamed and fell to the ground, her eyes closed.

"No!" he cried. "Malvina! No!"

When he reached her, he bent to a knee beside her. He lifted her head from the snow, his eyes sweeping over her in search of a bloody wound.

Relieved when he discovered that she hadn't been shot after all, but seemed to have fainted from fright, Red Wing sighed, then turned a livid gaze up at the butte. His eyes squinted angrily as he scanned the land overhead. Whoever had been there with a firearm was now gone.

But he didn't have to think twice about who it might have been.

Gerald Smythe.

Malvina had been right to suspect that he would not give up searching for ways to threaten their lives.

Today was proof that he would go to any length to rid the land of his woman, and surely himself.

It was apparent that this white man hated them with a vengeance.

Malvina moaned, causing Red Wing to turn his eyes back to her. She slowly opened her eyes, then clutched her abdomen when another searing pain swept through her womb.

She lifted sorrowful, frightened eyes up at Red Wing. "Our child," she sobbed. "I think I . . . am miscarrying."

Dreaming Shield came to them and knelt down on Malvina's other side. When he heard the words that meant that Malvina was perhaps going to lose her child, tears of regret splashed from his eyes.

Red Wing's heart felt as though it was being wrenched from his body at the thought of Malvina losing the baby.

Anger filled his being when he thought of why it might be happening.

Gerald Smythe had frightened Malvina into early labor!

Cassie Edwards

"Red Wing, I'm afraid," Malvina cried, pleading with her eyes. "So afraid."

"Do not be," Red Wing said, leaning to softly kiss her. "I shall take you home. You can lie warmly between the blankets. You will relax. The pains will go away."

Malvina grimaced when an even worse pain shot through her.

She closed her eyes, then drifted off into another fainting spell.

"He will pay," Red Wing whispered through clenched teeth as he gently lifted Malvina into his arms. "The evil white man will pay for this!"

No longer thinking about the downed deer and the victory of his first hunt and the glory that came with it, Dreaming Shield walked solemnly beside Red Wing as he carried Malvina to the sled.

Dreaming Shield knelt down beside the sled and parted the thick pelts so that Malvina could be placed between them, then sobbed angry tears as he snugly covered her.

"We must hurry home, Dreaming Shield," Red Wing said, rushing to his stallion.

Dreaming Shield ran to his own pony and pulled himself into the saddle.

He waited for Red Wing to turn around, back in the direction of their village. While waiting, he glowered at the butte overhead, knowing now that whoever had fired the shots had escaped Red Wing's wrath.

"If Red Wing doesn't find you, I shall," Dreaming Shield whispered to himself.

An idea came to him like a thunderclap. If he and Red Wing waited to search for the evil man

414

later, he would most certainly get far enough away *never* to be found.

But if Dreaming Shield went *now* and followed the man's horse's tracks, perhaps Dreaming Shield could find him and rid this land of the man.

He smiled at the thought of what that victory would gain him among his people.

If he killed the man who was responsible for Red Wing's woman losing her baby, how great he would be in the eyes of the Choctaw!

Dreaming Shield drew a tight rein and watched Red Wing ride away from him, then looked solemnly at the sled where Malvina lay unconscious.

This fueled his anger even more.

Wheeling his pony around, Dreaming Shield rode back to where Red Wing had dropped his bow and quiver of arrows. He left the horse long enough to get them, now carrying two quivers of arrows on his back, one on either side.

He gave one last lingering stare at the downed deer, then lifted his chin and rode away beneath snow-laden limbs of trees, his eyes intent on the butte overhead.

He rode until he found the incline that would lead him to the butte. Slowly he inched his pony up through the slippery snow, his heart skipping an occasional beat when the pony seemed to momentarily lose its footing.

"Dreaming Shield, ride ahead and tell the Shaman that we will need his medicine as soon as we get Malvina to the village," Red Wing said, glancing over his shoulder. He took a second, startled look when he found Dreaming Shield nowhere in sight.

He looked in all directions, then spied Dreaming Shield atop the butte on his pony. His heart sank at the sight, for he knew that Dreaming Shield had more than likely taken it upon himself to find the man who was responsible for the gunfire.

"No, Dreaming Shield!" he cried, drawing his horse to a stop. He shouted Dreaming Shield's name again, but either his voice had not carried that far or Dreaming Shield was ignoring him, for the child went on his way, soon disappearing from sight.

Red Wing was torn with what to do. He gazed down at Malvina, who was moaning in her sleep. He had to get her home. He had to do what he could to save the baby.

He gazed up at the butte. His heart ached to go for Dreaming Shield, to make sure nothing happened to him. He knew that Gerald Smythe was heartless.

And Gerald had surely seen Dreaming Shield with Red Wing and knew that he was associated with him in some way.

That alone would give Gerald cause to kill the young brave!

All that Red Wing could do now was get Malvina safely home and get her cared for. Then he would send several warriors to find Dreaming Shield.

Hopefully they would be in time to save him.

Sending his horse into a gentle lope, concerned that going faster might increase the chances of Malvina's losing the child from the jostling, Red Wing sent an occasional glance to her to see if she had awakened.

But she still lay there, limp and pale, an occasional moan whispering across her parted lips, her eyes closed.

Finally Red Wing entered the outskirts of his village. He began shouting for help, bringing people to their doors to see what was the matter.

Stands Tall came to Red Wing and ran beside the sled as he peered down at Malvina. "What happened?" he asked, giving Red Wing a troubled glance.

"Go for our shaman," Red Wing said, his voice drawn as his eyes met and held with Stands Tall's. "My woman may miscarry our first child. She is in pain. Hurry, Stands Tall. Hurry."

Stands Tall nodded and ran away.

Others came and followed the sled, staring down at Malvina, concern in their eyes.

When Red Wing reached his cabin, he slid quickly from his saddle. His people parted to make room for him as he knelt down beside Malvina. He watched her face as he unfolded the pelts from around her.

Still she slept!

Still she moaned!

Gently he lifted her into his arms. A young brave ran ahead of him and opened the door to his cabin. The sight of the young boy sent Red Wing's heart into a tailspin of despair. In his fears for his wife, he had forgotten about Dreaming Shield!

Stopping before entering the lodge, Red Wing looked through the throng of people, glad when Stands Tall came hurriedly toward him with the Shaman at his side.

"Stands Tall!" Red Wing shouted. "Gather together many warriors. Dreaming Shield may be in trouble! We were shot at. Without my

417

knowledge, Dreaming Shield left to go and search for the man. I fear this man may have been Gerald Smythe. If so, he won't hesitate at killing our young brave!"

"Where did you last see Dreaming Shield?" Stands Tall asked, his hand clasped onto his knife sheathed at his waist.

"Follow my horse and sled tracks into the forest," Red Wing explained. "You will find a downed buck. Look overhead. You will see a butte. That is where I last saw my son!"

"We will go for him, and we will bring him home," Stands Tall said, turning and instructing many warriors to follow him.

Knowing that Stands Tall would do his best to find Dreaming Shield, Red Wing went inside his cabin. They had not been gone long enough for the fire to be out. He welcomed its warm waves on his blistering cold face. He would soon have his woman absorbing the warmth also.

Bald Eagle came to Red Wing and stood on the far side of the bed as Red Wing laid Malvina on it. The Shaman began his low chants while Red Wing removed Malvina's coat.

"My wife," Red Wing whispered as he tossed the coat aside, then removed her moccasins. "You will be well. The child will survive. Bald Eagle will make it so!"

While Bald Eagle chanted and shook a gourd rattle over Malvina, Red Wing lifted the skirt of her dress and examined the small ball of her stomach, beneath which lay their beloved child.

Ann's Lace, a midwife who knew much about childbirth, came into the lodge. She knelt at the foot of the bed and parted Malvina's legs, then slowly and skillfully examined her while Red Wing looked on, horrified at what Ann's Lace might discover.

Ann's Lace withdrew her fingers and rose slowly to her feet, her eyes heavy with apology. "She is dilated," she murmured. "That means she is in the first stages of labor."

A mournful cry rose from between Red Wing's lips. He bowed his head, then looked at Malvina again. "I will not believe it is so until it happens," he said, taking one of Malvina's hands and holding it.

Malvina cried out again and her body tightened.

Red Wing's insides felt empty, for he knew that so often when a child is miscarried, the woman also dies.

"Do something," he said, gazing wild-eyed at the Shaman. He looked over at Ann's Lace. "If the Shaman's magic cannot save my wife and child, surely you know how. I have seen it before when you have come from a lodge where a miscarriage had been announced and you bring news that it was stopped. Work your miracle now, Ann's Lace. Tell me my wife and child will be all right."

"There is no more that I can do," Ann's Lace said solemnly. "We will have to wait to see what nature's plan is for your woman and child."

Ann's Lace sat down on the floor at the foot of the bed. She folded her arms across her chest and stared at Malvina.

Bald Eagle continued his chants and shaking his rattle.

Red Wing lifted Malvina's head and cradled her in his arms, his eyes never leaving her face, wincing when she cried out with pain, sighing when she seemed to be at peace again.

Thoughts of Dreaming Shield came to him in flashes. He gazed at the door, wondering if Stands Tall had yet found him.

If so, had he and his warriors been too late?

Was Red Wing to lose everyone today whom he loved?

Could he bear such losses?

Would he not also want to die if he lost his family?

The wails outside his lodge made him know that he was wrong to think of only himself and his losses when he had a village of people who depended on him and his leadership.

He knew that if he did lose those he loved today, he must go on for those who survived.

He was a chief now.

He loved all his people.

In a sense they were an extension of his family.

Distant gunfire brought his eyes up.

Wondering who had fired the gun, and why, he inhaled a frightened breath.

Chapter Forty-Six

Stands Tall had already passed the deer that had been left behind, and had gone to the butte. As he followed the tracks away from the butte, he heard a sudden clap of gunfire up ahead.

He rode hard toward it, stopping when he found one of the Choctaw warriors who had gone on a lone hunt bent low over a deer, preparing it for its return to his village and lodge.

"Gray Fox, it was your gun I heard firing only moments ago?" Stands Tall said urgently.

"That is so," Gray Fox said, nodding.

"Have you seen Dreaming Shield?" Stands Tall asked, relieved that Dreaming Shield had not been shot by the white man. "His pony's tracks lead this way."

"Yes, I saw Dreaming Shield," Gray Fox said, rising from the fallen deer. He gestured with one hand. "He went that way."

"Did you not question him as to why he was riding alone?" Stands Tall asked, frowning down at Gray Fox. "Did you not suspect that he was being somewhat careless going out alone? He is but a young brave. He should be accompanied by family while away from the village."

"I asked him," Gray Fox said, kneading his chin with his fingers. "But he did not reply." Then he arched an eyebrow. "I did wonder about why he carried two bows and two quivers of arrows. A boy of six winters is quite weighed down with such a burden."

"That should have been enough for you to know that things were not right with him and you should have told him to return home, or accompanied him on the mission," Stands Tall grumbled.

"I spied this deer," Gray Fox said, his eyes humbly lowered. "My family's needs came before Dreaming Shield's."

"If the child should die because you ignored the safety of the young brave, pity you, Gray Fox," Stands Tall said, his eyes flashing angrily. "You know as well as I how devoted our chief is to Dreaming Shield, to *all* our Choctaw children. They are the future of our people."

"I shall leave the deer and ride with you to find him," Gray Fox said, slipping his knife back inside the sheath at his waist.

"No," Stands Tall said flatly. "You have already done our chief a disservice. Nothing you do now will correct it."

Stands Tall sank his moccasined heels into the flanks of his horse and rode away. Again Stands Tall followed the pony tracks. Then a movement up ahead caused him to wheel his horse to a stop.

He moved his horse cautiously forward, his breathing shallow, his heartbeat erratic. He gazed cautiously on all sides as he proceeded, then stopped and breathed more easily when he found Dreaming Shield kneeling beside his pony, checking one of its legs.

Dreaming Shield looked up at Stands Tall as he drew tight rein beside him. "Stands Tall," Dreaming Shield gasped. "Why are you here?" He looked past him at the many warriors following. "So many have come with you."

Then Dreaming Shield paled. "Have you come to tell me bad news about my mother Malvina?" he gasped. "Did she die? Did . . . the child . . . ?"

"When we left the village, Malvina was still fighting for her and the child's lives," Stands Tall said, his jaw tight. "Red Wing sent us to find a young brave who foolishly set out on his own in the snow. What do you have to say for yourself and your reckless behavior that might have sent you to your death?"

"Red Wing's full attention had to be on Mother," Dreaming Shield said, rising slowly to his feet. "It was left up to me to find the man who fired the shots at my mother and father."

"And when you found him, what would you have done?" Stands Tall asked, sighing.

"The same as you, should you have found him after endangering your chief's life and his wife's," Dreaming Shield said matter-of-factly. "I would have killed him."

"And you are practiced at killing white men?" Stands Tall further demanded. "You are certain he would have not killed you first?"

"Are you ever certain that you will not be shot first when you are faced with danger?" Dreaming Shield said, then took a step away from Stands Tall when he realized how disrespectful what he had said to this older warrior must have sounded.

"You do and say things in haste that you must learn to control before you grow into adulthood," Stands Tall said, reaching down to place a hand on Dreaming Shield's shoulder. He gazed down at the boy's pony. "Your steed is injured?"

"Yes." Dreaming Shield looked woefully down at his pony's leg. "The snow hid a gopher hole beneath it. My pony stepped into it. I was thrown, but the snow cushioned my fall. But as for my pony, I . . . don't know."

"We Choctaw do what we can for injured animals," Stands Tall said softly. "The white man would shoot this injured pony without blinking an eye. We shall return him to our village and see to his leg and make it well again if it is meant to be well."

"May I ride with you on your horse to save placing needless weight on my pony's leg?" Dreaming Shield asked, gazing wistfully up at Stands Tall.

"Yes, that is best," Stands Tall said, offering the young lad a hand. "Come."

"I shall first place the two bows and arrows on my pony to prevent being awkward in your saddle with you," Dreaming Shield said, turning to tie the bows and arrows to his saddle.

Then Stands Tall lifted him onto his horse behind him.

Dreaming Shield held on to his pony's reins as

everyone turned back in the direction of the village.

"I never got even a glimpse of the white man," Dreaming Shield said, regretfully. "Again he evades the Choctaw. Do you think he will ever be stopped, Stands Tall?"

"Does a cat truly have nine lives?" Stands Tall said, laughing softly.

Dreaming Shield laughed, then clung around Stands Tall's thick waist with his tiny arms as Stands Tall led his steed down the steep slope that led to flat ground below.

Then they went on to the village.

Dreaming Shield slid from the horse as soon as he got his first glimpse of Red Wing's lodge. He wormed his way through the crowd milling outside the lodge, the women's wails reaching clean inside his soul.

When he stepped inside the cabin and saw Red Wing sitting beside the bed where Malvina was stretched out, pale, beneath a covering of blankets, her eyes still closed, his knees almost buckled from remorse to think that perhaps she was dead, and also the child!

Red Wing heard Dreaming Shield's entrance and his gasp of fear. He turned and his eyes brightened to see that his son was there, unharmed. He reached a hand out for him.

"Come to me, my son," he said thickly. "Fill my arms with your sweetness."

Dreaming Shield ran to Red Wing and moved into his embrace as Red Wing rose from the chair. "Father, is she dead?" he cried, clinging. "The child. Is the child also lost from us?"

Hearing the boy's despair, feeling it inside his

own heart too, Red Wing eased Dreaming Shield away from him and gazed down at him with wavering eyes. "My son, she is no better and no worse," he said. "Nor is the child. It is a game we play now of waiting. But soon we should know how it is to be."

Dreaming Shield moved to the edge of the bed. He knelt down onto one knee and reached a gentle hand to Malvina's face. "Mother, it is I, Dreaming Shield," he whispered. "Mother, please wake up. Look at me. Tell me you and the child are going to be all right."

As though his tiny, pleading voice had reached somewhere inside Malvina's unconsciousness, she fluttered her eyelashes, blinked her eyes, then slowly opened them.

Her lips dry, her brow clammy, Malvina first saw Dreaming Shield hovering low over her, then looked up and saw Red Wing. "My darlings," she whispered through dry lips. "You both . . . look . . . so afraid. I'm sorry if I gave you such a fright."

Relieved to see her awake and talking, Red Wing fell to his knees on the opposite side of the bed from Dreaming Shield. "My wife, do not worry about my feelings, or Dreaming Shield's," he murmured. "Tell me how *you* are feeling. Is the pain worse?"

"The pain?" Malvina said weakly. She reached a hand to her abdomen, feeling it through the blankets. Her eyes brightened when she discovered that she still had a slight ball of an abdomen, which had to mean that she had not miscarried in her moments of unconsciousness.

She looked up at Red Wing with a tremulous

smile. "There is no more pain," she said, her voice filled with joy. "And the child! He is still inside me! I shall not miscarry this child! I have surely passed the crisis."

Ann's Lace, the midwife, came into the lodge and knelt at the foot of the bed. She gave Dreaming Shield a frown, then nodded toward the door. "Child, this is no place for you," she said softly. "Leave now while I examine your mother."

Dreaming Shield hesitated, then nodded and left.

Ann's Lace placed her fingers deeply inside Malvina, then smiled at Red Wing. "I do not know how it has happened, but your wife is no longer dilated," she said softly. "She will not miscarry today, or perhaps ever. We must make certain through the rest of the pregnancy that she does not leave this bed unless to see to her private needs and her bath."

Malvina did not like the thought of being bed-fast, but she was willing to do anything to save her child.

"We will all do what is best for the child," Red Wing said thickly. He then looked over at Malvina. "And for my *wife*."

Malvina reached for one of his hands and squeezed it. "I feel so blessed," she murmured. "I truly thought that I was losing the child."

"You were, but by some miracle, you are no longer," Red Wing said, then smiled at Ann's Lace. "Please tell Dreaming Shield that he can return to his mother's bedside."

Ann's Lace left the house.

Dreaming Shield rushed back inside and knelt beside the bed again. "Mother, I went after Gerald

Smythe for you, but he got away," he said, then regretted having said it when Malvina's face grew even more pale than before.

"You did what?" she asked, her voice breaking.

"He was a foolish young brave today and will not do anything as foolish again, will you, my son?" Red Wing said sternly.

"I do see the foolishness in what I did," Dreaming Shield said, lowering his eyes. Then he looked quickly up again. "But someone has to find that man. He must be stopped."

"He will be stopped," Red Wing stated. "Had your mother lost her life today, and the child, and this man was the cause by frightening her with his gunfire, I would not have stopped, ever, until I found him."

Malvina reached a gentle hand to his cheek. "Red Wing, the gunfire was not the cause for my sudden false labor pains," she murmured. "I had them before the shot was fired."

"You did?" Red Wing said, arching an eyebrow.

"Moments before, I felt them but did not want to alarm you since I was not sure if they were false or true pains that might come with miscarrying our child," Malvina said. "I was going to the sled to rest when I heard the first gunfire."

"Then he is not the cause?" Red Wing said, feeling no less anger toward the man, for it did not erase the fact that he had been firing at them, to kill them!

"I am the cause," Malvina murmured. "I shouldn't have accompanied you on the hunt. That was foolish of me."

Stands Tall entered the lodge. He came and

stood over Malvina. She smiled up at him. "You smile?" he said. "Does that mean that the crisis is over? That you and the child are going to be well?"

"Both of us are doing quite well, Stands Tall," Malvina murmured, sad for him since he still had not found a woman to replace Pretty Cloud in his life.

"That is good," Stands Tall said, then turned and watched a young maiden enter with a basin of water. She was called Meadowlark and was much prettier than Pretty Cloud had ever been. He had not noticed her before, because she was from a different clan of Choctaw. Her parents had brought her to their village to live since their own people were lacking in food and shelter for the long winter ahead.

"Malvina, I have brought you warm water for bathing," Meadowlark said, casting a shy glance toward Stands Tall. "Ann's Lace instructed me to do so."

"Thank you," Malvina said, leaning up on an elbow. "I shall use it later." She caught the look in Stands Tall's eyes, a look of appreciation as he stared down at Meadowlark. "Stands Tall, I noticed when the door was open that it's getting dusk outside. Might you escort Meadowlark back to her lodge?"

Red Wing chuckled beneath his breath, now knowing for certain that his wife was on the road to recovery.

"Yes, I could do that," Stands Tall said, his eyes gleaming into Meadowlark's as she continued staring up at him. "Would you allow it, Meadowlark?"

Meadowlark softly nodded, then turned and walked slowly away. Stands Tall cast Malvina a broad smile, then went and took Meadowlark by an elbow and escorted her out of the lodge.

"You are a clever, conniving woman," Red Wing teased Malvina.

"Yes, and so I am," she teased back.

She reached her arms out for both Red Wing and Dreaming Shield. "Come to me," she murmured. "Fill my arms with your love."

One on each side of the bed, they leaned over her.

Malvina's eyes filled with joyous, thankful tears as they hugged her. "Our family still has a future," she whispered. "And oh, how wonderful it will be."

"Yes, twice blessed," Red Wing said, gathering her fully into his arms as Dreaming Shield crept away to leave them alone with their special privacy.

Chapter Forty-Seven

I love you, dear,
to love myself.
No earthly pride,
no common wealth.
For love is life,
'tis all too true.
I live my life,
just to love you.
—MARK ABBOTT, Choctaw

The long, dragging days of winter were past. The air smelled sweet of spring. The wharf at Fort Smith swelled with people as the first paddlewheeler of the season from Saint Louis made its way around the bend in the river.

Cradling her baby in the crook of her left arm, the blankets thrown loosely around him, Malvina anxiously watched the riverboat. "It's been so long since I saw Daniel," she said, giving Red Wing a glance as he stood beside her.

Dreaming Shield stood on Red Wing's far side, his black hair glossy beneath the brilliant rays of the sun.

"I, too, look forward to seeing Daniel again, and also Pretty Cloud," Red Wing said, smiling down at Malvina. He eyed the bundle in her arms. "Shall I hold our son?"

"Do you wish to?" Malvina asked, her arm sweating where Eagle Walking's blankets rested against it.

"Always," Red Wing said, taking Eagle Walking from her.

Dreaming Shield stood on tiptoe as Red Wing swept the corners of the blanket away from the child. "Is not Eagle Walking a handsome young brave?" he said, pride in his eyes. "Can *I* hold him?"

"Do you wish to?" Red Wing said, smiling.

"Always," Dreaming Shield said, laughing softly.

"One thing is certain," Red Wing said, giving his son over to Dreaming Shield. "Eagle Walking does not lack in love or attention."

He looked up just as the riverboat edged up next to the wharf.

Malvina's heart raced as she looked among those passengers on the top deck, searching with her eyes for her brother. When she saw him, her heart melted with happiness.

Then she gasped delightedly when she noticed something else as Pretty Cloud stepped up next to Daniel—a bundle in each of her arms, which had to mean that since they had seen them last, two children had been born to them.

"Twins?" Malvina said, then squealed when she realized that, yes, Pretty Cloud had given birth to twins!

She couldn't hold herself back any longer. She ran through the throng of people. Daniel came from the ship at a half run and lifted her into his arms and swung her around.

"Sis!" he cried. "Malvina, it's so good to see you."

Pretty Cloud stepped up to Malvina. Daniel turned to her and took one of the children into his arms. "Twins, Malvina," he said proudly. "We are the parents of a boy and a girl."

"You never wrote about twins," Malvina said, looking at one and then the other, as the blankets were drawn back to give her a look. She smiled when she saw the difference in the children. The boy had the skin coloring of his mother. Their daughter had the skin of her father.

"They are beautiful," Malvina said, then turned and beamed up at Red Wing as he came and stood beside her, Dreaming Shield having given his son back to his care.

"Let me see my nephew," Daniel said, peering into the folds of the blankets for his first look at Eagle Walking. "Isn't he handsome?"

A loud commotion down the street drew their attention. They turned and stared as a man was led down the middle of the street on a horse by two men, his hands tied behind him.

Malvina gasped. "Gerald Smythe," she said, paling. "That's Gerald Smythe!"

"Where are they taking him?" Dreaming Shield asked, shielding the sun from his eyes with a hand over them.

Malvina looked farther down the street. Her eyes widened when she saw a hangman's noose thrown over a tree limb. "He's being taken to a hanging," she said. "And I believe it's no one else's but *his*."

"I've wondered often what became of him," Daniel said.

"We've not seen him since that day he shot at us from the butte," Red Wing said, watching Gerald being fitted with the noose, as several people steadied his horse beneath him.

"Seems his crimes have caught up with him at long last," Malvina said, sighing heavily.

Malvina glanced down at Dreaming Shield. He was absorbed in what was happening. Something told her that it was not best that he watch a man die in such a vicious way, even though Gerald Smythe deserved it.

She placed a hand on Dreaming Shield's shoulder. "Son, look away," she murmured. "Don't watch. It's not a pleasant sight to see a man die at the end of a rope."

Dreaming Shield gave her a questioning look, then turned his back just as the horse was slapped, leaving Gerald hanging in the breeze as the horse rode away without him.

"Lord have mercy on his soul," Daniel said solemnly.

"Let's go home," Red Wing said thickly. "It will be good to have all of our family with us once again."

"Yes, let's," Malvina said, combing her fingers absently through Dreaming Shield's hair. She glanced one last time at Gerald Smythe, pitying him, yet glad that that part of her past was finally done with.

Chattering and laughing, she walked beside Daniel to the horse and buggy that awaited them.

"And besides twins, Malvina, I have another surprise for you," Daniel said as they reached the buggy.

"Oh?" she murmured. "What is it, Daniel? Tell me."

"I plan to bring my family to Fort Smith as soon as my teachings for the ministry are completed," he said, watching her eyes light up. "I will have my own church in Fort Smith. We will be neighbors."

Malvina's eyes misted with tears. She reached a hand to her brother's face. "Thank you," she whispered. "I have sorely missed you."

The night had been filled with much talk, merriment, and eating. It was midnight before everyone went to bed. Daniel and Pretty Cloud had gone to Daniel's cabin with their children. Dreaming Shield had soon followed to spend the night with them.

It was morning now. Malvina and Red Wing stepped outside their cabin and inhaled the wonders of the fresh air. They leaned into each other's embrace and watched the east for the rising sun.

Somewhere in the village someone was playing a flute. A small baby cried. Someone chanted. The smells were delicious, of smoke rising to the still dark sky, the smell of green willow branches burning.

Dust rose from the stamped-down earth in the center of the village as small tornadoes of dust swirled around in circles.

Cassie Edwards

"Isn't this a wonderful place to live?" Malvina asked, looking past the village, where she could see the white-blossomed dogwood trees and the purple of the lilac. "It's so peaceful."

"Yes, it is land the Choctaw, with savage pride, are grateful to call their own," Red Wing said, then took her hand and led her back inside the cabin. "The baby still sleeps. Dreaming Shield is still with Daniel and Pretty Cloud. Can you think of what a man and wife might do with such privacy?"

"I'm not sure," Malvina teased back. "Perhaps you'd best show me."

Red Wing whisked her up into his arms as he kicked the door shut. He carried her to their bed, his mouth brushing her cheeks and ears with light kisses.

Leaning down over her on the bed, his mouth seared hers, leaving her breathless and shaking.

She felt his hunger in the hard, seeking pressure of his lips.

She fed his hunger.

He fed hers.

"My husband, my wonderful Choctaw husband," she whispered against his lips.

Latest News From Cassie!

For those of you who are collecting all of the books of my Leisure *Savage* Indian Series, and have had problems finding some of the older titles, I am happy to report that Leisure has now made selected titles available to you for your convenience. Check your local bookstores or order directly from Leisure. It's easy! Call the Leisure telecenter at 1-800-481-9191, Monday-Friday, 10 A.M.-9 P.M. (EST) or fax them at 1-610-995-9274 anytime. You can also order on the Web from the Leisure online bookshop at www.dorchesterpub.com.

To receive my latest newsletter, autographed black and white photograph, and bookmark, write to me at:

> Cassie Edwards
> 6709 North Country Club Road
> Mattoon, IL 61938

For a prompt reply, please send a self-addressed, stamped, legal size envelope.

Thank you from the bottom of my heart for your support of my Leisure *Savage* Indian Series. I love researching and writing about our country's beloved Native Americans!

> *Ah-pah-nay,*
> Forever,
> Cassie Edwards

To read more about Cassie Edwards, visit her website at www.cassieedwards.com.

SAVAGE EMBERS

CASSIE EDWARDS

Before him in the silvery moonlight, she appears as if in a vision—her hair a vivid shock of red, her eyes a blazing blue. And from that moment, a love like wildfire rushes through his blood. Not one to be denied, the mighty Arapaho chieftain will claim the woman, brand her soul with his smoldering ardor, and fan the flames of unquenchable desire. Yet even as Falcon Hawk shelters Maggie in his heated embrace, an enemy waits to smother their searing ecstasy, to leave them nothing but the embers of a love that might have been.

___4546-X $5.99 US/$6.99 CAN

Dorchester Publishing Co., Inc.
P.O. Box 6640
Wayne, PA 19087-8640

SAVAGE SHADOWS

CASSIE EDWARDS

All her life, Jae lived in the mysterious region of Texas known as the Big Thicket. And even though the wild land is full of ferocious animals and deadly outlaws, the ebon-haired beauty never fears for her safety. After all, she can outshoot, outhunt, and outwit most any man in the territory. Then a rugged rancher comes to take Jae to a home and a father she never knew, and she is alarmed by the dangerous desires he rouses in her innocent heart. Half Comanche, half white, and all man, the hard-bodied stranger threatens Jae's peace of mind even when she holds him at gunpoint. Soon, she has to choose between escaping deeper into the dark recesses of the untamed forest—or surrendering to the secrets of passionate ecstasy in the savage shadows.

___52355-8 $5.99 US/$6.99 CAN

Savage Devotion
Cassie Edwards

Sailing the deep, clear waters of the Puget Sound, beautiful red-haired Janice Edwards is bound for a new beginning. Leaving behind the wealth and luxury she's known in San Francisco, she hopes to find a simpler, sweeter life in the towering forests of Tacoma . . . and a man who will love her for who she is, not what she has. But when the steamer *Hope* is wrecked by a sudden storm, Janice is rescued by a man like none she's even known. Tall, with muscular limbs and a powerful chest revealed by his buckskin clothing, he is a Skokomish Indian—from all she's heard, a savage to be feared. Yet in his gray eyes she sees tender caring, in his strong arms she discovers untold passion, and in his wild heart she will find . . . savage devotion.

___4735-7 $5.99 US/$6.99 CAN

Savage Grace

Cassie Edwards

From the moment he sees her, her lovely flame hair spread about her shoulders like a glowing halo, Standing Wolf thinks of no other. She is a vision—an angel with beautiful blue eyes that look deep into his and see his every emotion. She has rescued him, body and soul, and he knows that when he has finally claimed her as his one and only love, he will never leave her side. Shaylee has never dreamed that she will be given another chance at life and love. But Standing Wolf needs her as no one ever has: He is her destiny. As she nurses the handsome Cherokee warrior back to health, she longs to feel his hard muscled body beneath her fingertips and taste his sweet kisses. For only his touch can erase the pain of her past and unite them as one.

___4666-0 $5.99 US/$6.99 CAN

Dorchester Publishing Co., Inc.
P.O. Box 6640
Wayne, PA 19087-8640

SAVAGE FIRES
CASSIE EDWARDS

Josephine Taylor Stanton has given up on love after losing both her mother, and her desire to walk, in a train wreck. But when the tall, handsome Indian chief, Wolf, walks into her office, she is drawn to the proud Ottawa leader and longs to feel his strong arms surround her. Wolf has come to Jo to help fight for the rights of his people, but from the moment he sees her sweet smile, his heart is lost to her forever. Lying together in front of the crackling fire, he sees only the sparkling blue eyes and tender heart of a woman of courage and strength, a woman the Ottawa would be proud to claim as their own. And when he tastes her sweet kisses, her love speaks to his soul and unites them as one for all eternity.

___4551-6 $5.99 US/$6.99 CAN

Dorchester Publishing Co., Inc.
P.O. Box 6640
Wayne, PA 19087-8640

Please add $1.75 for shipping and handling for the first book and $.50 for each book thereafter. NY, NYC, and PA residents, please add appropriate sales tax. No cash, stamps, or C.O.D.s. All orders shipped within 6 weeks via postal service book rate. Canadian orders require $2.00 extra postage and must be paid in U.S. dollars through a U.S. banking facility.

Name_____
Address_____
City_____ State_____ Zip_____
I have enclosed $_____ in payment for the checked book(s).
Payment <u>must</u> accompany all orders. ❑ Please send a free catalog.
CHECK OUT OUR WEBSITE! www.dorchesterpub.com

Savage Joy

Cassie Edwards

Called Rain Singing by her Iroquois mother, Shanndel Lynn has lived all of her life in the white world, retaining nothing of her Indian heritage but her secret name. But when a group of Shawnee stop in town to spend the winter and she glimpses their handsome chief, she dons an old doeskin dress and moccasins, determined to meet the stranger.

___4480-3 $5.99 US/$6.99 CAN

Dorchester Publishing Co., Inc.
P.O. Box 6640
Wayne, PA 19087-8640

Please add $1.75 for shipping and handling for the first book and $.50 for each book thereafter. NY, NYC, and PA residents, please add appropriate sales tax. No cash, stamps, or C.O.D.s. All orders shipped within 6 weeks via postal service book rate. Canadian orders require $2.00 extra postage and must be paid in U.S. dollars through a U.S. banking facility.

Name_____
Address_____
City_____ State_____ Zip_____
I have enclosed $_____ in payment for the checked book(s).
Payment <u>must</u> accompany all orders. ❑ Please send a free catalog.
CHECK OUT OUR WEBSITE! www.dorchesterpub.com

SAVAGE WONDER

CASSIE EDWARDS

Hunted by the fiend who killed his illustrious cousin Crazy Horse, Black Wolf fears for the lives of his people, even as a flash flood forces him to accept the aid of gentle, golden-haired Madeline Penrod. Pursued by the madman who murdered her father to gain her hand in marriage, Maddy has no choice but to take refuge from the storm in an isolated hillside cave. But the breathtakingly virile Sioux warrior who shares her hideaway makes the nights far from lonely.

___4414-5 $5.99 US/$6.99 CAN

Dorchester Publishing Co., Inc.
P.O. Box 6640
Wayne, PA 19087-8640

Please add $1.75 for shipping and handling for the first book and $.50 for each book thereafter. NY, NYC, and PA residents, please add appropriate sales tax. No cash, stamps, or C.O.D.s. All orders shipped within 6 weeks via postal service book rate. Canadian orders require $2.00 extra postage and must be paid in U.S. dollars through a U.S. banking facility.

Name_____
Address_____
City_____State_____Zip_____
I have enclosed $_____ in payment for the checked book(s).
Payment <u>must</u> accompany all orders. ❏ Please send a free catalog.
        CHECK OUT OUR WEBSITE! www.dorchesterpub.com

SAVAGE TEARS

CASSIE EDWARDS

Bestselling author of *Savage Longings*

Long has Marjorie Zimmerman been fascinated by the Dakota Indians of the Minnesota Territory—especially their hot-blooded chieftain. With the merest glance from his smoldering eyes, Spotted Horse can spark a firestorm of desire in the spirited settler's heart. Then he steals like a shadow in the night to rescue Marjorie from her hated stepfather, and she aches to surrender to the proud warrior body and soul. But even as they ride to safety, enemies—both Indian and white—prepare to make their passion as fleeting as the moonlight shining down from the heavens. Soon Marjorie and Spotted Horse realize that they will have to fight with all their cunning, strength, and valor, or they will end up with nothing more than savage tears.

___4281-9 $5.99 US/$6.99 CAN